Praise for *Deadly Ties*

"Perfectly captures the culture and beauty of my home state, presenting an intriguing, masterful mystery along the way ... a thrilling read!"
— Jack R. Cotner, author of *Mystery Of The Death Hearth* and *Storytellin': True And Fictional Short Stories Of Arkansas*

"This latest book is not only the first novel of a new mystery series, it's a first class piece of storytelling. Excellently paced and plotted, it's filled with characters who, like real people, can give you a sudden jolt by revealing an unsuspected side. The Ozark mountain setting is vivid both as a realistic background and a place haunted by legends. Holmes creates a compelling puzzle in which old wrongs and rumors reach out from a past that is anything but dead—but nonetheless deadly indeed."
—Bethany Campbell, nationally bestselling author of *Whose Little Girl Are You?* and *See How They Run*

"I was hooked from the start. Terrific setting, a clever story line, and plenty of plot twists to keep you guessing right to the end. Wonderful characters and the dogs are awesome ... a sure winner!"
— Maureen Kidd, Therapy Dog Coordinator at The Glen Retirement System, Shreveport, LA

"Holmes' first mystery brings the reader to northwest Arkansas and into the world of Waterside Kennels. She uses historical fact and fable along with her knowledge of the region, dogs, and human nature to develop setting, characters, and most of all, intrigue. Well-paced and solidly woven together, one read of *Deadly Ties* leaves the reader eagerly awaiting the next book in the series."
—Barbara Alexander, retired librarian, writing professor, and avid mystery reader

DEADLY TIES

A WATERSIDE KENNELS MYSTERY

Susan Holmes

Elderstone Press
FAYETTEVILLE, ARKANSAS

DEADLY TIES

Elderstone Press
PO Box 1822
Fayetteville, AR 72702-1822

ISBN-13: 978-0-9898100-0-5

Visit the author's website: dogmysteries.com

Author's Note

THE IDEA FOR this story began with a news article about a cold case murder investigation of an unknown female in a rural Arkansas county. Initially logged in as Jane Doe #3 for the year, detectives now refer to her as Bone Woman. What kind of person, I wondered, could commit murder, burn the body, and stack the charred remains neatly beneath a tree? Was the killer a stranger or someone known to the victim—perhaps a family member or close friend? How did they meet, and why did she die? The questions lingered, and I tinkered with the idea of bringing Bone Woman into a novel.

About that same time, I met noted historian and folklorist Phillip W. Steele and was captivated by Ozark tales of buried treasure. As Mr. Steele notes in the introduction of his *Lost Treasure of the Ozarks* "considerable amounts of treasure still may be waiting to be discovered under Ozark soil."

Anyone wishing to learn more about Ozark legends might enjoy reading Mr. Steele's *Lost Treasure* publication or his *Ozark Tales and Superstitions*. I would also suggest the work of W. C. Jameson. His book *Buried Treasure of the Ozarks* provided hours of fun and was a source of inspiration for the plot.

As Mr. Steele and I discussed regional folklore, it occurred to me that a treasure hunt would be an intriguing backdrop to a murder mystery set in the Ozarks and thus *Deadly Ties* began. Recently, television shows have inspired many to take to the hills and fields in search of treasure, much to the chagrin of landowners. Consequently, I've taken creative liberties with locales in this book, inventing, reshaping, or fictionalizing many locations. While Beaver Lake and Eureka Springs are quite real, Barton County and Hogan County exist only in my imagination and within the pages of this series. I've done the same with organizations, events, and elected officials throughout the region.

A great many people helped in the research for this novel. The Benton County, Arkansas, Search & Rescue team let me tag along on training runs and answered endless questions, as did kennel owners, veterinarians, dog groomers, and pet owners. Patricia Amason created the dogs' American Kennel Club registration names. Maureen Kidd generously provided expert information about dog training as well as search and rescue strategies. I used AKC regulations and language for technical details as well as presentation of specific breed names, such as Cocker Spaniel or Labrador Retriever. In addition, I used the textbook *Scent: Training to Track, Search, and Rescue* by Milo Pearsall and Hugo Verbruggen, M.D. and Susan Bulanda's *Ready! The Training of the Search and Rescue Dog.*

Jerome Rose provided expert information and research support regarding the technical side of death and drowning. Jeff Sprott helped me work out fire patterns and evacuation logistics. Arkansas native and fellow writer Jack Cotner was my guide through the hills of the Ozarks and deep into caves. My thanks to beta readers Barbara Alexander, Maureen Kidd, and Jack Cotner for their keen eyes and excellent suggestions. My gratitude to Sally McCluskey for her enthusiastic support. Thanks also to everyone who helped nurture the cover design and interior layout from concept to creation. I'm grateful to all for their enthusiastic support and encouragement. Any mistakes are mine alone.

And finally, a note of gratitude for a life well lived with my own beloved Alix, found in these pages as Sweet Pea.

For Jack, who always believed.

Prologue

Doreen Crowley wasn't the smart type. She'd known that since the fourth grade, which she repeated three times. Doreen's teachers pronounced her hopeless. She left school at fifteen and pushed a broom through her uncle's grocery store for eight years, and then she drifted from one job to the next, waiting for Lady Luck to deliver a Prince Charming who would declare her beautiful and smart. Somebody who wanted her for more than one night, more than a casual good time.

And now that she'd found one, she meant for him to stay.

Doreen paced nervously about the room, the necklace dangling from her hand as she considered her options. She'd broken her own rule, the one about not taking anything expensive, or something that might be missed right away.

To keep it would be stealing, and she wasn't a thief. Souvenirs, that's what she took, something she could pull out when she needed to lose herself in memories.

This was no souvenir.

She could put it back, pretend she hadn't seen it, didn't know whose it was, but she wouldn't forget. Defiant, she shoved the jewelry in the small front pocket of her jeans. When the time was right she'd confront him, demand an explanation. And an apology. Let him say the woman means nothing to him.

And if she won't back off, Doreen thought, she'd have to get in her face. This was her man, her future, and nobody's going to say different.

She'd die before she let him go.

1

The unmistakable sound of trouble brewing sent Maggie Porter sprinting into the kennel office to discover two Schnauzers off leash and hell-bent on having a cat for breakfast. The dogs snarled and growled and fell over each other in their efforts to capture a tabby that crouched, hissing, within the fragile protection of a cardboard carrier. Maggie waded into the fracas, snatched the carrier out of harm's way, and pressed the intercom button. "All staff to the office, please."

The employment agency had promised to have someone at the kennel by eight that morning but the only person in sight was Mrs. Gruber, who appeared oblivious to the uproar her dogs had started. No newcomer appeared in response to the summons, but Maggie was relieved to see Bev Donaldson, the kennel's master groomer, hurrying to help. Handing over the cat carrier with a grateful smile, Maggie turned and collared the Schnauzers with a practiced hand. She wished she could hand the dogs to Bev as well, but Mrs. Gruber had been adamant when she'd called. "Dr. Sheppard assured me you would *personally* care for my darlings."

Angus Sheppard's decision to close his clinic for remodeling had generated welcome business at Waterside when the kennel first opened, although Maggie fervently hoped the vet hadn't made similar promises to all his clients—especially if they all had pets like these. She leashed the Schnauzers and held on to her temper while Mrs. Gruber fussed over each dog before signing the contract authorizing boarding, grooming, and emergency veterinary services. Departing in a flurry of tearful farewells, the woman left the door open behind her.

One of the Schnauzers strained forward but was thwarted by Maggie's firm grip on the leash. The other stared at her ankles. "Don't even think about it," she warned him.

"Tabby's just fine," Bev reported calmly as she returned. "Whose cat is that? I didn't see a name on the carrier."

"Haven't a clue. How did they get in? The door was locked."

"Guess they dropped him off while I was setting up in the back, and I didn't hear them. No harm done." A single mother of two young daughters and sole caretaker for aging parents, Bev had an endless supply of patience and tended to dismiss routine irritations with a shrug.

When she'd first returned to Eagle Cove, Maggie looked for a groomer to clip her aging Cocker Spaniel, Sweet Pea, and found Bev working in a cramped, smoke-filled room at Paradise Pets. The woman handled Sweet Pea with ease ("The trick is to work fast, before she falls asleep," she'd said). Maggie had been pleased when Bev accepted her offer to work at the newly renovated Waterside Kennels.

Her other full-time employee didn't have much kennel experience but he was turning out to be a great asset to the small team. Garrett Johnson had the right temperament for the job, was willing to lend a hand to any project, and he handled the dogs like a pro. Customers liked him. She counted it a bonus he could pick up a Saint Bernard with ease. Maggie was grateful she'd found two such dedicated, intelligent workers. Without them, the new Waterside would still be a dream.

The only other person currently on the payroll was Jake Turner, a part-time worker long past his prime. Thinking about her staffing situation, she sighed. Record unemployment all over the region and she still couldn't get decent help, Maggie thought irritably. At this point, she'd even give Doreen Crowley

another chance if she waltzed in and asked for her receptionist job back. Okay, so the girl's social skills were on par with
Mrs. Gruber's Schnauzers, but she had been good with the animals—at least until she'd quit without notice and left Maggie
scrambling for a replacement.

Glancing up at the sound of a vehicle, Maggie saw Garrett
pull into the large gravel lot that served as general parking
for staff and customers. He strode whistling into the office,
sidestepping quickly to avoid the Schnauzers lunging in his
direction.

"Morning. Who do we have here?"

"Meet Fritz and Hauser—Mrs. Gruber's darlings," Maggie
said dryly. "Booked in while she's off on a cruise. Can you
manage?"

"Sure. Hey, there's a dog outside. Not one of ours."

"I'll take a look." As Garrett led the Schnauzers out to the
double run reserved for them, Maggie filled a bowl with kibble
and set it outside with a bowl of water in plain view of the dog
she saw huddled beneath one of the cars parked in the lot.

Head low, tail tucked tight against his thin body, the dog
whimpered at the sight of food and edged forward. He snatched
a few pieces of kibble from the bowl and retreated to gulp his
prize.

Maggie was still watching him when Garrett returned to the
office. "No collar, no tags. I should call Animal Control."

"The no-kill shelter is full. They'll have to send him over to
the county, and you know what that means."

"Well, we've got plenty of room here for now. Find a spot
for him and I'll ask Dr. Sheppard to check him over."

With his clinic shut, Angus Sheppard had offered to drop
by the kennel on an as-needed basis. "Save you from driving all
the way down to Huntsville," he'd said. "Keep me from being
bored. Nothing on my calendar except catching up on some
reading—love that Jack Reacher character—and a fishing trip
or two."

If Angus had chosen that week to go in search of striper bass or catfish, she'd have to juggle her schedule to make time for the hour-long trip through the mountains. "Don't put him near the boarders until the vet clears him."

At the desk, Bev was skimming through the paperwork and glanced at the dog Garrett carried in. "Better let me give him a bath first."

"He sure needs one," Maggie agreed. "Hey, did you figure out whose cat that was?"

"He must be Oscar, he's the only tabby on the list. Lisa Jarrett's the owner, but I don't see her boarding contract."

Maggie groaned. "Filing is not my strong suit."

"It wasn't Doreen's either."

"Darn it, why did that wretched girl quit on me?"

"Maybe she thought the job was too much for her."

Maggie sighed. "Well, until I find somebody else, I'll have to do a better job managing this paperwork."

"And when are you planning to do that? You never take a day off as it is. You need more help around here."

Garrett returned for coffee in time to hear Bev's comment. "She's right. And we'll probably get busier after the open house."

"I must have been crazy, scheduling that so soon."

"It's good PR," Bev said cheerfully. "You haven't been here long. Folks can come out, see the place, get to know you. You can meet the owners of the hotels and the B&Bs—most don't accept pets, so they could send a lot of business your way."

"There are still a dozen things I need to do here. I want it absolutely perfect for the open house, that's all."

"Sure, we can do perfect. We'll get right on that, boss," Garrett said, straight-faced.

Maggie laughed. "So maybe I'm obsessing a little."

"Everything will be fine," Bev assured her. "Great timing, too. Who wouldn't want to be part of the 'Treasures of the Ozarks' fun? Pretty clever idea."

"With the Chamber of Commerce and the Merchants League kicking in money for our open house as part of that advertising campaign, I'd be foolish to say no," Maggie said, thinking about the precarious state of her bank account. "Now if I could just hire more staff, we'd be in good shape. I'm so desperate, I'd even welcome Doreen back."

"Why don't you try that new employment agency in Rogers? Maybe they'll have better luck finding somebody who's willing to drive out from town."

"Hey, my brother's got some time. He's taking a summer class at the community college, but if you can be flexible about his hours, he could probably help out," Garrett suggested. He refilled his coffee cup and stood. "I have to go exercise the boarders."

"Jake's supposed to handle that chore," Maggie objected. "Where is he?"

Garrett shrugged. "Anybody's guess."

"I heard he's digging for some relic hunters in the caverns around Rocky Branch," Bev offered.

Jake Turner had been employed at the kennel in various capacities for years, ever since Maggie's grandfather had owned Waterside. After her grandfather's death, Jake had stayed on as a caretaker when Maggie's father accepted a partnership in a veterinary practice in Florida and moved the remaining family to Tampa.

When she'd inherited Waterside from her grandmother, Maggie couldn't afford to keep Jake on in his former role, but she had been reluctant to dismiss him outright. Once the kennel reopened she'd offered him part-time work, worried the rigors of the job might be too much for a graying man whose leanness bordered on frail. Now, imagining Jake climbing rocks and clambering around caves, she realized he must be stronger than he looked.

"Well, I hope he strikes it rich, because he won't stay on my payroll if he doesn't show up soon," Maggie said tartly. "Okay, hiring just went to priority one. I'll call the agency in Rogers and see what they can offer. Garrett, if you think your brother would be a good addition to the team, I'd like to meet him."

"I'll bring him by this weekend."

TUESDAY BEGAN WITH a short rush as customers dropped off pets for boarding or grooming. Garrett handled the boarders while Bev greeted the grooming clients, many of whom had followed her from her previous job at Paradise Pets. Maggie filled in wherever she was needed, grateful she didn't have to fit any pick-ups into the schedule. Even though the offer of pick-up and delivery had generated much-needed revenue, she was still learning her way around, and Garrett's father, the Hogan County sheriff, had warned her about relying on GPS.

"Our Search and Rescue teams spend a lot of time finding tourists who think choosing 'shortest route' will get them where they want to go," Lucas Johnson had told her. "Unfortunately, the shortest route around here can send you down a logging road, up a mountainside, and into places where cell phone service is spotty at best." He'd handed her a map of the county. "Get a compass," he advised, "and keep it with this map in your vehicle. I don't want to have to send Search and Rescue after you."

Grateful she wasn't driving miles this morning, Maggie enjoyed her time helping customers. Once the rush subsided, she filed client records, prepared billing statements, and updated the kennel's expense ledger. She answered emails and reviewed online reservations requests before checking for phone messages. In addition to the typical mix of customers, suppliers, and telemarketers, there were a few hang-ups and one heavy breather. She shrugged. Wrong number, maybe, or just your garden-variety jerk.

She took a break to play with her own dogs before turning them loose in the grassy meadow serving as the boarders' exercise area. Hickory, oak, and mountain cedars provided welcome shade and a cool place to retreat as the day warmed. Her Labrador Retriever, Sam, bounded happily about, no doubt on the trail of the rabbits and other wildlife that crossed the meadow when the dogs were in their runs. Sweet Pea, her elderly Cocker Spaniel, dozed off while Mr. B, the Beagle Maggie had recently adopted, settled quietly beneath a cedar, showing little interest in his surroundings.

Leaving the dogs in the exercise area, Maggie returned to her chores. By early afternoon, she'd filed much of the paperwork and updated the computer entries. After a quick sandwich at the house, she was ready to get back to work. She was wrestling with the dead bolt key in the front door lock when she heard a vehicle approaching, moving slowly up the steep hill and twisting lane that led past her house to the kennel and continued eastward. Recognizing the veterinarian's truck, she waved.

By the time Maggie reached the kennel, the vet was already working. Angus Sheppard was a meat-and-potato-sized man, with a waistline that suggested a preference for his own home-brewed beer. He enjoyed creating exotic brews, but his latest experiment—apricot beer—had been a disappointment. "Tasted like shampoo," he admitted ruefully when she asked.

After a thorough exam of the stray, he declared, "Nothing a month of decent food won't fix. Anybody else you want me to check out while I'm here?"

With his Ford F-250 four-wheel drive pick-up truck packed full of veterinary equipment and supplies, he was the only vet Maggie knew who made house calls. Maggie found it hard to believe the man was her father's age. The difference, she decided, was attitude. Unlike her father, Angus Sheppard was a perpetual optimist.

Angus patted the stray, packed away his gear, and stretched to his full six feet. "I keep meaning to tell you, I like the way you worked around the old barn. Gave me some ideas for renovating my own place."

"I'm glad. Want to walk through and see the modular pens we installed? They cost more than traditional versions but you get more flexibility to manage your space."

"Lead the way."

It had been a challenge to find an architect and a general contractor who understood her vision for the kennel, and who could be trusted to stay on schedule while Maggie remained in Florida settling her grandmother's estate. The first architect she'd interviewed had dismissed her renovation ideas, agreeing only with the decision to gut the building. When she'd finally found the right team, she kept in regular contact by phone, email, and video chats. As the work progressed, she shuttled back and forth between Tampa and Eagle Cove to watch over the work with equal parts anxiety and anticipation.

Knowing that boarding can be a stressful experience, Maggie had designed a facility intended to pamper both owners and their pets. Anticipating that customers might enjoy a place to relax and visit with other pet owners, she'd added a customer lounge, installing comfortable sofas and armchairs in front of wide windows that framed a stunning view of Beaver Lake and the bald eagles nesting there. One wall held an oak sideboard, well-stocked with packaged snacks, hot beverages, and copies of the Pet Owners' Bill of Rights A refrigerator to one side held soft drinks and water. An old map of Hogan County hung above the sideboard.

On the low counter separating the office and lounge, Maggie had placed treats and toys to smooth pets' entry into the kennel. Hanging above the counter were the boarding kennel's accreditation certificate and the industry's code of ethics. Other documents attested to Maggie's certification as a professional dog trainer specializing in obedience, utility, and agility work. She was also certified as a handler and trainer in tracking and retriever work.

Another wall featured framed photographs, articles, and awards that chronicled the career of Maggie's grandfather, who trained champion retrievers in field work for thirty-one years. Maggie had grown up hearing stories about him from Gran, who had taken many of the photographs while accompanying her husband to the annual retriever championship trials.

The kennel Maggie vaguely remembered from childhood was up there, too, captured in grainy black and white. Only the outer walls of that structure remained. In addition to the office and customer lounge, she'd built grooming rooms, a compact kitchen, storage rooms, and a cattery. The rest of the interior was dedicated to training space and dog runs, with a small space for the on-site manager Maggie hoped to eventually hire.

As they walked along, a sleek black cat crossed the training arena, heading for the dog runs. "Is that a boarder?" Angus asked.

"No, that's Momma Cat. She came with the house," Maggie explained. "She has the run of the place. She doesn't have much use for people, but she likes being out here with the dogs."

They followed the cat into the open arena used for training sessions and foul-weather exercise. Collars, leashes, retrieving dummies, tracking harnesses, and portable jumps were shelved along the east wall of the arena. Another storage area held panels for additional kennel runs.

Maggie had chosen modular units for the indoor-outdoor runs along the west and south side of the barn. Doors at the end of each row led to the fenced exercise area. They stepped outside where Garrett was surrounded by a dozen dogs, prompting Angus to ask, "Do you let them all out at once?"

"It depends. If they're sociable, and their owners approve, they can have joint play time. Otherwise, they don't come out until the other dogs are back in their runs. And nobody's ever out here alone, unsupervised. My own dogs spend a lot of time here, too." She paused and then added dryly, "Those Schnauzers you sent me didn't pass the play test, by the way."

Angus shuddered. "They're a menace! Watch your ankles," he said darkly. "They've bitten my entire staff."

"I'm not sure if Edith Gruber's Schnauzers are a blessing or a curse," Maggie teased him. "But I am grateful. Without your help, I'd still be struggling to attract customers."

"You have a first-class operation here. Your grandfather would be proud of you."

"I wish I remembered him."

"Miles Raeburn was a hard man, but fair. And he was brilliant with dogs. Best I've ever seen."

Maggie smiled. "Gran used to say he could turn any dog into a champion."

"What do you think he would have said about this fellow?" Angus stopped in the shade of a pin oak where Maggie's Beagle sat quietly, watching the other dogs in the yard.

"I wish I knew. I don't seem to be making much progress."

Angus ran his hands expertly, gently, along the dog's body. The Beagle sat patiently, unmoving except to lift a paw when prompted. The vet patted the dog gently. "Physically, he's okay. But his other wounds are going to be a long time healing."

The Beagle had been part of a K-9 unit of a federal agency, sniffing out drug smugglers. Retired from active duty after being seriously wounded in the ambush that had killed four officers, including his handler, and without a family willing to take him in, the Beagle's future had been grim until Maggie adopted him.

Her decision had irritated her father. "He's never been anybody's pet. You're wasting your time."

Now, as Maggie looked at the Beagle, she wondered if he was right. "My father thinks Mr. B is a lost cause," she confided.

"Look at it from the dog's point of view—he's lost everything he's ever known. That can haunt you for a long time."

"I know what you mean."

2

By Friday morning, Maggie was relying on a steady infusion of caffeine to stay alert. What sleep she did manage was broken by a string of haunting dreams that left her sweat-soaked and awake long before dawn. Although she'd been plagued by nightmares as a child, they faded over the years but returned when she reopened Waterside.

Well, they can just go away again, she thought crossly as she yanked on jeans and grabbed her work boots. She had a kennel to run and with more training sessions booked, she needed a clear head for the job. Better cut back on the coffee or switch to decaf for a while, she decided.

The employment agency had yet to find anyone willing to take the job. "I had two lined up," the counselor reported. "The first guy turned it down because you board cats—he's allergic. The other one, very nice, would love to work out there, but he's the only family member with a driver's license, so he's responsible for driving everybody to work. Too bad you can't hire the whole family—great work ethic."

Jake appeared Tuesday afternoon and completed his chores but was gone again by the time Maggie went looking for him. Thank heavens Garrett's younger brother Rob had accepted her offer of part-time work, she thought. Starting next week, he could handle the morning pick-ups and deliveries.

As she drove back to the kennel after her morning run, she conceded she needed to offer perks like a flexible schedule or better pay. She made a mental note to update her "now hiring" message on the Merchants League's online job board.

Back at the kennel, she unloaded a young Dalmatian and two Yorkshire Terriers. Hearing the phone ring, Maggie hurried into the office and found Garrett's father, Lucas Johnson, on the line. The tone of his voice warned her this wasn't a social call.

"What can I do for you, Sheriff?"

"My boys were talking about your kennel last night, and Garrett told us about your receptionist who quit a while back. Mind telling me when you last saw her?"

Maggie wondered what Doreen had done to draw the sheriff's attention. "About six weeks ago."

"And she hasn't been in contact with you since then?"

"No. But unless you tell me she's committed some awful crime and is sitting in your jail right now, I'm going to swallow my pride and give her a call, see if she wants her job back."

Lucas sighed. "Might be another reason you haven't heard from her. I was going over ACIC reports—"

"ACIC?"

"Sorry, that's the Arkansas Crime Information Center. It's a statewide data system for law enforcement."

"And you're telling me this because …"

"Because Barton County had a Jane Doe turn up at the end of March. She didn't match anybody on their lists or mine, but I got to thinking about what Garret said. If you haven't seen or heard from her since then, it's possible the body could be—"

Maggie sat down abruptly. "Wait. Just wait. Are you saying Doreen's dead?"

"They'll need a positive ID to be sure. The Barton County folks can fill you in on the details, assuming it is her." When Maggie didn't respond, he sighed. "I shouldn't have dropped this on you. Never mind, I'll get somebody else to do this."

Maggie forced herself to breathe deeply. When she thought she could trust her voice, she said quietly, "It's all right, Sheriff. Where and when do I need to go?"

SHERIFF DAN MALONE pushed a box of tissues toward the young woman who sat across the desk from him. He hated this part of the job. Sometimes he wished he'd listened to his father and gone into the roofing business.

The young woman before him was more controlled than most, though, considering what he'd asked her to view. She identified the body without fainting or even losing her breakfast, although her few words had been spoken so softly he nearly missed them.

Now, as she accepted coffee and tissues with quiet thanks, he wondered what she was thinking. He cleared his throat. "I do appreciate how difficult this is for you, Miss Porter."

"Call me Maggie, please. What happened to her?"

The sheriff checked the file open on the desk in front of him. "Fishermen found the body near Lost Bridge back on the 23rd of March. The autopsy ruled accidental drowning by exclusion."

Maggie frowned. "How do you exclude a cause of death?"

"A lot depends on the circumstances," the sheriff explained patiently. "Sometimes it's what's *not* present that helps the most. Drugs, skull fractures, bullets, stab wounds, the obvious things." He glanced at the file. "Her blood alcohol was point oh-nine, and there was water in both lungs. Stomach, too.

"We see a lot of boating and swimming accidents around here," he continued. "Folks get to drinking, forget to wear their life vests. Doesn't take much more than that and it's death by stupidity, as one of my deputies is fond of saying.

"As to when it happened, well, factoring in the warmer-than-usual spring weather and judging from the condition of the body—skin, nails, blisters, et cetera, et cetera—all we can say for sure is that she hadn't been in the water very long. Maybe three days, no more than that."

"She was at work during spring break, or at least part of it."

Sheriff Malone flipped through his calendar and checked dates against the report. "That fits."

"That's when she died?"

"It's possible."

"And nobody knew who she was," Maggie said softly.

"We checked at the time she was brought in, of course. She didn't match anyone listed on the missing persons bulletin in the region. We checked ACIC and submitted our own Jane Doe report. Beyond that, not much else we could do." He shrugged. "We're stretched pretty thin, what with four of my deputies gone with their National Guard units."

"I didn't mean to sound critical."

The sheriff reached for the coffee pot and offered a refill. When she declined, he topped off his own cup. "There are some points I'd like to clear up for the report." When Maggie hesitated he added, "Call it curiosity. My staff say I'm detail-crazy."

"What can I tell you?"

"There was a large faded bruise on her right thigh. Do you recall seeing that?"

"Maybe." She shrugged apologetically. "Doreen was always bumping into things at the kennel. She bruised easily."

The sheriff checked off an item on the report before him. "Okay. Would you happen to remember a lot of smaller bruises, above her ankles? These looked more recent."

"I don't remember anything like that, but I'll ask my staff if they noticed anything."

"I appreciate that." He added a short note to the report, then glanced up. "Did the Crowley girl have anything that belongs to you? I can make a note for the next of kin."

"Two keys—one for the office, another for the gates. I'd left messages asking her to return them. It doesn't matter now, though. I had the locks changed."

"We didn't find any keys."

"She had a big key ring, with a purple unicorn on it."

"I'll check the evidence bag." He strode out.

Minutes later, he returned with a brown paper bag. Cutting through the tape sealing the bag, the sheriff emptied the contents onto the desk. There wasn't much: grubby sneakers, jeans, a long-sleeved shirt, and a denim jacket.

"No keys. No purse, no wallet, no driver's license. That's why she came in as the county's Jane Doe number seven."

"Oh," Maggie said faintly.

"Hey, now." He placed a steadying hand on Maggie's shoulder as she swayed in her seat. "Deep breaths," he advised. "That's it, just relax. Take your time."

Her hand trembled as she pointed to a locket protruding from the small front pocket of the jeans.

The sheriff picked it up carefully. "Fancy piece of jewelry. Don't think I've ever seen another like it."

"There are two of them, actually," she whispered.

"The Crowley girl told you that?"

"No." She slipped shaking hands beneath her shirt collar unfastened a delicate chain, and held up a locket. It was identical to the one he held. "They were made for Sarah McCullen and her daughter in 1820, and have been passed down through the women in my family ever since. I inherited this one from my grandmother."

They stared at one another. "And our victim had the other," the sheriff said slowly. "She some kind of kin to you?"

"No."

"If your grandmother had the locket you're wearing, who was supposed to have this one?"

"My mother. Margaret Raeburn."

"The artist? I didn't realize—we have one of her lithographs. My wife loves her work." When Maggie didn't respond, he laid the locket on the desk and picked up his pen, shifting back to business.

"So, your mother gave a family heirloom to somebody who worked in your kennel. Is that typical behavior for her?" When Maggie didn't respond, the sheriff persisted. "Why would she do something like that?"

"I don't know. I haven't talked to my mother in twenty years."

3

Sheriff Malone had clearly hoped for more information. That makes two of us, thought Maggie wearily as she drove back to Eagle Cove in a tangle of emotions.

The McCullen lockets had been in the family for nearly two hundred years, one generation's gift to the next. Trust her mother to break the tradition, Maggie thought bitterly. But why give it to Doreen?

Back at Waterside, Maggie filled Bev and Garrett in on the sad details of her trip to Barton County and dutifully repeated Sheriff Malone's questions. "Did Doreen complain about falling down or anything like that, back around spring break? Apparently she had marks—bruises, he said—on her legs, around the ankles."

Bev frowned. "I don't remember anything like that."

"She was always complaining about something," Garrett said. "Unloading supplies, hauling training equipment, you name it. To be honest, I tuned her out most of the time."

Maggie hesitated, then pulled her locket from beneath her shirt. "Did you ever see Doreen wearing a locket like this?" When the other two shook their heads, she sighed. "Just one more thing I can't explain."

"It *was* an accident, wasn't it?" Bev asked.

"That's the official verdict, yes."

"You don't sound convinced."

"I can't explain it, but I'm missing something important."

"Well, stop worrying about it. Whatever it is, it'll come back once you've had some time to rest," Bev said kindly.

Garrett looked troubled. "We were talking about the kennel last night, and I told my family about how Doreen quit on you, right in the middle of spring break when we were so busy. But she didn't quit, did she?"

"It's possible that's about the time she drowned."

"I suppose we'll never know," Bev murmured.

Maggie snapped her fingers. "Hang on." Leaning over the computer, she logged into her online commercial bank account and scrolled through the entries. "Doreen said she didn't have a bank account, so I didn't use direct deposit for her pay." She looked up. "And guess what? She never cashed her last paycheck."

The others fell silent as they considered the implications of that. "I'll pass this information along to the sheriff, just in case it might help," she said, rubbing her temples. She could feel a headache building.

"Do you have an address for her family?" Bev asked.

"I checked her file; nobody listed. Doreen never mentioned family. Either she was alone or she didn't want to claim any kin. Happens to the best of us," Maggie said quietly. "But if there *is* any family, Sheriff Malone—and I suppose your dad, too, Garrett—will trace them."

"Dad will find out." Garrett shifted the conversation back to business. "I have some chores to finish. Oh, and I meant to tell you yesterday—we're low on kibble. I called the feed store, and they can deliver this afternoon, save you another trip back into town. I asked them to send the usual order. Is that okay?"

"Best news I've heard all day."

LATER, WHILE UNLOADING the week's supplies from the whole-saler's delivery van, Maggie found herself replaying the scene in Sheriff Malone's office. As she carried in a sack of kibble, she exclaimed, "Her clothes!"

"Whose clothes?" Bev asked curiously.

"Doreen. She was wearing jeans and a long-sleeved shirt *and* a jacket. Remember how hot it was during spring break? Why was she wearing such heavy clothes?"

"Who knows? Maybe she'd gone on one of those cave tours—it's always cooler underground."

"So how did she end up in the lake?"

Garrett took the bag of kibble from Maggie and thrust it onto the shelf. "Most likely she went out in a boat."

"If she'd been out on the lake by herself and fell overboard, where's the boat?" Maggie's uneasiness grew into a full-fledged knot of anxiety. "And if she wasn't alone, who was she with? And why didn't they report the accident?"

"Ask my dad," Garrett suggested. "He gets the police and marine reports for the whole region."

"Good idea." Maggie hurried into the office and punched in the number of the sheriff's office. When Lucas Johnson came on the line, she repeated her questions. "It just doesn't make sense," she concluded. "Why was she wearing those clothes?"

"Who knows? Maybe she hadn't planned on swimming." Lucas sighed, but his voice was gentle. "Dan Malone called me about the locket you saw. Is that what's bothering you?"

Maggie slumped in the chair. "Nothing makes sense about this. Her clothes, the locket. It's obvious now she knew my mother, but she never mentioned her, or the locket. I wear my own every day; she must have seen it."

"If it will make you feel better, ask your mother about it, but I don't see a big mystery here. Those folks on the Barton County team are professionals. If they say the death was an ac-cident, that's good enough for me."

4

Jake Turner showed up for work Saturday morning just as Maggie began morning chores at the kennel. He came on foot, as usual, appearing at the top of the trail that led southeast over the hills to Buck Mountain and Hawk Hollow. His chin was covered in gray stubble, his jeans and shirt dusty, his boots caked in dirt. He had an old backpack slung over his shoulder and carried a pickaxe with an ease that belied his frail appearance.

He made no effort to explain where he'd been for the better part of the past week. He stood scowling at the ground while Maggie reminded him of his responsibilities.

"I need to know I can count on you," she said finally. "If you need to cut back on your hours, or if the job's getting to be too much—"

Jake jerked his head up. "No," he said hoarsely.

Maggie sighed. "Start by getting the boarders out. Then you can hose down the runs."

He was good with the dogs, she mused as he led the boarders out to the shady exercise yard moments later. Patient, too; she watched him hold the gate open for Mr. B, who plodded slowly up the path and into the yard. Leaving him to his work, she checked on her feline boarders before turning her attention to her household chores.

She cleaned out the spacious dog run behind the house and refilled the water buckets. She was amused to see Momma Cat stroll past her to join the dogs in the shade. Chuckling, Maggie latched the gate and went indoors.

Hiring a crew to handle all the house repairs would have been faster, but she'd already strained her personal budget with the plumbing and electrical work required to bring the house up to code. And money aside, she wanted to do the work herself, to put her own mark on the rambling place that had sheltered her family for generations.

When she wasn't in the kennel, she worked on the house. One of her first tasks had been to haul out the junk left behind by the last tenant and scrub away the grime that had accumulated over the years. She'd picked up a book about basic home repairs at the hardware store and learned how to replace broken window panes and patch holes in the drywall. She chose warm, rich paint colors for the walls to compliment the original woodwork. She ripped out the stained carpets and cracked linoleum, uncovering the original hardwood floors that gleamed like new after waxing. Returning her grandmother's prized Persian carpet to its place in the living room, Maggie had added a sofa and deep armchairs she found at auction to the tables and lamps she'd brought with her from Tampa. Shelves built under the stairs housed some of her grandmother's favorite books as well as her own collection of search-and-rescue, tracking, and training books.

A wide hallway led from the living room to the kitchen, a room that always reminded her of her grandmother. Tall windows flooded the space with light. Dominating one end of the kitchen was a fireplace with a fieldstone hearth. In front of the fireplace were two rocking chairs and the large braided rug Gran's mother had made when she'd been a new bride. An eight-foot-long trestle table stood on the far side of the room, surrounded by an unmatched collection of chairs. New appliances, added after the wiring was updated, gleamed against the warmth of the old maple cabinets. A plank door in the far corner opened onto a steep flight of stairs leading to the basement. Maggie had been down there just once since her return, when the electrician and plumber inspected the property. The place had always given her a bad feeling. She was glad they'd been engrossed in discussing code compliance so she didn't have to explain her hasty retreat to the kitchen above.

She considered the work still needed around the house. The only rooms she'd tackled upstairs were her bedroom and the bath. No rush, she decided. She wasn't expecting company.

Her work was interrupted by the repeated ringing of the kennel phone, which was connected to both the office and the house. When Maggie answered, she heard nothing but heavy breathing. "Jerk," she muttered after the fourth call, and switched the telephone to voice mail.

At lunchtime, she made a plate of sandwiches and carried it with a jug of iced tea over to the kennel. Jake was in the exercise yard with Mrs. Gruber's Schnauzers for company. Watching him gulp down the food, she found herself wondering about him. Local gossip had Jake living in an old cabin somewhere near Hawk Hollow and hiring out as a backwoods guide to anyone interested in exploring the region and searching for Civil War relics.

He'd probably found himself on the wrong side of the law at some point, judging from his reaction when he saw the sheriff's car in the parking lot one day. She also suspected a good portion of whatever money he made went to whiskey instead of food. As long as he was sober on the job, she didn't care.

"There's more food in the staff kitchen," she said casually. "Help yourself whenever you want."

"Don't need no charity," he muttered. He swallowed the last of the tea. "Gotta get back to work."

"You're welcome." Picking up the empty plate, she headed back to the house, her mood lifting as she admired the neatly landscaped grounds around the kennel. Some might question her decision to hire a landscape company for a business like hers—God knows her father would rail at the expense if he knew—but Maggie was confident she'd made the right choice. Rural didn't have to mean rough, and she'd included the expense in her renovation budget. She reminded herself to send a note of thanks when she paid the bill.

5

Sylvia Bridger was a tall gray-haired woman with a wiry frame clad in jeans and a tee-shirt that showed off lean muscles developed by years of hard labor in her landscaping business. Stepping out of her truck at Waterside Kennels Saturday afternoon, she knocked dust from her boots and surveyed the grounds with an expert's eye.

She'd taken a personal interest in this project when Maggie hired her company to landscape the kennel grounds, in part because her own property was just east of the kennel. Her family and the Raeburns had been the largest landowners in Eagle Cove since the Civil War, and the families had been close until the kennel closed and the property left to the haphazard care of Jake Turner. It was good to see the place regaining its old beauty, she thought.

There was professional pride, too, in having her hard work and design skills appreciated. The publicity from a job like this could draw more customers to her garden center on the outskirts of Eureka Springs. And in these lean economic times, she needed all the business she could get. She'd cut back on staff last year as profits dwindled. She put in increasingly long hours, hoping to generate more revenue—after all, she had a hefty mortgage, inventory to buy, payroll to meet, and taxes due. If she could land a couple more jobs as big as this one, she just might hold on until the economy turned around.

Much depended on the local reaction to Waterside. Maggie had only recently opened the renovated kennel, and her location had so far shielded her from intense scrutiny. Her return to Eagle Cove, however, had not gone unnoticed, reminding more than one person of things best forgotten. Would they let the girl make a fresh start, see the place as something new and innocent? Or would they rake up, yet again, the scandals and lies and ghosts that still lingered in all too many memories?

Sylvia genuinely liked the girl, and she was grateful for the work Maggie sent her way. She wanted to believe the girl's uncanny resemblance to her mother was no more than skin deep. Otherwise … well, she'd find out soon enough, she thought.

With an effort, Sylvia dragged her attention firmly back to the present as she saw Maggie climbing the sloping hill between the dock and the kennel, carrying a dripping collection of retriever dummies. Her retriever trotted happily alongside. "Don't you ever take a day off?" Sylvia called out.

"I was about to ask you the same thing. And if you don't count morning kennel chores, this is—technically—a day off for me. I've spent most of my time working in the house. Oh, and I took some digital photographs for my insurance agent. He says he's transferring everything from paper to the computer."

"I did the same thing last week. My agent told me she'd need a photographic record or a video if I ever file a catastrophic loss claim. A lesson from the Joplin tornado, I suppose, and the Colorado wildfires. Better safe than sorry."

"Agreed. Let me put this equipment away, and we'll go to the house for some iced tea."

While she waited, Sylvia looked around her, evaluating the work in progress. The rocky hillside was being transformed into a symphony of color. Beside the kennel stood a cluster of dogwood and redbud trees, new companions to the huge oaks and hickory giants that had graced these hills for generations.

Maggie's grandmother had planted masses of daffodils and irises decades ago. Their colors had brightened the early spring landscape and the warm weather had teased other flowering plants open early. Daylilies provided a bright orange splash against the green background of holly that served as a natural fence on the eastern side of the kennel. Trumpet vines were already twisting green leaves across a trellis at one corner, and drought-resistant grasses had been planted beside the split rail fence that edged the parking area. Window boxes, hanging pots, and large ceramic vases filled with a variety of flowering plants added still more color to the landscape.

Maggie stepped out of the office, locking the door carefully behind her. "This place looks better every day. I didn't expect so much color so soon."

Sylvia chuckled. "Weather in the Ozarks is notoriously unpredictable. This time last year, I was wearing flannel shirts and running heaters in my greenhouses. This year we're set for record-breaking heat. The lake's dropped another eight feet in the last month. We need rain or the only color we're going to see is dead brown."

"The plants you chose seem to like this weather."

"Make sure you keep watering anything in pots, and those young trees, too. Hard to say how long anything will survive in this drought."

"Good thing my great-grandparents dug those water wells. I'd hate to imagine how high my bill would be if I were on the county water system."

"I'll get my crew back out here in the next few days to check all the planting and fill the gaps in the edging. Then they'll start clearing out that deadwood along the lane. Ice storms did some serious damage over the past couple of years. You'd need an army to clear it all, but we'll make a start before fire season hits. Oh, and I took some pictures of the new sign we installed for you." The old Waterside Kennels sign had long ago fallen into the weeds. "I supervised it myself to make sure they did the job right. I didn't want them trampling the Echinacea and Rudbeckia beds."

At the younger woman's blank look, Sylvia grinned. "That's purple coneflower and black-eyed susan to you non-gardening types. You'll get nice contrast in color, although they won't bloom in time for your open house." She studied Maggie's face. "Something worrying you?"

"If you have some time, I could use a friendly ear."

"Two of them, at your service. Oh, almost forgot—I picked up your mail on my way in. It's in my truck."

They walked into the kitchen, where Sweet Pea was lying on a cushion beside the hearth. "Does that animal ever do anything besides sleep?"

"Not much. But if napping were an Olympic sport, Sweet Pea could win a gold medal."

Adding the mail she carried in to the stack already on the kitchen table, Sylvia listened in dismay as Maggie related her visit to the Barton County sheriff's office. "The only accident I've heard about recently was that drunk idiot who fell off the dam. And surely a drowning would have made the local news."

"I guess they're waiting to notify her next of kin." Maggie frowned. "I did try to reach Doreen when she didn't show up for work, but when she didn't return my calls, I just assumed she didn't want to work here anymore."

"I probably would have thought the same thing. The girl bounced from job to job, you know. She even worked for me at the garden center last summer. I'm not sure why she wanted to in the first place, unless it was to hook up with the college boys I hire for seasonal help. She didn't last long, anyway."

"Why not?"

"Couldn't stay focused on anything but gossip," Sylvia said shortly. "And the stories she'd tell! You could never be sure what was truth and what wasn't with that one."

"Gran would have said Doreen liked minding other people's business. She certainly seemed interested in mine—I caught her poking around in the house one day, not long after I hired her. I kept the doors locked after that. Then I had to fuss at her when I found her playing around on the office computer."

"How did she come to work here, anyway?"

"Dr. Sheppard mentioned she needed a job, and I was desperate for office staff. And my dogs liked her."

Sylvia looked over at Sweet Pea, who'd gone back to sleep. "I'm not sure how much faith I'd put in Rip Van Winkle there. And that retriever of yours loves everybody."

"You just haven't seen him riled up," Maggie retorted. "He can be downright intimidating when he doesn't like somebody."

"I'll take your word for it. But what on earth was Lucas Johnson thinking when he asked you to identify her body? Plenty of us around here could have done that."

"But I bet not many of you would have identified *this*." Tugging her locket from beneath her shirt, she held it out. "Look familiar?"

"Your grandmother's locket, of course. Leah always wore it, as I recall. What's that have to do with Doreen?"

"She had the matching locket, the one that belongs to my mother. Sheriff Malone showed it to me."

"Are you absolutely certain? I mean, you'd just identified a body, for heaven's sake. Isn't it possible you simply saw a locket that just looks like Margaret's?"

"The two lockets are identical," Maggie said flatly. "I wear Gran's every day. Doreen must have seen it, but she never said a word about having the matching locket. Why did she keep that a secret from me?"

"I don't know."

"Maybe that's not the only secret she was keeping. Maybe she did know my mother, knew she wanted to come back here to Eagle Cove. Maybe that's why Doreen wanted to work here, so she could be on the inside, tell my—"

"Stop right there," Sylvia commanded. "God knows you have every right to be upset, but thinking Doreen was working for Margaret, or that Margaret wants to come back to Waterside? No, that's just ... well, that's just not possible."

"Why not?" Maggie argued. "By rights, my mother should have inherited everything."

"Your grandmother knew exactly what she was doing when she passed Waterside to you. If Margaret really wanted this place, she would have found a way to get it a long time ago. She was good at getting anything she wanted," Sylvia said tartly. "She's made it plain she doesn't want to be here. She didn't even come back for her own mother's funeral, for heaven's sake."

"But—"

"Look, I wasn't going to mention this, but there was something in the *Times* yesterday. Seems Crystal Bridges museum—you know, the one built with all that Wal-Mart money—wants Margaret's work for their permanent collection. Which just goes to prove that your mother has bigger fish to fry than anything we've got out here in these hills."

Sylvia laughed softly, the sound diluting the tension that had gripped them just moments before. "Definitely bigger fish. And whatever price they pay, I bet it's a heck of a lot more money than she got way back when. I can remember when she made her first sale for a hundred dollars! A lake scene, on a canvas she'd picked up at a yard sale and painted over. Neither of us could afford to buy new canvas or frames back then."

Maggie was surprised. "I didn't know you painted."

"I could never compete with the likes of her. No, I gave up that foolishness a long time ago. And all that's best left in the past, where it belongs." She shook her head. "Now," she said briskly, "let's talk about more pleasant things. Sounds like you have a full house over there."

"Almost," Maggie agreed, grateful for the change of subject. "I think Dr. Sheppard sent every one of his customers here. I just hope he doesn't come to regret recommending Waterside."

"Don't worry about Angus. He's downright fussy when it comes to sending his customers anywhere. That's why he hasn't renovated his own place before—hasn't been a kennel within fifty miles that met his standards. Not until you came along, anyhow."

"I wanted to have a full staff before the open house, but that doesn't seem likely now. I've tried every temp agency in two counties. I reposted all the ads, and I'm going to ask the high school counselors if they know any teenagers looking for a summer job."

"Well, if that doesn't work out, Howard could lend a hand. Since the economy tanked there's not much call for his custom cabinets around here. He does great work, but takes forever to get anything done. He still works with one or two local build-ers, but mostly folks just go on down to the Home Depot in Harrison and buy ready-made. He hasn't had a big order in months, and he's flat-out bored. And when he gets bored, he gets stupid. He spends hours tinkering with the boat or wander-ing around with that fancy metal detector he bought last year. Thinks he's going to strike it rich any day now. A grown man, believing in treasure stories—absolutely ridiculous."

Maggie grinned. "Lots of retirees use metal detectors on the beach. Seems like fun. And you do hear stories about sunken treasure now and then."

"Not a lot of shipwrecks around here, in case that's escaped your notice," Sylvia said sarcastically. "But the doctor did say any exercise was good for his heart. If he's helping out at the kennel he won't land himself into trouble. I nearly had a heart attack myself when he came home all busted up last week."

"What happened?"

"Said he took a fall following some old map with a buddy of his. He looked like he'd been in one heck of a bar fight. Old fool's going to kill himself if he carries on this way. So you'd be doing me a favor if you just let him give you a hand around the kennel. And he always did love working with dogs."

Seeing Maggie's confusion, she explained. "You don't re-member? Howard was the kennel manager here for years. Of course, you weren't much more than a toddler then. You used to follow him around, just like the puppies. No children of our own, of course. I like to think he missed you more than anything else when he lost his job."

"You mean when we moved away?"

"No, it was before that. Howard and your grandfather had a falling out, a big one, and Miles decided to bring in a new manager. He never did hire anybody else, though. Just tried to do it all himself until his heart gave out."

"What did they argue about?"

She shrugged. "Same old thing, I expect. It would have been about the dogs, because Miles had only two passions in life—dogs and family."

"And all that was a long time ago, too." Sylvia glanced at the clock, then at the unopened mail on the table. "Why don't you get a start on that stack and I'll fix some iced tea?"

Maggie sighed as she opened the top envelope. "More bills from the plumber, I suppose. Did I tell you? He claimed Sweet Pea tried to bite him when he installed the new water heater."

Sylvia looked at the snoring spaniel and laughed. "Oh, right. Definitely one vicious canine."

"Gran would have set that plumber straight ..." Maggie's voice faded as she stared at the page before her.

"Leah had a quick tongue. Just don't let him bully you into paying more than the estimate without a darned good reason. Stand your ground, and you'll be fine."

"I think somebody is hoping otherwise." Maggie handed the letter to Sylvia. Letters and words had been cut from magazines and roughly pasted into the shape of a threat.

YOUR A **DIRTY** THEF
GO *BACK* HOME
OR
YOULL **B** SORRY

"Nasty."

"First crank calls, now this. Not exactly the Welcome Wagon, is it?"

"What kind of crank calls?"

"Just somebody breathing into the line. Kids with nothing better to do, I expect."

"Are you going to tell the sheriff?"

Maggie crumpled the letter and tossed it into the trash can. "I'm not going to waste his time on a heavy breather and some cut-and-paste idiot who can't spell. Now where's that tea?"

6

Thursday morning brought a flurry of business. Maggie juggled the telephone and customers, passing the dogs to Garrett and his brother Rob, who handled the animals with the same level of confidence his brother demonstrated. Bev took care of the cats. By nine-thirty all but two of the expected boarders had arrived, and Maggie turned her attention to answering the phone, returning calls, and tackling the paper monster on her desk.

At ten, Bev came into the office carrying two water bottles. Nudging files aside to clear a space on the desk, she set one down in front of Maggie, who was frowning as she hung up the phone. "Everything okay?"

"I just had the strangest phone call from Doreen's landlady, Abigail Simmons. Well, former landlady. Doreen moved out a couple of months back. Anyway, she'd heard what happened—her granddaughter is dating one of Sheriff Malone's deputies—and wanted to know if I was going to keep Doreen's dog."

"Doreen didn't have a dog."

"Miss Abigail insists she did." Maggie actually preferred employees who owned pets, finding they enjoyed their job more and had an easy rapport with customers. Bev had a terrier with the personality of a Rottweiler, while Garrett's family had three dogs, a couple of cats, and routinely fostered animals from the shelter. "And what's more, the dog is the reason Doreen moved out—right after he dug up Miss Abigail's azaleas."

"Oh my," Bev said, wide-eyed. "Miss Abigail's azaleas have won the blue ribbon in the spring garden competition for more years than I can remember."

"That would explain Doreen moving out. Or maybe not. Miss Abigail says Doreen told her she'd found her 'Mr. Right' and was getting married!"

"Wow! That's amazing, especially since the girl was hunting for a husband in casinos and dance bars—not exactly prime territory for the perfect man. When did all this happen? And why didn't she tell us?"

"No clue. Miss Abigail sounded quite surprised that I didn't know anything about it." Maggie paused, thinking. "For a girl who loved to gossip, Doreen certainly had her share of secrets."

"You're still thinking about that locket, aren't you?"

"I can't seem to stop thinking about it," Maggie admitted. "Sure, Doreen wore jewelry all the time, but it was beads and bangles and cutesy things you see from flea markets and street vendors. She loved to show off any time she got something new, remember? So how does a girl like that end up with an heirloom locket *and* a fiancé *and* a dog and never say a word about any of it? Does that make any sense to you?"

"Can't say it does, but then again this is Doreen we're talking about. Heck, maybe she made it all up."

"The locket's real," Maggie reminded her. "And if Miss Abigail's azaleas are anything to go by, we can be sure there *was* a dog at some point. The fiancé? That's anybody's guess." She picked up her water bottle and reached for her keys. "I was planning to run errands, but I'm going to go by the sheriff's first, see what he has to say about all this."

"Take your time getting back. We can handle things here."

MAGGIE FOLLOWED THE county road to the intersection with Highway 62 and turned in the direction of Eureka Springs. She was glad Garrett reminded her his father was working out of the local sub-station that week. That saved her from a long drive to the Hogan County courthouse where the jail was located.

She drove carefully, acutely aware the mountain roads were a far cry from the flat coastal highways where she learned to drive. Here, even the major highway running east-west at the top of the state wasn't much more than a twisted two-lane road winding through the Ozarks.

When Maggie walked into the sheriff's office, she found him busy on the phone. He pointed to a chair in front of his desk and continued his conversation.

"What's that, Miz Sternes? No, you are *not* within your rights to shoot them." He listened at length, holding the receiver from his ear as the caller continued in increasingly strident tones.

"I've got fences down and holes dug all over the place. And the noise! They're scaring my hens! I'll be giving a piece of my mind to those idiots. Treasures of the Ozarks, what rubbish! Maybe they thought this would attract tourists, but all I've seen are trespassers climbing the bluffs and destroying my property."

"You marked your property lines with purple paint and signs, right?"

"Yes, my boy used all that paint you gave me and we put up those 'no trespassing' signs too. Not that it did a lick of good," Mrs. Sternes spluttered. "Now get your deputies out here and arrest these criminals. What am I paying taxes for? I tell you ..."

By the time the sheriff finally hung up the phone, Maggie was chuckling quietly, her own worries set aside for the moment. "What was that about a posse, Sheriff?"

"Go ahead, laugh," he grumbled. "If I'm real lucky, I won't get reelected and somebody else can worry about Myra Sternes shooting up the countryside."

"Sorry, but if the editorial in last week's paper is any indication, you'll be chasing the bad guys for years to come."

"Just my luck." With a grunt, Lucas settled back in his chair and grinned at Maggie. "Setting aside some property owners' complaints, I've heard a lot of good things about this Treasures of the Ozarks campaign. I reckon the Merchants League came up with a winner this time around."

"Pretty clever," Maggie agreed. "An 'X marks the spot' treasure hunt to get people into restaurants and businesses and stores. And the prize packages are impressive."

"Treasure's a powerful attraction, even when it's nothing more than a publicity gimmick. There's even a couple of reality TV shows about diggers and treasure hunters. Wouldn't surprise me if we start seeing television crews around here, considering all the stories about gold and silver stashed in these hills."

"You're joking!"

"I never joke about buried treasure," Lucas said solemnly. "Stories about treasure have been part and parcel of Ozark legends for generations. Some credit De Soto and other Spanish explorers. Some like to believe it was Indians who operated gold and silver mines all across the Ozarks. There's a lot of Civil War treasure stories, too. Soldiers on the move—both sides—often buried their valuables to keep them safe from the enemy. Over the years, folks have found some interesting stuff."

"I can understand the interest in Civil War things, but does anybody actually believe there's gold or silver around here?"

"Yeah, they do, and in all sorts of places. You'll hear stories about old mines, and more than a few tales suggest there's treasure waiting to be found in caverns and caves under these hills. There's the Spanish Treasure Cave over near Sulphur Springs, for example, or the Lost Silver Mine down near Huntsville, and the Kings River Silver Mine. That's supposed to be somewhere around these parts. And of course, there's the legend of Mill Ford Hollow. That's the one my granddaddy liked best."

"I'd like to hear it."

"As the story goes, the last of the tribes were forced out of the territory back in 1825. Some of the white settlers didn't feel safe with all those Indians around, or maybe they just wanted the land for themselves. Not all white folk felt that way, and some—who'd lived in peace here for years—decided they'd go west, too. Early in the journey, the travelers crossed the White River at a place called Mill Ford. Legend has it that during that crossing, one of the tribal elders pointed downstream and told a story about Spanish soldiers who came through the Ozarks a long time ago, hauling a cargo of silver. When the soldiers attacked a local band, the Indians fought them off and claimed the silver for their own. They hid the cargo inside a cave near the Mill Ford crossing, and then sealed the place up."

"Interesting story," Maggie said politely.

"The story got passed along, as folktales do, through family gatherings and traveler's stories. Most thought it was just a tall tale until sometime in the 1920s, when two men sheltering from a storm found a couple of silver bars sticking out of the mud. Turned out to be the real thing, and pretty soon somebody remembered the old Indian story. The treasure hunters searched and searched, but never found anything else."

"And Mrs. Sternes' property is where the silver was found?"

"Pretty close. But some folks believe those bars were planted there to keep people away from the real location. That doesn't seem to stop treasure hunters digging up any place they have a mind to," he said wryly.

"Wait a minute. They made this lake back in the sixties, right? Could the treasure be underwater now?"

"It's anybody's guess. Some versions have the cave entrance on the limestone bluffs where the lake meets the White River. Some think it's close to where the dam is now. My granddaddy was inclined to believe it's on the eastern shore of the lake."

"Considering how low the water level is in this drought, any caves should be easy to spot."

"See? Treasure hunting is contagious. Just promise me you won't bother Miz Sternes' hens."

"Cross my heart," Maggie promised.

Growing serious, the sheriff pulled a note pad closer and glanced at it. "I'm glad you stopped in. My dispatcher took a call from Sylvia Bridger. She claims you're being harassed."

"I don't know if 'harassed' is the right word." Briefly, she told Lucas about the anonymous letter and phone calls.

"And this doesn't worry you?"

Maggie shrugged. "It's just a crank."

"Let me be the judge of that. Give me the letter."

"I threw it away."

"Any idea who might be unhappy with you living here?"

"I've just barely settled in, for heaven's sake. I haven't had time to make friends, let alone enemies. No," she said, shaking her head, "it can't be anything more than a prank."

"Say it's just some bozo looking for a cheap thrill. But do me a favor, will you? If that letter is still in your trash, drop it by here or send it home with Garrett so I can look it over. And if you get another one, promise that you'll call me. Right away."

"Okay. I actually came in to talk about something altogether different, if you have a few minutes, Sheriff."

"Just call me Lucas," he invited.

"Thanks. I actually came by to ask: do you know Abigail Simmons well?"

"Known her most of my life. Why?"

Maggie told him about the call she'd received that morning. "Any chance she's confused about all this?"

"Miss Abigail does get mixed up now and again," Lucas admitted. "But she's past ninety, I'd say she's entitled. When it comes to her garden, though, she remembers every detail right back to 1947 and her first blue ribbon at the county fair. Now, what can you tell me about this fiancé she mentioned?"

"Miss Abigail saw a man in a Jeep going to Doreen's apartment over the garage, but she never saw him up close."

"A Jeep, you said? She give you any details?"

"I didn't think to ask. Doreen never mentioned a man or a dog. Considering how much she loved to talk, I find that odd."

"I'll have a visit with Miss Abigail, see what she has to say. Meanwhile, what else can you tell me about the Crowley girl? Ever had any problems with her?"

"Nothing major. She was good with the animals, but couldn't seem to mind her own business. She liked to gossip about people. Including my customers."

"Some of them get upset, hearing tales spread about Fido?" Lucas asked, grinning.

"I guess that sounds pretty silly to a man in your line of work. But trust me, my customers are very serious about their pets and about their own privacy."

"So what kind of dog did Doreen Crowley have?"

"A 'black one' according to Miss Abigail. But Doreen didn't have a dog. At least, she didn't when I hired her. Of course, I still have Miss Abigail's address listed and apparently that's not accurate, so maybe I'm wrong about the whole thing.

"But if Miss Abigail's right … if the dog was with Doreen when she drowned, he could be running loose. The best case scenario I can think of is that he's with Doreen's fiancé, whoever that might be. Otherwise," she said grimly, "he's in trouble if he's out on his own in this heat."

Lucas dialed a number and spoke briefly. "Animal control will follow up," he said when he disconnected. "And I'll get working on an address. It's possible Doreen was living with this alleged fiancé. We find him, we could find the dog."

"If she was engaged, why didn't he report her missing?"

"One of the first questions I'll ask, soon as I find out who he is." Clearing his throat, he continued. "And speaking of the Crowley girl, I haven't had the chance to thank you for going over to Barton County. Identifying a body isn't easy at the best of times, and when it's a drowning victim … well, you were a big help. At least she didn't remain a Jane Doe for years."

"We have three ourselves," he said somberly. "And I'll tell you straight, it hurts me to think that somewhere, somebody is grieving for their daughter or their wife or their mother."

"Don't you know anything about these women?"

"Sure. Take our Jane Doe number one. Mid-twenties, five feet five, 125 pounds, brown hair, brown eyes. Her description matches thousands of women across the country. We found her along Highway 62, wearing nothing but twelve feet of rope, the kind folks use for clotheslines. You can buy it in any store.

"Now, the next one. We thought she'd be a quick ID. A teenager, probably not more than fifteen. A natural blonde. She had a butterfly tattoo on her left breast, and another tattoo, a rose, on her right ankle. You might have seen her on that show Unsolved Crimes. The episode's run twice but no results. She's not on the runaway list. Nobody's filed a missing persons report. Her fingerprints aren't on file. Officially, she's a nobody."

"That's terrible! And the other?"

"She's listed in ACIC as our Jane Doe number three, but to me, she'll always be Bone Woman." Lucas sank back in his chair. "She was found north of Polecat Mountain, right near the county line. Somebody walking his dog found her remains. Just a pile of bones beneath a big pine tree. They were stacked nice and neat, like somebody had taken a lot of care about it. The medical examiner confirmed the remains were human, and female, and they'd been burned."

The sheriff paused. "It happened a long time ago. But somewhere there's a family waiting for this woman to come home."

7

After leaving the sheriff's office, Maggie turned toward town, slowing to a crawl behind a motor home whose driver was inching around a hairpin curve. At the first side road she left the highway, bypassing the main thoroughfare to thread her way through the crooked streets of the historic loop toward the business district.

Now a thriving art colony, Eureka Springs was a fascinating example of a turn-of-the-century village. Often called "Little Switzerland," the town was famous for its quaint Victorian architecture with its profusion of turrets, cupolas, and gingerbread trim. Many of the town's hotels and inns were included in the National Register of Historic Places, several famous—or perhaps infamous—for ghostly sightings and other supernatural occurrences.

The historic Basin Spring with its famed healing waters had become the centerpiece of a lovely little park tucked in amongst hotels, restaurants, and shops filled with antiques, contemporary art, jewelry, and mountain crafts. The street was currently decorated with colorful banners emblazoned with the Treasures of the Ozarks logo; matching posters adorned lampposts and shop windows. Maggie wedged her truck into a parking spot a few blocks from the park and walked briskly to the bank to deposit customer checks. Added to the total from the weekly credit and debit card receipts, which were processed automatically, the deposit was the largest she'd made since opening the kennel. The resulting balance lifted her spirits so much she decided to heed Bev's advice.

"Do you good to enjoy some time away, remind yourself there's more to life than just cats and dogs," the groomer had said bluntly.

Not for her, thought Maggie. She'd gambled everything on her return to Eagle Cove: the money Gran left her and her own small savings, even the remains of her college fund. Maggie's father shrugged off her decision not to finish her degree, but reopening Waterside infuriated him.

"Haven't we had enough trouble there? What about William? You know he's fond of you."

Maggie had met William Lamont, graduate of Harvard Law and junior partner at Wedington, Hughes, and Lamont at a humane society fund-raiser sponsored by the Rotary Club. He'd invited Maggie and her family to similar events in the months that followed. "If we don't take care of our four-legged friends, who will?" he liked to say, but Maggie suspected it was less a personal passion and more a ploy to please his senior law partners, all generous patrons of the local animal shelter.

William had been baffled by Maggie's desire to reopen Waterside and predicted she'd come running back to Tampa just as soon as she got "that dog business" out of her system. Maggie tried to picture him laying a track for the dogs through a field full of ticks and chiggers, and failed. He'd probably sue the creatures for unlawful trespass, she thought with a rueful smile.

After completing her errands she stopped by the Chamber of Commerce to pick up a Treasures of the Ozarks poster and headed back toward the truck. Passing the New Orleans Hotel, her attention was captured by the window display of the Crane Gallery, where stone sculptures nestled in a bed of silk.

Impulsively, she went inside. The soft shades of the original brick walls provided a perfect backdrop to the fine art displayed on wide mahogany shelves and freestanding brass easels. The room was crowded, and it took Maggie a few moments before she spotted Nicholas Crane through the open door of his office, where he was on the telephone.

Nicholas had been among the first to welcome Maggie back to Eagle Cove. It had been he who encouraged her to join the Merchants League. He'd smoothed her way into the local community, introducing her to the bank manager, prominent business owners, and tradesmen. While she waited for him to finish his phone conversation, Maggie wandered around the gallery, admiring the work on display. Something about a lake scene done in oils sparked a memory, but it eluded conscious recognition. She was leaning forward for a closer look when she noticed Nicholas hurrying in her direction.

"Margaret." The single word vibrated with anxiety.

"Maggie."

"The resemblance startles me every time. You realize you're the very image of your mother, don't you?"

"I couldn't say," she said coolly. Noticing his flushed face, she relented. "I'm sorry, I didn't mean to interrupt you."

"You've rescued me. I swear, some artists would drive even a saint to violence. And I'm no saint," he said with a wink. "Now, tell me you have time for tea. I want to hear all about what's happening at that kennel of yours." Smiling, he led her to his office located at the rear of the gallery.

In his well-tailored suit he looked as though he should be a high-dollar art dealer in Chicago or New York instead of a gallery owner in a small Ozark mountain tourist town. He wore his black hair long, pulled back and caught at the base of his neck. He has the right face for that sort of hair, Maggie decided, studying him while he poured the tea.

"A man of many talents," she said, nodding toward the sketches and canvases scattered on the table behind his desk.

"Observant, aren't you?" He settled in the armchair next to Maggie. "I confess to enthusiasm for the arts. I dabble, nothing

more. And now that you're finally here, what do you think of
my little gallery?"

"It's lovely. And the window display is stunning. I haven't
seen that work before. Do you represent a lot of artists in here?"

"We show the work of quite a few, but I personally prefer to
limit my involvement to a select number each year."

"Weren't you the first gallery to host Art Walk?" The event
combined gallery exhibitions with meet-the-artist receptions
each month from May through October. Featuring the work of
both emerging and well-established artists, Art Walk had pro-
pelled several local artists to commercial success.

"That first one was my idea," he admitted modestly, "but
with my own obligations it wasn't possible to give Art Walk the
time and attention it deserved. Now that the Merchants League
is managing the project, all the galleries in town are participating. It's been quite a success."

"I read the League's annual report. Seems to have been a
prosperous year all round."

"It's been an uphill battle. When Branson hit the big time,
we found ourselves on the edge of bankruptcy. That's when
the Chamber of Commerce, the Historical Association, and the
Artist's Guild combined forces to launch the Merchants League
and win back customers. We had over a million visitors last year,
and that's not counting shoppers who find us on the Internet.

"We're doing a much better job now of coordinating events
to appeal to a wide range of visitors. It's proven profitable all
around. An excellent idea. Unfortunately I can't say the same
for *that*," he said, frowning at the poster Maggie held.

"The treasures campaign isn't the same caliber as Art Walk,
but it seems to be profitable in its own way," she protested.
"There are all sorts of businesses—my own included—that
people wouldn't have known about if they weren't on the map."

"That may be true, but the whole foolish campaign has re-
vived interest in the old silver legends. I warned the League
members this was a bad idea, but they didn't listen."

"Sheriff Johnson told me about those treasure tales. I got the impression he'd enjoy looking for treasure himself."

"He's not going to enjoy all the complaints he'll get," Nicholas said coolly. "Those of us who own property around the lake have had quite enough of these so-called treasure hunters. They have no respect for private property, none at all. They damage our land and throw trash in the lake. It's a miracle they haven't set fire to the hills already. And now I hear some of these idiots are actually using dynamite underground to try and break open passages in caverns on the eastern bluffs."

He shook his finger sternly at Maggie. "You own a good-sized chunk of Eagle Cove. I expect the miscreants will get around your way once they realize there's nothing worth finding on that side of the lake. Be careful—you're isolated out there."

"There aren't any bluffs on my part of the shoreline, so I doubt anyone would be interested in my property. Besides," she said with a laugh, "if any trespassers did get close to the kennel, they'll set off the noisiest burglar alarm in the world."

"Just be careful. Now, enough talk about trespassers and treasure tales. I haven't managed to get out your way as much as I'd like, and I hear the old place is looking better than ever. Is business picking up?"

"Yes, to the point where I seriously need more staff. I know it's not your field, but would you happen to know of anyone interested in clerical work for me?"

Nicholas frowned slightly. "I wish I did. Have you checked the Merchants League website lately? Remember, members have unlimited access to the site. There's a new section, too, where job seekers can upload their resumes."

"I'll take another look."

"I have personal experience in the trials and tribulations of starting a business. I pretty much did all this on my own. There was no Merchants League when I started out," he told her. "I was barely out of college and struggling to get established in the art world. Did you know I was your mother's first agent?

There wasn't much money at first, of course, but now her signature on a painting brings thousands of dollars."

Maggie drained her cup and set it aside. "I don't follow my mother's career. Now, if you'll excuse me, I should head back to the kennel. I'll let you get back to your customers."

"You're uncomfortable. I apologize." He rose gracefully and grasped her hands, his grip firm, uncompromising. "Let me make it up to you. I'm leaving later today for a business trip but have dinner with me when I return, will you? And not," he raised his left hand, as if making a pledge, "just because I'm an old friend of the family, and not because I promised to keep an eye on Charles' only daughter. I want to get to know you better." He escorted her to the front and held the door for her. "I'll call you soon," he promised.

NICHOLAS WATCHED MAGGIE as she walked away from the gallery, moving briskly through the tourists crowding the sidewalk. He really touched a nerve mentioning her mother, he reflected.

He'd been involved with that family, one way or another, for nearly twenty-five years, since he had hosted the exhibition for local artists that included Margaret Raeburn. He'd opened doors for that woman, he mused, and look how she repaid him.

He'd been as surprised as anyone when the daughter re-opened Waterside. Maggie couldn't have many happy memories there, at least not of that final year, when her grandfather died and the family seemed to fall apart. Nicholas recalled that summer clearly, when tempers had risen with the temperature, minor quarrels escalating into furious arguments with seemingly little provocation. He'd heard some of those arguments himself when he'd gone out to see Margaret in her art studio. Maggie was just a small child then, but certainly old enough to have been distressed by it all, and frightened.

He wondered if she'd heard the latest gossip making the rounds, whispers of wrongdoing and betrayal during that long-ago summer. Those whispers could turn into wildfire if new trouble erupted—and that could spell doom for Maggie's business.

If only she hadn't insisted on returning to Waterside, he thought uneasily. He found himself wishing she'd stayed in Florida and let the memories fade into dust, where they belonged.

MAGGIE REGRETTED REACTING so rudely to a family friend. He'd done a lot to help her settle in, she reminded herself. And it was only natural people would want to talk about her mother. After all, the family had been part of this community for generations, and people do like to talk, especially when one of their own is as famous as Margaret Raeburn. So get used to the attention, she told herself sternly. Think of it as free publicity for Waterside.

Before leaving town, she stopped at the grocery store, and again at the wholesalers to increase next week's order of kibble. She smiled in satisfaction at the thought of the additional reservations that had come in. The bills had mounted steadily during the kennel renovation, but if her luck held, she'd be able to repay the debt sooner than she'd thought possible. Thinking about bills reminded her she hadn't heard from her insurance agent after emailing the digital photographs last weekend. Maggie glanced at her watch. Plenty of time before she was due back to help feed and exercise the boarders. She decided to make a final stop.

Frank Taylor's insurance agency shared space in a historic building near Basin Park that housed his family's land survey business. Arkansas was just a territory when many of the surveys had been drawn, including one depicting what was now Maggie's property. The surveyors' journals on display in the office offered an intriguing glimpse into the untamed wilderness as it had been in the early 1800s.

Today, however, Maggie's attention was fixed firmly in the present. Her earlier high spirits faded as she listened to her insurance agent's request for more documentation. "I thought all you needed were photographs, Frank, to update my account. How is this going to affect my policy on the kennel?"

"We've discussed this. The kennel itself is covered as a commercial enterprise under a separate policy. It's the personal property account I'm talking about now. All I need from you is an inventory of contents and you're good to go."

"But I gave you that inventory months ago, when I got the last of the furniture out of storage," she protested.

"For the house, yes. But what about the other buildings I saw in those photographs?"

"One is a storage barn," Maggie replied impatiently. "My grandfather's tractor is in there, and I keep the lawn mower and that sort of equipment in there, too. The building next to the barn used to be an old greenhouse. It's empty now."

"And the third building?"

"My mother's art studio. Hasn't been used in years."

Frank was busy typing as she talked. "Okay. I've listed the storage barn with its contents, and the greenhouse. If you can send me a list of the studio's contents, we'll be all set." When Maggie didn't respond, he glanced up. "Problem?"

"I'm not going to use the studio," Maggie said flatly. "I don't care if it's insured or not."

Frank sighed. "You might change your mind if the building burned down. Look, how about this? Photograph the inside of the studio, or just use a video camera to record what's there. Send it along to me by email, along with a brief statement about the contents. I'll take care of the rest. Could you do that?"

He was doing his best and she was acting like a sulky four-year-old. Get a grip, she told herself firmly. "I'll take care of it as soon as I can."

8

Lucas Johnson telephoned on Saturday evening. She listened to his message amid several from the heavy breather. Maybe she should pay the extra fee and get Caller ID, she thought as she punched in the sheriff's number.

"Doreen Crowley rented a house out by Piney Point," Lucas told her. "That's in my jurisdiction. Property records show it's owned by a real estate holding company. We'll dig a bit, see what we can find. Meanwhile, we're still looking around."

"What have you found?"

"Her car, a purse, clothes. Dan Malone said you mentioned keys, but we didn't find any. I hope you changed the locks."

"Months ago," Maggie assured him. "What about the dog?"

"Didn't find one, but there was a box of dog treats on the kitchen table. It was hard to find anything at all, frankly. She wasn't much of a housekeeper."

"Miss Abigail seemed so certain about that dog."

"I didn't see anything other than the treats to suggest a dog had ever been there. But if it will put your mind at rest—and Miss Abigail's," he amended, "I'll ask the Crowleys if they know anything about a dog."

"She did have family, then?"

"A large one, from the looks of the address book I found in the bedroom. Parents, brothers, a sister, and aunts and uncles, all up in Missouri. The parents are driving down from St. Louis in the morning. Oh, and we found her cell phone. No surprises there, family and numbers to people and businesses around here. Your name, your neighbors, the veterinarian, a couple of art shops, that sort of thing."

"Nobody listed as boyfriend or fiancé?"

"Nope, but I'll ask the parents about that. And we'll put out a press release, ask anybody with information to come forward. The usual thing."

Maggie's throat constricted. "When you talk to her parents, could you ask about the locket? They'll want to keep it, I guess."

"I'll let you know. And that reminds me, have you looked for that letter you told me about?"

"I forgot," Maggie said guiltily. "And I'm sure you have more important things to do."

"Humor me, okay? I'll feel better if I can see it."

"Okay," she agreed reluctantly. Hanging up, she turned her attention to chores. She lined the bowls along the counter in the workroom and concentrated on the feeding ritual. Most of the boarders ate the premium kibble purchased in bulk from the wholesalers, but a few required special meals. Some owners, especially those with overweight or senior dogs, provided the dog's usual food. She scanned the roster posted on the white marker board above the counter. The dog's name, kennel run number, scheduled medications, and any special care notes were listed in neat columns. A separate board held similar information for the cats in her care. The bowls were numbered to match the runs to eliminate any mix-ups in food or medication.

After feeding the dogs, she checked on the cats. One rambunctious Siamese was busily tossing litter out of his box, spilling it into his water bowl and across the floor of the cage. "Whiskers, how many times do I have to tell you that the litter stays in the box?" Smiling despite herself, she picked up the cat, who draped one paw companionably around her neck and butted his head against her chin.

"Do me a favor, don't teach that little trick to the others. I've got my hands full as it is." Depositing Whiskers in the play area by the window, Maggie swept out his cage and cleaned and refilled his dishes. She returned him to his place with a stern admonition to play with his toys instead of the litter. Then she cleaned the rest of the cattery. Most of the feline boarders came right up when she opened their doors, eager for the personal attention. Maggie, who had never spent much time around cats before, found she enjoyed this time of day, and she fussed over each cat in turn before securing the cattery for the evening.

After retrieving the dog bowls, refilling water dishes, and cleaning the runs, Maggie exercised all the dogs before taking Mr. B for a leisurely stroll around the grounds. After that, she checked that all the runs were securely fastened and turned her attention to her own Labrador Retriever. Sam was officially registered with the American Kennel Club as Samson's Blue Delight. He'd already earned his Utility Dog certification and they were now focused on the AKC's tracking test.

We don't have much time to get ready, she thought as she walked with Sam along the path leading to the training grounds. The young dog, who came from the top-ranked Blue River Kennels, was living up to his exalted pedigree. Sam had begun his tracking education in the coastal scrub of Florida, and Maggie had underestimated the time they both needed to adjust to the rugged terrain of the Ozark Mountains. Lately, Sam had shown more enthusiasm for exploring his new surroundings than following the tracks laid by Garrett or Bev.

Sam wasn't the only one easily distracted. Their long stamina-building hikes took them across her land and around the sparsely populated hills south of the lake. Maggie loved their quiet walks through the old growth, reveling in the peace of the forest, the beauty of the red-tailed hawk, the flashing grace of white-tailed deer.

She understood, now, why her grandmother had steadfastly refused to sell this property. After the death of her husband,

Leah had left the property in the care of a real estate agent who leased the house to a steady stream of vacationers looking to rent a few weeks of heaven. Looking at the quiet hills around her now, Maggie was grateful the land had not fallen to developers the way much of Barton County had. Of course, they didn't have a Sam Walton or John Tyson attracting the world to Hogan County, she mused. And that was just fine with her.

She'd sketch this, she decided. She'd learned to draw before she could even write her name, and Maggie had spent many happy hours with her grandmother on art projects over the years. Her grandmother had insisted on framing several of the paintings, and Maggie had brought them with her when she returned to Eagle Cove. And that reminded her, abruptly, of the art studio inventory she'd promised her insurance agent.

"Blast," she said aloud.

Sensitive as always to her moods, Sam bumped against her leg, looking at her reproachfully. Maggie stroked the dog's head. He was too good a dog to ruin just because she was out of sorts. Impulsively, she changed direction and headed for the lake, taking the old logging road by the stone wall that marked the western edge of her property. As she neared the small building sitting close to the shoreline, Maggie pulled a retrieving dummy out of the backpack she carried and sent it soaring over the water. "Play time, boy!"

Sam leapt into the water. Taking the dummy in his mouth, he raced back to her, dropping it at her feet, begging for more. "Why not?" she agreed, kneeling. The dog sat rigidly at attention, his eyes never leaving her face. Maggie faked a throw, but Sam didn't budge.

"Takes more than that to fool you, doesn't it?" She threw it as far as she could, sending it farther out into the water.

"He sure is smart."

Startled, Maggie swung around. A little girl she'd never seen before peeked over the rock wall. The child, whoever she was, seemed to be staring at the dog with equal parts admiration, excitement, and longing. She was young, probably five or six, Maggie decided. Brown hair, tucked firmly into long braids, trailed down her back. Freckles splashed across her nose. Tiny suspenders over a bright yellow shirt held up equally small jeans.

Maggie sent the dog after the dummy again and walked over to the wall. "Sam *is* very smart," she agreed, smiling. "When he wants to be," she added.

The child giggled. "That's what my daddy says about me."

"Are you staying around here?" Maggie asked, remembering the rental cabins tucked in the woods above Eagle Cove. Where were the child's parents?

"We live up there." The little girl waved vaguely toward Maggie's house. Maggie was confused until she saw a cottage nestled among the trees halfway between her western boundary and the county road. She seldom walked this way but now remembered hearing the cottage had recently been sold.

"My name's Claire," the child added politely, holding out a hand after swiping it against her jeans.

Maggie shook hands. "I'm Maggie."

Sam rushed back up the slope, eager to play. He wagged his tail at Claire, who looked longingly at the big dog.

"Do you want to pet Sam?"

"I'm not allowed to go past the wall," Claire said, looking wistfully at the dog.

Maggie patted the top of the stone. "Sam, this young lady wants to say hello." As the 85-pound dog leapt up easily, the little girl shrieked and fell back a step, while Sam sat and solemnly raised a paw in greeting.

"He won't hurt you," Maggie promised.

Claire said breathlessly, "I'm not scared, really." She reached up and tentatively touched the dog's proffered paw. "Awesome." She watched as Sam, at Maggie's command, jumped off the wall and raced back down the slope after the dummy again. "I'm gonna ask Santa Claus to bring me a doggie."

"I think Santa's on vacation this time of year."

"Gotta ask early, before he runs out of puppies."

Maggie remembered her own pleas for a childhood pet and found herself hoping with a fierceness that surprised her that Claire's father wasn't like her own. And if he was, she hoped there was a Gran somewhere who would defiantly sneak a wiggling little bundle beneath the Christmas tree. "Even if Santa can't manage a puppy for you this year, you can always come play with my dogs. You've already met Sam, and I think you'll really like Sweet Pea. Of course, she's pretty lazy these days—" Maggie was interrupted by the sound of a man's voice calling Claire's name.

"That's my dad. I gotta go."

"Come over anytime," Maggie offered.

"I have to ask my dad if it's okay. Is that where you live?"

Maggie didn't have to turn around to see what Claire was looking at. From where they stood, the only building visible on Maggie's property was her mother's art studio. "No. My house is up near the kennel," she answered, pointing up the slope. "Tell your dad to follow the road that goes past your house."

"Thanks!"

The man's voice came again, louder.

"Coming!" Claire yelled, and ran toward the cottage.

Maggie watched until the little girl disappeared from sight. "Sam," she said, "I think we just made a friend."

CLAIRE'S FATHER ZAK lit his fourth and final cigarette of the day. Four was nothing compared to his days in Afghanistan when he chain-smoked three packs of English Ovals a day. Who worried about lung cancer when a sniper or a roadside bomb could take you out in a flash?

He'd survived three deployments and came home mostly intact, but his marriage hadn't been so lucky. Hardly surprising, considering Althea had essentially become a single mother while he was overseas, juggling part-time jobs to help pay the bills while raising an infant on her own and no family close enough to help. Making it worse, Zak had been part of a forward combat unit and unable to use email or Skype to stay connected to home and family. He'd returned stateside after his final deployment to discover Althea on shaky emotional ground and desperate for an unburdened life. The divorce was final eight months later.

Once the doctors at the VA medical center gave him the all-clear, Zak had flung himself back into civilian life, sending his clay sculptures and raku pots to the galleries and gift shops that had previously carried his work and had agreed to do so again. He'd leased an RV and set off with his young daughter on a cross-country journey, keeping the larder filled through sales at art shows, festivals, and fairs. Traveling had been a good decision, giving him time to smooth the ragged edges of his life. He settled into his role as a single parent with an ease that surprised him. But then, having a great kid makes being a parent easy, he mused.

They'd not seen Althea since she'd suffered a complete breakdown and was briefly hospitalized. She sent a Christmas card in February and there had been a short phone call at Easter. Zak glanced now at the letter he'd received today. *I've found a place in Springfield. I want to see Claire. My therapist thinks I'm stronger now.* For their daughter's sake, Zak hoped Althea had made some progress against the debilitating depression she'd sunk into during his last deployment.

He wondered where Claire was right now. She'd promised to stay close to the house, but he didn't see her from where he stood on the back porch. He called again, louder. Just as he was about to set off in search of her, he heard her answer and spotted a flash of yellow headed his way. From the direction of the lake, which was definitely in the forbidden zone.

He sighed. Swimming lessons coming up, he decided.

The lake wasn't the only hazard in Eagle Cove. He'd been seriously unhappy to discover a dog kennel so close to their new home. Nobody mentioned that when he'd first looked at property a year ago. He reminded himself to warn Claire to keep clear of that place, too.

Watching her run toward him, he thought again about Althea's request. He didn't want Claire to grow up believing her mother did not love her. Maybe Althea *was* getting better. He hoped so, for Claire's sake. He shoved the letter into his pocket as his small daughter launched herself into his arms.

"Oh, Daddy, she's beautiful and she let me pet him and he's really 'normous and I wasn't scared well maybe a little but not much but he won't hurt me—"

Zak managed to push a couple words into the flow. "Who's beautiful?"

Claire giggled. "The dog lady."

The dog lady? While he'd been up here thinking about Althea, his fearless daughter has been out in the woods meeting monster-sized dogs and God knows who. "Does this dog lady have a name?"

"Her name's Maggie. His name's Sam. He knows how to shake hands," Claire said with obvious awe.

"A true gentleman." Zak carried her into the cottage. Depositing her in front of the kitchen sink, he watched as she washed her hands. "A 'normous gentleman," he amended, and earned a flash of a smile from Claire.

"Maggie says I can play with Sam." Seeing her father's raised eyebrow, she added hastily, "If you say it's okay."

Zak decided he'd better give in gracefully. "I'll go check out your dog lady. But until I do," he said sternly, "I don't want you near that place alone. And absolutely no going near the lake without me, understood?"

She nodded.

Later, when her father came to tuck her into bed, he found her with crayon stub and paper in hand. "I'm asking Santa to bring me a Sam dog," she explained.

"Sweetheart—"

"Not a huge one, just a little one, like me. I promise I won't ask for dolls or a bike or anything else. Well, maybe crayons, if Santa has any extra."

Laughing, Zak hugged his daughter until she squealed in delight. "Honey," he told her, "You make your list, and I'll make sure Santa gets it, special delivery."

"Oh, Daddy! You're the best!"

Better ask the dog lady about puppies, he thought.

DOG CHORES WERE long over before Maggie remembered her promise to the sheriff to look for the anonymous letter she'd received. She wasn't thrilled at the idea of digging through the trash. At least it's just the household trash can and not the large commercial bin that serviced the kennel, she thought philosophically.

With floodlights illuminating the side yard, she brought Sam out of his kennel. "Watch," she commanded. Moments later, she smiled in grim satisfaction as she pulled the crumpled paper from the trash. Another five minutes of searching yielded the envelope. She shoveled the remaining trash back into the can and dropped both letter and envelope into a large mailer she'd picked up in the office. Returning Sam to his run, she checked the locks on the doors and windows before going to soothe body and mind in a cool bath and a soft bed.

9

Maggie was exercising the boarders early Sunday when Sweet Pea growled in warning. Whirling, she saw someone staring at her from the shadow of the old hickory tree. Even as a cry formed in her throat, she recognized the man and with an effort regained her composure. "Damn it, Jake! You could give somebody a heart attack sneaking up like that."

Jake Turner stared sullenly at her, saying nothing. Sweet Pea's growls had been replaced by a wagging tail. Maggie studied the man. She thought she could smell alcohol on him, although it was difficult to name any one particular odor. Jake was wearing the same clothes she'd nearly always seen on him, and he was again badly in need of a bath. Suddenly, Maggie regretted her harsh greeting.

"Sweet Pea's eyesight must be going. It's not like her to growl at you." She paused, and then asked quietly, "I haven't seen you in days, Jake. Where have you been?"

He was silent so long, Maggie didn't think he had heard. Finally, he shook his head, looking confused. Staggering closer, he mumbled, "Work. Gotta work."

"It's Sunday. You don't work on Sundays, remember?" When he stood silently, staring bleary-eyed at her, she added, "Go home, okay? You're on the schedule for Tuesday. Come back then and we'll talk."

Jake reached out a trembling hand, touched the locket Maggie wore. "You gotta be nice to me, Margaret. You don't want me to tell, do ya?"

MAGGIE'S EFFORTS TO make sense of Jake's comments had been interrupted by the incessant ringing of the telephone, with only the heavy breather on the other end. This is really getting irritating, she thought.

Jake had obviously mistaken her for her mother, but he'd never done that before. Was it possible Jake had seen Margaret recently? And had he seen Margaret wearing *her* locket? Had she been in Eagle Cove? If she had been here, why hadn't Nicholas, or Sylvia, or even Angus mentioned seeing her? And why would she bother to come back now, when she hadn't for her own mother's funeral? "What am I going to do?" she wondered aloud.

For years, Maggie's grandmother resisted changing her will, perhaps hoping her daughter would one day find her way back to the family she'd abandoned. Leah's final will was written just a year before her death. Maggie fought against the panic that flooded through her. What if her mother decides to contest that will? Waterside was her whole life now, and she'd fight anybody who tried to take it away from her.

What was the secret Jake's not supposed to tell? Did he know that Margaret had given her locket to Doreen? What possible connection could there be between those people?

Maggie wished for someone close to talk to. She supposed she could wait and talk this over with Sylvia, who'd promised to stop by later that day, but Howard was coming to help with evening chores, so a confidential chat wasn't likely.

Howard had agreed to lend a hand but rebuffed Maggie's offer to pay him for his time. "I still have a few customers wanting cabinet work done," he'd told her. "And I've got another iron or two in the fire. Glad to help you when I can, of course."

Whatever those other irons were, she didn't want to know, Maggie decided. He was a couple inches taller than Sylvia with a thick frame that made him appear much bigger than his slender wife. There was something odd about Howard, but she couldn't quite put her finger on it. He had an odd habit of moving quietly, almost as if he didn't want Maggie to notice him.

Don't borrow trouble, she told herself. Howard's problems, whatever they might be, were no business of hers. And she had enough on her own plate, which brought her full circle to her mother, that locket, and her own questions.

When in doubt, follow E.T.'s advice, Maggie thought, and dialed her father's telephone number in Tampa. He'd known Jake, so perhaps he could explain the man's strange behavior. When her father didn't answer she dialed another number and heard a familiar voice answer after the fourth ring.

"Tell me you've come to your senses and are coming home."

"I never lost my senses, William."

"How else would you explain your behavior this past year? I wish you'd leave all that dog stuff to Jane Goodall and come home like a sensible girl."

"Jane Goodall works with chimpanzees, not dogs."

"I'm sure you understand my point," he said stiffly.

"Actually, I couldn't reach Dad, and wondered if he might be golfing with you this weekend." William and Charles were members of the same country club, and Maggie knew the two men were on the links most weekends.

"No golf—too much rain down here. And I've not seen much of your father since you ran off to live with those hippies in the sticks."

"I didn't 'run off' and you know it. And you'd be surprised what kinds of people call this area home. Musicians, artists—"

William snorted. "Hippies."

"Even lawyers," she finished sweetly. "And did I mention enough golfers to attract a PGA tournament here every year?"

"So they visit. And then they go right back to the real world."

She thought of a half-dozen rejoinders, rejected each one, and let the silence speak for her.

"I was just leaving for the Wedington's party."

"Well, don't keep your boss waiting on my account."

"Sarcasm doesn't suit you, my dear. And it's hardly reasonable of you to criticize me for meeting my professional obligations."

"I'm not feeling reasonable. Have a good time at the party." Maggie hung up, more depressed than before. Her own fault, she thought. William's priorities were firmly focused on his career and whatever could propel him into a full partnership, a secure seven-figure income, and a permanent place on the society page. She felt a tug of remorse, but if she were honest with herself she had to admit there hadn't been any serious emotions involved—for either of them. Just a prop for his career, she realized. Well, goodbye and good luck, Gran would have said.

Now, as Maggie replaced the phone on its stand in the kitchen, she found herself using her grandmother's habit of counting to a hundred to give herself time to calm down. She made it to thirty before the phone rang again. She lifted the receiver and heard, once again, the sound of heavy breathing.

"Get a life," she snarled and banged the receiver down.

The afternoon slipped by as she paid bills and filed receipts for household expenses, repeating the process in the kennel office with Sweet Pea settled at her feet and customer records covering the desk. Each file contained contracts, grooming needs, special care information, emergency contacts, and the name of the client's vet. Many of the files also held photographs. "A recent picture helps avoid mix-ups and can be useful in an emergency," Maggie had explained when a customer asked.

Now, as she considered the thick stack to be filed, she groaned. She hated filing. That's why she'd hired Doreen in the first place, she thought crossly, and immediately felt penitent. It's not as if the girl ran off to another job, she told herself sternly. The girl's dead. Stop being a jerk.

Maggie opened the customer database, which was automatically updated as reservations came in. She printed weekly and daily calendars; staff members checked the printouts and organized their workload accordingly. Arrivals, departures, training sessions, grooming appointments, and pick-up/delivery requests were included in the printout. An attached list showed the names of boarders and the kennel run or cattery cage they'd been assigned. Checking the week ahead, Maggie was pleased with the number of reservations, noting multiple pick-ups requested. Thank heavens Garrett's brother Rob is handling those now, she thought.

A few hours' work saw most of the customer records neatly filed away. Next, Maggie worked on the kennel's website, uploading new photographs and checking that the online request forms were functioning properly. She planned to offer discount coupons to advertise the puppy socialization classes and different kinds of training sessions. Twitter and Facebook accounts, Maggie thought, should keep people interested in Waterside.

After cleaning the cattery, Maggie gave her canine boarders another play session outdoors in the shady field. Nearly every run was occupied, including the run usually occupied by Maggie's own dogs; Garrett had relocated Sam and Mr. B to the large kennel behind the house. Maggie roused Sweet Pea from her nap, and with Sam and Mr. B, headed for a long walk around the kennel grounds.

Mr. B showed no interest in his surroundings. When the Beagle stopped for the third time, Maggie turned toward home. She walked slowly, letting the Beagle set the pace. Sweet Pea ambled companionably alongside, while Sam trotted ahead. After securing her dogs in the large run behind her house, she headed for the kennel to await her neighbors' arrival.

10

Although Waterside was only a short walk from their house, Sylvia was careful to set a slow, leisurely pace. She'd bullied Howard into a getting a complete physical exam, and the doctor had recommended rest and light exercise.

"Lots of folks don't realize how stressful retirement can be, especially if you go from full-speed busy to full-stop couch potato," Dr. Henry had told them. "Ease into it, that's my advice. Find a new hobby, maybe go back to doing something you did before. And cut down on that smoking."

"I told Maggie you'd always enjoyed working with dogs," she said now. She deliberately kept her tone light, casual.

"You should have asked me first," he muttered.

"All you have to do is lend a hand now and then."

"I've got plenty to keep me busy. I went over to Brennan's yesterday to pick up the cherry wood for that hutch you've been after me to make. And I'm working on the boat—"

"In this heat? You're going to give yourself a heart attack!"

"Doc said there wasn't much wrong with me."

"Sure, nothing wrong, unless you count your sky-high blood pressure and those chest pains you put down to indigestion. First sign of trouble, mister, and you're going straight back to see that doctor," she warned him.

"Quit nagging, will you?"

"Well, just remember we're here to give Maggie a bit of help tonight, that's all. It's nothing like it used to be around here, so don't go getting yourself all worked up again."

"It's a bit late for that," he said bitterly.

EVENING CHORES WENT quickly with three pairs of willing hands. Howard demonstrated his knowledge of kennel operations as he moved through the routine, taking care of the canine meals, leaving Maggie free to clean the cattery. Sylvia volunteered to exercise the boarders while Maggie hosed down the runs and Howard patrolled the yard for waste and debris. Noticing one of the newcomers was a digger, he insisted on filling in the hole and then walked the perimeter to check the fence line. By the time the Bridgers left, the shadows had grown long and the air was marginally cooler.

Inside the house, lamps controlled by automatic timers flicked on, and Maggie moved inside, contemplating her own dinner. Spaghetti, she decided, and garlic bread. She set the water to boil for the pasta, and was reaching for the bread when she heard an indignant yelp.

She sighed. "It's your own fault, you know. Why don't you sleep on your pillow so I won't trip over you?"

Sweet Pea looked at her with reproach and didn't move.

"I'm sorry, okay? I suppose you don't want spaghetti, either. How about chicken?" A tail wagging furiously was her answer.

After dinner, Maggie left Sweet Pea snoring peacefully on a pillow and wandered around the house, trying to decide what to do next. There was plenty to keep her busy, but she sensed her restlessness wouldn't be curbed by doing laundry or stripping that dreadful paper off the guest room walls. There was probably another ugly layer underneath, and another beneath that one. The image made her shudder. She hadn't used that room since she moved in, and she wasn't likely to use it anytime soon, so that chore could wait.

Her wandering took her through the house and back again to the kitchen. Looking down the hall, she realized the front porch was dark. That light should be on, she thought nervously. She ran to the front hall and slapped the light switch, but the light didn't come on. After all that money spent rewiring the house, she thought irritably, it better not be a faulty switch. No, probably just a burned-out bulb.

She found a replacement and dragged a stool out to the porch. Slipping on work gloves in case the bulb was still warm, she stretched upward, surprised to find the bulb loose in its socket. That was weird, she thought. Two quick twists and the light was back in operation.

She stepped down, and saw the white envelope on the welcome mat. Her name was typed. No return address. Her pulse quickened as she unfolded the single piece of paper inside.

Daughter OF **SIN**
STEALINGS **A** C**RIME**
Get out **NOW** OR *youLL* PƏy

Maggie's hands shook as she dialed the sheriff's office.

A harried dispatcher identified herself as Paula Sue. "I'm taking calls for three counties. Who are you looking for?"

"Sheriff Johnson."

"He's out on a rescue, him and half the county. But you can dial 911 if it's an emergency."

"Um, could I just leave a message, and ask him to call me when he has time?" Maggie made herself speak calmly. "Tell him I got another letter. Anonymous, like the first one—"

"We're stretched real thin tonight, but I can send a deputy out your way, soon as they can spare somebody."

When Maggie declined, Paula Sue continued briskly. "You did right calling in," the dispatcher assured her. "I'll make sure he gets this. Meantime, you said you're at a kennel, right? Keep a dog with you tonight. Make you feel better."

Maggie hung up and, after a moment's hesitation, retrieved the large mailer holding the first letter from her desk drawer and dropped the latest letter inside. She double-checked all the locks, collected her three dogs, and took them upstairs to her bedroom. "You're all on guard duty tonight," she informed them, and crawled into bed to stare at the ceiling and wonder who wanted her gone.

THE SHERIFF HADN'T called by the time Maggie and her crew handled their Monday morning chores. Garrett and Rob exercised the boarders, giving each of them individual attention before the temperature climbed too high. The Weather Channel had predicated upper 90s with a heat index of 105 or higher by afternoon. Maggie made a mental note to set out the larger water bowls for the dogs.

Sam, who'd spent his early years along the hot, humid Gulf Coast, appeared oblivious to the heat and begged for attention. Maggie wished she had a track laid for him to work, but she needed another person for that, and none of her staff could help until later in the day, when the scorching heat would make a tracking session unbearable. Instead, she grabbed her pack and canteens and took Sam, with Sweet Pea and Mr. B trailing behind, up to the open meadow near the training grounds. The older dogs settled in the shade and watched as Sam and Maggie worked through obedience drills before playing the 'Search' game.

Time and again, Maggie threw the weighted glove that was Sam's favorite retrieving object into the tall grass. "Search!" she commanded, and walked alongside as the dog searched for the article carrying Maggie's scent. No matter how far she threw the glove, or how she tried to confuse him by sending the glove into the woods one time, heavy brush the next, Sam always found it, standing over the article to indicate its location. By nine-thirty, Maggie had enough. She led the dogs home to find Lucas Johnson waiting for her on her porch, looking haggard.

"Been out all night," he explained, passing a slow hand across his face. "Thought I'd swing by here on my way home."

"Coffee first, before you fall over," Maggie said firmly, and led him inside. She watched in silence as he drained the mug she pushed into his unresisting hands. She refilled his cup and took a sip from her own. "Bad night?"

"Oh, yeah. Couple of amateur treasure hunters set off some black powder in Chimney Rock Caverns. Blew a good-sized hole in the bluff and got themselves trapped in the cave-in that followed. Took us all night to tunnel through and haul them out of there. Concussion, broken bones, and looking like they'd both been kicked by mules. They're just lucky somebody out on the lake saw the explosion and called it in, otherwise we might not have found them," he said wearily.

He paused to sip the coffee. "Let's talk about you. Paula Sue said you got another letter."

"It'll keep. Get some rest. We can talk about it tomorrow."

"Might as well let me have a look, long as I'm here. When did you get this thing?"

"It must have arrived while I was in the kennel last night. I didn't hear a car, though, and the dogs never barked."

"Any strangers been around?"

Maggie shook her head. "Sylvia and Howard came by last night to help with evening chores, but I haven't seen anybody else. Except Jake, yesterday morning," she added with a frown.

"Jake Turner still hanging around here?"

"You know him?"

"He's spent his share of nights courtesy of the county. Misdemeanors, mostly. I'll have a talk with him."

Maggie sighed. "He's scheduled to work tomorrow, but whether he'll show is anybody's guess."

"Any other employees or neighbors I should know about?"

"Garrett and Rob, of course, and Bev Donaldson, my groomer. I trust them all absolutely," Maggie replied instantly. "And the Bridgers have been friends of the family for years." She handed Lucas the envelope containing the letters. "I think this has something to do with my mother," she admitted.

Lucas opened the envelope and grunted at the sight of the crude letters. Handling the paper at the edges, he studied each piece in silence. "Interesting theme, stealing."

"I can't imagine anything I've done that anyone would consider stealing. All I have is Waterside and this property. I inherited it from my grandmother."

"And this reference to your mother?"

"My mother ran off with a married man twenty years ago," Maggie said quietly. "I suppose taking another woman's husband might be considered a kind of stealing."

"Have you discussed these letters with your parents?"

"My father doesn't want to talk about anything connected to this kennel. Actually, we don't talk much at all. And as for my mother—I don't even know where she is."

Lucas studied Maggie's face. "I'm real sorry to hear that," he said quietly. He drained his cup and got to his feet. "Okay if I hang on to these letters for a while? I want to get them checked for prints."

"Keep them," she answered tersely. "I don't want to see them again."

"I'll let you know if we find anything." Lucas replaced the letters in the envelope. "Anything else I should know? What about those phone calls, still getting those?"

"My heavy breather? Oh yeah, you can set your watch every weekend by him. Or her," she amended.

"Only on weekends, huh? That's odd."

"Tell me about it."

"My mother had a problem a while back with some jerk who liked to call her after dark and say nasty things. It rattled her at first, and then she got mad. Bought a whistle and blasted him but good one night," he said with a grin. "That was the end of that problem."

"Quite a woman," Maggie said, smiling.

"She sure is," Lucas agreed. "Hey, talking about mothers reminds me. I asked the Crowleys about that locket you found. They swore they'd never seen it before, and they want you to have it. You can pick it up at the Barton County sheriff's office."

11

There had been a time in Howard Bridger's life when he'd been passionate about many things, dogs and women included, when he hadn't worried overmuch about trespassing on the rights of others. That was before his world crashed down around him.

He'd learned his lesson, tried to mend his ways. He'd turned his woodworking hobby into a successful carpentry business and mostly made it home every night for dinner. He had a good life, one he didn't want to lose. When the old desires flickered back to life, he told himself he could handle it. And for a while, he did.

Until Waterside reopened, and it started again. What on earth had he been thinking, to get involved with *her*? That had been a huge mistake. He'd known it from the start, but he couldn't stop, even with disaster staring him in the face.

Whatever that doctor liked to think, Howard knew his problems didn't have a thing to do with retirement. Working at the kennel was making everything worse. He should never have gone back there, he realized. If he wasn't careful, that place could be his doom.

He was desperate for a decent night's sleep, when he didn't wake with hot pain stabbing his chest. He'd tried passing it off as heartburn or too much caffeine, but he knew Sylvia didn't believe him. Thinking about his wife, he broke out in a sweat, worrying what she might do if she ever learned the truth. He'd lost so much already. He couldn't risk losing Sylvia, too.

It all depended on Maggie. How much did she know? And would she tell?

MAGGIE STARED AT the small building by the lake that had been her mother's art studio. "I wish I hadn't promised Frank I'd do this," she said aloud. Sweet Pea poked her nose against Maggie's leg. "Okay, let's get this over with."

The leasing agent had delivered the complete master set of keys, but none of the keys on the heavy ring fit the sturdy padlock hanging on the studio's door. Maggie remembered seeing a smaller bunch of keys, but couldn't recall where. Frustrated, she stomped off to the storage building and rummaged around until she found what she needed. Returning to the studio, she unscrewed the hinge plate holding the padlock to the door frame, and smiled in satisfaction as the hardware fell away from the door. The master set of keys did include one that opened the simple lock set in the doorknob. When the door swung quietly open, she decided that the agent must have oiled the hinges when he added the padlock.

Taking a deep breath, Maggie stepped across the threshold. Glass domes set in the ceiling flooded the room with natural light. Easels and large work tables dominated the floor of the studio. Cans of turpentine and thinner stood on the worktables, along with crumpled tubes of Cadmium red, Hansa yellow, and Prussian blue. Mayonnaise jars and coffee cans had been pressed into service to hold brushes and pencils. A pair of folding screens hid a small kitchen and bath. Sunglasses lay on the table by the door, a pair of sandals on the floor.

Maggie breathed in the scent of turpentine and brush cleaner. Sketches were scattered on the table next to a large easel which held a blank canvas. A wall calendar, showing a snow-covered barn, hung above racks of paintings. If you over-looked the dust, she decided, the studio looks as if the artist had just stepped out for a minute. She sank into a chair as the memories flooded back.

Three months after Margaret abandoned the family, Maggie's father grimly instructed his lawyer to begin divorce proceedings and acquired a partnership in a vet clinic in Tampa, Florida. But before Charles could move himself and his young daughter, Maggie's grandfather suffered a fatal heart attack. When Maggie's nightmares began, the doctor diagnosed separation trauma and warned that taking the child away from her grandmother would only intensify the problem. Unable to deal with his daughter's nightly screams but unwilling to stay in Eagle Cove, Charles grudgingly asked Leah to move to Tampa.

Maggie knew her grandmother sacrificed a great deal for one lonely child. And in losing her grandmother, Maggie had lost her surrogate mother, counselor, mentor, and dearest friend.

Maggie forced her thoughts away from the painful memories. Listen to Sylvia and leave the past where it belongs, she thought. Working quickly, she photographed the room, pausing now and then to jot comments on the pad. She'd almost completed her notes when she heard a child's laughter. Crossing to the open door, she saw the little girl Claire, arms flung wide, dancing along the top of the rock wall marking the property boundary. Following closely was a tall, slender man.

Claire spotted Maggie. "It's the dog lady, Daddy!"

Her earlier sadness dispelled by the girl's obvious excitement, Maggie grinned and walked over to the wall. "Nice to see you again," she said to the little girl before turning her attention to the man. That short haircut could be his conservative side, but she thought he probably cropped it to keep those curls in check. His jeans and simple shirt mirrored Maggie's clothes.

His handshake was brief, firm. "I'm Claire's dad Zak. Zak Henderson," he added with a smile. "And I suspect your name might be something other than the dog lady."

"It's accurate," she admitted. "But most people call me Maggie. Maggie Porter."

"Where's the big doggie?" Claire asked.

"He's up at the kennel. It's just Sweet Pea with me today." Maggie pointed to the spaniel who'd followed her out of the studio. "Come on over, say hello."

Zak set his daughter down on Maggie's side of the wall before jumping over himself. He looked down at Sweet Pea, who was standing patiently as Claire petted her. "Well, Maggie Porter, if all your dogs are like this one, I think I can stop worrying about living next door to a kennel."

Maggie smiled. "Sweet Pea's one of a kind. But all my dogs are well behaved. And the boarders are always secured, I promise you." Looking at the small girl crooning over Sweet Pea, she spoke softly. "You do realize, don't you, your daughter has her heart set on a dog of her own?"

"She's too small."

"Dogs come in all sizes, you know," she teased him gently. "Why not let her join my obedience sessions? She can start on the basics, and you can decide if she's ready to own a dog. No fee, of course," she added hastily when he hesitated.

"Doesn't she need a dog first?"

"She can work with Sweet Pea, if you'll agree." Maggie smiled at his look of surprise. "I'll have you know you're looking at Champion Penelope's Yorkshire Windsong, UD. That stands for Utility Dog," she explained. "In her day, Sweet Pea was unbeatable in the obedience ring. She'll take good care of Claire."

"I guess that's okay—"

"Yippee! You're the best, Daddy!"

"I'm heading up to the kennel now," Maggie told them. "It's play time for the boarders. Want to come up and look around?"

"I'd like that, but some other time. I'm on duty at the co-op in a little while. How about a rain check?"

"Can I play with the doggies, Daddy? I'll be good, I promise!"

"The sitter's coming for you," he reminded his daughter. "She's probably got something special planned."

"She's welcome to bring Claire over any time, assuming that's okay with you. Oh, and I'm having a preview session at the open house this weekend. Some of the owners from the last class will show off their dogs, and you can visit with them and decide if you're interested."

"That's a good idea. We'll be there," he promised.

TWO HOURS LATER, Maggie greeted Claire and her sitter, who seemed just as interested as Claire as they toured the kennel and helped exercise some of the boarders and the stray dog Maggie had taken in.

"Who's that?" Claire pointed to the Beagle sitting quietly beneath a tree.

"That's Mr. B." Maggie walked over to pet the dog. The Beagle thumped his tail in recognition, but made no other move.

"Why doesn't he play with the other doggies?"

"Mr. B used to be a police dog," Maggie explained patiently. "He was hurt, so they retired him. I think that makes him sad."

"Mr. Bridger's retired," Claire said, puzzled. "But he's not sad." Taking the dog biscuit Maggie offered, she knelt down. "Here, doggie," she coaxed. "Want a treat?" When the dog didn't move, she handed the biscuit back to Maggie. "I guess he doesn't like me," she said, dejected.

"We just need to be patient. It might be a long time before Mr. B is better." Impulsively, Maggie hugged the child. "I'm glad you came to visit, Claire, and I'm going to tell your mom and dad that you're welcome here any time."

Claire kicked a pine cone. "I don't have a mom, well…I do but not really. She got sick and moved away when I was a little kid."

Maggie's heart ached for the child. "That's hard. I haven't seen my mom in a long time, either."

Claire squeezed Maggie's hand. "You know something? When I grow up I want to be a dog lady just like you!"

RETURNING TO THE art studio after seeing Claire safely off with the baby sitter, Maggie tried to summon the energy to finish the inventory, but the only thing that came was a half-formed sensation of having done this already. That doesn't make any sense, she thought. Closing her eyes, she willed herself to be quiet, to wait for the memory to surface.

When they'd moved to Tampa, Charles had refused to let the movers pack anything from the art studio. Maggie had been in the kitchen, playing with her dolls, when she'd heard Gran and her father arguing. Charles had been rigid in his refusal, and in the end it was Gran who inventoried the studio, recording names and descriptions of every painting, finished or not.

That was it. Gran's notebooks. Gran had always been a meticulous note taker, recording every detail of life at home and in the kennel. She'd used inexpensive three-ring binders, one for each year she'd managed the household. Those records, Maggie remembered now, were among the many personal items that she'd shipped back to Eagle Cove and had yet to unpack. If she could find Gran's inventory, she'd make a copy for the insurance agent and be done with it.

Maggie was anxious to get away from the art studio and shut the door on the memories she'd dredged up. "Come on, Sweet Pea, time to go." She was about to lock the door when a Mercedes bumped cautiously down the road and pulled up in front of the studio. Nicholas Drake stepped out and tossed his Ray-Bans onto the leather upholstery. GQ meets the Ozarks, she thought in amusement, taking in his exquisitely tailored suit and highly polished loafers against the backdrop of thickly forested hillside.

Sweet Pea growled.

Nicholas looked amused. "That's quite a guard dog."

"It's nothing personal. We only know one other person who drives a Mercedes, and he's not overly fond of dogs." She knelt down to put a reassuring hand on the spaniel. "Relax, Sweet Pea. He's a friend," she said firmly. She looked up at Nicholas. "I'm surprised you risked that beautiful car of yours on this old logging road."

Nicholas said absently, "I saw you from the road above." Nodding at the padlock lying on the ground he asked sharply, "Having trouble?"

"My by-the-book insurance agent insists on a complete inventory of the entire property. Give me a minute to lock up, and we'll go up to the house."

"Why don't you let me take care of the inventory for you? Frankly, you look exhausted, my dear. And art *is* my business," he reminded her.

"Thanks, but I've decided to use the inventory from Gran's household records. Frank—my agent—will just have to wait until I unpack them."

"Care for some help?"

"I don't think you're dressed for sorting through cartons in a dirty basement."

He looked down and grinned. "You may be right. I'm heading down to a political meeting in Berryville," he told her, "which gave me the excuse to drop by here and repeat my invitation to dinner. Are Thursdays good for you?"

Maggie shook her head, regretfully. "Most Thursdays I offer obedience classes."

"Perhaps I should introduce you to Delilah."

"Who?"

"She's my incredibly beautiful and unbelievably dim-witted Labrador Retriever."

"How old is she?"

"Just coming up on a year, but I haven't had her as long as that. Thought I'd train her myself, but one or the other of us is useless at the end of a leash."

Maggie laughed. "Some are easier to train than others, but no dog is hopeless. Why don't you bring her over?"

"Only if you promise to have dinner with me."

"It's a deal."

12

Maggie checked the computer printout and noted the names of boarders scheduled for departure. She and Sweet Pea had been in the office since five-thirty. With the printout as her guide, she collected the special foods, medicines, and miscellaneous paraphernalia belonging to the departing animals.

Garrett and Rob arrived at seven. "Knew we'd have an early crowd," Garrett said with a yawn.

Maggie handed Rob a can of Coke and poured a cup of coffee for his older brother. "I don't know how I'd do all this without you."

Garrett grinned. "Remember that, will you, when I ask for a raise?"

"Absolutely," she agreed. "Hey, if you have a spare moment today, could I impose on one of you to shift some boxes out of my basement? I need to go through my grandmother's records."

"Sure," Garrett and Rob said in unison, making Maggie laugh. At seventeen, Rob was a slightly smaller carbon copy of his older brother, with the same cheerful outlook and polite manners. Those two make a great team, Maggie thought as she watched Rob follow Garrett out the door.

Bev arrived next with a large box of pastries. "I looked at the schedule and decided we'd need sugar *and* caffeine to get us through the day."

"You're an angel!" Maggie cried gratefully. She poured coffee for both of them. Handing Bev a mug, Maggie studied the woman's face. "Everything all right?"

The groomer shrugged. "Headache."

"You should have stayed home."

Bev sipped her coffee. "Not with five dogs to groom this morning and the wolfhound at noon. And home's too quiet this week. The girls are with their father."

"At least take the afternoon off."

"Maybe after the wolfhound." With a wave, she headed down the hall to the grooming area.

"Not maybe. Definitely," Maggie called after her.

The morning exodus was in full swing when Jake arrived. He began cleaning the exercise yard without being told, leaving Garrett to ferry dogs from the runs to their owners while Rob left to collect a couple of new boarders.

Oscar, the tabby that had been terrorized by the Schnauzers was scheduled to go home that morning. His owner, Lisa Jarrett, appeared while Maggie was in front of the kennel dousing a fire in the trash can.

A customer's careless cigarette had ignited the contents, sending Maggie dashing for the hose. Whoever it was hadn't paid much attention to the news. Just that morning, the forestry service had raised the fire danger for the Ozarks to the second highest threat level.

Lisa waited impatiently while she completed her task, and appeared unmoved when told about the tabby's traumatic experience. "Dogs are afraid of *him*, not the other way around."

Maggie bit back her irritation and handed Lisa a contract. "Take a blank contract home with you," she suggested, "and you can always get one from my website. If you have to leave Oscar unattended again, you can just put the completed contract inside his carrier."

Lisa shrugged and paid her bill. "Lot of work just for a cat," she complained.

Thank heaven that attitude isn't common among my customers, Maggie thought. Most were devoted animal lovers, and their joy at being reunited with their pets, no matter how brief their separation, always warmed her heart.

Five more customers arrived within minutes of each other, Edith Gruber among them. "Help yourself to coffee or a cold drink, and we'll bring your pets up to you." Maggie pressed the intercom. "I need Fritz and Hauser, Sadie, Duke, Princess, and Kiki to the front for pick-up, please." She paused, then added, "Bev to the office, please."

When Bev appeared in the hall, Maggie asked, "Do you feel well enough to watch the front while I help with the boarders?"

"No problem."

In the back, Garrett was swearing and nursing a thumb.

"Who bit you?" Maggie asked anxiously.

He pointed toward one of Mrs. Gruber's dogs. "He didn't break the skin, but man, it was close. And I can't find their leashes," he added in frustration.

"Relax, I brought some from the office." Together, they sorted out collars and leashes and led the dogs to the front.

Just after ten, Maggie collapsed onto a sofa as Bev sagged against the counter. "I think that's the last of them. Give me a minute to catch my breath and I'll help you finish your work so you can go home and rest."

"I wouldn't mind an afternoon off," Bev admitted. "Especially since I'm booked solid for the next week. Which reminds me, are you still taking reservations for next weekend?"

"We can take a couple more, but we'll need all the portable pens," Maggie answered as Garrett walked back in. Noticing the cobwebs and dust he was brushing off his shirt, she asked in surprise, "I thought you were going to take a break. What on earth have you been doing?"

"Moving those boxes, like you asked," he responded. "Good thing you decided to get that stuff out of the basement, it's full of spiders and mice."

"I thought that's what cats were for," Maggie grumbled. "Momma Cat better start earning her keep."

She was still muttering when Nicholas telephoned a few minutes later. "I just read the paper. Your father is not going to be happy when he finds out about a death at your kennel—"

"Nobody died at Waterside, Nicholas," Maggie said quickly. God, that's all she needed. A rumor like that could seriously damage her business. "It's true that one of my employees did have an accident but—"

"I'll be there as soon as I can."

"I've got a training session scheduled—" Maggie began, then realized he'd already hung up.

Bemused, she returned to her chores in the cattery. She ran the vacuum, then cleaned each of the cages in turn, talking to the cats as she brushed their coats. One Silver Tabby worried her; neither food nor water had been touched, and the litter was clean. When Maggie opened the cage, the cat hissed and backed into the corner, ears back, tail twitching.

"Okay, okay. Have it your way," Maggie said quickly. She secured the door and hurried through the rest of the work, drawing a soft growl of protest from a disappointed Calico. "Sorry, little one," she said, depositing the cat in the play area. "Entertain yourself, will you? I need to check on your neighbor."

Back in the office, she pulled the Silver Tabby's file. The cat was scheduled to board for another two weeks. She scanned the information sheet for any mention of medical problems or behavioral disorders. Nothing. Angus Sheppard was listed as the cat's regular veterinarian; Maggie called and, getting his answering machine, had to content herself with a message and a request for a callback "soonest."

Collecting Sweet Pea from her pillow, she headed for the training arena and a session with two puppies.

If she'd had only one terrier puppy in her care, Maggie would have included the dog in the regular obedience session. But these were two mischievous six-month-old Cairn Terriers with attention spans as short as their legs, and Maggie knew they could turn her well-controlled obedience class into a shambles in the blink of an eye.

Inside the arena, she tucked Cleo and Tiffy into a small crate, arranged so the puppies had a clear view of the training area. A short game of ring toss perked Sweet Pea's interest and stirred the puppies to clamor for their turn. Next, Maggie worked Sweet Pea, both of them enjoying the long-familiar routine of heel, sit, stay, stand, down, and come. She ended the session with a short period of play.

The terriers, now quivering with excitement, were put through their paces in turn. The dogs had known neither collar nor leash before coming to stay at Waterside. Since then, they'd learned quickly, clearly enjoying the routine. Another session or two, and they should be ready to join the class, Maggie decided as she handed the puppies to Jake, who was supervising playtime in the exercise yard.

A Mercedes pulled into the parking lot, gravel spurting from beneath the tires. She recognized Nicholas' car as it halted abruptly a few feet from the fence bordering the dog runs, setting off a barking frenzy. Maggie stormed toward the parking lot. "Are you crazy? You can't drive like that around a kennel!"

"I was worried about you, Margaret. Are you quite sure you're all right?"

She controlled her voice and her temper with an effort. "I've told you before. My name is not Margaret."

"You're as independent as," he hesitated, then continued smoothly, "a cat." He glanced around, saw Jake staring at them. "Is there someplace we can talk privately?"

Maggie eyed him warily. She was sure he'd been about to compare her to her mother, and she wasn't in the mood for that. She hadn't missed the emphasis placed on her name, either. Studying his contrite expression, she told herself he hadn't meant to upset her. Leaving Garrett in charge of the kennel, she offered her unexpected guest a glass of iced tea.

Nicholas went straight to the point of his visit. "I want you to know I'm sorry I wasn't in town when this news came out." He paused, then continued more quietly. "The death of someone you're close to must be extremely upsetting."

"Doreen and I weren't close at all. She worked for me. Period." And the girl had that locket, she reminded herself.

"The paper said it was an accidental drowning?"

"Apparently. Personally, I'm not convinced."

"Did you discuss your concerns with the sheriff?"

"Yes, but he didn't think the clothing was an issue."

"Well, then, surely he knows best? After all, he deals with this sort of thing all the time. I couldn't do that job myself. I've seen one body in my life, and that was quite enough."

"Was it someone you knew?"

"As far as I know, they never identified her. They didn't even call it a body, just 'human remains.' More accurately, it was just a pile of bones. That was enough to haunt my dreams for a long time," he admitted frankly.

Abruptly, Maggie remembered the unidentified victims the sheriff had talked about. "Are you talking about the one Lucas calls Bone Woman?"

"The sheriff told me it was a female, but that's all he ever did say." He paused. "That's why I came charging over here, butting in the way I did. I know personally how awful this whole thing can be.

"I know all about guilt, too," he continued. "If I had taken the time to walk around my property more often, would I have found that woman in time for her to be identified? If you hadn't hired this employee—what was her name? Noreen?—would she have ended up in the lake the way she did?"

"Her name was Doreen. And I guess we'll never know," Maggie said quietly. She heard her name over the intercom and rose. "They need me in the kennel."

Nicholas rose, too. "Anytime you want to talk, call me."

Impulsively, Maggie kissed his cheek. "I really do appreciate you watching out for me," she told him warmly.

"Just remember you're not alone."

SHORTLY AFTER NOON, Zak knocked on the office door and strolled in when Maggie looked up, smiling. "Am I interrupting?"

She gestured toward the paperwork. "I wish you would."

"I can relate. Last Christmas, my accountant gave me a book called *Get Organized.*"

"And are you?"

"If I ever read the book, I might be," Zak said cheerfully. "I suspect it's buried under the stack of papers on my own desk, but I'm afraid to look."

"I tell myself if I just work on the accounts every day, I wouldn't have this problem."

"Let me know how that works for you. Personally, I think you need to spend more time on stuff that matters."

"Such as?"

"Food," he replied promptly. "Eating a balanced diet. You know, like macaroni and cheese."

"Is that an invitation?" Maggie inquired, laughing.

"Claire wants to cook, and since I didn't think you'd be tempted by hot dogs and beans or peanut butter and jelly, I persuaded her to put macaroni and cheese on tonight's menu. The assistant chef—me—will provide the boring stuff which, according to my daughter, is anything green and good for you."

"I wouldn't miss it for the world. What can I bring?"

"It's all taken care of. We'll see you about six-thirty."

"GO HOME, BEV," Maggie said. "It's obvious you need some down time."

"I'd love to," Bev admitted. "But I totally forgot Garrett will be gone. He's helping his dad this afternoon."

"That still leaves Rob and Jake and me for now," Maggie said firmly. "And by the time Rob leaves for his class, most of the chores will be finished." She glanced at the clock and reached for the intercom. "Garrett to the office, please."

"Did you see that message about an afternoon pick-up?" Bev asked. She pawed through the papers littering the desk, muttering under her breath. "I know I put it right here … here it is. A new client, going out of town, needs you to board his dog."

"No problem. I'll call him later."

"He's catching an afternoon flight. And you know what airports are like these days. He asked for a pick-up soonest." Bev looked resigned. "I better stay until you get back."

"Absolutely not. Who is he, and where does he live?"

"Corbin, I think he said. The address is in Hickory Cove."

Maggie looked at the map and stifled a groan. She'd have to drive miles around the lake to get there. She wished she had a boat. The only option seemed to be a road—little more than a thin line on the map—on the lake's east side. It appeared to be a shortcut. She'd take that route.

She was still wondering how to juggle her schedule when Garrett came in. "Hey, Bev just reminded me that you're working with your dad this afternoon, so you'd better get a move on. And you, Bev. Go home. Now."

"Don't yell, I'm going," Bev said meekly and followed Garrett out the door a few minutes later.

Maggie telephoned Sylvia Bridger. "Do you think Howard would be willing to keep an eye on the kennel for a couple of hours?" she asked without preamble. "I need to drive over to Hickory Cove, and Jake will be here by himself."

"Call you right back," Sylvia said briskly. Moments later, she told Maggie, "Howard didn't answer, so he must still be out in that boat of his. He promised me he'd be home before noon, though, to get those fund-raiser letters out in the mail for me." Sylvia volunteered several hours a week to the local chapter of the March of Dimes. "I'll make sure he's there within the hour.

Will that do?"

"That's terrific," Maggie replied gratefully. "I'll be back as soon as I can."

Before leaving, she checked on Jake, who was dragging a shovel across the yard. "When you finish with that, the Shelties in run 28 need to be exercised. Give everybody fresh water, too. If you need help, ask Mr. Bridger; he'll be by in a little while."

13

The temperature edged toward the upper nineties and dust billowed around the truck as Maggie drove cautiously down County Road 207, dodging ruts and the large stones strewn across the ungraded surface. She thought she must have missed the turnoff when she finally spotted the name Corbin on a mailbox leaning atop a rotting post. Maggie tapped her horn to announce her arrival, and eased the truck up the faded track leading to the house.

No answer at the door. Frustrated, Maggie walked around, and banged on the back door, listening to the sound fall away in the silence. Looking around, she saw nothing to indicate anyone lived here. The house looked as though it had been unoccupied for years. Either Bev got the address wrong, or—remembering the name she'd spotted on the mailbox—it was more likely this was somebody's idea of a stupid joke. Retreating to her truck, Maggie tried her cell phone but couldn't get a signal. Too far from a tower, she supposed with a sigh. The cove was adjacent to one of the many wildlife conservation areas that edged the lake, and signs of human habitation were few and far between.

She wondered what was happening at the kennel, and was reassured at the thought of Howard being there to help Jake and keep an eye on things. When she pulled in nearly an hour later, though, she didn't see either Howard or Jake.

Instead, she saw dogs. All of them.

The boarders were loose, she realized in horror. Gates and doors stood open and she could see dogs running freely across the grounds. Charging into the kennel office, she slammed the door closed just as four dogs, barking wildly, came toward her. "Howard! Jake!" she yelled. "What the devil is going on around here?"

No answer. Inside the customer lounge, she saw a Saint Bernard slobbering over a bag of treats. "Get off, Beauford!" Maggie ordered the huge dog. The terrier puppies Cleo and Tiffy had run in behind Beauford and promptly hid under the sofa. Maggie hauled them out and dumped them unceremoniously into a crate she'd left in the office.

Grabbing a handful of leashes, she made a quick detour to check that the cattery was secure and then whistled for the dogs, snapping leashes at random as they clustered around her. Maggie didn't waste time sorting the dogs into their assigned quarters but instead shoved them into the first runs she came to, shutting gates and doors as she went.

She swallowed a sob of relief when she saw the perimeter gate was still latched. If they'd made it through that gate, she thought, she could have lost them all.

The boarder's list showed twenty-six dogs, not counting her own, in the kennel that day. Mentally counting the number she'd already secured, she surveyed the yard and counted tails. Slowly, deliberately, she counted again. No mistake. Three dogs were still loose somewhere.

Frantic now, she ran through the grounds again, shouting as she went. "Howard! Jake! Where are you?" She bolted toward the parking lot and stopped short at the sight of Howard coming up the path, a cigarette dangling carelessly from his lips, wearing headphones and swinging a metal detector slowly in front of him.

"Howard!" She ran over and thumped him on the shoulder. "God almighty, Howard, what are you doing?"

He pulled off his headphones. "Got my new metal detector today, thought I'd check it out," he said happily. Then, sharply, "What's wrong?"

"They're gone."

Howard looked bewildered. "Who's gone?"

"The dogs," she said furiously. "The boarders were running wild when I got here. I caught most of them, but three are still missing."

"Are you sure?"

"I counted. Twice."

The color drained from Howard's face as he heard Maggie's terse explanation. "Where's Jake?" he asked, looking around him.

"He's gone, too."

"He was in the kennel not more than twenty minutes ago." Howard shook his head. "The dogs haven't been loose for long, that's for sure. We better look for Jake, make sure he's all right."

"I'm more concerned about the dogs," Maggie retorted. "Go get the roster—it's on the front desk—and we'll sort the dogs into their assigned runs. Then we can see who's still loose. And put that cigarette out!"

She ordered Sam into a down-stay while Howard hurried inside for the clipboard that held the roster. Maggie forced herself to act calm. She checked off the animal's name as Howard secured each one in its assigned run.

"There's a Beagle under that big cedar," Howard reported finally, mopping the sweat off his face. "And I count three runs—numbers two, twelve, and fifteen—still empty."

"The Beagle's mine; he won't go anywhere. He's in run number twelve with Sam. That leaves two runs unaccounted for." Frowning, Maggie flipped through the list again. "Okay, run number two holds Cleo and Tiffy. They're up in the office."

"So who's supposed to be in run fifteen?"

"There's no name—" Maggie broke off as she heard Sylvia calling her. Maggie hurried out to the front, Howard following closely, and found Sylvia striding into the customer lounge, arms firmly fastened around the stray.

"I nearly hit this pathetic mongrel," she announced. "He's not one of yours, is he?"

"*That's* who's supposed to be in run fifteen!" Maggie exclaimed. She collapsed onto the sofa, exhausted. "I didn't lose any after all."

"What are you talking about? And what's that dreadful noise?"

A steady whining had grown to a fevered pitch with their arrival. "That would be Cleo and Tiffy," Maggie said with a sigh and pushed herself back on her feet. "They're supposed to be in run number two."

Howard waved her down. "I'll take care of them," he told her. He reached for the dog. "I'll put this one back, too."

Sylvia tightened her hold. "He really *is* one of yours? He looks dreadful! And what was he doing out in the road?"

"He's a stray I took in—and you should have seen him before Bev cleaned him up," Maggie replied wearily. "As for the rest, well, it's a long story." She rose unsteadily to her feet. "I have a missing employee to find. I'll let Howard fill you in on what's been happening here."

Minutes later, she spotted Jake far down the slope from the kennel, sprawled beneath a pine tree not far from the art studio. Prodding him, she watched in disgust as he mumbled his way awake and raised a shaking hand to shield his eyes.

"Why aren't you up at the kennel?" she demanded.

"Told me to come down here, wait." He looked confused.

Maggie didn't even try to hold onto her blistering temper. "Howard's the only person here, and he wouldn't say any such thing," she snapped. "You stink of whiskey. Did you start drinking before or after you let the boarders loose?"

Jake squinted up at her. "Huh?"

"If any of those dogs had been injured or lost, you'd be looking at criminal charges. As it is, you're fired," she said flatly.

"I'll pay your wages until the end of the week, but I never want to see you again. Understand?"

"I wouldn't hurt no dog."

"I want you off my property in ten minutes." When Jake didn't move, she added, "Or I'm calling the sheriff."

"It ain't right. I'm telling you, it just ain't right."

"**BUT WHY WOULD** Jake Turner do such a thing?"

They were in Maggie's kitchen. After Maggie had checked all the boarders again and tested the gates, Sylvia had all but dragged her to the house, insisting she rest and cool off before tackling the evening chores. Now, pushing Maggie into a chair at the kitchen table, Sylvia pulled a pitcher of iced tea from the refrigerator and poured tall glasses for everyone before joining Howard and Maggie at the table. "He won't ever win Citizen of the Year, but I can't imagine Jake harming an animal. He's never done anything like that before."

"He was drunk," Maggie said in disgust. "I've told him over and over I won't tolerate cigarettes or alcohol in the kennel, and he got drunk anyway. If I hadn't come back when I did ..."

Sylvia stared at her husband. "You promised to watch the kennel for Maggie. Where were you?"

I *was* here," he replied defensively. "I just wanted to test out the new equipment—"

"Playing with your damned toys again!"

Maggie hurried to calm marital waters. "Really, he's been a great help," she assured Sylvia. "I'd still be sorting dogs into runs if Howard hadn't been here."

Howard shifted uncomfortably. "You should use self-closing hinges on all the gates and doors. I can go by the hardware store in the morning, pick up some if you want."

"Thanks, Howard. I don't know what I'd do without you two—" she stuttered to a halt, staring at the door in the corner of the large room.

"What's the matter?"

"The basement door is open. I keep that door locked."

"Howard," Sylvia ordered, "go check." As her husband obediently disappeared down the stairs, Sylvia turned to Maggie and gripped her hands. "My goodness, girl, you're shaking!"

Moments later, Howard climbed back up the stairs. "Nothing but cobwebs," he assured them as he washed his hands at the sink.

"Oh!" Maggie remembered. "Garrett moved some boxes out of the basement for me yesterday."

"Well, there's your answer," Sylvia said calmly. "The boy didn't shut the door properly."

After the Bridgers had gone home, Maggie went back to the kennel and checked all the boarders again. She'd feed them now, she decided, and call it an early night. But as she was filling bowls, she abruptly remembered Zak's dinner invitation. She was too tired to be good company, but halfway to the phone she realized she didn't have the Henderson's telephone number. There's always directory assistance, or she could just run over to make her apologies.

Ten minutes later, she stood on Zak's front porch. "My turn to ask for a rain check. I really am sorry."

"Sit down," Zak ordered. "You look exhausted."

Settling into the rocker he pointed to she said, "It's been a one awful day." Quickly, she related the day's events, finding Zak an attentive listener. "It's a miracle I didn't lose any of the boarders," she concluded. "There's nobody else there right now and I can't afford to leave the kennel unguarded for long."

"I agree," Zak said calmly. "Go on back and we'll bring dinner to you."

"But—"

"You have to eat. Besides, do you want to tell my daughter she grated all that cheese for nothing?"

"I *am* hungry," she admitted.

"We'll be right behind you."

Thirty minutes later, Maggie surveyed a large wicker basket Zak deposited on the table in the kennel's customer lounge. "Plates and silverware, too?" she exclaimed in surprise.

"It's the show box," Claire explained. She perched on a stool, watching critically as her father unpacked the basket, setting out salad, bread, macaroni, and foil-wrapped fish onto plates.

"Still hot," he noted in satisfaction. "Lemonade or iced tea?" he asked Maggie.

"Iced tea, please."

After her initial hunger was satisfied, Maggie sighed with pleasure. "Everything is wonderful," she said. "So, what's a show box?"

"One of the first things I learned about the art show circuit," Zak said, "was that the food was terrible, unless you like corn dogs, Indian tacos, polish sausage, and awesome blossoms."

"What's an awesome blossom?"

"A Vidalia onion, peeled like a flower, then battered and deep-fried."

"I take it you're not an onion fan?"

"I like them, but I don't think they constitute one of the four basic food groups."

"So Daddy made us a show box," Claire put in.

"Shows are long. They usually run ten, twelve hours at a stretch. And that's not counting the time you need to get the exhibit booth ready every morning, or the time it takes to lock down at night. Anyway, I wanted our lives to have some semblance of normalcy—is that a word?—even if we were living like a roving patrol. The RV had a kitchen, so I'd pack us a decent breakfast and lunch every morning and take it with us."

Maggie admired the basket's interior, divided into sections to hold flatware, dishes, and storage containers. "This looks very organized!"

Zak grinned. "I learned a few things the hard way. Before I discovered Tupperware, I used regular dishes to store food. One time, I put a bowl of peaches in with our sandwiches and

I loaded the basket onto the hand truck, like I usually do when I have to haul stuff a long way. Well, by the time we'd got to our exhibit space, the peaches and all the juice had spilled over everything in the basket and just about everything else I was hauling. The ants had a field day!"

"It wasn't too bad," Claire said. "We got polish sausage for lunch!"

After dinner, they toured the kennel, with Maggie double-checking that every gate was securely latched. After a final check of the grounds, they wandered through the soft twilight toward Maggie's front porch with Claire trotting alongside Sam. Mr. B and Sweet Pea brought up the rear.

Two paddle fans offered the hint of a cooling breeze while citronella candles discouraged mosquitoes. The furniture dated back to her grandparents' days and was shabbily comfortable. "The kind you can put your feet up on," Maggie told Zak, who stretched out on the chaise lounge.

"Or paws," Zak agreed, glancing at Sweet Pea who had jumped up beside Maggie.

"Before you did the RV thing, was this home for you? I mean, did you grow up around here?"

"No. My dad was career military, so home was wherever they sent him. I did my own gig in the service, and then came looking for a place for us to call home. Once I saw Eureka Springs, and then Eagle Cove, I knew this was it."

"From soldier to artist—that's quite a change."

"I always wanted a career in art," he said. "Back in grade school I had this awesome art teacher who let me stay in during recess and sketch. When she showed me how to work with clay, I was hooked. I studied ceramics and sold my first piece before I'd finished school. Then came Afghanistan."

"You were married?"

"A few years. Althea didn't want me to sign up, but national service is a tradition in my family. We were in Georgia when Claire was born and I went overseas the first time."

She tried to imagine what that had been like for Althea. A young wife and new mother, a long way from home, scraping by on a soldier's pay. Maggie felt an unexpected rush of sympathy. "Sounds like deployments are rough on the entire family."

"By the time I finished my last tour, she'd had all she could take. She took off, and I got a new gig as a single parent," he said lightly.

"So how did you end up traveling in an RV?"

"I needed money, so we hit the road. Art shows, craft fairs, street festivals. I picked up supplies along the way and rented kiln time when I could. It's nice to travel," he said thoughtfully, "when you know you can go home anytime you want."

"I lived in Florida from the time I was five, but this—" Maggie gestured around the property. "This is where I knew I belonged."

"Has this property been in your family a long time?"

"My great-great-something settled here back when Arkansas was still a territory, and my grandfather built the kennel after his discharge in '46. My grandmother said he trained dogs for the War Department. When he opened Waterside, people would send him dogs from all over the country to train. He must have been wonderful," Maggie said wistfully.

"Didn't you know him?"

"I was younger than Claire when he died. I don't remember too much from that time." Restless, Maggie stood and leaned against the porch railing, watching the child tossing sticks for Sam.

"I think he would have been proud of what you've accomplished here," Zak offered.

She smiled wryly. "He'd no doubt have something to say about my management skills. I haven't been able to keep more than a few workers at a time, even in this economy. And look at Jake—he's worked here since my grandfather's days, but I had to fire him, and just when I can't afford to lose any more staff." At Zak's questioning glance she added, "You might have seen the article in the local paper about the young woman who drowned. You know, Doreen Crowley?"

"I didn't connect that with your place."

"She used to work here. She didn't show up for work one day. Sheriff Malone thinks she probably drowned about then."

"That's rough."

"I just assumed she'd quit without notice. You wouldn't believe how often that happens. But she didn't quit—she died. Even if it didn't happen at Waterside, rumors can cause all sorts of problems I don't need."

"I'm a good listener," Zak said quietly. "And you sound like somebody who needs to talk."

"The sheriff thinks I'm imagining things."

"What does he think you're imagining?"

Hesitating only briefly, Maggie plunged into a detailed narrative, pouring out everything she knew or suspected about Doreen's death. "And I can't stop thinking about that dog Abigail asked about, or why Doreen was wearing my mother's locket, or those clothes!" She took a deep breath and let herself be momentarily distracted by the sight of the little girl throwing a ball for Sam. She looked back at Zak and saw he too was watching the child.

"There seems to be a lot of unanswered questions." The sight of Sam racing after the ball as it rolled down the slope had him rising from his chair. "Claire, stay in the yard where I can see you. I don't want you near the water."

"The water—that's it! Doreen would never have gone near the water voluntarily."

"Why not?"

"Listen. About three months ago I was running a training session with a retriever out in the lake. I ran overtime, had another customer waiting. So I asked Doreen to put the equipment away. She refused to get the dummies from the water, said swimming wasn't in her job description. Made me mad, to be honest. At this kennel, everybody pitches in wherever there's work to be done. But Doreen flat-out refused. Said she wasn't going near the water, period."

"Why not?" Zak asked, perplexed.

"She said she nearly drowned when she was a kid. I can't believe I forgot about that until now." Maggie paced along the porch, her mind racing. "Don't you see? She was afraid of the water. She refused to go anywhere near the dock, so why would she get into a boat?"

"So you think—"

"I think that makes it murder."

14

Lucas was clearly irritated when she reached him the next morning. "That just makes an accident even more likely. She couldn't swim, and she panicked."

Maggie was feeling pretty irritable herself. She hadn't managed more than a couple hours of sleep, broken by a string of bad dreams that left her with the mother of all headaches. "She wouldn't have gone near the water on her own."

"How come her family didn't say anything about this?"

"Who knows? Maybe it never occurred to them that her death could have been anything other than an accident."

"You're making something out of nothing," Lucas growled. "But if it will make you feel better, talk to Sheriff Malone."

"I'll do that." She hung up and called the Barton County Sheriff's office, where a recorded voice invited her to hold for a dispatcher, record a message for routine matters, or dial 911 for emergency assistance. Frustrated, Maggie left a brief message and dropped the receiver back into place. Count to a hundred, she told herself, and then get back to work. The loss of yet another employee meant more work for her.

Rob and Garrett and Bev volunteered to help with the work Jake had been doing, but she knew they had a full load already. The kennel was her responsibility, although their reactions to yesterday's news made it clear they all felt a sense of ownership.

"Who would play such a mean trick?" Bev demanded.

Rob studied the map hanging on the wall. "Hickory Cove isn't much more than a speck on the map. We could ask Dad to check, see if anybody's actually living out there."

"I don't want to bother your dad about this. Nothing criminal happened, unless you count me wasting two hours of my time driving around in this miserable heat."

"Yeah, but look what happened at the kennel, with all of us gone," Garrett pointed out. "That was pretty weird. I mean, Mr. Bridger used to work here, a long time ago. Right? And Jake—well, so maybe he drinks more than he should. And okay, he's done some dumb stuff now and then. But endanger animals? That doesn't sound like something either of them would do."

"They're both getting on," Maggie said wearily. "Jake's behavior lately has been increasingly erratic, and Howard was distracted. I shouldn't have left them here on their own with so many animals to watch."

She sighed. "Look, I know we're stretched thin already. And I appreciate Howard's offer to help out around here, but he's got some health issues and I don't want to add to his stress. As for Jake … well, his drinking is too much of a liability. I'll pick up the slack until I can hire somebody else."

Maggie turned her attention to the morning schedule as the others went back to work. In addition to a scheduled tracking session, she had a potential client coming in who was interested in obedience training. To build her business, she offered a no-cost, no-obligation initial consultation; the response so far had been slow but steady. Dog people talked to one another, and a trainer with a good reputation could prosper or be bankrupted by word-of-mouth alone. Competitive obedience and field work were her specialties, skills she knew would set her apart from other kennels in the region.

Today, Maggie was surprised to see Nicholas appear at the kennel with a lovely retriever fighting the leash. "*You're* my nine-thirty appointment?"

Dressed casually in jeans and a chambray shirt, Nicholas still managed to look elegant. "I trained my first two dogs myself, but Delilah is beyond me," he confessed.

Delilah, Maggie learned, was a slim beauty of impeccable breeding. Nicholas told her Delilah had been sired by a Westminster champion; she'd inherited the conformation but not, as far as Maggie could see, any keen desire for training. Even as Maggie studied her, she yawned repeatedly.

"What kind of training have you done with her?"

"Just the basics. She's not very good at any of it."

"Does she like to work?"

Nicholas shrugged. "I have no idea."

"Let's find out, shall we?" She led them into the training arena, where she'd laid out some equipment.

"Is this where you work all your dogs?"

"Most of the class work, yes. Some trials are held outdoors, so I also have training fields and working trails in the hills behind the kennel. But we don't need that much space today. I just want to get a feel for what Delilah's interested in, and get some sense of her current abilities."

Maggie watched critically as Nicholas coaxed the retriever through a basic routine of sit, down, and stay. The stay wasn't successful; as soon as Nicholas turned his back, Delilah jumped to her feet.

"I did warn you," he said ruefully.

"Let's try something else."

Taking Delilah, she walked briskly around the arena, making frequent turns. The dog lagged, then heeled widely, and finally crowded Maggie as they walked along. Next, Maggie selected a lightweight wooden dumbbell and faced the dog. "Take," she directed, using an upbeat, encouraging tone as she held out the dumbbell. Delilah mouthed the dumbbell and dropped it with a yawn.

"Are you interested in competition?"

"That depends on whether you can train her."

"I can," she said confidently. "She needs a lot of work, but more than that, she needs to learn to enjoy herself. Did you notice those yawns? That's anxiety—she's nervous. So let's start by getting her more comfortable around people and other animals," she suggested. "We can set up a schedule now, if you like. If you're planning to handle her yourself at a show, it would be best if I could work with both of you."

They walked back to the parking area, discussing details. Pausing beside his car, Nicholas said bluntly, "It's obvious you're tired, my dear. We should have done this another time."

Maggie brushed aside his apology. "It's been a bit crazy around here," she conceded. "But I appreciate your business."

"At the very least, I'll call in a few favors with the Merchants League and get some people out here to help with your open house."

Definitely a knight in shining armor, Maggie decided with a grin.

Inside, she found Garrett in the equipment storage area, collecting tracking equipment. "Rob says one of his buddies came by and laid that track you wanted," he told her. "And Mrs. Bridger called to say Mr. Bridger will install those new hinges for the gates this week. She also said he can be here Saturday if you need him."

"Terrific," Maggie said gratefully.

"Speaking of the open house, Rob and I can help Saturday morning if we can use your dock. I need to be on the lake in the afternoon. Dad says there's been more trouble with relic hunters around the lake, so he's asked reserve officers and Junior Sheriff's Academy graduates to help with shoreline patrols. All the campgrounds and parks are packed in this heat. Ought to be a zoo," he said cheerfully.

"You're welcome to use the dock any time," Maggie assured him. "Are you interested in a law enforcement career yourself?"

Garrett shrugged. "Maybe. Right now, I'm just helping my dad. And I like working here."

"You know, there's a lot of opportunity to work with dogs in public safety. Search and rescue teams are always looking for tracking dogs and well-trained handlers. You've already seen a few dogs in action, so you have a good idea of the basics. I have a couple of new dogs coming in soon for advanced tracking work. Want to shadow me while I work with them?"

"Definitely!"

"Good. Right now, though, I'm taking Sam up to the training fields." Outside, Sam jumped up eagerly at the sight of the tracking harness. Maggie was loading the dog and equipment into the bed of her truck when Zak walked up the drive.

"Just dropped Claire off at a birthday party. What did Sheriff Johnson have to say about your theory?"

"He shot it down."

"Why?"

"I gather her parents accepted the accidental drowning verdict without protest, so Lucas didn't put much faith in Doreen's story about being afraid of the water."

"He thinks she made it up? Why would she lie?"

"Who knows? Maybe she just didn't want to do what I asked. Anything's possible, I suppose. I've thought about this until my head hurts and there's something that just doesn't make sense, but for the life of me I can't figure out what it is."

"Did you tell him about firing Jake?"

"No, but I'm sure Rob and Garrett will pass the news along. Meanwhile, I have a kennel to run and dogs to train, and this morning I need to work Sam. Want to come along?"

"About the only thing I know how to track is my budget, and I don't do that very well," Zak admitted.

Maggie chuckled. "You don't have to actually do anything. I've already had a stranger lay the track, and I'll handle Sam."

"You're on."

They climbed into Maggie's truck and drove slowly along the winding road made long ago by her grandfather, passing through the woods above the house and across a small meadow.

"Why do you need a stranger to lay the track?"

Patiently, Maggie explained. "I need to match the type of track that the AKC uses. That's a 440-yard track with three to five changes in directions. This track was laid by a friend of Rob's who's never been to the kennel. Sam knows the scent of Bev and Garrett and Rob almost as well as he knows my own, so now they only lay track for the dogs I'm training. Otherwise, I run the risk of Sam tracking *them,* instead of the track that's been laid."

"You know a lot about it," Zak observed.

"If I've learned anything, it's that all dogs learn at their own pace. Take Sam, for example. He's a fast learner, the kind of dog who likes to be challenged. Demands it, really. Tracking one or two scents over and again bores him."

The truck rolled to a stop a short distance from an orange flag waving above the meadow grass. Thirty yards farther stood a second flag. Maggie didn't know which map had been used; without personal knowledge of the track, and without turn stakes to guide her, she would have to trust Sam's instincts and nose completely.

At the first flag, she put the harness and leash on Sam, checking for proper fit while Sam nosed the ground eagerly. Zak stood several yards to the rear, watching. "I'll time you, if you like," he offered.

Maggie shook her head, her hands busy with the harness. "Not necessary, thanks. There's no set time limit at an AKC test so long as the dog's working. And I never hurry at the start, because dogs need time to become familiar with the scent."

"What are the flags for?"

"They indicate the starting location of the track. We're using two flags, thirty yards apart, to show the direction of the track." Satisfied with the fit of the harness, Maggie opened the bag containing a shirt worn by Rob's friend and let Sam sniff thoroughly. "Remember to stay well back and don't interfere with the track in any way. Okay?"

She didn't wait for Zak's reply. "Find it, Sam," she commanded in a clear, firm voice. Smoothly, quickly, Sam moved out, working slightly to the right of the line between the two starting flags. Maggie did not snub the leash, trusting the dog's superior nose. She'd ask Rob if his friend was a smoker; she knew Sam shied away from exceptionally strong scents, preferring instead to work a step or two off the track.

Some forty-five yards after the second flag, Sam quartered briefly. Maggie debated snubbing the leash as her dog cast back and forth, but then resolutely stood still. That extra moment was all, apparently, that Sam needed; he turned at right angles from the first track, head high, moving steadily. Maggie concentrated on keeping the leash clear of tangling brush, or anything else that might tug on the fabric and signal a correction where none was needed. Sam, working hard, never wavered after that initial turn. Twenty-five minutes after passing the first flag, Sam nosed the glove lying in tall grass.

Maggie raised her arm to signal the find, as she would at the AKC test. Then, knowing Sam's love of retrieval, she instructed the dog to bring the glove to her. "Take it!" Maggie directed, standing perfectly still until Sam, glove in mouth, came around to sit directly in front of her. "Drop," she commanded, and the dog dropped the glove neatly at Maggie's feet. Picking up the glove, she gave one final command. "Heel!"

Sam moved smartly around Maggie's right, circling behind, and ending with a solid sit in the perfect position. "All done!" Maggie exclaimed, using the release words to signal the end of the tracking session. "Good boy!" More praise followed as Sam danced happily about, standing still long enough only for Maggie to remove the tracking harness and leash. She sent the dog flying ahead of her, back to the truck near the starting point, with a single sweep of her arm.

Maggie turned toward Zak, who'd followed unobtrusively. "That's only the second time we've tried a track so long and complicated. I think he did well."

"Great job," Zak agreed.

They walked slowly back to the truck as Maggie reviewed and analyzed the practice test, praising Sam's skill and criticizing her own faults. "When I started training Sam, I made the mistake of dropping just one item along the track. That's okay for basic tracking, but the advanced tests require dogs to find multiple items. One day, the tracklayer accidentally dropped a sweatband. I had a devil of a time convincing Sam to keep going. We're much better now." She glanced at the man walking beside her. "Sorry. Am I boring you?"

"Not at all. And no need to apologize; I do the same thing myself after a show. On the circuit, we call it a post-mortem."

Maggie shuddered. "That's a little too close to home."

"Sorry, poor choice of words. So Sheriff Johnson refuses to consider the girl's drowning might be anything but an accident?"

"He thinks it's likely Doreen panicked and fell in."

"He's not in charge of the investigation, is he?"

"The two sheriffs are working together to close the case," Maggie explained. "To be fair, Lucas did suggest I talk with Dan Malone. I've left a message."

When they reached the truck, Maggie loaded Sam before turning to Zak. "Thanks for listening."

"Glad I could help." As they drove toward the kennel, he asked, "Something else bothering you?"

"Family issues, and who wants to listen to that sort of stuff? It's just something I need to sort out for myself."

"I can appreciate that." As he climbed out of the truck, Zak said, "Thanks for letting me tag along. You looked great."

"The credit belongs to Sam. He's a great dog."

"Actually, the subject of dogs is what brought me over this morning. I thought maybe you could give me some ideas about a dog for Claire. A small one," he added quickly.

"Tell me what you're looking for. Besides size, I mean. Do you want the dog for companionship or protection? Who's going to be responsible for daily care—you, Claire, or both? That makes a difference," she warned. "Some of the terrier breeds, for example, require a lot of coat maintenance. If you have allergies, you might consider a Poodle, although their hair needs a lot of attention. A Cocker Spaniel would be a good choice. There are quite a few puppy mills in the region, though, so do your homework and check the breeder carefully."

"There's more to this than I thought."

"What kind of dog did you have as a kid?"

"I never had a dog."

Maggie looked at him in astonishment. "Never? We'd better start at the beginning, then. Some of my customers have agreed to bring their dogs to the open house this weekend, to help me promote my obedience sessions. You'll be able to see several breeds in action, plus a couple of mixed-breed dogs adopted from the shelter."

"I saw some posters advertising the open house when I was in town yesterday. The Chamber of Commerce is calling Waterside 'the newest treasure of the Ozarks.' With publicity like that, I expect you'll have a big crowd. Claire and I will be happy to pitch in."

"That would be great," Maggie said happily. "Do you think Claire might like to hand out the dog and cat goodie bags? She could keep Sweet Pea with her, if you approve."

"She'd love it. I'm looking forward to seeing the dogs work."

"There's an AKC show coming up in Tulsa soon, too. You should go, take a look at the dogs, talk to some breeders, get a better idea of all your options."

"I wouldn't know what I'm looking at. Would you go with us? Show us around?"

Maggie willed her heart to settle down. Don't make too much out of it, she warned herself. He's a conscientious father, wanting to do right by his daughter. That's all. She nodded. "I'm very fond of Claire. If Garrett can cover for me, I'll go."

Maggie found herself replaying that conversation through the rest of the day's work. The kennel was quiet as she exercised the boarders after supper, with her own dogs joining the activity. Returning to the kennel, Mr. B was last in line as usual, and Maggie smiled as she nudged the gate behind him. Those self-closing hinges are terrific, she thought. Garrett told her that Howard had finished the installation while Maggie had been out with Sam and Zak.

Inside Mr. B's run, she tucked an extra biscuit beside his bedding. "It's a bribe," she confessed. The Beagle ignored the biscuit and settled on the blanket with a weary groan. Sam, in the opposite corner, eyed the biscuit with interest, but made no move to take it from the Beagle. Maggie gave Sam a biscuit of his own before securing the run for the evening.

The Beagle's continued melancholy worried her. She'd tried him in the house with Sweet Pea, who liked the company, but Mr. B had nervously strayed to the door, clearly anxious to return to his kennel run. After the third unsuccessful attempt, Maggie gave up. She knew the dog had spent his working years living in a kennel, and he was obviously uncomfortable in the house. Still, she didn't want him to be isolated, so she had created a spacious corner run, large enough to accommodate both her Labrador Retriever and the Beagle. The two dogs shared the space in companionable accord, moving to the run behind the house when Maggie needed the kennel space for paying customers. Mr. B took the occasional shifts in territory with the same equanimity he showed for everything else.

After putting the kennel kitchen in order, Maggie walked through the building, checking that all was secure. She'd do a final walk-through before she turned in. Now, though, she was looking forward to her own supper. While she ate, she'd check the listings in Canine World for the dates for that Tulsa show.

15

The forecast for record-breaking heat didn't deter the crowds enjoying the open house festivities. Nicholas had worked with the Merchants League staff to deliver a truckload of canopies and chairs, providing extra shade and comfort for visitors. Garrett and Rob arrived early to clean the runs before setting up the equipment for agility and obedience demonstrations, then stayed to give guided tours of the kennel and exercise grounds. Maggie cleaned the yard after exercising the boarders and checking that everything was ready. She coiled the water hoses neatly beside the taps and made a mental note to remind smokers to use the sand buckets she'd set around the kennel instead of tossing cigarettes into the grass.

Bev turned up with her parents and daughters, all clamoring to be part of the day's activities. Maggie sent the girls to help Claire greet the visitors and hand out goodie bags, while Bev's parents headed for the cattery with their two inquisitive Siamese cats peeking out from their carriers. Bev had brought along her own terrier to demonstrate basic grooming techniques.

Maggie was grateful for their help as she was kept busy greeting visitors, running the agility demonstration with Sam and a couple of clients' dogs, and answering questions about the training and services available at Waterside. Sweet Pea spent an hour with the girls at the welcome booth and then ambled over to settle down with Mr. B, who had retreated to the deep shade beneath the junipers at the far side of the exercise yard. With the boarders safely secured in their runs, the yard gates had been propped open so people could come and go as they liked. Maggie knew Sweet Pea wouldn't stray from the premises, and the Beagle seemed content to stay close.

Several of the obedience clients had come by with their dogs and, while waiting for their scheduled demonstrations, wandered through the crowd greeting people and introducing their canine companions.

Representatives from the Chamber of Commerce and the Merchants League turned up, passing out paper fans featuring the Treasures of the Ozarks theme. With temperatures in the nineties, the fans were a welcome addition as visitors toured the grounds, with the more adventurous clambering up the hillside to the training fields and the tracking demonstrations scheduled throughout the morning.

Maggie had prepared information flyers for pet owners and offered special packets for those managing guest houses, B&Bs, and hotels, including generous discount coupons for their customers. By noon, she was running low on her marketing materials, and Zak volunteered to print additional packets.

Angus Sheppard came by to show his support and stayed to help Howard Bridger, who was in charge of keeping the coolers filled with ice and soft drinks. The two quickly attracted a large audience as they handed out cold drinks and reminisced about Maggie's grandfather and the champion dogs that had come through Waterside in the old days. Angus pointed out that Maggie was continuing that tradition of training dogs for the field and urged visitors to watch the field demonstrations taking place that day.

The demonstrations proved immensely popular, and the appointment book filled rapidly as guests took advantage of the special discount coupons Maggie had printed for the occasion.

The final demonstration of the day had been scheduled in the indoor training arena, where the cool air provided a welcome respite from the fierce heat outside.

"A well-trained dog is a wonderful companion but an untrained dog can be a nuisance to the entire community," Maggie told the small crowd assembled in the training arena.

The turnout for the obedience demonstration session was better than she'd expected. Claire was there with Sweet Pea, Nicholas had brought Delilah, and a dozen prospective clients gripped leashes of assorted breeds and sizes.

Earlier, Maggie pointed Zak toward a seat at the end of the row, against the wall. "Don't smoke that in here," she'd warned him, frowning at the cigarette in his hand. Now she noticed him watching her dogs with a bemused expression. He'd agreed to keep Sam at his side until Maggie called for him during the demonstration, but both of them were surprised when Mr. B had also settled quietly beside Zak's chair.

Addressing the group, she outlined the program she'd prepared. "In obedience sessions, we work on the basics: stand, sit, and down. You'll also learn heeling—with and without a leash—plus different stay exercises and the recall. We won't be doing serious work today, though. This is your chance to meet some of the dogs and their owners who've completed the basic obedience course and decide if you want to participate."

"I'm interested, but my wife thinks it's a waste of money," admitted one man who held a shivering Lhasa Apso on a tight leash. "She says I can do the same work at home."

"You *can* train a dog by yourself," Maggie agreed. "Attending a class like this socializes the dog, and gives you a chance to see how others work. If you're having trouble, we can work on solutions together. Take the way you're holding that leash, for example. We'll practice holding the leash loosely, so that the snap hangs straight down."

She smiled as he self-consciously relaxed his grip. "And you *will* work with your dog on your own, in between classes. In class, you'll work around other dogs. Our goal is to develop good citizenship skills. That means teaching your dog to be well-mannered in all situations, and not to be intimidated by strangers, other dogs, or unfamiliar noises. A well-trained dog is a happy dog. And that takes dedication, patience, and discipline.

"But don't confuse discipline with punishment," Maggie warned. "Correction is limited to what's necessary to get the job done, and it doesn't mean endangering your animal. I will not tolerate verbal or physical abuse of any animal, and that includes using dangerous or excessive equipment. You should use the lightest possible collar and leash. Nylon or leather leashes work best, and we'll only use nylon slip collars during class. You'll find all the equipment you need right here. You *won't* find any prong or spike collars—I don't allow them in my kennel."

"My breeder told me that's the only kind worth using," a woman objected. At her side, a Rottweiler pup strained against his heavy choke collar and chain leash. "He says one correction with a spike collar works better than a dozen pulls on those soft collars. And besides, Adolph will grow out of a nylon collar."

"If you correct properly, you won't need frequent pulls on the collar. Besides a risk of damaging vocal cords, spike collars motivate through fear. That's not the way I train."

Maggie paused to look around the group of interested faces. "Any other questions or comments?"

"When I trained my last dog, the instructor used treats as a reward for doing an exercise properly. Is that all right?"

"Treats can used for positive reinforcement, but I'd suggest using food sparingly. Try praise and attention. Use your happy voice, toss a favorite toy, and enjoy play time with your dog to reinforce positive behavior. By the way, you'll find snacks for both you and your dog in the customer lounge."

She paused as the group chuckled. "Now, I'd like you to meet a couple of recent graduates from the program."

Two people, with dogs held on a loose leash, entered the training arena and lined up next to Maggie. Maggie put her hand on the arm of the person standing next to her, a self-assured woman standing calmly beside an adult German Shepherd. "Novice classes aren't just for puppies," Maggie told the group. "Meet Rebecca Peabody and her dog Lobo. Rebecca found Lobo, who's about two years old, at the animal shelter. What was he like when you got him, Rebecca?"

"Awful," the woman said. "I thought he'd pull my arm out of its socket when I first tried him on a leash. He tried to run all the time. He was afraid of everything and everybody, especially the kids. I nearly took him back to the county shelter, but they don't have room to keep dogs for long and I couldn't bring myself to let such a gorgeous animal be destroyed. Then a friend suggested obedience training, and I signed up for Maggie's basic course." Rebecca stroked the dog fondly.

"If you want a dog that will walk nicely at the end of a leash, a dog that behaves well in public, obedience training can help. Lobo's a good example. He was uncomfortable around people, and other dogs intimidated him. We spent a lot of time working on socializing the dog. It took a while and a lot of hard work by Rebecca and her children, but he gradually improved."

Rebecca nodded. "He's part of our family now."

"Lobo and Rebecca are going to demonstrate heeling on leash. Ready?"

"Ready." Both handler and dog moved confidently through the routine, walking briskly so that Lobo trotted along, then running when Maggie called for a fast pace, turning at her command. Lobo remained attentive and eager, obviously enjoying himself. When they finished the exercise they resumed their place to the sound of applause.

"If you're interested in competitive obedience, you're in the right place," Maggie said as she moved to stand next to the second person in line, a young teenager with a Labrador Retriever nearly the size of Sam. "This is Samantha Cooper and her dog Gizmo. They've already earned two legs toward Gizmo's Companion Dog title. A leg," Maggie explained, "is a passing score of at least 170 out of 200 points in a class at a show. To earn the CD title, you and your dog must pass at least three times by different judges, and the passing scores have to be all in Novice A or Novice B categories."

"What's the difference?" someone asked curiously.

"Novice A is for new exhibitors with their first dogs. All other dogs compete in Novice B, including any dogs you train for another person. I've asked Samantha to demonstrate the off-leash recall. In this exercise, you ask the dog to break a sit-stay command, and while you're standing at a distance, have the dog come to you." She glanced at the young handler. "All set?" At the girl's nod, Maggie ordered, "Leave your dog!"

Samantha told Gizmo, "Stay!" and walked briskly away toward the far end of the long arena. When she was more than thirty feet from Gizmo, the girl turned and faced the dog squarely. Leaving her hands hanging naturally at her sides, Samantha smiled and called her dog, then stood unmoving as the dog approached and sat directly in front of her. "Heel!" she commanded, and again stood motionless as the dog moved smartly around her, finishing at her side to enthusiastic applause.

The remaining time passed swiftly. Maggie introduced three other clients and had them work their dogs, then used Sam to demonstrate a few advanced techniques and fielded more questions. Finally, she divided the audience into smaller groups.

"Socialization is important for both dogs and their owners. Spend a few minutes getting to know each other, and then help one another practice the novice stand."

Maggie moved between groups, demonstrating the technique, correcting where needed. "There's no need to sound like a drill sergeant," she told one group. "When you're teaching a new exercise, never raise your voice or give a 'tough' correction."

"I work around a lot of machinery," one man said apologetically. His shepherd-collie mix looked resigned to his owner's bellowing voice. "Noisy. Stressful, too. Takes me a while to unwind."

"Don't train when you're tense, or in a bad mood. Your dog deserves the best you can offer. Come early, enjoy the trails and walking paths, or just relax in the customer lounge."

"I'll give it a try," he agreed.

The next group included Claire and Nicholas. "I was just about to hire this youngster," Nicholas said, nodding toward a beaming Claire. "That spaniel is perfectly trained. I can only dream of the results she'll get with Delilah here."

Claire giggled. "Sweet Pea belongs to Maggie," she told the others. Then she asked, "What's Sam doing, Maggie?"

Sam had circled the group and was now wiggling intimately against Delilah, who looked bored with his fervent attention. Maggie hooked her fingers in his collar and ordered, "Sam, off!" The retriever turned anguished eyes on her but obeyed.

Maggie knelt beside Delilah and examined her. Sitting back on her heels, she looked up at Nicholas. "She's in season. I'm sorry, Nicholas, but she can't be in class until her cycle passes."

"How long will that take?" he asked, dismayed.

"It varies. I don't know how long she's been in heat, but you're welcome to bring her back just as soon as she's out of season. Meanwhile, you can put her in one of the portable pens until you're ready to leave."

Resigned, he led Delilah out as Maggie called a halt to the session, thanked everyone for coming to the open house, and reminded them to pick up their discount packages on their way out. The crowd slowly dispersed until only Nicholas and Maggie's neighbors remained. Unexpectedly, a drunken voice ripped through the arena.

"You gotta give me my job back." Jake Turner's voice was laced with equal parts belligerence and whiskey.

With a growling Sam at her side, Maggie hurried to intercept her former employee. "You better leave, right now. I've told you before to stay off my property. Go. And don't come back."

With a violent curse, Jake hurled a bottle over Maggie's head. The cheap glass smashed on impact as he advanced, stopping abruptly when Sam lunged, snarling, against her restraining grip. "You're gonna regret this," Jake cried. Turning, he stumbled out of the building.

Shaken more than she cared to admit, Maggie hugged Sam. "Thanks, boy," she whispered, and looked up to see the others standing protectively behind her.

"Are you all right?" Howard demanded.

Maggie nodded. "I'd been feeling guilty about firing Jake, but not anymore."

"That man's trouble," Nicholas said flatly. "Be careful."

"I agree with Nicholas," Zak said later as he helped her clear up broken glass and roll out clean matting. "If you see Jake around here again, I think you should call the sheriff."

"I'm just glad nobody was hurt." Leading the way into the customer lounge, Maggie handed Zak a cold drink. "I don't think he'll be back." She gazed at Claire, who had thankfully dozed right through the confrontation. "Is it your daughter you're worried about? I wouldn't do anything to jeopardize her safety."

"I know that," he assured her. "She'll be gone for the next few days, anyway. She's going to visit her mother in Springfield," he confided in a low voice.

"Claire said she never sees her mother."

"Althea's changed her mind. I only hope, for Claire's sake, that she means it."

"It's tough growing up without a mother."

"Your folks are divorced, you said?"

"Yes, I grew up with my father. And Gran." Sinking into one of the overstuffed chairs, she waited until he'd settled himself on the couch beside his sleeping daughter. "Did I tell you that Doreen's parents swore they'd never seen my mother's locket before? They asked the sheriff to give it to me." She sighed deeply. "Doreen never mentioned the locket—or my mother—to me. What's the connection? Where could they possibly have met?"

"Your mother is a very big name in the art world," Zak said thoughtfully. "And practically every other building in Eureka Springs is an art gallery. I can't see her being here without the whole town knowing about it. Do you know if Doreen ever worked in Colorado Springs? Maybe she met your mother there."

"I've no idea, but I doubt it. She certainly wouldn't have been a part of my mother's social group. But this business with the locket is just part of the puzzle."

"What else is worrying you?"

"The more I think about it, the more convinced I am that Doreen's death was no accident."

"Officially, the case is closed."

"If the sheriff won't do it, fine. I'll investigate on my own."

"But you said you don't know much at all about the girl," Zak argued.

"I know she had my mother's locket. So I'll start there."

"With the locket?"

Maggie's voice was low. "No, with my mother."

16

Zak sighed in relief as he headed home. Visits to the VA medical center always left him feeling a little depressed, even when his appointments went well. The counselors called it a kind of survivor's guilt. Zak understood it on an intellectual level; he was one of the fortunate ones, and he knew it.

As he drove, he found his thoughts wandering back to Maggie. When Sylvia Bridger's garden center came into view, he wondered what she had to say about Maggie's decision to seek out her mother.

Inside at the register, Sylvia was deep in conversation with a customer. Watching her, Zak realized this was a woman who loved her job, the sort who wasn't afraid to get her hands dirty. She and Maggie were a lot alike, he decided.

After the customer left, Sylvia and Zak walked among the greenhouses while he shared his concerns. "She's determined to find the connection between her mother and Doreen. Bit tricky, when you consider she doesn't know much about Doreen and hasn't spoken to her mother in, what, twenty-something years?" He hesitated, then decided to dig a little. "I gather her mother's departure was a bit of a shock for Maggie."

"For everyone," Sylvia corrected. "That was a terrible day. Margaret's parents and her husband Charles had gone to the field trials, leaving her at home with young Maggie. When they got back, Margaret was gone. They found the child in the basement. Leah told me later that the latch must have fallen into place and the child couldn't get out."

Zak's throat constricted at the thought of a little girl alone in a dark basement.

"If it hadn't been for her grandmother, I don't know what would have happened to Maggie," Sylvia confided. "Charles might be a decent man but he's useless as a father. It didn't help that every time he looked at Maggie, he'd see Margaret—the girl is the spitting image of her mother. Fortunately, Leah was there for her. But she's gone now, and Maggie's basically alone."

He was still thinking of that when he retrieved his daughter from the children's park where she and Bev's girls were dancing in the splash pool under the watchful eyes of Bev's parents. He wondered if Maggie had ever enjoyed play dates as a child. Probably not, he thought sadly.

Pushing that thought away to consider later, Zak did his best to sound cheerful. "I talked to your mom again. She's really looking forward to your visit, and said she had a couple of surprises for you. Isn't that great?"

"But why do I have to go *now*? Maggie promised I could watch her and Sam trap."

"That's track, not trap," Zak corrected with a smile. "And you can watch her track another time. Your mom wants to spend some time with you, and that's a good thing, right?" Zak glanced over. "Hey, it's not forever, just a few days."

"You're just saying that 'cause you don't have to go."

"We'll have a picnic when you get back," he promised.

"Maggie, too?"

"Maggie, too."

17

After the usual morning rush, Maggie was kept busy updating paperwork and handling the phone. At the moment, she was pondering where to put Mrs. Latham's Greyhounds and the other newcomers when they arrived the next day. If she moved Sam and Mr. B to the run behind the house, split their usual corner run in half, and set up the portable runs, she could make it work.

The morning sped by. With Rob's help, she shifted her dogs, along with their bedding and water bowls, to the run by the house before helping Garrett slot the modular units into place.

Checking the cattery, Maggie was disturbed to see the Silver Tabby still hiding in the corner. Berating herself for not asking Angus about the tabby when he was there for the open house, Maggie placed another call but reached only his answering machine. Frustrated, she left a brief message, urging him to call.

At lunchtime, a customer arrived to pick up her Persian cat. "Was she very difficult?"

"Pookah seemed a bit sad this past week," Maggie admitted. "Did you tell her how long you'd be gone?"

"Tell a cat? Of course not!"

"I know an animal psychologist who recommends telling your pets where you're going and when you'll be back. Animals can suffer separation anxiety, too. Try talking to her next time."

"Anything to keep Pookah happy."

Watching them leave, Maggie shook her head. If only her own problems could be fixed that easily, she'd be in like Flynn, as Gran used to say.

Concentrate on one thing at a time, she counseled herself. Like hiring another employee. Business was picking up rapidly; the open house had prompted a flurry of interest in training sessions and obedience classes. Kennel reservations for both dogs and cats surged. One B&B owner, Julie Palmer, called to say she was updating her website to include a link to the kennel.

"I used to accept pets," Julie told her, "but cleaning carpets, repairing damaged furniture, and getting the poop off my lawn was just too much aggravation. But now you're here, your dogs are adorable—with better manners than some of my guests— and Waterside is classy. So I'll nudge people in your direction, and maybe you could do the same for me."

"I'd love to. Send me your link, and I'll add it to my website. And next time you're out this way, feel free to drop off some brochures—I'll put them in the customer lounge." They talked a few minutes more before they disconnected. Laughing out loud, Maggie scooped up Sweet Pea and hugged the little spaniel close as she danced around the office. The phone rang again and still holding Sweet Pea she sank into her chair, breathless, and answered the call. It was Sheriff Johnson and, as usual, he came straight to the point.

"I heard you had some trouble with Jake Turner."

She refused to let the subject of Jake sour her good mood. "Would that be the trouble when I fired him, or the subsequent 'you're gonna regret this' trouble?" she asked lightly.

"My boys told me about that stunt with the dogs. They did not, however, say he threatened you. I'll be having a word with them about that."

"It was at the open house. Pretty much everybody had gone home by then. Garrett and Rob, too," she added quickly.

"Walk me through it, why don't you?"

"Short version? He showed up drunk, demanded his job back, and tossed a bottle of whiskey over my head. I had my dogs with me, and a couple of people were still there—um, Zak, Howard and Sylvia, and Nicholas. It was a little scary, I admit."

"You want to press charges?"

"Not as long as he stays off my property."

SHE WAS TALKING with Bev when she heard Sam, who was with Mr. B in the run behind the house, barking steadily. "I better go check that out."

"Holler if you need help."

Maggie hurried toward the house, where she was surprised to discover Nicholas once again on her front porch. "You're getting to be a regular around here," she told him, smiling. "Is Delilah still in season?"

He frowned. "Definitely. I made the mistake of taking her to the park. A huge Alsatian practically assaulted her!"

Sympathizing, Maggie asked Nicholas to stay for lunch, then notified Bev she'd be at the house for a while. "Let me check on Sam, then I'll put something together. Sandwiches okay?"

"Yes indeed." Nicholas agreed. As they walked through the house toward the kitchen he added, "I was wondering if you'd care to tour Crystal Bridges tomorrow. The art is really spectacular."

"I wish I could, but I can't manage a day off right now." She entered the kitchen, then froze in place when she saw the large window overlooking the side yard standing open, its screen missing. Outside, Sam was still barking feverishly. "I didn't leave the window that way. I need to check the house—"

"I'll do it. Wait here," Nicholas ordered.

Maggie ignored him. As she checked the first floor she followed his progress, one creaking board after another, through every room on the second floor. Moments later, he was back, shaking his head.

"No one here." Crossing to the window, he leaned out and looked down, then grabbed the screen which had fallen to the ground. He inspected the sash critically, and pointed to the hook and eyelet catch. "It's loose," he told her. "Look around, see what's missing."

"I don't have anything worth stealing."

"A burglar wouldn't know that," he admonished. "And it might not have been a regular thief. We all heard Jake threaten you."

"He was drunk," she protested weakly. "I can't believe he really meant it." As she spoke, Momma Cat stalked through the kitchen and jumped onto the window ledge where Nicholas had replaced the screen. She meowed irritably, pushed against the frame, and the hook slipped free of its anchor and the screen fell away. Leaping gracefully across the ledge, the feline disappeared from view.

"Momma Cat," Maggie cried in relief. "She must have been in the house when I left this morning. Looks like she decided to make her own door."

Maggie went out to settle the dogs and afterwards busied herself serving tea and sandwiches. She decided to bring up the subject of her mother before she lost her nerve. "When I dropped by your gallery a couple of weeks ago, you wanted to talk about my mother. I'm afraid I was quite rude to you then. I'd like you to tell me about her now."

"My dear, what would you like to know?"

"I know she's been here recently. Did she visit your gallery?"

Nicholas choked on his iced tea. "My gallery would be the last place you'd find her."

"Why?"

"It's no secret I once offered Margaret an exclusive contract. I've told you I got her started in the business. I sponsored her exhibit, helped her make the right connections, convinced people she was a good investment."

"She must have been grateful."

"She turned me down," Nicholas said flatly. "Then her work showed up in Colorado Springs."

"Oh, Nicholas, I'm sorry. I never considered how my mother's behavior might have affected anyone outside the family."

"Wounded pride," he admitted. "But it was a very long time ago, and twenty years is much too long to hold a grudge. Now, tell me, what on earth made you think Margaret was here?"

"It just seemed possible. I've been trying to figure out how Doreen Crowley came to have one of the McCullen lockets." Maggie fingered her own locket as she spoke.

Nicholas' face was flushed. "The dead girl had that locket? How do you know that?"

"This one I'm wearing came from my grandmother," Maggie explained. "My mother had the matching locket. Of course, for all I know, my mother could have sold it years ago and Doreen bought it from a traveling jewelry salesman."

Maggie pushed back her chair. "Let's forget it," she suggested, and was relieved when Nicholas began to describe the new Crystal Bridges museum.

THE SUN WAS low in the sky by the time all the boarders were fed and exercised. After the staff departed for the day, Maggie found the silence around the kennel that evening oddly oppressive. She was dispirited and lonely, and questioning her decision to pursue the connection between her mother and Doreen. She knew she'd upset Nicholas earlier in the day, although he'd done his best to wave away her concern.

She remembered, suddenly, Sylvia's warning that some things are best left alone. Maybe she's right, Maggie mused. Maybe it's time to just let it all go, and concentrate on the here and now. Maybe this was one mystery that wasn't going to be solved.

The office phone rang. She debated letting it roll to voice mail, then sighed and answered the line. "Waterside Kennels."

"Angus here. That Silver Tabby? Afraid I can't tell you much. I only boarded her once. I do remember we had to move her to the far end of the back room after the hair dryers in the grooming room freaked her out. Her owner said she's the same around vacuum cleaners. Oh, yeah, and she likes to watch television. She's a Cubs fan."

"Baseball?"

"Right. Hope you have cable," Angus said with a laugh.

She hung up, muttering to herself. "Next, the dogs will expect Lassie."

"Personally, I prefer Rin-Tin-Tin."

Maggie spun around to see Zak in the doorway.

"Talking to yourself?"

"A bad habit," she admitted. She studied his face, measured his mood. "Your ex-wife's been here," she guessed.

"Picked Claire up earlier today. Back in a week."

Maggie flicked the light switch and ushered him outside, locking the door carefully behind them. "I'm not the best company tonight, but if you're in the mood to share dinner, I can offer spaghetti or chicken—your choice."

"Spaghetti, if you'll let me cook."

"I hoped you'd say that."

Over plates of pasta, Maggie told him what she'd learned from Nicholas. "I had no idea my mother treated him so badly."

"Considering the price of her paintings, I can understand his attitude. On the other hand, your mother did what she thought best for her career. And exclusive contracts are not always in the artist's best interest."

"Why not?"

"Contracts like that can place all kinds of limitations on the exhibition or sale of an artist's work. Sometimes the limitation is by city, other times it's regional. I've even heard of a few agents demanding nation-wide control and the right of refusal when a museum wants a piece on loan, or if a gallery wants to show a piece."

Zak gazed at her. "I've been thinking about all this, and a two-pronged approach might be best. We need to check out your mother, but we need to consider Doreen, too."

"We?"

"If you're right about this, somebody made Doreen's death look like an accident, and they won't take kindly to your interference. This could be dangerous. And I'd like to help. So," he said briskly as he cleared the table, "let's go out to the porch— it's cooler—and make a list."

When they were settled, dogs scattered about, fans moving slowly overhead, Zak picked up a pad and pencil. "Start with Doreen. Was she from these parts? Who knew her?"

"Her family's from Missouri, according to the sheriff. Who knew her? Well, obviously everyone at Waterside. Garrett, Bev, Jake, myself. The wholesaler's delivery drivers, I guess. She used to rent an apartment from Abigail Simmons. And she worked for Sylvia Bridger before she came here."

"What about Sylvia's husband? Did Howard know her?"

"I suppose so. He probably met her at the garden center. That's everybody I can think of."

"I knew her, too."

"You did?"

"She came into the co-op a few times earlier this year, signed up for a beginner's painting class. I'm not sure why, frankly. Spent more time asking questions than she did painting. Never finished the course, either."

"What did she ask about?"

"How to tell original paintings from assembly-line originals."

"There's a difference?"

"Oh, yeah. There are big-time sweatshops—like the village of Dafen in China, for example—that turn out so-called original oil paintings by the thousands every month. The artists themselves are paid pennies for what's called 'piecework.' They might copy a single painting hundreds of times. Might be an old master, might be a contemporary piece, but it's never their own work. The real artist might not even know they've been ripped off until knock-off copies of their work show up in places like Wal-Mart."

"That's terrible!"

"The art world is full of forgeries, didn't you know? The sweatshops like Dafen are some of the very worst to my way of thinking, but they're not alone. Take commercial studios, for example. They hire a roomful of art students to paint multiple copies of an original painting, assembly-line style. The copies are signed by the name of the studio's 'official' artist and sold as originals under one signature."

"Good heavens. Is that legal?"

"I wouldn't do it, but it's a matter of ethics. If the original painting was created by the artist who signs the copies, well ..." Zak shrugged. "I've seen worse."

"Do you suppose Doreen thought my mother did that?"

"I've no idea what she thought, but I can't believe your mother would do such a thing. She's got something special and I don't know too many artists who have the talent or ability to reproduce her style. I certainly couldn't."

Maggie paced in frustration. "So what do we have? We still don't know who stood to gain by Doreen's death. Did she have something somebody else wanted? Was she killed to keep her quiet? And if so, what did she know?"

Zak frowned over his list. "There's no insurance involved, at least that we know about. That leaves out financial gain, probably. What about property? Did she own anything valuable?"

"Not likely. I think her job here as a receptionist was the most money she'd ever made, and that's not saying much. She spent her money as fast as she made it. Doreen liked to gamble at the Indian casinos across the state line, go dancing at the clubs." Maggie sank into a chair. "This isn't getting us anywhere."

"Okay, shift gears. Tell me about your mother."

"You probably know more about her than I do. I can tell you my father hired a private detective after she left," she said slowly, allowing the memories she'd long suppressed to return. "The detective found out she hadn't touched any of the family money."

"Didn't that seem suspicious?"

"Not really. My parents did have joint accounts, but Gran said my mother opened a business checking account of her own when her artwork started selling. I don't know if the detective ever looked at that."

"Did she have money of her own? I mean, were your grandparents wealthy?"

"My grandfather built a thriving business as a dog trainer, but they weren't rich. It was Gran's parents, actually, who had money. Certainly not a fortune by today's standards, but you and I would call it a lot. Gran was very frugal, and her money came to me. That's how I could afford to reopen the kennel. Even so, I'm carrying a sizable debt for the renovation costs."

"Did the investigator find anything else?"

"He gave my father some newspaper clippings about my mother's work in a Colorado Springs gallery. My father wrote him a check and told him to go away. Gran packed the investigator's reports and the clippings away," Maggie said, blinking furiously to hold back tears. "I used to sneak up to the attic and read them."

"I have some connections among the Colorado Springs art crowd. Can you remember which gallery it was?"

"Whispering Creek."

"I think I know a couple of artists who have their work there," Zak said in satisfaction. "They should know her. Even if they don't, there's a good chance they'll know who she's friendly with on the art circuit, and we'll talk to those people. Somebody has to have seen her around, maybe even been in a show with her at some point."

"I'll ask people around here."

"Good idea. There was a lot of talk at your open house about your family, and your mother in particular. Gossip and speculation, from what I heard. Still, your family was well known. If there are any secrets about your mother, it's a safe bet that somebody around here knows. Play your cards right, and maybe, just maybe, they'll tell you."

"I'll see what I can find out." Maggie stood and stretched. "This business is making me paranoid—even the smallest things have me looking over my shoulder. Today, for example. I came over for lunch and found the kitchen window wide open and the screen knocked out. So of course I immediately thought somebody was in the house—"

"Did you call for help?"

"Didn't need to. Nicholas was here with me. We checked the house but didn't find anything. Then Momma Cat strolled in, pretty as you please, and proceeded to demonstrate just how she knocked the screen loose to let herself out." Maggie laughed shakily. "And aren't you tired of listening to me whine?"

"Maggie—"

Sam surged to his feet and barked sharply. Zak jumped up at the sound. Maggie twisted around and saw the sheriff's SUV coming up the road.

"Oh, God. What now?" Her knees buckled and she sank down to sit on the porch step, flanked by Sam and Sweet Pea. Zak stood protectively at her back. Mr. B surprised her by coming to stand beside Zak as the vehicle rolled to a stop.

Lucas Johnson stepped out, waved. "Just making the rounds, folks. Everything okay out here?"

Maggie hadn't realized she'd been holding her breath until she let it out with a whoosh. Summoning a smile, she greeted the sheriff and offered him a drink.

"Wouldn't say no to something cold."

Maggie hurried inside for another glass and the pitcher of sweet tea, and returned to the porch in time to hear Zak asking Lucas for news of Jake.

"Nothing yet, but we'll keep looking. But that reminds me of something I meant to tell you, Maggie. After my boys told me about that wild goose chase of yours to Hickory Cove, I checked it out. Place used to be owned by the Corbins all right, but the old couple passed away some years back. Nobody's been there in a long time. Whoever sent you out there must have known that."

"So it was just a stupid prank?"

"Maybe, or maybe somebody wanted to be sure Jake was alone in the kennel that afternoon."

"There's usually several of us around during the week," Maggie objected. "There's no way anyone could have anticipated most of us would be out at the same time, or that Howard would have left Jake alone."

"You spend most of your day in the kennel, don't you?" Lucas asked abruptly.

"Of course," Maggie answered, puzzled. "Why?"

"Maybe they were interested in the house, not the kennel."

Zak looked thoughtful. "Would anybody in the kennel even notice if somebody was at the house?"

"Probably not," she admitted.

Lucas nodded. "So somebody might have wanted to make sure this place was empty. It wouldn't have mattered if there were a dozen people over in the kennel."

"But why?"

"Well, that's the question, isn't it?"

"Your mother's paintings," Zak suggested.

"They're all in the studio."

"Which you can't see from the house. And unless you've been inside that building, you can't tell it's an art studio, either. If anybody's after any of her work, maybe they figure you have some of it here, in the house."

"Why didn't your mother take all that with her when she left?" Lucas wanted to know.

"From what my grandmother told me, my parents had been arguing for days and one day she just left. Maybe she didn't think it was worth the effort to take all that with her. She took a couple of suitcases, that's all. She left everything else behind. Anybody who knew the family probably knows that."

"Her work is pretty valuable these days, isn't it?"

Maggie looked helplessly at Zak, who answered for her. "One painting just sold for six figures, and there's another big sale coming up. I don't know about you, Sheriff, but that's enough motive for me."

"It's a possibility. Maggie, do you have an inventory of these paintings?"

"My insurance agent asked me that," she said with a sigh. "Gran made a list of everything before we moved."

"Make another," Lucas suggested. "And do it soon."

18

By the weekend, all but two counties were under burn bans following the driest month ever recorded across the state. Wildfires had already scorched hundreds of acres with more fire likely as the hot, dry conditions continued. Reports of a grass fire near Hawk Hollow south of Eagle Cove had Maggie checking that hoses were properly connected to the multiple faucets installed around the kennel.

After cleaning the cages and supplying all the cats with fresh food and water, she turned her attention to the Silver Tabby. Ignoring her growls of protest, Maggie deposited the feline in the play area. "You need exercise," she said firmly, "and while you play, I'm going to redecorate your quarters." She moved the dishes, bedding, and litter pan to a large corner cage, hung a small cloth over part of the cage door, creating a private corner, and pinned a sign to the cloth saying, "No vacuuming!" Finally, she carried in the small television from the customer lounge, set it on a table against the far wall, and turned the channel to the Chicago station. "You'll be happy to know the Cubs are playing at Wrigley today," she said as she deposited the cat in her new quarters.

After cleaning the dog runs, Maggie felt the weary pride of labor invested in her own business. She smiled wryly as she remembered one customer who said, "How sweet to spend your day with all these cute animals!"

Sweet isn't quite the word for it, Maggie thought as she hosed down the last run. Kennel work was hard labor. Maggie took pride in a clean kennel, and had trained her entire staff to meet her high standards of care. "Treat all boarders as though they were your family pets," she'd instructed.

When she went back in to check the cattery, she was pleased to see the Silver Tabby peeking out from behind the curtain, looking interested in her surroundings for the first time. Maggie shook her head, smiling.

After an hour of paperwork, interrupted only by the now-predictable calls from the heavy breather, she pulled out the lawn mower and worked on the yard around the house. Sweet Pea drowsed in the shade as Maggie weeded flower boxes and cut the ivy back from the screens, coaxing the trailing vines to curl around the porch railing. She found a bird bath stored in the old barn, and dragged it back to rest between the flower beds. She wanted to set out the lawn furniture as well, but that would have to wait until she could ask Garrett or Rob to make another trip to the basement.

Late in the afternoon, Maggie sprawled on the porch with Sweet Pea snoring beside her and surveyed the results of her labor. Checking her watch, she estimated Sylvia should be home from the garden center. Remembering Zak's suggestion, she decided it was time to ask her neighbors more questions about her mother. Before she could change her mind, she headed for the telephone.

Sylvia sounded pleased by the invitation. "I just got home. Let me shower and change, and we'll be over."

A short time later, as the three of them settled beneath the paddle fans on the front porch and Maggie offered iced tea, Sylvia asked, "Everything all right at the kennel?"

"It's actually been quiet the last few days."

"I suppose that pitiful stray has gone to the shelter by now."

"Not yet. They're short of space, and anyway puppies and cute dogs are most likely to be adopted first."

"Living at the county shelter would still be better than roaming wild, I suppose."

"They don't have the money or space to keep animals indefinitely. If he's not adopted quickly, he'll probably be put down."

"You're not going to let that happen, are you?"

"I can't keep him indefinitely either," Maggie pointed out, and watched a series of emotions flicker in Sylvia's eyes.

"You don't like dogs," Howard reminded his wife.

"I didn't like that last one of yours. Looked like a black wolf. Now, that little stray, there's something special about him. Maggie, you just can't send him to the shelter."

"We'll see." Privately, Maggie thought the stray had already found his next owner, even if Sylvia didn't realize it yet. Smiling, she let the conversation wander from dogs to the weather to local politics and back to dogs again before Howard gave her the opening she wanted.

"Your grandfather would have enjoyed the field dog trials at Blue Mountain this year," he told Maggie. "Some real champions turned out for the competition."

"You probably trained your share of champions yourself."

"Me? No, I just helped Miles—he was the real pro."

"Howard's much too modest," Sylvia declared. "He handled all the day-to-day work here. Ran the place entirely when Miles was out in the field."

"You never went to the trials yourself, Howard?"

He shrugged. "Back then? No, somebody had to look after the kennel. Miles didn't run a big boarding operation like you've got, but he usually had a handful of retrievers here in training, and of course he couldn't leave them alone. He hated to travel without your grandmother, and your father was always busy."

"And my mother?"

He stared at the ice cubes in his glass. "She would have been with you, wouldn't she?"

"Or down in her studio," Sylvia said quickly. "Margaret didn't like dogs very much. Said she couldn't paint with all the barking. That's why she had that studio built where she did, at the very edge of the property."

"If she thought a few retrievers were noisy, she'd really hate the place now," Maggie said sardonically.

"You don't really think Margaret's coming back to Eagle Cove, do you?"

"I think there's a good chance she's already been here, and recently. Sylvia, do you remember me telling you about the locket she gave to Doreen—" She was interrupted by a groan from Howard as his glass broke, splashing tea in a wide arc.

"Sorry." Howard grimaced and flexed his fingers gingerly. "Clumsy of me."

Sylvia jumped up. "Chest pains again?"

"It's just a muscle spasm."

Maggie hurried to remove the broken glass. They hovered anxiously until Howard waved them both away, insisting he was fine.

Sylvia settled into another chair, this one closer to her husband. "I've heard something about Doreen that might interest you," she told Maggie. "Some of my crew heard about her drowning, and were talking about the last time they saw her."

"When was that?"

"Right around spring break, I think. We were doing some work for that new bank, the one next to the artist's co-op. Anyway, Miranda told me Doreen had been bragging about 'rolling in money' real soon. And Jessie Lynn—who could match Doreen story for story when it comes to gossip—claims Doreen showed them a pretty necklace, said it was her ticket out of here."

"A necklace! Was it my mother's locket?"

"You don't really believe your mother would give that to a girl like Doreen, do you?"

"Is there another explanation? Howard, what do you think?"

"I dunno—maybe the girl got it from a pawn shop."

Maggie shook her head. "How many paintings has my mother sold over the years? I seriously doubt she's ever had to pawn anything. No, that doesn't make any sense."

"Giving family jewelry to Doreen doesn't make much sense, either," Sylvia pointed out.

"So where did Doreen get that locket? Her family said they'd never seen it before. They insisted the sheriff give it to me."

"Well, then, that's the end to it," Howard said, clearly relieved. "Let it go, why don't you?"

"I need to know the truth. And my mother may be the only one who can tell me. Sylvia, would you ask around, see if she's stayed in contact with anybody?"

"I guess so," Sylvia said reluctantly. "All right. If it means so much to you, I'll do it."

ZAK TURNED OFF the county road and drove slowly down the dirt lane leading to the cottage. He'd followed up on his promise to Maggie and contacted colleagues in Colorado Springs, beginning with an old friend he'd known since high school.

Nathan Wheeler had been pleased to hear from him. After catching up on events in their lives since they last worked the art show circuit together, Zak explained the reason for the call.

"Margaret Raeburn is a seriously good painter," his friend Nathan said. "You've seen her work, right? Man, if I could paint like that—"

"Stick to pottery," Zak advised. "So what's she like? Besides being a brilliant painter, I mean."

"Never met her," Nathan said regretfully. "I guess public appearances aren't her kind of thing. Can't say I blame her. I mean, with every gallery in the country clamoring for her work, why would she slog through the mud with us commoners?"

"Do me a favor, will you? Ask around, listen to the circuit gossip, see who knows her."

"Why all the interest?"

"I'll explain soon," Zak promised. "Hey, send me a couple of pieces and I'll show your stuff to some of the galleries here. Pottery sells big in these parts, and the tourists will love your work."

After promising to stay in touch, Zak disconnected and dialed the number for the Whispering Creek Gallery, where Margaret Raeburn's work was sold. After a short delay, he found himself talking to Jefferson Fulbright, the gallery's owner.

"Does all her business through her agent," Fulbright said after hearing Zak's request. "I've never met the woman myself."

"That's not typical, is it?"

"Margaret Raeburn is a very well-known name in the industry, and her agent is one of the best in the business," the owner pointed out. "Actually, I carry the work of several I don't know personally. Leo Shotweiler represents them all. Damned good at his job, Leo is."

"How can I reach Mr. Shotweiler?"

"If there's some problem with a painting—"

"Nothing like that," Zak assured him. "Family business. I'm calling on behalf of her daughter."

"I didn't know she had a daughter."

"About Mr. Shotweiler—"

"He's on vacation. Out of the country, actually."

Zak groaned.

"Celebrating his 25th wedding anniversary in style," the gallery owner continued. "Treated his wife to a cruise around the Greek islands."

Zak gave his own name and number, as well as the number to Waterside Kennels, and pressed the gallery owner to pass that information to the agent as soon as he returned from vacation. "It's important," he told him.

19

Reporting the results of his phone labors, Zak said, "Your mother seems to be something of a recluse. As far as I could find out, she doesn't socialize with anyone attached to the gallery, I don't think she's on the show circuit, and nobody I talked to has ever met her."

"How is that possible?"

"She has a very high-priced agent," Zak said simply. "The owner told me his gallery carries the work of several artists he's never met. In the art world, being eccentric is a marketing plus."

"What did the agent have to say?"

"Haven't tracked him down yet." He told her about the anniversary cruise. "But there's something else I can do while I wait to hear from him. I'm going to check to see if your mother signed on for an exhibition tour."

"I thought you said she's not on the show circuit."

"An exhibition tour is different. Artists sometimes agree to display their work at museums and cultural arts centers across the country, and quite often the artist will make an appearance."

"So?"

"So I'll check the exhibition schedule for events in Kansas City, St. Louis, Memphis. Tulsa and Dallas, too, while I'm at it. That would put her within driving distance of us. It still doesn't connect her with Doreen, but maybe we'll get lucky."

"St. Louis," Maggie repeated thoughtfully. "Doreen was from St. Louis."

"I'll start there," Zak promised. "I'm working at the co-op from one to six tomorrow. I can make some calls then."

"I'll do some more checking of my own. When I talked to Howard and Sylvia, the conversation made Howard nervous."

"Any idea why?"

"No. But when I mentioned the locket, he broke his glass."

"What made him nervous, the locket or Doreen? Or was it you talking about your mother?"

She paused, considering. "I got the impression he knew my mother better than he wanted to admit."

"Ask Howard what he knows about Jake Turner, too."

"Why?"

"Both Jake and Howard worked for your grandfather years ago. They've known each other a long time and they were here alone the day the dogs got loose. Maybe there's more to either of them than we know."

"Okay," Maggie agreed, and offered dinner. "Spaghetti or chicken?"

"Is that all you ever eat?"

"Pretty much," she replied cheerfully. "I make a mean bowl of soup, too. And you should taste my fruit salad."

"Not tonight. I have steaks in the fridge. Be right back."

Over dinner, they discussed Claire's growing interest in dogs. "I admit, I'm warming up to the idea of a dog of her own," he told her. "She enjoys watching you work."

"Speaking of work, I've entered Sam in the next round of obedience trials in Tulsa. And I'm handling a dog for one of my clients."

"Will you be doing the same kind of thing I've seen so far?"

"Yes, but also retrieves, scent discrimination, and jumps. Sam already has his Utility Dog title, so he's done it all before."

"If he already has the title, why compete?"

"Two reasons, really. We're working on his UDX title—that's Utility Dog Excellent," she explained. "I'm also working on his tracking certification, but that's a different test."

"And the second reason?"

"Good advertising. A good chunk of my income comes from training dogs, and demonstration is the best marketing tool I have. A lot of dog owners want to see their dogs win awards, but don't want to handle the training or the competition themselves. So Sam and I go to the trials, he makes me look good, and I get more customers."

Zak cleared the table. "Want a cheering section?"

"Absolutely. If you like, you can start this week. Sam's at his best when he's working in front of an audience. You can tell me when I make a mistake."

"How will I know what you're supposed to be doing?"

Maggie rummaged through the paperwork on the table and found the AKC rule book. She tossed it to Zak, who looked dismayed by its size.

"Changed your mind already?" she teased.

"Not on your life," he replied with a grin. "By the way, I promised Claire a picnic as soon as she gets back from her mother's. She told me to be sure and invite you."

"I'll bring the marshmallows."

Before leaving, Zak suggested Maggie move Sam into the house. "At least for tonight," he said. "I've seen him when he's angry, and only a suicidal burglar would face a dog like that. Bring him in tonight so I won't have to worry about somebody trying to carry you off."

"You've just given me an idea," Maggie said suddenly. "Oh, I wish I had a boat."

"Why?"

"I have an idea. Meet me at the dock tomorrow morning and I'll explain."

20

Maggie exercised all the boarders before leaving a resigned Sam on guard duty in the kennel. "I'll make it up to you, big guy," she promised before hurrying down to meet Zak.

"Sheriff Malone told me Doreen had quite a few bruises when they found her," she said as they walked along the shore.

"So?"

"So she was quick to point out any bruises she got on the job. Said manual labor wasn't in her job description. She complained about every bump and scrape, but I never saw any serious bruises. That tells me she got those after I last saw her."

"She was a receptionist. No offense, but how hard could that be?"

"Waterside is a fluid operation," Maggie explained. "We all have primary jobs, of course. Bev handles the grooming, Garrett and Rob take care of the canine boarders, and I do the training and whatever else needs doing. Doreen worked the front desk, but she was expected to pitch in wherever necessary, just like the rest of us."

Zak gazed up the hill toward the kennel. "Pretty fancy setup you've got here. Of course," he admitted frankly, "I don't know a thing about dogs, let alone a boarding kennel. Do they all look like this?"

"More frugal, less frills. Most are bare-bones operations working on a shoestring budget. Without Gran's money, I would have gone the same route, pouring all my money into the basics. I'm luckier than most."

"I'd say you've made your own luck."

"Let's hope it holds until we figure this out." She paused, thinking. "If Doreen fell from a dock like this, I don't see how she could have gotten those bruises. She might have bruised her knee, or even her shin, but there's no way she'd get the kind of bruises Sheriff Malone described—almost a ring of bruises, I think he said. Plus, the water is pretty shallow by the dock, especially in this drought. If she'd fallen off a dock, all she'd have to do is stand up to be out of danger."

"But she wasn't found near your dock, was she?"

"A fisherman found her body out by Lost Bridge." Maggie shuddered. "There must be a boat involved. But whose?"

"Did they find alcohol in her system?"

"More than the legal limit. Being drunk might explain why she was out in on the lake at all, given her fear of the water. I'm guessing she was in a boat with somebody she trusted."

"Reasonable."

"Now all we need is a boat to prove it."

"One boat, coming up. I called Sylvia last night; we can use Howard's. She thinks you need a little of the three Rs. You know, rest and relaxation."

"That's only two Rs," Maggie said suspiciously. "What's the third?"

"Romance, of course."

"Romance?"

"Well, I could hardly tell her we want to try out possible murder scenarios, could I?"

"I guess we could go out when Garrett's here to watch the kennel," Maggie said uncertainly.

"I thought of that, too. Howard is bringing the boat along," he checked his watch, "in about thirty minutes. Sylvia's coming too, and they're both going to stay in the kennel until we get back. So go get ready and meet me back down here in half an hour."

HOWARD'S BOAT WAS a sleek twenty-footer with a white fiberglass hull, bench seating for six, and storage compartments cleverly built into the deck. Its compact size and powerful motor made it easy to handle as Zak navigated past other craft into the main channel.

They drifted along, tossing out theories and considering possibilities. An hour later, they were no closer to a solution than before. Maggie slapped on another layer of sunscreen, adjusted her life vest, and offered the bottle to Zak, who shook his head, all his attention focused on the puzzle before them.

"Maybe she was bound and gagged," he suggested. "You say she was afraid of the water. Wouldn't she have screamed blue murder if somebody had tried to force her into a boat? At the very least, she'd have put up a fight."

"The sheriff said there weren't any defensive injuries. If Doreen had been tied up, the autopsy report would have mentioned marks on her skin from the ropes, or tape residue or bruising around her mouth if she'd been gagged."

Zak steadied himself against the side rail as the craft rocked in the wake of a passing speedboat. "Maybe she just lost her footing and fell overboard," he said wryly. He turned toward the stern and cursed as he tripped over a long pole lying on the deck. "Another stunt like that and *I'll* fall overboard. I should have stowed this away with Howard's metal detector and his other gear." As he picked up the pole another boat sped past, setting their own bobbing wildly once again.

Maggie stumbled and the pole caught her smack across her shins. "Ow!" She steadied herself against the side rail. "That hurt!"

"Are you okay?"

Maggie stared, transfixed, at the pole. "That might be it! What if Doreen tripped over a pole just like that?" She grasped the pole and swung it round experimentally. "Or maybe she was pushed from behind and fell. She might have knocked her shins against the side as she fell overboard."

"That would account for some of the bruises. But how do you explain a whole ring of them?"

"I can't. Maybe we're just wasting our time out here."

"Hey!" Zak dropped the pole and dropped down to the deck. "Are you willing to try one more experiment?"

"What—" Her breath left her in a rush as he wrapped his fingers firmly around her ankles, jerking her off her feet, and in one powerful move, thrust her up and over the side of the boat and into the water.

By the time Maggie resurfaced, choking and spluttering, the boat was several yards away.

"I think it's time to call the sheriff," Zak said as he pulled her back on board.

21

Lucas Johnson was not impressed. "She fell in the water and drowned. Her parents believe it. Dan Malone believes it. I believe it. Why can't you?"

"I'd bet everything I have she was not out there alone on the lake when she drowned," Maggie retorted. "You don't want to believe she was afraid of the water? Fine. I don't care. But those bruises, Lucas. How do you explain those?"

Silence.

"I'll talk to the coroner," Lucas said finally. "And in the meantime," he warned, "keep your murder theories to yourself. I don't want to fish *your* body out of the lake," he said darkly, and slammed the phone down before Maggie could reply.

The following week was a blur of activity. Garrett, assisted by his brother, handled the daily arrivals and departures, escorting the dogs from the runs to the owners while Maggie managed the intercom, telephone, and customer billing in between retrieving cats as their owners called for them. Bev arrived early every day and disappeared into the grooming room, emerging only to collect the next animal on her grooming schedule. By Wednesday afternoon, she looked ready to drop.

"You don't look well," Maggie said, concerned.

"You're a fine one to talk. When's the last time you had a decent night's sleep?"

"Can't remember," Maggie admitted. Her nightmares now included horrid dreams of being thrown overboard. She'd wake long before dawn, screaming and thrashing and gasping for air, to find herself tangled in the sheets with Sam and Sweet Pea standing guard beside her.

There was still no word from Lucas. Patience, she counseled herself.

Patience, though, was in short supply. On the pretense of thanking him for the use of his boat, Maggie had dropped by to see Howard, hoping to persuade him to talk, convinced he knew more than he'd let on. She hoped he'd confide in her if she got him alone, but so far that hadn't happened.

Face facts, she jeered as she attacked the pile of paperwork on her desk. She missed Zak. She hadn't seen him since their boat excursion, and they'd spoken just once, briefly, by phone.

"We'll need to wait on our picnic," he'd said when he called. "I think Claire picked up some kind of bug when she was visiting her mother. You probably wouldn't appreciate us passing a virus along."

Without Zak's company, the week dragged by. Maggie busied herself with kennel chores and training sessions, spending her spare time working with Sam. She tried several times more to talk to Howard, but each time she ventured by the Bridger home, no one answered her repeated knocking.

Friday morning, Lucas delivered a bombshell.

"Consider this an apology," the sheriff said gruffly. "One of the Crowley cousins has corroborated the dead girl's story. Said they were at a summer day camp, kids were horsing around in the lake, and Doreen went under. A camp counselor was right there and pulled her out, no problems. Told the parents she was never in any danger. This cousin, however, says Doreen freaked out, insisted she nearly drowned."

"She *was* afraid of the water, wasn't she?"

"Looks that way, although her folks didn't realize it. Seems she was prone to exaggeration as a child, and with the camp counselor saying differently, nobody took much notice of the girl's story.

"As to your theory about the bruises around her ankles and how that might have happened, I've asked Barton County to review the case in light of this new information. We just might be looking at something other than accidental death."

He cleared his throat. "There's something else. According to the same cousin, the Crowley girl was indeed planning to be married."

"So Miss Abigail was right!" Maggie exclaimed. "When? And who? And why hasn't he come forward?"

"As to 'when,' just as soon as the groom tidied up some loose ends, according to the cousin. 'Who' is anybody's guess. The cousin says Doreen called her in March, swore her to silence. Told her she wanted to surprise everybody."

"There's no way Doreen could have kept something like that a secret. And why would she want to, anyway?" A thought struck her. "Unless he was still married to someone else."

"That might explain why he hasn't come forward," Lucas agreed. "I'll pass your ideas along to Dan Malone."

Maggie hung up and went in search of Bev. "I think it's time I had a talk with Miss Abigail."

BEFORE DRIVING INTO Eureka Springs, Maggie gave Sam a solid workout, and then put a few of the boarders through their scheduled training sessions. It was two o'clock before she reached Miss Abigail's B&B.

"I appreciate your taking the time to talk with me," Maggie told her hostess after she'd accepted a tall glass of iced tea.

"Afternoons are usually quiet here," the elderly woman informed her. "My guests enjoy visiting the shops and browsing through the galleries. We'll have plenty of time for a nice chat." Miss Abigail settled herself more comfortably among the cushions and reached for her knitting.

"I hope it won't upset you, but I'd like to ask you a few questions about Doreen."

Miss Abigail's eyes filled with quick tears. "That dear girl, such a tragedy."

"Did she live here long?"

"Nearly four years," the elderly woman said. "Such good company. I always enjoyed her stories, made me forget my aches and pains. She could tell some marvelous stories about all sorts of places and people—including you!"

"Me?"

Miss Abigail nodded vigorously. "My goodness, I feel as though I know you and your lovely animals personally. Now if *you* had trained that dog of hers, the creature would never have dug up my prizewinning azaleas or annoyed my guests."

"I appreciate your confidence in me, but I have to confess I didn't even know Doreen had a dog. Or a fiancé."

"You could have knocked me over with a feather when she told me she was getting married. Oh, I knew she had a gentleman friend, she talked about him all the time."

"But you've no idea who he was?"

"We were never introduced," Miss Abigail said stiffly. "I'd encouraged her to bring him to Sunday dinner but he was working, or going out of town, or they'd already made plans. Always had some excuse. No, I never met him, although I did see him from a distance once or twice when he brought the girl home."

"What kind of car did he drive?"

"A Jeep. Black, with lots of shiny bits. And one of those wind-up things on the front."

"A winch?"

Miss Abigail nodded. "My grandson Eddie has one of those. He says it comes in handy when somebody gets stuck, or trees block the road. He was awfully busy when those ice storms hit last year. He's in Search and Rescue," she added proudly with a wave of one hand that sent her ball of yarn tumbling off the chair.

"I look forward to meeting him." She bent to retrieve the yarn. Straightening, she tried to hand it back, but the woman's attention was focused on the locket Maggie was wearing.

"That looks so familiar," Miss Abigail said with a slight frown. "Now where have I seen that before?"

Maggie's pulse quickened. "It's one of a pair. This one belonged to my grandmother. Recently, I've learned that Doreen had the other one. Perhaps that's why mine looks familiar. Do you remember her showing it to you?"

Miss Abigail shook her head doubtfully. "That girl never had anything as lovely as that. Or as valuable."

"What about her engagement ring?"

"She had no such thing. I did find that a bit curious."

Maggie decided not to share her suspicions that Doreen had been seeing a married man. "Perhaps he couldn't afford one."

Miss Abigail sniffed. "To hear Doreen tell it, he could have bought her a dozen diamond rings. She said he was an important business man, but she would say that, wouldn't she? God bless her soul, but the girl did love to tell stories." Sniffling, Miss Abigail excused herself.

When she returned moments later, it was clear she was ready for a change of subject. "I do believe you're the very image of your mother. My dear late husband enjoyed her work particularly. We purchased several paintings at her very first show, all those years ago. At the Crane Gallery, it was."

Miss Abigail's eyes were suddenly alight with mischief. "You look so much like her, I suppose it's no wonder somebody would mention that old gossip."

"Gossip?"

"All that talk of an affair, my dear. Your father was furious, but naturally none of us believed she'd ever divorce him. There was you, for one thing."

"But she did leave."

"Not with anyone local, I can assure you. Women kept a tight hold on their husbands back in those days, myself included.

And it wasn't one of the town's bachelors, either, because they were all still here long after she left. So you just pay no mind to those ridiculous stories about your mother and Nicholas Crane."

"Nicholas!"

"If your mother was keeping company with someone other than your dear father—and I'm not saying she was—it was most obviously *not* Nicholas Crane."

Maggie didn't know which statement to tackle first, and finally settled on the last one. "Why was it obvious?"

"Your mother didn't like him," the old woman said tartly. "Claimed he was trying to control her life. And once your mother got a bee in her bonnet about something, well, she couldn't be told different."

"I know Nicholas offered her an exclusive contract. Could that be what she meant by control?"

"I think Nicholas didn't approve of the men she was keeping company with. In fact, he said as much to my dear husband George. Yes, indeed. She set more than one tongue wagging."

No wonder the old woman had liked Doreen so much, Maggie thought. Two peas in a pod, as Gran would have said. Aloud, she asked dryly, "And whose name did they wag about?"

"Oh, more than one, my dear girl. But there was many a whisper about Angus Sheppard."

"My veterinarian?"

"Always making an excuse to run out to Eagle Cove," she said craftily. "And it couldn't have been business, could it? With your own father in the same line of work?"

"You said there was more than one name," Maggie prompted.

"You'd better ask your neighbors about that. I imagine the Bridgers know quite a bit more than I do. And I wouldn't like you to think I'm just a gossipy old lady."

The return of Miss Abigail's guests saved Maggie from a reply. Thanking her hostess, she made her excuses and fled.

OVER THE YEARS, the Bridger's dining room had gradually become Sylvia's domain, with invoices, payroll sheets, and seed catalogs littering the surface. When they actually sat down together for a meal, it was more often than not at the small kitchen table or on trays in the den, with a television show serving as conversation.

It hadn't always been like that, Howard mused. He hovered in the doorway with the day's mail in his hands, wondering if he should just leave it on the hall table. She didn't like to be disturbed when she was in there, and she looked as though she was concentrating fiercely, hunched over the table and hands busy with something he couldn't see. He'd just drop off the mail, he decided, and then take the boat out for a while.

He cleared his throat as he walked in, not wanting to startle her, but she jerked upright with a gasp, one hand pressed hard against her chest as she glared at him.

"Are you trying to give me a heart attack?" she demanded. "What are you doing here, anyway? You were supposed to be out this afternoon."

"Sorry," he said automatically. He'd been apologizing for years, not that it seemed to make the least bit of difference. He knew it would take more than apologies to repair what he'd done. Still, he had to try.

"I've told you, leave the mail on the hall table."

"I just thought ..." his voice trailed off as he looked at the materials scattered on the table. Saw what she'd cut out of magazines, the jar of paste, the cheap white paper. "You're going ahead with your plan? I thought we agreed—"

"I never agreed, I just said I'd think about it. And I have."

"I hope you know what you're doing."

"I know what might happen. It's a risk I have to take."

"And if it ends badly?"

"Then I'll put an end to it, once and for all."

BACK AT THE kennel, Maggie sorted through a stack of phone messages. One of them was from her insurance agent, who had called to remind her of the inventory. So, after checking on the boarders and exercising her own dogs, Maggie spent the afternoon unpacking the boxes Garrett had shifted from the basement to the old pantry.

Nine boxes later, Maggie stared at the studio inventory her grandmother had completed nearly twenty years ago. In her meticulously neat handwriting, that dear woman had recorded everything from tubes of paint to canvases in different stages of completion. Some of the finished canvases had obviously been titled by the artist, but many of the entries bore short descriptive phrases or titles Gran had created to identify the work.

The box in which Maggie found the inventory also contained a number of loose newspaper clippings. One titled "Exhibition by Local Artists" caught Maggie's eye, and she sat down to study the yellowing newsprint.

"Margaret Racburn is a rare talent," she read aloud. "The artist herself does not claim any one school of influence, but Hans Gabriel of New York's American Museum has praised the artist for her genius in what is considered a daring interpretation of the traditional landscape." The other reviews appeared equally flattering in their comments.

Maggie was about to return the reviews to the box when a quote by Nicholas Crane caught her eye. She read it aloud. "Sylvia Bridger, a longtime resident of Eagle Cove, was recently offered the opportunity to display her work as part of a regional exhibition that culminated with the highly acclaimed work of Margaret Raeburn. Bridger's landscapes may have been inspired from the same locales but there the similarity ends. Indeed, they are best described as amateur ambition unfulfilled."

Poor Sylvia, Maggie thought indignantly, flinching at the vindictive tone. Why on earth would Nicholas say such a thing?

"I CAN'T POSSIBLY recall something I said to the press so many years ago." Nicholas dismissed the subject with an airy wave when she confronted him a few days later.

"Sylvia told me about that exhibition. It was very important to her," Maggie said sternly.

"You must understand, my dear, that an art exhibition is an expensive undertaking. There are literally thousands of artists who pass through the system in the course of a year, yet few have sufficient talent to be offered a show. It is a rare honor, undeserving of the cavalier attitude some artists display."

"Does that mean you didn't want Sylvia's work?"

"Your mother's voice should not have been diluted by amateurs," Nicholas replied simply. With practiced skill, he steered the conversation toward lighter subjects, and pressed Maggie to spend the afternoon with him.

"I'm afraid I can't." She was still feeling indignant on Sylvia's behalf, but she did have other obligations. "I have an appointment with my insurance agent. I've been promising him a copy of the studio inventory, and he's getting impatient. And I have an obedience class starting this evening."

"I'm beginning to doubt my Delilah will ever see the novice competition."

"She'll get there eventually."

"If you're still willing to take on the challenge, I'd love for you to work with her. I have business out of town in the next few days, but after that? I really would like to see her achieve some semblance of obedience in my lifetime."

"Call me when you get back. We'll set up an appointment."

22

The arena at Waterside was crowded for the obedience class. Maggie noted the Rottweiler and his handler hadn't returned after the demonstration during the open house; no surprise there. She was pleased to see the Lhasa Apso, Missy, was back, along with everyone else who'd come to the preview.

Claire was there, working quietly with Sweet Pea. She'd arrived with her sitter, who explained Zak wouldn't be there. "Staffing problem at the co-op. Two employees just eloped."

Now, as Maggie joined the group that included Claire, she asked, "Everything okay here?" She'd demonstrated the basic technique for the novice sit, and the class had divided into smaller groups to practice the drill. As Maggie watched, Claire knelt beside Sweet Pea, her right hand pulling slightly at the collar, left hand gently pushing in just above the hocks on the rear legs, and folded Sweet Pea's legs into a sit.

"Looking good, Claire," Maggie praised the young girl. "Remember to give the command at the same time you push against the legs." She smiled and added, "Sweet Pea knows the drill by heart, but the other dogs need to hear the commands."

"I will," Claire promised. She was quieter than usual but seemed content to be working with Sweet Pea. Maggie had hoped to talk to the youngster, but the sitter appeared as the session was ending and whisked her away. Oh, well, Maggie thought, she'd see her tomorrow at the obedience trials in Tulsa.

Or maybe not, she thought as she listened to Zak's apologies later that evening. "Most of the artists have shows booked this weekend," he explained. "And somebody has to be here. With Bill and Judy on their honeymoon, the only somebody is me."

"Okay."

"No, it's not," Zak said vehemently. "I really wanted to be there for you."

"Another time."

"Claire had her heart set on going—"

"I'd love to take her with me," Maggie interrupted. "She's no trouble at all."

"You think you can keep up with two dogs *and* a little girl for the entire day?"

"I have hidden talents."

"I promise not to say 'I told you so' when you get back. When will that be, anyway? In time for dinner?"

"Doubtful. My client is a talker. She'll insist on discussing every detail of Hillary's performance."

"I'll keep the coffee warm," he promised.

"WE COULD HAVE done better," Maggie said, gratefully accepting the proffered cup of coffee following her grueling drive back from Tulsa.

"Maggie was great," Claire informed her father, and yawned. "I helped too," she said proudly. "Sam and me—"

"Sam and I," her father corrected.

"Sam and I," Claire repeated obediently. "We was good. I did everything Maggie said and Sam did too and he didn't pull on his leash or anything and then she got a green ribbon and got their picture took and I saw a zillion dogs and everybody was nice and we had ice cream—"

"After sandwiches and milk," Maggie interjected hastily.

"Who got the green ribbon?" Zak asked with a smile.

"Hillary qualified for her second leg in open competition. That's why we're so late, actually. Mrs. Johannsen wanted to go over every single detail. Twice."

"And Sam? How did he do?"

"Not one of his better days. He was distracted by a female who'd come into season. Compared to her, of course, the ring held zero interest."

"Couldn't you, um, cool him down?"

"The judge is a stickler for the rules, and there's nothing in the rule book about cooling off periods. Actually, the rules are explicit, she shouldn't have been entered if she's in season."

"That happened in your obedience class, didn't it?"

"Delilah is the first female dog Nicholas has owned, so this is all new to him, but the Utility ring is no place for beginners. That handler today should have known better." Maggie yawned. The energy that had carried her through the day had faded on the long drive home, and by the time she'd sent Garrett on his way, she was struggling to stay awake.

"All quiet," Garrett had reported cheerfully. "Mrs. Malloy picked up Checkers and the vet stopped by."

"Who's sick?"

"Nobody. Dr. Sheppard said he was out this way, and mentioned he'd come by next week." Garrett grinned. "He's bored."

"Sylvia thinks he's allergic to vacation."

"She and Mr. Bridger came by, too. He helped with evening chow. Nice guy," Garrett commented. "And Mrs. Bridger seems awfully attached to that stray. Asked me what his breeding might be. I told her American Dog."

"You should be a diplomat," Maggie told him with a smile. "Everything else quiet, then?"

"There was one weird thing. No problem," he added quickly. "The dogs were restless this afternoon, kept barking off and on. I walked around—everything looked fine. But you know that building down by the lake? The one you said was a studio?"

Maggie nodded, tense.

"When I went down there, the door was open. I took a quick look around but everything seemed okay, so I checked all the windows and locked the door for you. You might want to think about putting a better lock on that door. The one you have on there now is pretty lame."

Now, as Maggie sipped her coffee, she realized she hadn't asked Garrett what time he'd found the studio open. Could one of her visitors have entered the studio? But why?

"I guess it's a good thing I gave Frank that inventory," she said aloud. Noticing Zak's startled expression, she explained.

"Have you checked that inventory yourself?"

"No, but I kept a copy. Are you thinking what I think you're thinking?"

"That's entirely too complicated for me to follow at this hour. I was about to suggest you go through the place and compare your list with what's there."

"I can think of a dozen other things I'd rather do, but you're right. Want to help?"

"First thing tomorrow suit you?"

"As soon as I finish morning exercise."

MAGGIE DRAGGED A couple of chairs over to the table in the center of the studio. "I should have brought the vacuum cleaner." Cobwebs decorated the corners, and somewhere a fly buzzed angrily. She settled herself more comfortably in her chair and glanced over the inventory. "This is more your territory than mine. How do you suggest we do this?"

"Divide and conquer. Give me the list and I'll go through the supplies and whatever equipment I can find. Why don't you inventory the paintings? Check off each one on the list as you find it. Start in one corner and work your way along the wall."

"Okay." As she sorted through canvases and frames, she told Zak how much she'd enjoyed Claire's company at the obedience trails. "I think you exaggerated about her being a handful."

Zak chuckled. "Maybe a bit. I'd like to take the credit, but she's terrific. Makes me look like a great parent. That's probably why the committee put me in charge of the children's activity for Summerfest."

"What's that?"

"Eureka Springs always has a festival during the peak tourist season. The season officially kicks off with the May Festival of the Arts. High-profile gallery shows and exhibits. Summerfest is more laid back. It's a nice mix of arts, crafts, and general fun stuff. This year, of course, they're advertising it as part of the Treasures of the Ozarks campaign, which means we'll have more financial support than usual. That means more prizes, and something special for the kids. This year, it's storytellers."

"You're going to read books to kids?"

"It's part of the Ozarks oral history project. These storytellers share folklore, frontier tales, stories from the region. And treasure tales, of course."

"What I know about kids wouldn't fill a water bowl, but wouldn't they have more fun if there was some kind of activity connected to the stories they're listening to?"

"Such as?"

"Treasure hunting seems this year's favorite activity. How about a kid-sized version of the Treasures of the Ozarks map? And speaking of treasure, did you see that news story about old silver turning up in St. Louis? I knew about black market sales in Florida—all those shipwrecks—but St. Louis?"

"Doesn't seem like pirate territory to me."

"Maybe it's some of that Spanish silver the sheriff told me about," Maggie said with a wink.

"Too bad we don't have any silver for prizes. Hey, we could ask the bank to donate some silver dollars."

"Great idea! Do you think the downtown merchants would be willing to donate small prizes for the treasure?"

Zak grinned at her. "How could they refuse? Everybody loves a treasure hunt."

They discussed details as they worked. Finally, Maggie put down her pen. "I've found most of the ones on the list."

"What's missing?"

She frowned. "I'm not sure. I found three canvases that don't match the inventory, and I don't see the one titled 'The Herb Garden.' And there's a note here that says 'plus paintings tbd from gallery.' To be determined?"

"Hmm ... more likely she meant 'to be delivered.' Maybe she's talking about the paintings from your mother's first show."

"I'll ask Nicholas," she said and pulled out her phone and called the Crane Gallery.

"Good heavens, you can't possibly expect me to remember mundane details like that from twenty years ago!" he protested after she explained the reason for the call.

"I wondered if you kept an inventory from that show."

"I'd have kept a record of what sold, of course, but that won't help you. My assistant would have overseen the return of anything that remained. And before you ask," he said, anticipating her next question, "that person no longer works for me."

"It's probably not important anyway." She disconnected and looked at Zak. "Another dead end."

"What about the ones you found that aren't on the list?"

"Two are lake scenes," Maggie replied. "But I haven't the faintest idea about the third one."

Zak studied the painting she held up for his inspection. "I didn't realize your mother painted abstracts."

She studied the crimson and black splotches. "I can see why she left it behind," she said wryly. She shrugged and replaced the painting in the bottom rack. "We've ended up with more, not less, than we expected, unless you count the 'tbd' paintings."

"Maybe she had them shipped to Colorado," Zak suggested.

"Anything's possible, I guess. Pretty much shoots down your theory, though."

"The equipment checks out, too." He looked around the room, frowning. "Your mother left in the summer, right?"

"Right."

Zak strode across the room and studied the temperature control panel on the rear wall. "I thought it was awfully warm in here—the unit is set on heat, not cool. And why is the calendar open to December?"

"It was probably the real estate agent. He took care of repairs, things like that. Maybe he was curious, looked around."

"I thought you said the building was closed up when you moved to Florida."

"It was. But Gran must have arranged for maintenance. In fact, I know she did, I saw the bills and her canceled checks when I was looking for the inventory. I found a padlock on the door here, so somebody's been looking after the place. It might even have been Jake, he was the caretaker here for years. Whoever it was, he kept the place in good shape." She shrugged, uninterested. "One of them was probably in here, checking the heating system. I should have done that with the air conditioning, too. Set it now, would you?"

Shutting the studio door firmly behind them, Zak looked around the yard and spotted his daughter chasing after Sam, who was dripping wet and carrying a stick proudly in his mouth.

"How many times have I told you not to go near the lake alone?" Zak asked sternly.

"Sam went swimming, but I didn't, honest!"

"Then just how do you explain being wet?" her father inquired. Before Claire could respond, Sam shook himself vigorously, spraying everyone.

"That would do it," Maggie said ruefully.

"Hmm. I think a swimming lesson is long overdue. How deep is it along the shoreline here, Maggie?"

"You can wade for several yards before it drops off," she assured him. "Better put on a life vest, though, just to be safe. You're welcome to check in the barn. I brought several with me from Florida, but they might be too big for Claire."

"That's okay. I'll run into town while I'm thinking about it."

"Get swim booties, too. The lake has a rocky bottom."

Claire tugged at her father's arm. "Can Maggie come swim with us, Daddy? Please?"

"Well?"

"Count me in!"

MAGGIE SPLASHED THROUGH the shallows before stretching out in the afternoon shade of the pines. From there, she could see the front of the kennel, as well as most of the exercise yard. She'd left a disappointed Sam back at the house.

"Sorry, pal. You can come swim with us another day."

Now she reapplied sunscreen and smiled contentedly as she relaxed, lulled by the sound of their laughter. She dozed, awakening a short time later to find Zak kneeling beside her.

"Sorry to interrupt your nap," he murmured. "But one of the dogs sounds awfully excited."

Groggy with sleep, it took a minute before Maggie identified the sound in the distance as Sam's frenzied barking. She shoved her feet into her sandals and grabbed her bag. "Sounds like a problem. I'll go check."

"We'll be up there in a minute," Zak called as she scrambled up the slope. "Shout if you find trouble."

The kennel was still securely locked, the dogs milling about but quiet. Maggie was conscious of a tightening in her chest as she hurried down the path and approached the dog run behind the house. Sam was still barking steadily.

Maggie opened the gate and grabbed Sam's collar as he attempted to lunge past her. "Steady, boy," she said quietly. Even Mr. B looked worried, she thought nervously. The Beagle was standing rigidly, staring at Sam. "Let's check it out, fellas."

Leaving the gate open, she released her grip. The dog hurtled around the house. Maggie rushed after him to find him pawing at the porch mat. A flash of white caught her eye. Oblivious to Zak and Claire, who were hurrying toward her, Maggie tugged the single sheet out of the envelope with trembling hands, forcing herself to notice details: plain envelope, no return address, no postmark. Her name and address were typed, just like the others.

"Oh, God. Not another one."

"What do you mean, not another one?" Zak read over Maggie's shoulder. "What is it? And how many have you had?"

"If it's like the others, it's somebody's idea of a nasty joke. This is the third one I've received."

"Why didn't you tell someone?"

"I told Lucas."

"And what did he do?" Zak demanded.

"There's not much he could do. It's probably a prank."

"One might be a prank. Two is stupid. Three makes it a threat in my book. Call the sheriff."

DINNER WAS LONG over. Claire had been put to bed under protest in Maggie's guest room. "I'm afraid the room's a bit of a mess," Maggie said apologetically after they had tucked the little girl into bed, with Sweet Pea curled up beside her. "That wallpaper's on my list, but—"

"For Pete's sake! There's a lunatic running around and you're worrying about interior design." Zak steered her by the shoulders onto the porch and pushed her gently toward a chair. Sam, still on guard duty and clearly disappointed at not having found an intruder earlier, crouched protectively beside Maggie's chair.

"I've got a few words for the sheriff. This must be Jake Turner's doing, and I bet he's behind the other problems you've had, too. I want to know why he's not in jail."

"If Jake is guilty, we'll get him," Lucas said an hour later. He'd gulped down a glass of iced tea and was making inroads on another while he listened to Zak. Now, he looked straight at the younger man. "We have no evidence that points toward Jake or anyone else yet. No fingerprints or identifying marks on the letters. We don't have a thing to go on. Yes, I agree Jake had opportunity, but what about motive?"

"He lost his job," Zak shot back angrily. "How much motive do you need?"

"And there's the wording of the notes themselves. Jake's barely literate. Smashing that bottle of booze is more his style. And yes, before you ask, we are looking for him. We'll find him. In the meantime, if you have any other suggestions that might help, I'm all ears." Lucas sighed. "I wish I could say I'll make this my top priority, but then I'd be lying. We're stretched real thin right now, and that's a fact."

Maggie became aware of the scent of smoke, the soot on the sheriff's boots. "Has there been another wildfire?"

"No. This time it was one of the old buildings downtown by Basin Park. The Taylor's business burned down this afternoon."

"My insurance agent works there!" Maggie cried. "Was anyone hurt?"

"Nobody there at the time, luckily, but the whole place is a write-off. Arson, from the look of it," Lucas said grimly. "In this drought, it's a miracle it didn't spread to the other buildings on the street. The whole county is a tinder box."

"Why would somebody want to burn down a land survey company? Or an insurance agency?"

"I've heard some folks are angry with the Taylors over their stand on the Hobbs Mountain issue," Zak volunteered.

Maggie stared blankly at him.

"There's a fight to keep a landfill off of Hobbs Mountain. Some big corporation wants to clear-cut the land, use it for a dump. Environmentalists are opposed, arguing the place is unstable, and a landfill will poison the water supply. Since Beaver Lake supplies water to the entire region, that's a big deal. The case is in the courts right now, but tempers are riding high all around."

"What do the Taylors have to do with a landfill?"

"Everyone in the Merchants League—except Frank and his

brothers—threw their support behind the environmentalists," Zak explained. "The Taylors abstained. They own a good-sized piece of that land, and the family is split on the issue. The old-timers want it kept safe from development, but the younger Taylors think it's the right time to sell."

The sheriff swallowed the last of his iced tea and set the glass on the table beside his chair. "Whoever it was, we'll find them. I've put in a call to the arson team in Little Rock. I'd just as soon let the pros take care of it." He looked at Maggie. "Let's talk about you. How does this letter compare to the others?"

Wordlessly, Maggie handed him the latest threat.

Lucas read the note aloud: "When doggies die, ABKA says bye-bye." He frowned. "What the hell is ABKA?"

"The American Boarding Kennels Association," she told him. "Although it hasn't been called that for a few years now. They changed their name to Pet Care Services Association, to include pet sitters and groomers. At least, they did before they went bankrupt. If something should happen to the kennel or any of the animals in my care ..."

"This letter's different from the others. There's no mention of your mother or you. This threat is specific, and the dogs are the target." He looked somberly at Maggie. "You need better security around here, at least for a while. I'd suggest a good alarm system. I hope you can afford it."

"It doesn't matter how much it costs."

"Check the supercenter store down in Harrison," Zak suggested. "And I think you should wire the house, too. Whoever it is, they've broken in here already—"

"The note was on the porch," Maggie objected.

"Remember the open window?"

"What window?" Lucas asked.

Tersely, Maggie explained. "Nicholas was here and we both saw Momma Cat knock the screen out."

"That doesn't mean somebody wasn't here," Zak persisted. "Maybe whoever it was came back today and the dogs scared them off so they dropped the letter on the porch and ran."

"I'll get an alarm for the kennel, but I can't spend that kind of money on myself."

"Has it occurred to you that all these strange happenings could be related?" Lucas asked. "I hear you've been asking people about the Crowley girl and about your mother and that locket of hers. Now, your mother—that's family business and I reckon it's none of mine. But I'd be obliged if you would remember that folks know the Crowley girl worked for you. It's bound to leak out soon—if it hasn't already—that we're investigating the circumstances of that girl's death.

"When things start escalating in an investigation, that could mean that somebody's getting angry or worried. I'd say somebody's got a secret, maybe a whole bunch of secrets, and I don't reckon they'll take kindly to those secrets seeing the light of day. Seems to me somebody is trying to scare you away."

"I don't scare that easy," Maggie said defiantly.

"Call me a sexist or a chauvinist or whatever you want, but I'd feel a lot better if you weren't out here by yourself," Lucas said calmly. "Why don't you let Garrett camp out here until I get to the bottom of this?"

"He wouldn't want—"

"Yes, he would. My oldest daughter is getting married in August, and the place has turned into wedding central. Trust me, he'll jump at the chance to get out of the house for a while."

"I can juggle my schedule a bit, but I'd feel a lot better if Garrett was here," Zak admitted.

"Don't I have any say in this at all?" Maggie said plaintively, but her heart wasn't in the protest. This latest threat had shaken her to her core, and she was sick to her stomach with fear.

"I'll have a word with Garrett when I get home. In the meantime, lock up tight, keep your eyes open, and don't do anything stupid. And keep him with you," he said, pointing to Sam.

As he rose to leave he said, "I'm not ready to hang this one on Jake, not yet anyway. It's a long stretch between letting dogs loose and making drunken threats to actually killing animals. I'm the first to admit that alcohol has addled his brains, but I just can't imagine Jake deliberately hurting any animal."

In the silence that followed the sheriff's departure, Maggie looked at Zak. It seemed a lifetime since they'd been swimming that afternoon.

He gazed calmly at her. "How about loaning me six feet of your living room floor?"

"More trouble to come—is that what you're thinking?"

"I think the sheriff's right. Somebody wants you to leave Eagle Cove."

"What threat could I possibly be? I haven't even been here very long. And besides," she added miserably, "I don't want to leave."

"That makes two of us."

23

By the following Friday, Maggie found herself wondering if she was overreacting. The week had passed quietly. No more letters, no intruders, no new crises. Garrett's younger brother Rob was working at the kennel all day now that the first summer term was over, relieving Maggie of some of the routine chores. The obedience session had gone off without a hitch, and the weekend boarders who arrived early Friday morning filled all available runs. Contracts signed with two new clients interested in competitive obedience bolstered both her bank account and her self-esteem.

With Garrett staying in the assistant manager's quarters in the kennel and Zak at the house, Maggie had found herself relaxing a little more every day. That's something good that's come out of the bad, Maggie thought as she entered the New Orleans Hotel to attend the quarterly meeting of the Merchants League. The days she'd shared with Zak and Claire had been some of the happiest of her life.

She paused to thank Julie, the B&B owner she'd met at the open house. "I appreciate the business you've sent my way," she told her.

"Ditto," Julie said, smiling. "Hey, I'm glad I saw you today. My neighbor is fostering a couple of dogs from the shelter, and they're making her crazy. I was hoping you could give her some suggestions on handling them. They don't take kindly to other dogs—or most people, come to think of it—or I'd have suggested your obedience class."

"Have her call me and we'll work something out. No charge, since she's working with the shelter."

"That's really generous. I didn't see much of that when I lived in Dallas."

"Is that home for you?"

"Nope. I'm a home-grown girl. After college, I went the corporate route—big city, big money, at least until the bottom fell out, and then I hightailed it back home to help my aunt run the B&B. She passed away last year. Even with old family connections, it's still a struggle making a go of it. Trying to find enough help—I stand a better chance of finding that buried treasure," Julie said with a sigh.

"I know exactly how you feel," Maggie confided. They chatted a few moments longer before Maggie caught sight of her neighbors and excused herself. Howard's reaction when she'd asked questions about her mother and Doreen still puzzled her, and she was sure he knew more than he'd said.

Spotting an open seat next to Sylvia, she hurried to claim it. "I've missed seeing you around. How's business?"

"Drying up, like everything else in this drought. About all I seem to sell these days are pond liners, hoses, and rocks."

"Landscape work must be brutal in this heat."

"I'm only working mornings. If the economy doesn't turn around soon, I'll have a lot more time on my hands."

"Good thing you have a hobby," Howard said slyly.

"What kind—"

"Never mind," Sylvia cut her off and abruptly changed the subject. "Hey, there's Angus. Now that's what I call dedicated, somebody who comes to meetings while they're on vacation. I guess he didn't want to miss the trolley vote."

The narrow, winding streets, heavy traffic, and limited parking discouraged many tourists from driving downtown. The trolley system with its low all-day rates and frequent stops allowed customers to travel comfortably throughout the entire village and along the adjoining roadways with ease. Now, though, the traffic committee of the city council wanted to eliminate the all-day fare and raise ticket prices, a proposal that infuriated most business owners.

The hour passed swiftly as the council representative's speech was followed by spirited discussion. When the votes were tallied, a small cheer went up among the crowd. The decision to oppose the council was unanimous, and a contingent would be out in force when the city council voted on the issue at its next meeting.

As the meeting adjourned, several members clustered around Maggie, congratulating her on the success of her open house and wanting to learn more about the kennel. An owner of a small inn suggested Maggie contact the Historical Association. "I know you've spoken to the B&B and hotel owners, but don't forget the luxury guest homes and inns. Convince the Historical Association to include information about Waterside in their advertising and everyone would profit."

Another member had a more personal concern. "No kennel will take my Pit Bull," the woman said challengingly. "They all say the breed's too dangerous."

"I accept all breeds," Maggie said calmly. "You're welcome to visit Waterside with your dog. After you've had a look around, I'll be happy to discuss boarding options for your pet."

"That's a nice change," someone remarked. "Paradise Pets won't let customers past the front desk, even by appointment."

Maggie was reluctant to criticize the competition. "They might have had security problems in the past. Kennel owners take the safety of your pet very seriously. At Waterside, one of my staff or I will be happy to escort you through the kennel."

You're a fine one to talk about safety and security, Maggie chided herself as she made her way back toward Sylvia, who was deep in discussion with Nicholas Crane and Angus Sheppard.

If those folks ever got wind of that latest letter, she thought, they'd think twice about letting her care for their pets. She hoped the few people who knew about the letters didn't gossip. Judging from the sudden silence that fell as she approached, though, she guessed rumors were already circulating.

"Don't stop talking on my account."

"Sylvia's been filling us in," Angus informed her. "What's the sheriff doing to find that scoundrel Jake?"

Maggie looked askance at her neighbor.

"Zak told me. He's worried. What can we do to help?"

"Try talking about something else," Maggie suggested tartly. "Honestly, I appreciate your concern, but I think we're blowing this whole thing out of proportion. And Lucas says these incidents may not even be Jake's doing."

"The man threatened you in front of a roomful of people," Nicholas pointed out. "He lost his job through his own incompetence but he blames you. That makes him a candidate in my eyes. And if that damn sheriff is too stupid to see it, it's time we get a Republican back in the job."

"Lucas will find out who's doing this," Maggie said firmly. "And I am not going to be scared away from Waterside."

"Any other trouble, besides the letters?" Angus asked.

Maggie was unwilling to discuss her problems so publicly. "Everything's fine. The only excitement we've had lately was when an employee accidentally tripped the new alarm."

With Garrett's help, Maggie and Zak had installed a simple alarm system in the kennel. She'd intended to discuss the new procedures with Bev and Rob on Monday. What she hadn't planned, however, was that her conscientious groomer would arrive for work two hours early and trigger the alarm, tumbling Garrett, Maggie, and Zak out of their beds. It took two aspirin and several cups of coffee before Bev stopped shaking long enough to apologize for "scaring the daylights out of everyone."

Garrett had patted her on the back and yawned. "At least we know the thing works."

Now, Maggie smiled at the group. "Everything's fine. With the exception of the mice Momma Cat is catching, everything is alive and well at Waterside."

"It's no joking matter," Nicholas said sternly. "What does your father have to say about all this?"

"I can sort out my own problems, thank you very much. And don't even think about calling him."

"Oh, dear," he murmured.

"You didn't!"

"Ease up, Nicholas," Angus said calmly. "The girl's no fool. If she needs help, she'll ask." He winked at Maggie and changed the subject to an entertaining and highly improbable version of his most recent fishing trip.

As the group prepared to leave, talk shifted back to the meeting. "I'm glad it didn't end like the last vote," Sylvia said with obvious satisfaction.

"Was that the Hobbs Mountain issue?" Maggie asked.

"Our most recent controversy," Nicholas said with a nod. "Although I feel obligated to point out that we did achieve a near-unanimous decision in the end."

"Except for the Taylors," Angus said quietly. "Although none of them voted against it. They abstained, not that some of these hotheads understand the difference."

"Was it arson or accident?" Nicholas asked curiously.

"The Taylors must have an idea," Angus said, nodding as Frank Taylor hurried toward them.

"Maggie, I'm glad I caught you. I'd like to have a word with you about your policy."

"Of course."

The older man hesitated, glancing at the curious faces around him. "Perhaps I could walk you out?"

"It's all right, Frank. These folks probably know more about Waterside than I ever will." She paused. "I was glad to hear no one was hurt in that fire. But I'm sorry that you lost all your work, and those wonderful old maps and tools."

"Many of those maps are on file in the state archives—we had copies. As for the rest, well, you can't hold on to the past too tight, or you'll miss the here-and-now, as my grandfather liked to say. And we still have some of the really important items, they were stored in a fireproof safe."

"I'm glad."

"We'll rebuild. And most of my paperwork is stored on the company server, so it's not as awful as you might expect. What I did lose, however, was the paperwork that had been on my desk. I'm afraid your file with the studio inventory was part of that. Did you by any chance keep a copy of that inventory for yourself?"

"I do have a copy." She thought briefly. "I think I actually left it in the studio."

"Good," he said with obvious relief. "I'm setting up a temporary office in Pine Mountain Village, and should be back in business sometime next week."

"Give me a call when you're set up, and I'll bring the inventory over to you," Maggie promised.

24

Claire was fascinated as Maggie put her retriever through several obedience drills. "Can he do any other neat stuff?"

"How about playing the Search game? Give me your socks, and we'll see if Sam can find *you.*"

Giggling, Claire pulled off her socks and stuffed her bare feet back into her sneakers. Maggie let Sam sniff the items, pulling then away only when she was sure the dog had the scent. "Stay," she commanded. Using a new piece of rope from her backpack, she twisted the rope around one of the socks and dragged it out of the dog's sight, dropping it beside a rotting log where the small object was well camouflaged. She zigzagged back across the meadow and around the blackberry brambles near the creek before rejoining Sam and Claire.

Holding out the remaining sock, Maggie let the dog sniff again. When she was confident he had the scent, she told him, "Find the sock, Sam! Search, boy!"

The dog seemed to understand the target wasn't the little girl standing so close, and bounded away across the meadow. Maggie and Claire could hear him thrashing through the tall grass and glimpsed the tip of his tail as they trailed behind.

Moments later, the dog stood at attention over the log, signifying a find. "Bring it in!" Maggie called.

"That's so cool!" Picking up the sock that Sam had dropped on command, she squealed as she realized the fabric was soaking wet. "Good thing we didn't use my shirt," she said with a giggle.

"It's too hot to do any more work. Let's go see if we can talk your dad into a swim before supper."

"Okay," Claire agreed happily. "And we're going to the dog show tomorrow, right?"

"Right you are." As they walked back along the dirt track, Maggie said casually, "You haven't said much about your visit with your mom. Did you have a good time?"

"It was okay," Claire muttered, her voice barely audible.

Maggie glanced at Claire and was alarmed to see her crying. "What's wrong, sweetheart?"

"I don't want to go live there," the little girl whispered, clutching Maggie's leg. "I want to stay right here!"

Soothing the child, Maggie felt a rush of affection for this pixie of a girl. Drying the little girl's tears, she said briskly, "Let's go find your dad."

ZAK KEPT HIS feelings in check all through a quiet talk with his tearful daughter, and through the hours between dinner and Claire's bedtime. Now, with Claire inside with a coloring book, crayons, and Sweet Pea for company, he stalked the length of Maggie's porch, careful to keep his voice low. "Althea can barely take care of herself right now. What kind of crazy scheme is she thinking of, and why wouldn't she talk to me first? It's not as if I ever tried to keep her away from Claire."

Maggie's heart ached for this man and his beautiful daughter. "Think she'll try to get custody?" She stroked Sam, taking comfort in his protective stance beside the porch swing. From the safety of his corner, Mr. B watched them.

"Who knows? Maybe she honestly believes she can be a full-time mom again."

He dropped onto the swing beside Maggie. "Apparently, this all started when Althea said she had some exciting plans for Claire's birthday party. Claire, of course, thought her mother was talking about coming here. One thing led to another, and Althea said she wished Claire lived in Springfield with her. Took me quite a while to convince my daughter I wasn't trying to get rid of her." He checked his watch. "Time to say good night," he said. "Care to join me?"

The stormy emotions had taken their toll on the small child, who teetered on the edge of sleep as Zak tucked her in. "Can Sam come to my birthday party?" Claire asked drowsily, petting the big dog as he stood next to the bed. "And Sweet Pea and Mr. B, too?"

"Absolutely. Here's a nice coincidence—my birthday is coming up soon, too," Maggie said as she kissed the little girl.

"Are you gonna have a party, too?"

"Oh, I'm too old for parties," she answered lightly. "Now, go to sleep, or you won't be awake for the dog show tomorrow."

"Yes, ma'am!"

THE TULSA DOG show was already underway when Maggie arrived with Zak and Claire. "This is a great way to start shopping for a dog," she told Zak. "You're going to see lots of dogs today. There are plenty of breeders and handlers here who will be happy to answer your questions once they've finished their ring work."

"Shouldn't you be showing Sam today?"

"Sam's entered in obedience trials. This is an all-breed dog show. That means the focus isn't on obedience, but on the dog's overall appearance and structure. The judges you see today are experts in specific breeds and groups. Basically, they compare each dog against the breed's official standard."

Zak watched the dogs in the ring before them. "Those dogs are all different kinds," he objected. "How is that fair?"

"The Bulldog, Dalmatian, Poodle, and the Chow Chow do seem different, don't they? Some say they don't have enough in common with any of the breeds to fit in the other groups. Dogs compete in one of seven groups: Sporting, Hounds, Working, Terrier, Toy, Non-Sporting, and Herding," Maggie recited, ticking them off on her fingers. "This is the Non-Sporting group."

Zak eyed the dogs as they trotted past. "If you say so."

Maggie laughed, already counting the day a success. Claire dashed happily from one ring to another, questions spilling out faster than anyone could answer. Zak seemed to be enjoying himself, too, asking questions, clearly wanting to better understand this passion of Maggie's. For her part, knowing that Garrett and Rob were caring for the boarders gave Maggie the freedom to relax and enjoy herself.

They entered the exhibitor's tent, where portable tables and crates were stacked in long rows. "We can walk through, but we have to be careful not to get in anyone's way. The handlers don't have much time to get the dogs ready." Maggie stepped to one side as a handler hurried toward the ring with his charge.

"Look at that funny little sheep!" Claire said delightedly.

Maggie smiled. "That's a Bedlington Terrier." Turning to Zak she said, "A friend of mine will meet us after she's finished with the Toy Group. She handles Chihuahuas and Pomeranians."

"A toy breed. Is that what you'd recommend, then?"

"I think you should see as many breeds as you can before you make up your mind," Maggie said firmly. "That's why I wanted you to come to this show."

"I like them all," Claire said happily.

"I think Santa might spring for one puppy, but that's all— unless your dad wants to open a kennel of his own."

"One puppy will do us just fine," Zak said firmly.

The Poodles were first along the aisle, drawing oohs and aahs from the excited little girl. As Claire reached out impulsively to pet a Miniature Poodle, Maggie restrained her. "Never touch a dog without permission. Always ask first."

While Zak and Claire watched a handler demonstrate the art of combing out a topknot on a Standard Poodle, Maggie wandered over to the next aisle where the Cocker Spaniels had been assigned space. Admiring the animals being groomed, she forgot to watch her step, and stumbled against the man in front of her. "Sorry," she said automatically. Looking up, she was astonished to find she'd run smack into her own veterinarian, who was talking to a thin woman holding a badly behaved Cocker. Both the woman and the dog looked in need of some pampering, or at least a good brush out. The small dog shivered, whether from excitement or fear Maggie couldn't tell. He certainly didn't appear ready, or particularly eager, for the ring.

Angus seemed flustered by her presence. "Uh, Maggie, this is Bertha Hawkins. She runs Paradise Pets. "You probably know each other already, seeing how everybody seems to know everybody else in this dog business," he said in an obvious effort to make conversation.

Maggie extended her hand and smiled politely. "I saw you at my open house, didn't I? I'm sorry we didn't have a chance to talk, but I hope you enjoyed visiting Waterside."

The woman smirked. "I hear you're having some problems there. Oh, yeah, I've heard the talk. That kennel of yours might look all fancy right now, but there's some saying you won't last a year. Be a right shame, wouldn't it—you work your heart out and one day it's all gone. Yeah, that would be a real shame." Bertha turned on her heel and, clutching the whining spaniel tightly to her chest, hurried down the aisle.

"She's a real bucket of cheer, isn't she?" Maggie glanced at Angus for a reaction, but he was staring after Bertha and didn't respond. "Paradise Pets sounds so familiar. Oh, that's where Bev used to work."

"Excuse me, will you?" Without waiting for a response, Angus hurried off. Bemused, Maggie turned to find Zak and Claire right behind her.

"What's her problem?" Zak asked.

"I think it's safe to say she's not a fan of Waterside—or me." Consciously setting that little episode aside to think about later, Maggie turned her attention back to the reason they came. "Let's go find my friend Karen and see what you think about a Pomeranian."

DRIVING HOME FROM Tulsa, Zak brought up the subject of his schedule. "I'm booked for a couple of out-of-state shows later this summer," he told Maggie. "And I need to put in some time at the co-op and turn out more inventory. At least Garrett will be around, but I wish I hadn't committed to those shows."

The idea didn't appeal to Maggie, either, but she could hardly expect them to stay with her indefinitely, and Zak had business obligations of his own. That realization and the need to assert her independence prompted her to encourage Zak to move back to his cottage. "I think word about the new security system has scared off whoever it was."

"You're sure you'll be all right?"

"Positive. I promise to shout good and loud if I need help."

The next day passed quickly. Garrett helped with the morning exercise and chow routines, and then Maggie insisted he take the rest of the day for himself. "You haven't been out in your boat all week," she reminded him. "Everything's quiet here. You need some down time. If I need help, the Bridgers can be here in a flash."

After cleaning the equipment used during training sessions and the weekly obedience classes, she turned her attention to the grooming area. Bulk supplies were kept in a large storage closet at the far end of the room while rolling carts and open shelving held items needed daily. Maggie restocked the shelves with protein and medicated shampoos, and added several bottles of whitener and rinse. She needed to order more flea and tick control products from the wholesalers; Angus had warned her the insect problem would worsen over the summer.

She took a break at mid-morning to exercise some of the boarders, and was laughing over the antics of a Parson Russell Terrier when Sam suddenly growled, his attention focused on a man standing on the crest of the hill high above the kennel, staring at her. Even at that distance, Maggie easily recognized Jake Turner with a backpack slung over one shoulder. Her attention sharpened when she realized he was carrying a pick axe, and was relieved when he made no move to approach her and finally turned away, disappearing over the hill.

Although her property included almost two hundred acres south of that hilltop, Maggie hadn't bothered with the expense of fencing that land, in part because several hiking trails crossed her southern boundary leading into the wildlife conservation area and, eventually, around the southern fingers of the lake. Following her neighbors' advice, she'd applied splotches of purple paint to the largest trees and boulders along a line north of the trails and added a few 'no trespassing' signs for emphasis.

She'd spotted a few hikers along the trails but none had come close to her training fields. Seeing Jake so close, though, she decided to tell the sheriff she'd seen him and she resolved to keep a closer eye on her property. She secured the boarders and then directed Sam up the hill, where his relaxed demeanor convinced her Jake had left the area.

Returning to her labors, she turned her attention to the customer lounge, followed by the kitchen, training arena, cattery, and kennel runs. Maggie swept, mopped, vacuumed, scrubbed, and polished until her back ached. She finished her labors with an application of disinfectant to guard against parvovirus, pseudorabies disease, and canine distemper.

Looking good, Maggie thought with satisfaction. Even the office was presentable. She'd spent two hours on paperwork alone, but it was worth it, she thought, surveying the neat desk and clean counters. She'd even updated the mailing list for the promotional postcards she planned to send, offering current customers ten percent off their next boarding fee. With the renovation of Angus Sheppard's clinic nearly complete, Maggie anticipated a drop in business. She hoped to offset that drop by offering discounted rates for returning customers.

By the time Maggie printed the last customer bill, it was time to feed and exercise the boarders again. One unsociable Boxer, Bruno, needed to be exercised alone. "He's not polite toward small dogs," the owner had warned. "Thinks they're chew toys."

Maggie had just released Bruno into the yard when Sam, in his corner kennel, leapt to his feet with a deep growl that raised the hair on the back of Maggie's neck. Pacing the length of his run, Sam began to bark insistently, a sound Maggie had come to think of as his intruder bark. Around her, the boarders in their runs quickly joined in enthusiastically. The noise was deafening.

"Quiet!" Maggie yelled, and was gratified when the noise dropped a few decibels. She secured the boxer in his run and moved to stand beside her retriever. "Good boy, Sam," she said quietly. Dropping to the dog's side, Maggie slid her trembling hands around Sam's neck, his strong muscles reassuring beneath her hand. Movement down near the water caught her attention.

"Somebody's out there, Sam," she whispered. Fear was pressing down against her chest, making it difficult to breathe. Oh, God, she thought. Why did she pick today to be independent? Why didn't she just confess she liked sharing her house with Zak, and with Claire?

Get a grip, coward, she jeered. Ordering Sam to stay and watch, she groped her way along the wall and found the shovel she used earlier to clean the exercise yard. She hefted the heavy tool, uttered a quick prayer for courage, and motioned to Sam to lead the way.

Some part of Maggie's mind was working on autopilot, processing details in a detached manner. She could hear the boarders barking, but all her attention was focused on Sam as he hurtled down the piney slope, adding her furious yells to the dog's wild barking. She skidded to a stop, looking about her in frustration. She didn't see anyone close, but there were a couple of boats moving out into the open waters of Beaver Lake.

Maggie rarely noticed the boats out on the lake, although she could recognize the Bridger's boat as well as Garrett's sleek craft and his father's pontoon boat. Now she cursed her inattention. What at Waterside was important enough to risk possible arrest? Maggie had gone over nearly every inch of the kennel during her cleaning marathon. Surely, if anything could have been hidden there, she would have found it by now.

More questions without answers, she thought in frustration as she climbed back up through the pines. At the top of the slope, she paused at the wrought iron bench Zak had retrieved from the basement, and was startled by the sound of footsteps. Sam growled softly but made no effort to escape Maggie's restraining hand. "Who's there?" she called warily.

Howard came into view. "Just me. I was working on my boat when I heard the commotion here. Sylvia insisted I come over."

Maggie let go of the shovel and waved him to the seat beside her. "Somebody was down by the dock. Whoever it was seemed in a hurry to leave."

"Might have been kids looking for a place to camp. Or some of those blasted treasure hunters trying to move into my territory," he said with an obvious attempt to lighten her mood.

She supposed it was possible. The nearby wildlife area was a popular destination for hikers, boaters, and birdwatchers alike. Although overnight camping was supposed to be restricted to marked sites, she knew people often disregarded that rule. "You're probably right. I guess the weird stuff around here— and what happened to Doreen—has me jumping at shadows."

"The sheriff said Doreen drowned. An accident."

"He's changed his mind. Hasn't he talked to you again?"

His hands trembled as he lit a cigarette. "Why me?"

"He's talking to everyone who knew her."

Something close to panic flashed across Howard's features, reminding Maggie that he'd reacted oddly before when Doreen had been mentioned. Doreen's sister had spoken of 'loose ends' when discussing the purported engagement. Could one of those loose ends have been a divorce?

Her last efforts to discuss Doreen with Howard had been an exercise in frustration. He'd blamed that broken glass on a muscle spasm, she remembered. Now she wondered if it could have been something else. Had he been involved with the girl? Instinct told her he was hiding something.

"You know something, don't you? You might as well tell me, unless you'd rather wait for the sheriff."

"It was never supposed to be serious," he said miserably.

"When did it start?"

"About a year ago. Some buddies and I used to meet at the café across the road from the garden center. Doreen had just started working in the garden shop. Anyway, she came in one day, overheard us talking about metal detectors. We were organizing a hunt, and she wanted in but didn't have any equipment. So I said she could tag along. One thing kinda led to another."

"Led to an affair, you mean? An affair with a girl who worked for your wife and loved to gossip. Did you really think Sylvia wouldn't find out?"

"The fact is, my wife and I haven't been ... well, close, for a long time now. I was just looking for some company."

"Right," Maggie said sarcastically.

"Hey, only a saint would turn down what that girl was offering. Oh, it wasn't just physical," he added defensively. "She was really interested in me, in what I was doing. Like I said, I just wanted some company. But then ..."

"Doreen wanted something more?"

"She always wanted more. I thought I could handle her. But Sylvia must have gotten wind of it all, because she fired her. Oh, she said she was cutting back on staff because of the economy, but she has a way of getting rid of anything—and anybody— she thinks is a threat." He shot a look at Maggie. "She wasn't too pleased when she found out you'd hired Doreen."

"If she'd had a problem with that, she should have said something—which she never did."

"She wouldn't, would she? But I knew she was watching close, so I told Doreen we better lay low for a while. I expected her to throw a fit—she had her claws in me but good by then—but she just blew me off." He frowned, remembering. "She'd been acting weird for a while, though. She'd been asking a lot of questions, wanted me to get her inside Margaret's studio. I never did, of course," he added hastily. "I told her I didn't have any keys. I guess she got bored with me after that, 'cause she stopped coming around."

"Did that bother you?"

"Couldn't exactly object, could I?"

The silence stretched out between them.

"When did she die?" he asked.

"During spring break, probably. Why?"

"About the first week of March, I stopped by her place to talk her into going on a relic hunt with me. She had a couple of canvases on the kitchen table, but she tossed a sheet over them before I could get a closer look. Acted mad that I was there at all, and practically shoved me out the door. Told me she wasn't interested in relic hunting any more."

"Did she say why?"

"Told me she had a line on a different kind of treasure."

"What do you suppose she meant by that?"

"Who knows? It was probably just another story she made up." He paused. "Truth be told, I was kinda relieved. If she was busy with somebody or something else, I figured I could stop worrying about her spilling the beans about us. My wife would never forgive me if she knew, especially after everything that happened at the kennel with ... well, that was a long time ago."

Maggie recalled what Sylvia had told her: "Miles and Howard butted heads a lot that year. It would have to have been about the dogs, because Miles had only two passions in life—dogs and family."

What if it hadn't been about dogs? What if Maggie's mother had been the reason they'd argued? Was it possible her mother had an affair with her best friend's husband? And if they'd been involved before, were they still involved?

"Doreen wasn't your first fling, was she? I've heard the rumors about my mother. Was it you she was having an affair with?"

"Does that really matter?"

Maggie ignored that. "If you were involved with her all those years ago, maybe you still are. Have you seen her? Did she give you her locket? A little memento of your time together?" she asked bitterly.

"You can't possibly believe—"

"I'm not sure what I believe any more. Maybe Doreen knew you'd been meeting my mother, knew she gave you her locket. And _you_ gave the locket to Doreen, so she wouldn't spill your nasty little secret." Suspicions hardened into a dead weight inside her. "You might as well tell me now, because I'm not going to let this go."

Howard's breathing roughened, and sweat covered his brow. "I haven't seen Margaret for twenty years."

"My grandfather fired you. He must have had a reason."

"Miles had suspected for a long time that Margaret was carrying on, and he didn't see any need to look further than his own yard. I'll admit I was a handy target, being here at the kennel every day. Miles and Leah were away for days at a time, and your father was busy with his vet practice."

"And my mother?"

"Working in her studio," he said hoarsely. "I'd make some excuse to go down there. I liked to listen to her singing while she painted. Sometimes I'd just watch, then make myself walk away. Other times, I'd convince her to get out, take a break."

"Wait a minute." Maggie held up her hand, tried to make sense of what Howard was saying. "Did you or did you not have an affair with my mother?"

He laughed shortly. "Hard to have an affair with a little kid hanging around," he said. "You were always there, playing in the studio while she worked. She kept you close. I didn't mind, at least most of the time. If we went walking through the woods, or out in the boat, you were always there. Don't you remember?"

Mutely, Maggie shook her head.

"If you only knew how much sleep I've lost worrying about what you remembered, what you'd tell my wife."

"What did you think I'd say?"

"Can't you just leave it alone? Whatever happened between your mother and me was a very long time ago. When she left, she walked away from all of us. I was willing to give up my home, my family, and my career for her, and she walked away without a word."

"You were in love with her," Maggie said quietly.

"I thought I was." He lumbered to his feet, exhaustion sharpening the craggy face. "About Doreen ..."

Maggie sighed and rose to stand beside him. "I'm not going to tell Sylvia, if that's what you want to know."

"Thank you," he said humbly. He turned to leave, then paused. "That locket. I couldn't say anything before, and I might be wrong, but—"

"What?"

"Doreen liked to take things. Key chains, watches, stuff like that. Called them souvenirs. Once, she took my St. Christopher's medal. She said it was a hobby of hers. Bragged about it, actually. Said she could take something from right under your nose and you'd never know it."

"What's your point?"

"You've been saying all along you think Margaret has been back around Eagle Cove. Maybe she has. And maybe Margaret's locket became one of Doreen's souvenirs."

25

Maggie's wide front porch had become her refuge from the confusion and stress in her life. Zak hauled the rest of the furniture up from the basement, and Maggie placed a small sand bucket on the porch to accommodate her guests' smoking habits. Although Zak was down to two a day and sometimes not even that, she'd noticed Howard lighting up more often.

After evening chores she headed to the porch with her own dogs, knowing Zak and Claire would probably come by to enjoy the evening with her. She was pleased to see them coming up the drive as she came around the corner of the house.

From their vantage point on the porch, the adults could keep an eye on Claire, who was romping around the yard with Sam. Mr. B lay on the porch next to Zak, indifferent to the child's efforts to coax him away from her father's side.

"He's always following you around," Claire said accusingly. "He likes you more than he likes me." Her bad mood evaporated in a rush of giggles when Sam dropped a soggy tennis ball in her lap, eyes begging for another round. She threw the ball and ran after the big dog as he bounded away.

"She's right, you know, he does seem to like being with you. Maybe you remind Mr. B of his handler."

Zak stroked the Beagle's head affectionately even as he shook his head. "Do I look like a cop to you?"

"You have the brains for the job." She appreciated his attention to detail as they discussed Howard's confession. "I guess we can rule him out as the alleged fiancé," she said, frowning.

"Why are you so sure?"

"He broke off the affair with Doreen months ago."

"We can't corroborate that," Zak pointed out. "And we only have Howard's word for it that he's not involved with your mother these days."

"Why would he lie about not seeing my mother? And why would he lie about Doreen?"

"Maybe he's afraid of what Sylvia would do. I don't know. All I'm saying is, keep an open mind. And until Doreen's killer is caught I say we don't rule out any suspects."

"Suspects," Maggie repeated. "We're back to motive again. Why would anyone want to kill Doreen?"

"Why does anyone want to kill another person?"

"To get something that person has? Something valuable. That's one reason."

"How about revenge? Or greed?"

"Love, or maybe hate. A lover scorned, that sort of thing."

"Go back to your first idea," Zak said, "and turn it around. Instead of killing to get something, what about somebody killing to *keep* something they have?"

"To keep another person from taking it, you mean? As in defending your property against thieves?"

"Or maybe killing to keep others from learning a secret."

The pair considered possibilities. Overhead, the old paddle fans creaked, an offbeat accompaniment to the chorus of tree frogs and crickets.

"I don't think the motive was to get something from Doreen," Zak said finally. "We've already decided she didn't own anything worth stealing, right?"

"Howard suggested Doreen might have taken my mother's locket. A souvenir, I think he said. Assume for a minute that's true. What if that wasn't the only valuable thing she'd stolen?"

"And somebody killed her to get it back—whatever 'it' might be."

"It's as likely as anything else we've considered."

Zak bolted upright. "What if the locket itself was the reason she was killed?"

"Are you seriously suggesting my mother would—"

"No, but what if somebody else knew Doreen had your mother's locket and wanted it?"

"There's a couple of big holes in that theory. First, it's not worth an amazing amount of money. Sure, it's valuable—to me—but mostly because it's a family piece. So that leaves out robbery. Second, why didn't the killer just grab the necklace before dumping her in the lake?"

"Was she wearing the locket when she drowned?"

Maggie closed her eyes, visualizing the scene with the Barton County sheriff. "The locket fell out of her jeans pocket when Sheriff Malone dumped the evidence bag on the desk. I think if she'd been wearing it, the killer would have seen it, taken it from her."

"Okay, so the killer didn't see it, but knew she had it—somehow. He gets rid of her and goes looking for the locket."

"What makes you so sure the killer is a he?"

"Figure of speech. Let's just say whoever it was didn't realize Doreen had the necklace on her."

"Maybe they thought she hid it somewhere. Her house, maybe? Which, according to Lucas, had been a real mess. Maybe the killer had been there, searching," Maggie said slowly. "But the sheriff said there was no evidence of a break-in."

"Doreen's keys were never found, were they?"

"No. So they were searching for my mother's locket—"

"And when they didn't find it, they decided to search here," Zak finished for her. "But why go to such extremes over a piece of jewelry? That piece, in particular?"

"I've been a coward," Maggie said suddenly. "I've avoided talking to the one person most likely to know the answer to these questions. I suppose I've never forgiven my mother for leaving. But it was her life, her choice to leave, wasn't it? I chose, too—I chose to come back, to make my life here.

"We made different choices, but our lives are still connected, aren't they? No matter how much we might want it different, we're still connected. What's that saying about 'the ties that bind'? Waterside seems to be the tie that binds, doesn't it? I mean, it's the one thing, besides the locket, that connects my mother, me, and Doreen."

"There might be an art connection, too. Who knows you've been inventorying your mother's studio?"

Maggie sighed. "Half the town, probably, since my insurance agent mentioned it at the Merchants League meeting last week. Several people heard him."

"Didn't Howard say that Doreen wanted to get into your mother's studio? She was interested in art, we know that. She signed up for that beginner's class, remember?"

"And she tried to keep Howard from seeing the paintings she'd been working on. Assuming Howard was telling the truth about that, of course."

"Let's say he is. If so, it would appear that Doreen was interested in your mother, and specifically in her art. Why?"

"I don't know, but first thing in the morning, I'm going to call that gallery in Colorado and get some answers."

"The owner wasn't very helpful the first time around."

"Maybe I can use the family connection to get what we want. We just need a phone number, or even an email address. How hard can that be?"

The next morning, however, she was too busy to follow through on her plan. A family showed up with two skittish young dogs they'd taken in, asking for help integrating the dogs into their crowded household. After that, Maggie evaluated a lovely Dalmatian pup. "She's a sweet little thing, Mr. Cooley. Bring the kids for the next session, if you can. The sooner Elsie is socialized toward the children, the better."

The afternoon was taken up with caring for the boarders and routine chores, interrupted by the persistent heavy breather. Garrett, who'd taken to answering the phone, reacted with a rude suggestion, then turned bright red when he saw Maggie hovering in the doorway.

"I should have thought of that," she said, trying hard not to laugh at the look on his face. "They won't call back today, so maybe you could give me a hand with that fence repair."

"Sure thing."

Although the temperature was still in the upper nineties, a stiff breeze off the lake made outdoor chores bearable. The Bridgers came by in the late afternoon. Sylvia went straight to the run occupied by the stray dog, while Howard volunteered to help Garrett wrestle a new section of chain link into place. Even if she suspected his motives were less than pure, Maggie appreciated the gesture. She wasn't the one he hurt by having an affair, she told herself. If anyone is entitled to be angry, it's Sylvia. If somebody decides to tell her about Howard's involvement with Doreen, it would serve him right, but she wasn't going to get involved.

THUNDER GROWLED ACROSS the water the following week, raising hopes all over the drought-stricken region. High winds and heavy storms spawned tornado activity across the plains. The storms swept through Kansas and down into Oklahoma before falling apart at the edge of the Ozarks. Zak and Claire joined Maggie and the Bridgers as they listened to the wind crashing through the trees and watched whitecaps thrashing the lake's normally placid surface. To the west, thunderheads packed an impressive display of lightning but failed to deliver desperately needed rain. To the north, the sky was ominously red, with a smoky haze blurring the horizon.

"The fire crews will be out all night again. These winds are sure to make their jobs a nightmare," Sylvia predicted.

Howard reached for the pitcher of iced tea. "The fire marshal was on Channel Five earlier, talking about evacuation plans. How are you going to handle the kennel?"

Maggie summarized the contingency plans she'd developed. "Angus is reopening soon, and he'll have room for my boarders in his new clinic if there's an emergency," she told the group. "That's Plan A, assuming Eureka Springs isn't at risk. Plan B is to move everybody to the fairgrounds southwest of town. They've already opened all the livestock barns for anyone needing a place. If I have to evacuate to the southeast, I've set up a reciprocal agreement with Eric Whitehorse and his son at the Madison County Kennels. That's Plan C. They're driving up soon, to see the place."

"Eric's been in the business since your grandfather's time," Howard said. "Trains bird dogs, mostly. Miles worked with him a lot."

Zak looked concerned. "I think Garrett or I should be with you when he comes."

"Any particular reason?"

"He knows dogs, he knows your family, and you're in the same business," Zak said bluntly.

"You think he might be responsible for those letters?"

"I've known him for years," Howard protested. "He's harmless."

"That's what everyone said about Jake," Zak reminded them. "Look how that turned out. Until we get to the bottom of all this, I'm presuming all suspects guilty until proven innocent."

"Don't you have that backwards?"

"Cops and the courts have to play by those rules—I don't."

TUESDAY WAS ANOTHER busy day. Maggie printed bills, processed credit card transactions and handed out receipts. Some customers liked to linger and chat. And some just liked to complain, she thought with a mental shrug as she turned her attention to Mrs. Jessup, who'd apparently been born with a belligerent personality and saw no reason to change.

"What's this charge? I'm not gonna pay for something I didn't ask for."

"We had to treat Duchess for fleas when she came in."

"I don't like that stuff, it smells."

"It's in your contract, Mrs. Jessup." Maggie pulled a copy from the file and circled the relevant paragraph. This was a familiar argument. Although she discussed the contract in detail with all new clients, most simply signed the form without actually reading it, never questioning anything until they received their bill. "I have an obligation to all my customers to control parasites. If we find fleas or ticks when an animal arrives, we have the right to treat infested animals at the owner's expense." She glanced at Mrs. Jessup's bill as Garrett delivered the sweet-tempered mixed breed. "I see here that Bev gave Duchess a bath, too."

"And how much is that going to cost me?"

"There's no charge for the bath. Bev remembered you don't like the smell of flea treatments. All part of our service."

"I suppose that's all right, then."

"You might want to try one of the flea control products you can use once a month. Just a little dab on the dog's back, no mixing, no spraying. No bad smells, either. If you're going to Harrison you can pick some up at that big pet store, or Dr. Sheppard can help you with that when he reopens."

After Mrs. Jessup and Duchess departed, Maggie drove to Eureka Springs where the Boyden sisters and their young Cocker Spaniel, Henry, waited for their weekly training consultation. With Rob at the kennel to help Garrett and Bev, Maggie didn't fret as much about the time she was spending away from the kennel. And the additional training fees brought her one step closer to getting out of debt, she reminded herself.

The session sped by. The women approached dog training with the same dedication and attention to detail they applied to their work as healthcare professionals. She'd seen the Boyden sisters in action when she'd stopped by the hospital to donate blood, and they'd begun training Henry soon after that, progressing steadily. Now they were working on the long sit and return exercise.

"He just won't stay once the leash is off," Chelsea Boyden reported.

"That's common at this stage," Maggie assured her. "I'd like to try something I learned from an Australian dog trainer." She went out to her truck and returned holding a hammer and a very long stake.

"What are you going to do?" Linda asked, puzzled.

"I want Henry to get used to the idea of the long sit off-leash, so we'll start by letting him see the leash in front of him." Maggie drove the tall stake firmly into the ground, and then circled the yard with Henry, finishing up several feet behind her original position.

With Henry on-leash in the heel position, she put her hand in front of Henry's face, palm facing him, and said firmly, "Stay!" Then she walked away from the dog, careful to step off with her right foot as a further signal for the dog to stay in place.

When she was six feet away and next to the stake, Maggie turned and faced the dog while still holding the leash. She was careful not to make eye contact with Henry, who might use that as an excuse to break from his stay command. She dropped the end of the leash over the stake, alert for the slightest movement from Henry. When he started to get up, she walked quickly back to the dog, chastising him in a stern voice. She put him back in position and gave the command, "Stay!" When he obeyed, she praised him, then moved back a few feet, returning when Henry moved again.

Patiently, she repeated the process again and again, gradually moving farther away. By the end of the session, she was confident the spaniel wouldn't break. Maggie ended the training session with Henry's favorite game of ring-toss.

"Practice using the leash and the stake for the next few days. Once Henry gets used to this, we'll try it with the leash off the collar."

"But he won't stay if he knows the leash is off," Chelsea objected.

"We'll let him think the leash is still connected. I'll dangle the snap at his side, and I'll lay the leash along the ground as I walk away, so Henry can see it. I'll walk a few feet at a time, so I can be close if he breaks. We'll increase the distance gradually.

"Once he's comfortable with that, we'll work without the leash. You'll need to practice the exercise for longer periods of time. I know you're busy people, but you can do this exercise while you're working around the house. Try it next time you wash the car, or when you're weeding the garden."

Maggie was updating Henry's training log when a beeper sounded. "We're on ER duty this month," Chelsea explained. "They're pulling staff from all over to help because of the fires."

"I didn't realize there have been so many burn victims."

"We've had a few. But burns are just a part of it. Some have been injured by falling equipment, or hurt cutting the firebreaks. Lots of respiratory complaints because of the smoke. Heatstroke is a real problem, too. Then there's the usual summer problems. Hikers fall off the bluffs, kids break a leg sliding into second base, and idiots who think it's okay to drink as long as they're driving a boat instead of a car."

As she drove home, Maggie considered Chelsea's comments. Doreen had been drinking when she died. What if the person who'd been in the boat with Doreen had been drinking as well? Could the person have feared arrest for DUI, or whatever the term was for operating a boat while under the influence of alcohol? And if so, could it have been an accident, after all?

As she approached the turnoff to home, a battered Chevy pickup that had been idling by the mailboxes suddenly pulled out onto the road, fishtailing before crossing the center line directly in front of Maggie's smaller truck. The Chevy's driver hunched low over the wheel, face camouflaged by sunglasses and a ball cap worn low.

Maggie slammed on her brakes but nothing could save her from the imminent collision. She swerved to the right but the road was narrow and the shoulder little more than a wedge of rocky ground.

Metal screamed as the larger truck crashed into the smaller Ford Ranger, knocking it sideways. Maggie tried desperately to maintain some sense of control, but the steering wheel was wrenched from her grip as the force of the collision sent her truck careening off the road. Tires bit into the shoulder, throwing up a shower of gravel across the windshield, and in the next second the vehicle lurched sideways and crashed down the steep hillside.

Maggie heard herself screaming, heard a horn blaring. Her head snapped against the window with an angry crack as the truck continued to slide down the hill. Her legs slammed into the dashboard and then against the steering column. The seat belt locked up and pinned her torso painfully in place. The airbag deployed, sending powdery dust through the cab. Training dumbbells and other equipment stored behind the seat flew free and pummeled Maggie as the truck continued its downward plunge toward the ravine a hundred feet below.

The hillside itself seemed to crumble beneath her. A torrent of dirt, uprooted trees, and rocks of all size thundered down the slope and past the truck. Window glass shattered beneath the force of the falling debris. Twenty yards down, the truck slammed into a massive oak and came to rest on its side, two wheels spinning in the air, the driver's side pressed against the earth. The roof of the cab bulged inward, delivering another slashing blow to her head as boulders bounced down the hill and against the vehicle.

Black dots whirled before her eyes, out of sync with the pain kicking against her skull. She struggled to unfasten her seat belt, but her fingers wouldn't respond. Maggie looked out the passenger window above her. She could see blue sky and the branches of a white oak. She twisted in her seat, frantic to get out, and then froze at the sound of metal grating against stone. She couldn't have moved, even if she'd wanted to. The back end of the truck slid, then held. She wanted to keep screaming, but her voice didn't seem to be working, either. The black dots grew larger, obscuring her vision, and she slid into oblivion.

26

With a supreme effort, Maggie forced herself to open her eyes. She was lying in an unfamiliar bed, surrounded by bright lights and bustling people.

"You're in the emergency room," a voice said soothingly. "My name is Dr. Coventry. You've had an accident."

"It wasn't an accident." When Maggie tried to sit up, nausea swept over her.

"Not so fast," the doctor warned. She helped Maggie back to a prone position and resumed her examination. "What's the last thing you remember?"

"Going over—" The words caught in her throat. She swallowed, tried again. "There was a truck. It hit me. I couldn't hold on. I went over the edge."

The doctor pocketed her penlight and made a note on a chart. "You'll live," she reported cheerfully. "X-rays show a wicked concussion, three broken ribs, a twisted right knee and a badly sprained left hand. Your left shoulder was dislocated; I've reduced that and immobilized your arm. You'll need to wear that sling for a while, give that shoulder a chance to heal properly. Oh, and you had a nasty gash on the back of your head, so I put in twelve stitches. They're the self-absorbing kind, they won't need further attention. Relax for a few minutes, and I'll go get your family."

"I don't have—" Maggie began, but the doctor had already gone. She closed her eyes, and was fading back into blackness when someone took her hand. She opened her eyes to find Zak standing at her right side.

"Hi," he said softly.

"How did you know I was here?"

"The paramedics saw the kennel logo on the side of your truck. They called the kennel, and Garrett called me." Zak gently stroked her arm.

"It wasn't an accident. There was a truck—"

"You can tell me later. Dr. Coventry says you're supposed to be still and rest. So relax, okay?"

Chelsea Boyden pushed a wheelchair in. "Your room's ready upstairs, Maggie."

"I can't stay—the boarders—" Maggie struggled to sit up, then fell back when the room started to spin crazily and her stomach heaved.

"Don't worry about the kennel," Zak said. "Garrett and Rob are there. I can help with the evening chores, and I'll stay at your house, make sure everything's okay. Now do what the doctor tells you. Get some rest, and we'll take care of everything."

"Dr. Coventry wants to keep you overnight for observation," Chelsea informed her. "Can't take any chances with a head injury. So if you can tear your hands off this gorgeous man—" the nurse winked at Zak—"I'll get you upstairs."

Maggie did as she was told. Although she didn't like the idea of any kind of hospital stay, she was too tired to argue. All she wanted to do was sleep.

"We'll be here to take you home as soon as the doctor clears you," Zak promised.

LUCAS ARRIVED THE next day while Maggie was contemplating her lunch with dismay. "I think it's alive," she said, pointing to the quivering mass of gelatin.

"I'm certainly glad *you* are. After seeing what's left of your vehicle, I'd call it a miracle."

"How did I get out of the truck?"

"That was your second miracle. Donnie Ray Bowles—he's on our county Search and Rescue team—drives that road every day. He saw skid marks and one of your fenders and stopped to check. When he saw your truck he called for help and climbed down after you. He had you stabilized and ready for transport when the paramedics arrived on scene. Took a while; they had to bring you up the hill in a Stokes basket. Donnie Ray stayed with you the whole time, didn't let go until they had you safely in the ambulance."

"He's a real hero," Maggie said fervently.

"Your truck is still there. We'll get Buck Sanders to haul it up and tow it to his garage. Now, do you feel up to telling me what happened?"

He listened carefully while Maggie related what she could remember of the moments leading up to the crash. "Would you recognize the truck if you saw it again?"

"I doubt it." She shrugged slightly, careful this time not to move too quickly. "I didn't have much time to notice details, Lucas. It just looked like another old clunker to me. You know, more rust than paint. Or maybe it was primer—it was sort of a gray color. And big tires," she remembered.

"What about the driver?"

"Something familiar about him ..." she tried to concentrate and failed.

"It was a man?"

"Maybe," she admitted. "I only had a quick glimpse before he hit me."

The sheriff asked her a few more questions, jotted down her answers, then flipped his note pad closed. "I have a couple things to tell you. First, somebody tried to break in to your house last night."

"Oh, my God. Claire—"

Lucas held up a hand, restraining her when she would have climbed out of bed. "The little girl and her father were with my boys in the kennel at the time."

"What happened?"

"Garrett says that big Lab of yours was outside and carrying on something fierce. Says you call it his intruder bark—is that right?" At Maggie's terse nod, Lucas continued. "Garrett decided to take a look around. He found your kitchen door jimmied open and called me.

"Whoever it was, they used a crowbar on the lock and nearly pulled the chain right out of the wall. Dog probably scared them off. Garrett said the house looked okay. When you get home and feel up to it, have a look around, see if you notice anything missing."

Maggie tried to control her trembling. "What's the other thing you need to tell me?"

"There was another letter."

"Oh, God."

"This one was in your mailbox. Sylvia picked up your mail and gave it to Zak. He saw the letter and called me." He pulled out a clear plastic envelope and held it out for her.

Trembling, Maggie read the words pasted on the page:

Bye Bye **BAD** girl

Maggie fell back against the pillows, her heart pounding. She slapped her right hand over her mouth to hold back the terror she could feel building in her chest.

Lucas pressed a glass into her hand. "Take a sip," he said kindly. "You've had a bad shock. Give yourself time to settle."

When she thought she could speak without screaming she asked, "Whoever was in that truck really meant to hurt me, didn't they?"

"I don't know for sure, but until I find out I'm assigning a deputy to your area," he said grimly. "I've already given Garrett his marching orders, and either he or Rob will be on site at your kennel at all times."

Zak said much the same thing when he arrived an hour later. "You might as well get used to having company. We've worked out a schedule to keep the kennel running, and you don't go anywhere alone until we figure out who's behind all this."

When Maggie remained silent, he continued. "I walked through the house with the sheriff. We double-checked all the doors and windows, and Garrett's there right now, putting a new lock on your kitchen door." He looked at her soberly. "After I take you home, I'm going over to Harrison and get more supplies and install an alarm system in the house."

"I don't know how I'm going to afford it. I have to buy another truck and the hospital bill—"

"I'll pay for the alarm."

"I can't take your money."

"You need an alarm system now, and I can afford it. You pay me back when you can. Plus, you make sure Santa gets the right puppy for Claire."

"I'll train it, too," she said firmly, trying to blink back the tears his generosity had spurred.

"Deal. Look, Maggie, I know you're worried about money, but frankly, I'm more worried about you."

Maggie was crying in earnest now, huge gulping sobs. When she could talk, she said, "Nobody's really worried about me since ... since Gran died."

Zak hugged her. "I think it's getting to be a habit of mine, so you better get used to that, too."

Maggie laughed shakily. "So, Santa, when do we go puppy shopping?"

27

In the days following the crash, Maggie was astonished by the people who called to wish her well or sent flowers or offered their assistance during her convalescence. A contingent of elderly ladies from town came bearing gifts of homemade jelly, chicken soup, and enough casseroles to feed the entire staff.

"We all went to school with your grandmother, God rest her soul," one told Maggie. "Now, we'll put these away for you, shall we? And then we'll tidy up a bit before we go."

"Gran was blessed to have such good friends," Maggie told them. "And so am I."

Now, sitting in the office for the first time since the accident, she talked to Zak between phone calls. "It's a bit overwhelming, but in a good way. So much support, even from people I don't really know. Everybody's working hard, except me."

Zak handed her a cup of coffee. "You're supposed to be resting," he said sternly. "Doctor's orders, remember?"

"I feel guilty knowing you're all working so hard."

"Hey, we volunteered."

Garrett had insisted on picking up most of Maggie's chores in addition to his own, even offering to lead the obedience class. "Good thing I read those training books you loaned me," he said with a smile. Rob was doing all the pick-ups and deliveries and filling in for Garrett when he was off the premises.

Bev cleaned the cattery in addition to all the grooming and kept the office running with Zak's help. When he wasn't working at the co-op or in the office or at Maggie's side, Zak ran errands and did the shopping. The Bridgers pitched in with evening chores, and Howard came by most mornings to help where needed. Even a few customers had dropped by to offer help exercising the boarders or play with the cats.

"I appreciate all your hard work, too," Maggie told Zak.

"You're just trying to butter me up so I won't yell about you being out of bed."

"Did it work?" she asked hopefully.

"Not a chance." Zak checked his watch. "You've been up for hours. Don't you think you should rest now?"

"I feel fine," she assured him. Emotionally, it was true. The outpouring of concern touched her deeply, making her feel a part of the community for the first time.

One of the first things she'd done after leaving the hospital was to have Zak take her to meet Donnie Ray Bowles. "I didn't think anybody would find me down that hillside," she'd told the young man. "I owe you my life."

"Just in the right place at the right time, is all," Donnie Ray responded. "I surely am glad to see you up and around."

"I don't actually remember too much," she confessed.

"Probably better that way. Although, if you have to have an accident, this county is a good place to do it," he told her with a grin. "Out here, most folks have at least basic emergency response skills. I was an Army medic, and there are other vets around here with similar training. You can get certified by taking classes at the community college, too. You don't have to look far around here to find an EMT or a fire fighter or a reserve sheriff's deputy. Quite a few of us are in Search and Rescue, too, so we stay pretty busy."

He winked at her. "We're going to count you as our Stokes basket rescue refresher training. That's going to come in handy. We're always busy with whitewater and cave rescues in the summer, and we spend a lot of time finding lost tourists. We use the Stokes to haul them out of holes and ravines."

"I don't know what I could possibly do to repay you for what you did for me, but I'd like to try."

"Tell you what, maybe you could think about joining our SAR team. It's a good group. Hey, you know one of 'em. Ben Springer? Says he's in one of your obedience classes."

"Oh, sure. He has a German Shepherd—Gretal."

"That's the one. He's interested in training his dog for SAR work, but that's a ways off. For now, we borrow Barton County's K-9 unit, because we don't have a dog of our own. Ben said I should ask you about your Lab."

"I haven't done any search and rescue work but Sam's an excellent tracker, and he's a fast learner. I'd be honored to help."

"Get yourself back to 100 percent first."

Physically, she was improving every day. The worst of her headache was gone, and at least she didn't feel as bad as she looked. She'd abandoned her usual jeans and boots in favor of lightweight cotton dresses that effectively hid most of the bruises, which were turning yellow and green and black.

The Boyden sisters had come by the previous evening with a basket of herbal teas and assured her the hideous colors would soon fade. They'd checked her shoulder and cautioned her about doing too much too soon. Pamper yourself, they'd said.

"And that couldn't possibly include paperwork," Maggie said aloud. Seeing Zak's startled look, she related the Boyden sisters' comments. "So let's do something fun," she suggested. "We still don't have a really good treasure map for the kids' Summerfest program. Want to work on that over lunch?"

Zak agreed. They'd found a collection of Ozark treasure stories and he sketched several maps based on those stories, but none of them seemed quite right to Maggie. Over lunch, she remembered she had seen a treasure map, and recently—when she sorted through her grandmother's boxes. "My mother's sketchbook! Let's go look."

In minutes, Maggie found what she was looking for. "I think I was four, or maybe five," she mused, flipping through pages. "I wanted to be a pirate for Halloween. Gran sewed my costume and my mother told me treasure stories while she drew a map. Said it was our secret. Funny, I'd forgotten all that." Her voice softened, remembering.

Zak peered over her shoulder. "Her pencil sketches are nearly as good as her paintings," he observed. "She drew part of the town, but most of this map is around the lake. It won't take me long to add more details around town with places for the kids to go. We should make up some clues to go with the map. What about prizes? Did the merchants come through?"

"Eight stores so far have promised prizes; I'll give you the list. Three restaurants offered family discount coupons, but we still need a few more donations. Nicholas is coming out for lunch tomorrow. Maybe he can help us get some more prizes."

"Better bring him up to date on what we're doing. Officially, he isn't part of the Summerfest committee, but he does have a lot of influence in the Merchants League," Zak reminded her. "We need all the goodwill we can get."

"Good idea."

Over lunch the next day, she handed Nicholas a copy of the altered map and the clues she and Zak created. "We want it to be a challenge, of course, but most of all fun."

Nicholas groaned. "I can see it now—we're going to be overrun by grubby little urchins."

"Don't you like children?"

"Certainly, as long as they belong to somebody else and are kept far away from my gallery."

"Well, you better post a guard at your door, because you're going to see a lot of kids. We thought the treasure hunt would keep them busy."

"Is the map your own creation?"

"I found one in my mother's sketchbook. Zak adapted it."

"Why not use your mother's map?"

"Give me a minute and I'll show you." She went into the office and returned moments later with sketchbook in hand. She flipped through the pages until she found the map and showed it to Nicholas. "My memory's a bit hazy, but I think she used some old map she'd found to draw this one. See how there's just a little bit of the town sketched in? We needed more details for this project, so Zak made the changes we needed."

"Your mother always did have an eye for detail," he murmured. "And Zak is a better artist than I thought."

"He added town landmarks and moved the 'X marks the spot' to fit with the Summerfest location. That reminds me— we still need some more prizes. Think you can persuade some of the merchants to contribute?"

He seemed absorbed in studying the map and didn't answer. "Nicholas?"

"Hmmm?" he said absently.

"Are you dreaming about buried treasure?" she teased.

"Treasure is very serious business," he admonished her, returning the sketchbook and sliding the map she'd given him into his pocket.

"Consider that your own personal treasure map," Maggie told him, laughing. "Just be sure to pass a copy along to the publicity committee. Remind them to plant the clues or the kids won't be able to find the treasure we've hidden."

Nicholas saluted briskly. "Aye, aye, Captain."

28

Maggie pulled into the grocer's parking lot slowly, not yet accustomed to the large panel van her mechanic had delivered. "It's the only loaner vehicle available," he'd apologized. "The AC works great, so at least you'll be cool until your new Ranger gets delivered."

"I wish it was an automatic," Maggie said to Zak, who had declared himself bodyguard for the day. "But I'll get used to it. I'm just glad to be doing something. It's about time I got back to work." Seeing him frown, she added quickly, "Hey, it's only shopping. I promise not to lift anything heavy."

"Fine. You can push the cart while I load the groceries," Zak said calmly. "And don't even think of picking up a single bag of kibble when we get to the wholesaler's warehouse."

Selecting groceries took longer than she'd expected. People kept stopping them to chat or commiserate or just plain gossip. They ran into Angus Sheppard and two of his grandchildren, who wanted to talk about the Summerfest treasure hunt. While Zak patiently answered their excited questions, Miss Abigail hurried up and threw her arms around Maggie, who held back a groan.

"Oh, you darling! I'm so very glad to see you're all right. I've heard such dreadful rumors, you simply can't imagine, and yet here you stand, unscathed."

"You wouldn't say that if you could see my bruises." Maggie glanced at her cart, wondering how to politely extricate them before her frozen foods thawed. Miss Abigail was still talking, but Maggie had totally lost track of the conversation.

"Such a beauty, just like her mother. Isn't she, Angus?"

The question seemed innocent enough on the surface, but Maggie was startled to see Angus' smile disappear. A muscle ticked along his rigid jaw. She wondered what she'd missed.

It wasn't until Zak had loaded the weekly supply of kibble from the wholesaler that she remembered Miss Abigail's earlier hints about an affair between Maggie's mother and Angus. Could it be true? Had Angus been having an affair with her mother? Was he the reason she'd left Eagle Cove? And, more importantly, could he be the reason she might have returned?

As Zak slowed for the turn onto the dirt road leading to the kennel, Maggie closed her eyes, not wanting to see again the scene of her accident. To distract herself, she shared her thoughts about Angus with Zak, who was easing the van along the rough road with careful attention.

"Even if there was something all those years ago, I just can't see Angus connected to Doreen," she concluded. "Okay, he'd seen her at the kennel, but I don't remember him paying much attention to her."

"Maybe Miss Abigail was just trying to rile him up," he suggested as he parked the van and began unloading.

"She does enjoy minding other people's business," Maggie admitted. "But I just can't see Angus having any kind of relationship with Doreen. He's a grandfather, for heaven's sake."

"You think affairs are only for the young? Howard was involved with her, and he's the same age as Angus."

"The more we learn about that girl, the more I realize I never really knew her at all," Maggie murmured. "She worked for me. I should have known her better than I did."

"Maybe she didn't want you to know that side of her. Maybe she thought you wouldn't have approved."

"Well, whatever the truth turns out to be, I'm going to remember she was good with animals, and Sweet Pea liked her."

"A good memory to hold onto," he agreed. He finished unloading the supplies. "Okay, you're set for now. Garrett, Rob, and Bev will be here all afternoon, and then Howard will come over to exercise the boarders and help with evening chores. If you need anything, all you have to do is holler."

"I doubt I'll do anything more strenuous than walk down to the dock. Today wore me out," she admitted.

"You did pretty good, considering it was the first time you drove anywhere since your accident."

MAGGIE NAPPED THROUGH the worst of the afternoon heat and awoke feeling sore and irritable. She wandered down to the kennel, where everything was quiet and calm. Most of the cats were following Maggie's example and sleeping through the afternoon, with only a few young felines playing energetically. The dogs, including her own, were inside enjoying the air-conditioned comfort of their runs.

Maybe a little exercise will improve my mood, Maggie thought, and decided to walk over to visit Sylvia. She found Garrett and told him where she was going.

"Give me a minute to tell Rob and I'll walk with you."

"Honestly, there's no need. We haven't had a speck of trouble since I got out of the hospital."

"Sorry, boss. You're stuck with me or one of the others until my dad says different."

"Have you had any time off in the last couple weeks? Bev and Rob are here, and Howard will be along soon. Why don't you take a break and go enjoy that boat of yours?"

"I went out on the lake for a couple hours today, while you were napping. So no worries there."

Resigned, she collected Sam from his run and waited for Garrett in front of the kennel. "Why don't we take the shoreline path?" she asked when he joined her. "It's practically a straight shot from my dock to the Bridger's place, and at this time of day there's plenty of shade on the path."

Garrett agreed, and used his cell phone to let Rob know their plans. He let Maggie set the pace and they walked slowly along as Sam splashed happily through the shallows.

Sylvia's house had been built close to the lake, just a few yards off the path that connected the two properties. Garrett found a stick and tossed it for Sam as Maggie walked up to the front door and rang the bell.

Sylvia stepped out, scissors in one hand and reading glasses in the other. "I thought you were supposed to be taking it easy. Climbing that hill is not easy," she said sternly. "And what are you doing out here all by yourself?"

"Garrett and Sam came with me. We skipped the hill and took the lake path." There was an awkward silence until Maggie cleared her throat. "You're busy. I should have called first."

"No, it's okay. Let's go out on the deck. There's plenty of shade." Sylvia led the way through the house, moving quickly. Just as the two women settled into deck chairs, the phone rang. "Stay here while I get that. Then I'll bring us some iced tea."

Maggie looked over the deck railing and realized Garrett had seen them come out on the deck and was now wading in the shallows and throwing more sticks for the dog to retrieve. She was laughing as Sylvia came out carrying a tray of iced tea and a cordless phone. "Why do people call you and then put you on hold?" she asked crossly. "It's one of the developers, fussing about the pond liners they ordered. I told those idiots three feet wasn't deep enough for a big koi pond here, but they wouldn't listen. You need a bare minimum of four feet, and even then you run the risk the fish won't survive the next bad freeze we get. And they need deep water in this extreme heat, too— yes, Niles, I'm here. What's the problem?" she said into the phone.

Maggie stood up, caught the older woman's eye. "I'll call you later," she murmured. Sylvia, her attention apparently caught by

Niles and his problems, didn't seem to notice as Maggie went back into the house. She walked down the hall and was tugging at the door when the clutter in the dining room caught her eye.

Boxes and packing materials occupied most of the floor space, but it was what was on the table that captured Maggie's attention. She saw newspapers and advertising fliers and a stack of pages that looked like they'd been torn out of the magazines scattered across the table. Scissors and glue stood beside several jars of acrylic paints and some strange materials Maggie couldn't immediately identify.

Sylvia had followed her into the house and watched with a curiously frozen expression. "I didn't want you to see all this," she said quietly.

Maggie felt as though the floor was tilting beneath her. Her mind numbly registered that the table held all the materials used in the threatening letters she'd received. It can't be true, she told herself. It wasn't possible. Or was it?

The first letter had been in a stack of mail which Sylvia had handed her, saying she'd picked it up from the mailbox. The next two had been left on the porch and could easily have been delivered by someone who was a frequent visitor, somebody who lived close by and could choose her activities with little fear of discovery. And the fourth letter, Maggie remembered grimly, had been handed to Zak by Sylvia, who claimed she found it in the mailbox.

Sylvia, who'd pretended to be her friend.

"I should tell you—"

Maggie cut her off in mid-sentence with a sharp wave of her hand. She was doing her best to block out the reality that lay before her, but Sylvia's next words could crush her defenses. She couldn't think, didn't know what to do next.

"I'm leaving." She was careful to keep her voice, her words, neutral. "I'm not feeling very well after all." Shutting the door quietly, she headed for the path where Garrett and Sam waited to take her safely home.

Maggie held her misery on a firm leash, but she couldn't stop her thoughts tumbling wildly. The first two letters referred to my mother, she remembered. What if the letter writer wasn't a jealous competitor after all, as Zak had suggested, but instead someone who hated her mother?

Had Sylvia resented Maggie's mother for her success when her own career had died an early death? Did she blame Margaret for that lost career? Or was it even more personal than that? Did Sylvia believe Howard had an affair with Maggie's mother? Had Maggie inadvertently opened old wounds—and made herself a target—by returning to Waterside?

How long must she pay for her mother's sins?

29

Zak glanced at Maggie as he hauled a folding chair out of the vehicle. He added the chair to the crates stacked on the roll cart and began to push it carefully along the cobblestone street. "You'll scare the kids with that frown."

"Then ask somebody else to run the treasure hunt."

"There isn't anybody else available. The artists will be working their booths and this is one of the busiest days of the summer for the galleries and shops. Besides, the treasure hunt was your idea," he reminded her.

"Yeah, but that was before I joined the ranks of the walking wounded," she muttered.

Zak glanced at her, then turned to his daughter. "Hey, isn't that your friend Melanie over there with her mom? Why don't you go say hello, we'll be right behind you." He waited until Claire was out of earshot before complaining, "I haven't had a moment alone with you in days. Tell me what's been happening. How did it go with Sylvia?"

Zak had persuaded her to confront Sylvia with her fears and suspicions. "I'm still trying to figure out what to say," she confessed. "She's called a couple of times, but I put her off. Just thinking that she could do such a thing makes my stomach hurt—along with the rest of me." She had a killer headache, no doubt caused by another string of sleepless nights.

"I cannot imagine her doing anything to hurt you."

"You were the one who said everyone was presumed guilty until proven innocent," Maggie pointed out irritably, and then relented when she saw his expression. "Sorry. I shouldn't be taking my mood out on you."

"That's what friends are for. Hey, why don't you head over to the bakery before you check in? Mrs. Kaplan makes the sweetest pastries in the world. You might want to skip her coffee, though—it's strong enough to make the spoon stand straight up in the cup."

"Caffeine and sugar—sounds perfect."

They reached the main street where exhibitors were unpacking and setting up their artwork. It was only six-thirty in the morning, but the streets were already crowded as exhibitors and shop owners hurried to unload stock before the downtown area closed to vehicle traffic at eight o'clock. When they reached Zak's space, Maggie waved good-bye and, after a stop at the bakery, headed for the town square, designated as "treasure central" for the day.

The treasure hunt got off to a roaring start as children of all ages clamored to participate. "The treasure may be hidden in more than one location," she reminded the treasure seekers, handing out maps and a short list of rules. "We're hunting for silver that might have been hidden by Spanish soldiers. The soldiers left clues behind so they could find the treasure again. In fact, Mr. Goodberry told me he saw one of those clues just this morning outside his store." She pointed in the direction of the old five-and-dime, whose owner had good-naturedly agreed to put the first clue among the advertisements posted around his door. "And even if you don't find the Spanish treasure, there's plenty of other cool stuff to be found!"

Maggie spent an enjoyable hour handing out maps before being relieved by another volunteer from the Merchants League. She wandered along, enjoying the sights and sounds of the festival despite the headache that lingered behind her eyes.

Tourists and locals alike crowded the streets. Children were everywhere, and nearly all of them held a treasure map. The boy scouts were selling lemonade, sweating as they hauled their wares through the crowd. Dogs of all sizes and colors wandered freely, napping in the shade or frolicking with children in the little park, where a splash pool provided a cool respite from the heat. There was a long line at the pony rides, and it was standing room only at the magician's tent.

Maggie stopped by the Crane Gallery to greet Nicholas, who was at his door where two small boys quarreled fiercely over a clue. She hurried to separate them before they came to blows. "It's only a game," she said sternly.

"Maybe to you," one yelled rudely as they ran off.

"Who knew there'd be such interest in a silly treasure game?"

"Never get between a boy and his treasure," Nicholas warned her.

"Are you sorry you're not out there searching with them?"

"I prefer my treasure in the form of commissions today."

Leaving him at his door, Maggie wandered among the exhibits, watching craftsmen make brooms and baskets, tapping her foot to the dulcimer music, and listening to the storytellers who had drawn a sizable crowd in the shade of tall oaks.

She stopped to listen to a woman dressed in a style Maggie imagined was common among frontier women long ago. Sturdy boots peeked out from beneath the hem of her skirt, and the simple cotton blouse she wore looked homespun. Her steel gray hair was tucked beneath a bonnet.

"This here story has been handed down through my family ever since 1826," the woman told the audience. "That's about the time the first Yokum—that'd be Jamie Lee Yokum—settled along the big river herabouts. My family farmed the land downriver from the Yokum place, which is how I come to know this tale."

"This land belonged to the Chickasaw tribe, and they were good neighbors, always sharing what they had. They were good traders, too, and pretty near famous for their beautiful silver jewelry. They always had plenty of silver but nobody knew—'cept the Indians, of course—where it all came from. Some said it was from a silver mine, and some claimed it was Spanish silver, but nobody knew for sure.

"When the government decided they wanted the Indians' land, the Yokums traded some of their wagons and supplies in exchange for information about the source of that silver. As the story goes, the Indians shared their secret with Jamie Lee. They told him where he might find some of that silver, and he told his brothers. Times being what they was, and money being about as hard to come by as an honest politician, the Yokums decided to use that silver and make their own coin. They minted their own dollars with that there silver. For years, people all over the Ozarks used the Yokum dollars as legal tender."

The storyteller looked across the crowd. "Well, you can probably guess what happened next. The federal government didn't take too kindly to somebody else making money. They didn't like the competition, my granddaddy said." There were chuckles and murmurs of agreement from some in the crowd.

"The federal agents confiscated all the Yokum dollars they could get their hands on. What they really wanted was the source of that silver, but Jamie Lee wouldn't tell 'em where to find it. After a while, the agents gave up and went back to Washington."

The storyteller paused for a sip of lemonade. "It wasn't long after that when Jamie Lee Yokum passed away. His two brothers died soon after, crossing the Rockies on their way out to California. Those men were the only ones who knew the Indians' secret and they took that secret to their graves, but they did leave some clues in letters they'd written to their cousins. Over the years, a lot of people have searched high and low for that silver, but nobody's ever found it. But who knows? Maybe you'll be the one to learn the truth about the Indian Silver Legend."

The crowd applauded enthusiastically as the story came to a close. Maggie glanced at her watch and realized she'd have to hurry if she was going to have time to browse through the rest of the show before heading back for another shift at the treasure booth. She decided to start at Zak's booth.

All the artists had erected shade canopies over their ten-by-ten squares, and Maggie noticed that most of the potters displayed their wares on simple board shelves. Zak's space, though, was dramatically different. He had created a miniature gallery look in his square by displaying his raku pottery on freestanding pedestals, using a series of interlocking panels covered in a soft gray to form a backdrop for the shimmering colors of his work. Zak had shown Maggie a sample of his work before, but this was the first time she'd seen a collection of his on display.

"Very professional. I'm impressed," she told him. "But I didn't know there were two artists in the family." A small table in one corner of his exhibit held hand-thrown bowls made by Claire. The display included a picture and a short biography of the young artist.

"She sold three pieces this morning. She's a natural with clay and one of these days she's going to be better than her old man." The pride in his voice was unmistakable.

"She's lucky to have such a supportive dad." She thought of her own father, who had never been interested in her achievements; she'd stopped trying to win his approval a long time ago. Thank heavens she'd had Gran. Without her encouragement, she might never have found the courage to try to carve out a place for myself in a field where legends lived large. And without her grandmother's expert advice and assistance, she might never have developed the skills needed to run her own business. A lot to be grateful for, Maggie reminded herself.

Zak was asking her something, and she wrenched her attention back to the present. "Sorry, I was woolgathering, as Gran would have said. I missed your question."

"I asked if you'd been through the entire show yet."

"No. Why?"

Zak grinned. "Because there's something you definitely need to see." He asked the artist in the neighboring space to keep an eye on his display and led Maggie to another booth several rows away, its small space crowded with customers.

As Maggie waited for a glimpse of the artwork on display, she heard someone ask, "Is this a plaster mold?"

"The masks are actually a papier collé. That's a form of collage. I use mixed paper—newspapers, magazines, whatever I have—to build up the three-dimensional shape. After that I add other items to the masks or the canvas, and sometimes both, to match the theme."

"That can't be—is that Sylvia?" Maggie murmured.

"See for yourself."

The customers moved on. Maggie came face to face with Sylvia Bridger, who said nothing as Maggie stared at the artwork on display. "*This* is what you've been doing?"

Mounted on canvas, each mask was a unique creation. Some were round, others oval, in a variety of sizes. Fascinated, Maggie moved slowly, admiring the work. "This one is very simple, but it has a lot of power," she commented. Against the sky blue background of the canvas, the mask was covered in waving stripes of red and white fabric, as though the person and the flag were a single entity. The words 'duty,' 'honor,' and 'country' stood out in sharp relief against the blue background.

Maggie realized the next mask matched the shape of her own face. The canvas had been painted before the mask was added; she recognized the scene as the shoreline of Eagle Cove. Sylvia had covered the mask with a series of overlapping images of dogs, with a single black cat added to the scene. A leather leash hung on the right side of the canvas. "That's me!" she cried in astonishment. Turning to Sylvia, she said simply, "I had no idea."

"It took me a long time to realize that I don't have the talent for traditional art," Sylvia confessed. "Working with paper has always been a hobby of mine, but I never considered it art. Not until I took some mixed media classes at the co-op and got the idea for making these masks, anyway."

"They're incredibly original," Zak praised Sylvia. "You've got my vote for a blue ribbon prize."

Sylvia blushed. "I still can't believe anyone will pay for these."

Maggie dug into her pocket. "I want the one with the dogs."

"Of course you can have it, but I can't let you buy it."

"Selling art is just as much a business as selling plants," Maggie insisted. "So how much?"

"Let's settle something first. You thought I sent those letters, didn't you?"

The deep sadness in Sylvia's eyes was more than Maggie could bear. "I didn't know what to think," she admitted. "So much has happened lately, I guess I just let my imagination run wild."

"I thought you'd laugh at what I was doing. I should have known better. You're not like … well, you're not like that."

Another surge of customers came in. Maggie asked Sylvia to put a 'sold' sticker on the mask she'd selected. "We'll argue about the money later."

On her way back to the town square, Maggie saw Claire playing in the splash pool with two other girls, all three laughing and shrieking as they danced through the water. She waved, and the girls came running over.

"I found her, Maggie!" Claire said excitedly.

"Found who?"

"My puppy! Well, she's not really a puppy, but she's pretty and sweet and she smells good and—"

"Take a deep breath and start from the beginning," Maggie instructed, smiling indulgently as the child obeyed. With the other girls chiming in at frequent intervals, it took a few minutes to hear the whole story. The object of all the fuss was a canine of unknown background, now up for adoption by the local animal shelter.

"A shelter animal might be a good choice," Maggie said thoughtfully. "I'll talk to your dad."

"I knew you'd say yes!"

"Don't get too excited until I check her out," she warned. "And what happened to your hat?" She tried but failed to keep her stern expression from sliding into a smile.

"I traded it for a whistle," the little girl explained, dragging the shiny object out of her pocket. "Just like yours!"

The little girls were sunburned and grubby and obviously having a wonderful time. Maggie rummaged in her purse for sunscreen and smeared it liberally across Claire's nose and shoulders. "Your dad packed juice in the cooler, but I added sodas when he wasn't looking," she said with a grin. "There's plenty for your friends, too."

"You're the best!"

IT WAS A week after Summerfest. The children's treasure hunt had been declared a stunning success, and there was already talk of planning a fall harvest festival continuing the treasure theme. For Maggie's part, she was just glad everyone was happy. She sat now on her porch with Claire, the dogs, and Garret. Overhead, the paddle fans creaked and labored to provide some relief from the unrelenting, scorching heat. She'd been trying, without success, to convince Garrett she didn't need a bodyguard.

"No, ma'am. I'm with you until my dad says different." There'd been no further incidents, but Garrett had insisted on staying close whenever Zak wasn't around.

"I worry that I'm abusing you, taking all your time. It's summer. You should be enjoying yourself with your friends."

"I get out some on the lake most days, which is plenty. And just maybe you haven't had any problems lately because you haven't been alone. By now, I'm guessing half the county knows that you've got a lot of security around here."

"I don't mean to sound ungrateful."

"Hey, you've had a rough time lately." He pointed to the northwest where blackened hills smoldered and smoke hung heavy on the horizon. To the south, other fires burned. "You want to worry about something, worry about that. A lightning strike started those, and we'll probably see more. Over a thousand acres have burned already. My dad said tankers are dropping water on the fire, and they called out the Guard to help."

"Any chance the fire will get this far?"

"Not likely. But that's not the only fire out there. There's one down near Berryville. Kids playing with bottle rockets set that one off. We're keeping an eye on that one, too. Hey, did you know Rob qualified for the junior firefighters? If the fires get over to this side of the lake, we might both get called up. But Zak will be here so you won't be alone."

"I think I'll give Eric Whitehorse a call in the morning. We might need to adjust our evacuation strategy, just in case we're cut off from both the town and the county fairgrounds." She gazed at the lake. "The logical choice would be the lake as an evacuation route, assuming that one, I had a boat and two, I had a safe place to go once we're out on the lake."

"Plenty of islands out there. I'd go for Deer Island—the Corps of Engineers patrols regularly so help is close by."

"Now all I need is a boat big enough to hold all the animals."

"My family has a pontoon boat, hasn't used it but a couple of times this summer. It has a big platform where we put tables and chairs. You could stack travel crates there. Be a tight fit, but it could work. Worth checking out, anyway."

Garrett's cell phone rang. He spoke briefly and then disconnected. "Zak says he's heading for home, wants us to meet him there. Rob's in the kennel. I'll walk you over."

They arrived at the cottage a few moments later. The door was ajar, but no one answered her knock. "Zak?"

"Surprise! Happy birthday, Claire! Happy birthday, Maggie!" Lights blazed as her friends and neighbors tumbled out of various hiding places. Sylvia and Howard were there, and Bev had brought her daughters along to enjoy the celebration. And there was Zak, standing there grinning at her.

"Surprised?"

"Absolutely. I knew you were doing something for Claire, but I had no idea you'd include me, too. You're wonderful!"

Garrett grinned. "He's been planning this for weeks."

"I had a lot of help," Zak insisted. He knelt down, hugged his daughter and spoke quietly so that only Claire and Maggie could hear. "Your mom really wanted to be here. She sent you a present and wants you to know she loves you very much."

"A present? For me?"

"Especially for you," Zak confirmed. "And she wants you to go visit again soon, whenever you're ready."

"Do I have to?"

"No, you don't have to, but I hope you'll give it some thought. She wants to tell you how sorry she is for making you upset." He looked up as Maggie knelt beside them.

"Remember how I told you Mr. B had been hurt, and it was taking him a long time to get better?" When the little girl nodded, Maggie continued. "You've seen for yourself, he's a little better now. It's going to take your mom time to get better, too. It may take a while before she can spend a lot of time with you. Just remember that your mother really does love you. A little visit might be fun for both of you. You could show her how to make those beautiful clay pots of yours, and I bet she'll want to hear all about that puppy you asked Santa to bring!"

"Really?"

"Really," Zak said firmly. "And speaking of presents, I see some right over there, waiting for you."

"Oh boy! Can I open them now?"

"After we eat," her father said firmly. Ushering everyone into the dining room, Zak settled Maggie and Claire at the head of the table. "Save room for cake and ice cream," he advised.

After a meal of grilled steak, baked potatoes, zucchini, and tossed salad, Claire opened her presents, exclaiming over each one. Maggie was glad she'd slipped Claire's present into the house last week. "Doggies!" the little girl shrieked, sliding her small arms through the straps of the backpack covered in Dalmatians. Laughing, Claire ran off to play with Bev's two girls.

Maggie was delighted with her own gifts. From Howard and Sylvia she received a khaki vest with pockets, perfect for field work. Bev and Garrett presented her with a book on advanced tracking techniques. Claire had given her a hand-braided cord for her training whistle, and from Zak there was one of his raku bowls. He'd also given her two flashlights.

"I noticed you have a lot of flashlights, but they're pretty big. I hope you can use these," he said with a smile.

"These are great," she said enthusiastically. One was a miniature Coleman lantern, scarcely two inches tall and designed to clip onto her belt loop. The other looked like no flashlight Maggie had ever seen. Shaped like a credit card and encased in plastic, there was a wedge of white at the top.

"It's called a Flashcard. The bulb's good for two years. It's waterproof, too. Wait a minute, I'll get the lights." When the room went dark, Maggie obediently pressed where he'd indicated, and was amazed at the pale, soft light that illuminated part of the room.

"Fantastic!" Maggie looked around the room, feeling a warm rush of happiness. "Thank you," she said. "I'm very grateful. For tonight, and a lot more. Friendship, for starters. I don't think I could have survived this past month without your support. 'Thank you' just doesn't seem enough."

"That will do just fine," Sylvia said gently, hugging Maggie as she and Howard prepared to leave.

Bev and her daughters followed them, with Garrett on their heels. "I'll go relieve Rob at the kennel," he told Maggie.

Claire was packed off for a bath before bedtime. A short time later, Maggie went in to say good night. "Sweet dreams," she told Claire, and reached out to switch off the lamp.

"Daddy always turns on the night-light first."

"Smart Daddy," Maggie said lightly as she turned on the small light.

"Sometimes I wake up and get scared," Claire confided.

Maggie gathered the child close. "I'll let you in on a secret, sweetie. I get scared of the dark sometimes, too."

Claire settled back against the pillows with a smile. "My mommy doesn't like me to sleep with the light on. But I knew you'd understand. You have pretty lights all over your house." She yawned, and was soundly asleep before Maggie finished straightening the covers.

Downstairs, Zak was out on the porch. The lamps were on in the living room, spilling light out onto the porch, pushing the shadows back, making a warm and inviting place.

As Maggie hesitated in the doorway, Zak smiled and moved to one side of the swing in unspoken invitation. She relaxed against the soft cushions beside him with a sigh. Beyond the porch, the sounds of the night drifted by—an owl, bullfrogs, cicada.

"You're really good with my daughter," Zak said softly.

"You heard?"

"Mm hmm." He paused. "If you want to talk, I'm a good listener."

"I know," she said. Her voice was thin, barely audible above the creak of the swing. The minutes passed by, unbroken by conversation. Trust him, she told herself, he'll understand. "Do you have nightmares?"

"Sure, a few now and again. What about you?"

"The same one, over and over."

She was running down the hallway, trying to find her way out. She could hear the voice calling her name, over and over. She ran faster, afraid to call for help, afraid the voice would find her. She fell against a door, and the knob turned beneath trembling fingers, and she fell down into darkness. Hide.

She wedged her small body behind something big and heavy, the brick wall rough against her back. Pressed her hands tight against her face, trying not to breathe, not to scream.

He was coming.

"It never changes," she whispered. "I know he's out there, in the dark, waiting."

"You've had this same nightmare all your life?"

"Every night when I was Claire's age. I told Gran, and she used to leave a light on." Maggie's voice dropped even lower. "I've tried, I really have, but it's no good. I'm still afraid of the dark."

Defiance crept into her voice. "It's no use trying to talk me out of it. My psychiatrist tried, twice a week, for years. 'Let go of the past,' she said. 'Monsters go away in the light of day.' But she was wrong, you know. Monsters don't go away. They never, ever go away." Her voice broke on a sob.

Zak wrapped his arms around her, hugging her close. "Maybe they don't," he said. "But you don't have to face them alone. Not anymore."

30

New fires had broken out near Sugar Mountain, threatening Eureka Springs as strong winds whipped the flames through timber at breakneck speed. Garrett and Rob divided their time between the kennel and the emergency response crews. Park rangers closed the hiking trails, parks, and campgrounds around Beaver Lake. As smoke darkened the horizon and thickened the air, the fire service issued pre-evacuation notices, warning everyone to pack essentials and be ready to move quickly if conditions deteriorated.

Eric Whitehorse came up from Huntsville to tour the kennel and review evacuation plans. "It'll be a tight squeeze, but we'll make it work," he told Maggie and Zak after he toured the facilities. "Just be ready to move 'em fast if you have to."

He listened with interest as she discussed using the lake as an evacuation route. "Smart thinking. Let me know if you need help finding a boat."

"Garrett's dad offered his pontoon boat. I think I can stack the crates under the shade canopy. Garrett and Rob will strap everything into place ahead of time, so we can leave in a hurry if we have to. Worst case scenario, we can head for Deer Island and set up a temporary shelter."

"Let's hope it doesn't come to that, but it's good to be prepared, just in case," Eric agreed.

They talked a little longer. When Maggie brought up the subject of expenses, he refused to discuss costs he might incur. "Your granddaddy helped me through lean times on more than one occasion. I reckon I'm just returning the favor."

Watching him drive off, Zak said, "I can't see him as your anonymous letter writer. Whoever did write them wants you out of Eagle Cove, and doesn't seem to care how it happens. Those letters were full of hate."

"Hate," Maggie repeated. "I met someone, just recently, who was really hateful. Now who was it?" She thought for several moments and then gave up, frustrated by her inability to remember. "I'm too tired to think straight," she admitted.

She hadn't had a full night's sleep in weeks. She slept fitfully, when she slept at all. At a time when other businesses were struggling to get by, the kennel business was booming. Customers apparently believed the proximity to the lake made Waterside a safe choice. Maggie hoped they were right but kept on with her evacuation preparations, just in case. She followed the suggestions Eric Whitehorse had given her, keeping leashes and travel crates close at hand. Fortunately, she had enough crates to use for her primary plan to evacuate with Eric's help, as well as the others strapped into place on the pontoon boat tied to her dock.

She added contact information to the daily boarder listing and set up a Dropbox account for off-site file storage. The dogs were confined to their interior air conditioned runs, and Maggie spent much of her time exercising them in the training arena. Outside, long hoses were hooked up to every water spigot. Shovels and rakes were placed around the kennel. Sylvia sent a crew out one afternoon to trim branches and shrubbery away from the kennel and house so flying sparks wouldn't ignite the buildings if the fire got close.

The grinding workload and news of fires blazing across the county kept Maggie from thinking too much about her other problems, but her fears returned in force a week after her birthday party when she woke to find her bedroom in darkness and Sam nudging her hand. The big dog was growling low in his throat. Sweet Pea was awake, too, and staring at the door. Someone, or something, was downstairs. There was a muffled thud, a curse, and then all was quiet again.

Maggie speed-dialed Zak's number before she realized there was no dial tone. The line was dead. Don't panic, Maggie ordered herself. The alarm would have sounded if anyone had climbed in a window or forced a door. But feeling Sam's rigid muscles beneath her hand, she thought panic might not be an unreasonable response. Garrett's in the kennel, she reminded herself. If there's somebody down there, she'd hit the alarm and he'd come running.

Grateful her arm was no longer in a sling, she quickly pulled on jeans and a shirt, slipped her feet into shoes, picked up her hickory walking staff, and released Sam with a whispered "Find it!" The dog raced out the door and down the stairs, barking fiercely. Behind him, Maggie groped along the wall until she found and pressed the switch. Nothing. Retracing her steps, she armed herself with a sturdy flashlight. Directing its powerful beam down the stairs, she stared in amazement at the familiar figure sitting on the bottom step, holding his head. Blood streamed from a deep gash on his forehead.

"Howard! What on earth happened?" She dropped the staff and rushed down the stairs, Sweet Pea on her heels. Sam backtracked through the hall; from the dog's behavior, it was apparent there was no one else in the house.

"Son of a bitch pushed me," Howard muttered, anger in his voice mingled with raw pain.

Maggie hurried into the bathroom and returned with a wet towel, pressing firmly against Howard's forehead, wincing as he groaned. "Who was it?"

"Too dark to tell." He pulled the towel away, paled when he saw the blood staining the cloth, and pressed it back into place.

"That needs stitches." Maggie stood up. "I'll get help."

"No!" Howard tried to rise and fell back against the stairs.

"Yes," she said firmly. "You need medical attention."

Gripping her hands, he spoke with an effort. "He might still be out there. Call Zak." Howard's face was gray and sweating.

"The phone's dead. Electricity's out, too."

"Shit."

"The kennel," Maggie said suddenly. "I put in a separate line when we installed the alarm system."

"Probably dead, too."

"If somebody had gone near the kennel, we'd have heard the dogs. Garrett's there. He'll come running when he hears the alarm." But when she pushed the alarm panel by the door, nothing happened.

"Alarm's not working either," she told Howard, and tried to think through her options. "Hey!" She grabbed her training vest, which she'd left on the banister post earlier that evening. Digging into a pocket, she pulled out her cell phone and speed-dialed the kennel. "I need help, right now." Disconnecting, she dialed 911 and requested a deputy and an ambulance. She was calling Zak when Garrett burst through the door.

"EIGHT STITCHES AND a mild concussion," Sylvia reported tiredly from the hospital the next morning. "They're still running tests. Just a precaution, they say."

Maggie was in the kennel office. She poured more coffee and sank into a chair, the phone cradled against her shoulder. "Has he told you what happened?"

Sylvia sighed. "Bits and pieces. He's been having trouble sleeping. Last night was no exception, so he went for a walk. He says he saw somebody holding a flashlight in one hand and something flat in the other. He thought it was you, of course. When he got to your porch he saw the front door standing wide open. Considering what's been happening, he decided to check it out."

"And nearly got killed for his trouble. This is my fault."

"Of course it's not. It will take more than a bang on the head to put that man six feet under. Just put that thought out of your mind, and tell me what's happening with you. Did Lucas get the utility companies out there yet?"

"Repairs promised by end of the day. And Zak is installing some gadget that sets off the alarm automatically when the power is interrupted."

Their conversation had put the worst of Maggie's fears to rest, but as she tried to concentrate on kennel chores, Maggie realized something was nagging at her thoughts. Who was the person Howard said he'd seen? And how did this mysterious figure manage to vanish in the time it took Howard to reach the house, and then reappear, just in time to knock Howard into the corner post of the banister?

And why didn't Sam pick up a stranger's scent? Maggie was struck by a frightening thought: what if there had been no one else in the house last night? Could Howard be lying? And why would he want her to think somebody had taken something from her house?

Don't jump to conclusions, Maggie warned herself. She reacted badly over those cutouts on Sylvia's table, and she'd been wrong about that. She could be wrong about this, too.

But what if she was right?

31

Security around the house and kennel was tighter than ever. Rob and Bev were at the kennel through the day. Garrett was still staying in the manager's quarters in the kennel, taking over in late afternoon and doing double-duty whenever Maggie had to leave the premises. Zak and Claire were once again in temporary residence.

"If you're going to have any more crises in the middle of the night," he told her, "I'd rather be on scene. This way, I can watch over both you and Claire."

The latest crisis, and Howard's insistence that the intruder had been carrying something out persuaded her to make a careful search. Something flat, he'd said. A book, perhaps, or could it have been a painting? Suddenly, she remembered Gran's notebooks and bolted into the office, which still held the boxes from the basement.

She sighed in relief when she found every year accounted for, then frowned when she realized the contents looked as though they'd been rifled through. She clearly remembered repacking everything from her grandmother with care. Someone had gone through these boxes.

She was still sorting when Zak returned. "God bless them, Bev's parents are taking all three girls to the community pool. So my afternoon's free. What are you doing?"

Maggie described the search she'd made. "The only thing that seems out of place is right here, in these boxes of Gran's. I'm trying to figure out what's missing."

"You're going to hurt yourself trying to move this stuff." He pointed to a chair, he said, "Sit. I'll do the lifting." He swept the contents of the desktop into Maggie's lap and, picking up an empty box, placed it on the desk beside her chair. "Start with that lot, and then we'll go through the boxes. Any chance your grandmother made a packing list?"

"Not that I recall. But I went through most of these when I was looking for the studio inventory, so I have a pretty good idea of what should be here." She glanced at the paperwork Zak had dumped in her lap. "These are bills I need to pay and some tax receipts." She shoved them in a drawer and took the files Zak passed to her. "These are my grandfather's. Gran kept the account books for his training business." Rapidly, she flipped through the paperwork and returned it to him. "Nothing seems to be missing here. What's in the next box?"

They worked their way through the remaining boxes, sorting and organizing as they went. Handing the last batch of paperwork to Zak, Maggie sighed. "Well, that was a lot of work without much to show for it." She glanced up and saw him staring at the boxes he'd stacked against one wall. "What is it?"

"Where's your mother's sketchbook?"

"On the kitchen table, I think."

They sorted through the materials scattered across the table, and then searched, again, every room in the house. "There's only one other place to look—"

"The studio," he finished for her.

They went through everything carefully, but the sketchbook was nowhere to be found.

"I better call Lucas, let him know," Maggie said wearily. "I guess I misjudged Howard. I thought he might be lying about seeing someone. But with the sketchbook missing—"

"Unless he took it himself," Zak said slowly.

"If he had wanted to steal something, he wouldn't have to break in to do it. As a matter of fact, that's true for quite a few people. And that sounds way too paranoid, even for me."

"Maybe there's something in the sketchbook he doesn't want you to see, or maybe it's something he wants for himself."

"But why anyone would want to steal an old sketchbook at all—that doesn't make sense. What do they hope to gain?"

"Money," Zak responded. "Face it, anything with your mother's name on it is likely to fetch a high price. When her agent calls back, better let him know her work's been stolen."

ANGUS CALLED WITH a welcome distraction and an invitation to a reception the following week at his newly renovated clinic. "Bring your dogs. My niece is organizing the party as part of the 'Pals for Paws' fund-raiser for the animal shelter."

"We'll be there. And I'll bring my checkbook."

"Much appreciated. Bring your bodyguards, too."

"For a man who's supposed to have been on vacation, you certainly seem well informed."

"I've been keeping an eye on you. Chalk it up to being an old friend of the family, or maybe just a nosy old man. That leads to the other reason I called. If you're going to be home later, I'd like to come by. I have some news you're going to want to hear."

"You're always welcome," she assured him. "What—"

"Think you can have your neighbors there, too?"

"Okay, but what—"

"I'll explain when I get there."

BY LATE AFTERNOON, the usual crowd had gathered on Maggie's front porch, speculating about what news Angus might have. Claire was in the living room, engrossed in a new coloring book with Sweet Pea at her side. Sam and Mr. B were on the porch.

Another dog had been added to the mix; Sylvia had gone over to the kennel and reappeared with the stray.

"You're always saying dogs need social time," she said defensively.

"Does this mean you want to adopt him?"

Sylvia nodded. "I'm going to call him Charlie."

Garrett appeared from the direction of the kennel. "Rob's staying until I get back," he assured Maggie. "Came over to tell you Dad's on his way here. Dr. Sheppard called him, asked him to come over and bring his handcuffs." As everyone stared at him, he shrugged. "Your guess is as good as mine."

Sylvia snorted. "It's all those thrillers he reads. He thinks he's some super-sleuth."

Despite the heat, Maggie shivered. Beside her, Sam whined softly and edged closer. She stroked him absently, grateful for the presence of her friends around her.

"Here comes Angus," Howard announced.

"And Dad's right behind him." Garrett walked over to his father's vehicle. Their voices were too low to carry to the porch.

Maggie's attention shifted to Angus, who was holding the door open for a passenger who seemed oddly reluctant to step out of the vehicle. Angus tugged the woman to her feet, and Maggie gasped at the venomous look the woman threw her way. Sam growled, deep and low, and Zak leaned closer.

"She looks familiar," he whispered.

"We saw her at the dog show in Tulsa, remember?" Maggie dropped her hand to Sam's broad head. "Watch," she said softly. Sam stood alert at her side as the new arrivals approached. At a nod from his father, Garrett took up a position by the steps while Lucas followed the others up onto the porch.

At Maggie's quiet invitation, Angus politely held a chair for the woman. She looked as though she might refuse, then with a muttered curse dropped into the seat.

The sheriff leaned against the porch railing. "What's all this about, Angus?"

"People talk, word gets around. We all know Maggie's had some trouble recently. Those letters—"

"How do you know about that?" the sheriff asked sharply. "That's not common knowledge."

"It's not much of a secret. I heard about from Sylvia at the Merchants League lunch. From what she said it was pretty obvious it had to be somebody local. Anyway, I had some time on my hands, so I decided to do some digging, see what I could learn. Which brings me to how we all came to be here today." He smiled at the people gathered there, clearly enjoying his moment in the spotlight.

"Get on with it, Angus," Sylvia said irritably.

"I asked myself: who stood to lose if Waterside Kennels stayed in business? And that letter mentioning the ABKA— how many people around here even know what that is? The letter writer had to be somebody in the dog world, so I started asking questions. Everywhere I turned, somebody mentioned Bertha Hawkins here." He pointed to the glowering woman seated in front of him.

"So I decided to set a little trap. I went to the Tulsa dog show. I saw Bertha there and told her that we had something in common. I said we both lost customers to Waterside."

"Angus!" Maggie exclaimed. "You can't possibly—"

"Of course it's not true, but I needed to gain Bertha's confidence. And it worked. Just the mention of Maggie's name was enough to make her spitting mad. And then you walked up when I was talking to her at the dog show, and anybody could see she was practically bursting with hatred for you. That's when I knew she wrote those letters."

"I remember—she owns Paradise Pets!"

Lucas had listened without interruption. Leaning forward, he asked soberly, "Proof, Angus?"

"Right here." Angus pulled a white envelope out of his pocket. "She was getting ready to mail it when I caught her. It didn't have any prints," he said quickly, as the sheriff raised an eyebrow in his direction. "I watched her wipe it clean while she was walking into the post office."

"Interfering with mail is a federal offense."

"I know that," Angus said indignantly. "I grabbed it before she dropped it in the slot."

"I don't want to know what it says," Maggie said quickly. She looked at the woman. "Why would you do such a thing?"

"Your kind thinks you can take whatever you want," Bertha said bitterly. She looked at the sheriff. "I was just protecting my own. Been losing customers ever since Miz Moneybags here opened this place. It wasn't fair. She stole my best groomer."

"I didn't steal anyone," Maggie retorted. "I offered Bev a good working environment and a decent salary. That's more than you ever did for her." She took a deep breath. "That's why you wrote those letters?"

"Knew Bev would come back if she lost the job here. That good-for-nothin' husband of hers never gives her a dime."

"Why bring my mother into your little vendetta?"

"What? Oh, yeah. That girl who worked for you—"

"Doreen?"

"The one who drowned, right? She told Joylene over at the beauty parlor that your ma ran off with some married man. Joylene told me. I thought it was funny, Miz High-and-Mighty having a whore for a mother."

Zak laid a restraining hand as Maggie jumped up with a snarl that matched Sam's. "Watch your language," he warned the woman. "What about those phone calls—was that your doing, too?"

"Got her riled but good, didn't it?" Bertha said with a smirk. "Oh, yeah. I enjoyed that—or I did until *you* started answering the phone," she said, turning to glare at Garrett.

Maggie was disgusted. "Get out of my sight and count your blessings I don't have you arrested on the spot."

"Not so fast," Lucas ordered as the woman edged toward the steps. "Miz Hawkins, do you own a gray Chevy pickup?"

Bertha licked her lips nervously. "That wasn't my fault!"

"Answer the question," the sheriff ordered.

"I never meant to hurt her," she muttered.

"That was you in that pick-up? I could have died!"

"I just wanted to scare you, shake you up a little, maybe."

Lucas ticked off a list of charges. "Terroristic threatening, vehicular assault, leaving the scene of an accident. I can probably add trespassing, breaking and entering, criminal assault—"

Bertha looked bewildered. "What are you talking about?"

"You're saying you weren't here on the day of the accident?"

"Okay, so I was here. That's not a crime!"

"Depends on what you did."

"Didn't do nothing. Saw she had company, so I left."

"What made you think Maggie had company?"

"There was a Jeep. Parked off the road by the house."

"Describe it," Lucas ordered.

"It was a Jeep, for chrissake."

"Try again."

"Black," Bertha said grudgingly. "With a great big silver thing on the front bumper."

"A winch?" It matched Miss Abigail's description of the vehicle driven by Doreen's fiancé.

"Yeah, maybe. I'd seen it here before."

Lucas pulled out his handcuffs. "Bertha Hawkins, you have the right to—"

"Free speech—ever heard of that? I got every right to say what I want!"

Lucas ignored her outburst and continued to read the Miranda warning. "Garrett, put Miz Hawkins in my patrol car."

TWO DAYS AFTER Bertha's arrest, Maggie answered the phone and heard Lucas on the line. "Has something else happened?"

"I'm just calling with an update. Thought you'd like to know we found Jake. He's in the Madison County jail. Been there a few weeks now. Seems he tore up a fair bit of some property and got in a brawl with the landowner's son. He'll be doing time for assault on a juvenile, trespassing with criminal intent, and a couple of other charges. But he's looking at more time if the feds have their way. I had a call from them just this morning."

"What do federal agents have to do with Jake?"

"He's been bragging to another inmate about finding old Spanish silver. The feds have been sniffing around ever since some of the stuff turned up on the black market in St. Louis. They're heading over to interview him today. And they just might have a case. When he was arrested, he was on the White River, where the bluffs are full of caves. He had digging tools and enough black powder to do some serious damage. They found traces of silver in his backpack."

"If he's been in jail all that time, he didn't break in here."

"Looks that way. If anything else happens, give me a call."

Maggie, on the verge of sharing her fears about Howard, stopped herself. If he was innocent, she'd hurt a good man. If he was guilty, another few days wouldn't matter. By then, she was determined to discover the truth, whatever the cost.

ON SUNDAY MORNING the wind shifted around to the southwest, pushing heavy clouds ahead of a strong line of storms marching across the plains. The meteorologist on Channel Five put a chance of rain back in the forecast for the first time in four months. When sunlight broke through the murky sky, Maggie turned the boarders out into the yard and decided to spend a few hours doing fieldwork before she went into town. Garret was off duty and Rob was covering the kennel with Bev so she and Zak could attend the reopening celebration at Angus' veterinary clinic. Going to the party seemed the least she could do, considering how much Angus had done for her.

The Hawkins woman signed a statement admitting she ran Maggie off the road and harassed her with letters and phone calls, but swore she'd done nothing else. Her knowledge of Doreen's death appeared to be limited to the information in the paper. The mention of a locket brought no reaction at all.

"It was worth a try," Lucas had said on the phone late yesterday. "But I'm confident she never met your mother, or Doreen either. Bertha and her husband Jed moved here from Texarkana just a few years back.

"We set up an anonymous tip line for the Crowley case," Lucas continued, "and we'll check every lead that comes in. Meanwhile, don't let your guard down. One of my boys stays in the kennel at night until we get this mess figured out."

"Your family has gone above and beyond for me."

The sheriff chuckled. "You're actually doing me a favor. If the boys were home, I'd have to arrest somebody for sure, because it's only a matter of time before this wedding nonsense drives one of us to murder. So do me a favor and keep them busy out there, will you?"

"Absolutely." She'd come to depend on having Garrett or Rob on the premises, and promised herself that she'd find the money, somehow, to give them both a raise.

And she needed to find a way to repay Zak for all he's done, she mused. After Bertha confessed, Maggie insisted Zak and Claire return to their own cottage. He agreed, reluctantly, but she wasn't surprised to find him close by during the day or sharing the porch in the evenings. He'd enrolled Claire in the summer day camp Bev's girls attended; Maggie missed the little girl's cheerful chatter but was happy to see her making friends.

It was time to concentrate on her business. A new client had brought in his young retriever; after evaluating the dog's skills it was clear to her that Chloe needed a lot more field work before she could hope to pass her Hunting Test.

Maggie dressed for the work in lightweight clothing, mindful of the excessive heat warnings. Although it meant extra weight, she couldn't resist donning the vest she'd received as a birthday present. Two large pockets in back held water bottles, freeing her oversized front pockets for the miscellany she carried. She dropped a leash and collar into one front pocket and ID, sunglasses, tissues, and lip balm in the other. She draped Claire's braided whistle cord around her neck, and smiled as she transferred the Flashcard from her purse to an inside pocket.

The training session took longer than expected. "I don't care if every canine in her pedigree was a champion at Westminster," Maggie fumed afterward as she shoved her gear haphazardly onto the shelves and threw her vest on top of the pile. "The only way Sasha will pass a Hunting Test is if the bird falls into her mouth and the judges are blind."

"It could happen," Rob offered cheekily.

"Not in my lifetime," Maggie grumbled. "Oh, great. Look at the time! I'm going to be late."

ANGUS STEERED MAGGIE away from the crowd that had gathered to celebrate the grand reopening of his clinic and toward a small group by the desk. "We've been filling Nicholas in on the latest news," he said with the whisper of a conspirator.

"I doubt she'll see a day of jail time," Nicholas was saying frostily as they approached. "Too many liberals in the justice system these days."

"I don't want Bertha to go to jail," Maggie said quietly. "It's enough for me to know that she won't write any more letters."

"But the letters are just a part of the crime," Nicholas remonstrated. "What about breaking into your home? Margaret's studio? And attempted murder—she ran you off the road, for God's sake. Surely even that idiot Johnson can come up with enough evidence to convict her on something."

"Bertha is convinced I ruined her business."

"So all this wasn't about your mother, after all?"

"Lucas doesn't think so, but I'm still not sure. There's her locket, for one thing, and that inventory discrepancy in the studio. Plus my mother's sketchbook is still missing."

"But what can you do?" Howard wanted to know.

"Talk to my mother. Or I will as soon as I figure out how to reach her. Zak has a lead on her agent. Mr. Shotweiler will call me as soon as he returns from vacation."

"When will that be?" Nicholas asked.

Maggie admitted she didn't know. "But in the meantime, I'm going to use the time to go through the rest of Gran's boxes. And I'm going to go through the studio again."

"Any particular reason?" Angus asked, refilling glasses.

"I'm looking for answers."

32

Maggie and Garrett were still busy with evening chores when members of her obedience class arrived. Several of them were on the volunteer fire crews, and they'd asked for a special make-up session. Others, including her neighbors, had asked to join in. Nicholas called to say he was bringing Delilah. "I hope she won't be a complete disgrace," he said mournfully.

Phil Olsen had made a habit of arriving early to unwind from his noisy job before participating in a training session. He drove up while Maggie was cleaning the runs. Turning his shepherd-collie mix, Percy, loose in the fenced yard, he said briskly, "You could use some help, and I need the exercise. Hand me that hose. I'll finish cleaning the runs while you handle the dogs."

"You're a life saver," Maggie said gratefully. She heard the rest of the class arrive and chatter among themselves as they put away the jumps and dumbbells from an earlier training session and sorted out collars and leashes.

Ben Springer wandered in with his German Shepard. "Donnie Ray says hey."

"Tell my favorite EMT 'hey' right back."

"Your favorite?" he scoffed. "You should see the rest of us in action!"

"You're all heroes to me," she assured him. "So, have you known Donnie Ray a long time?"

"Did a couple of tours in Afghanistan together—that's where we picked up our medic training. Most EMTs around here are also part of the fire crews or SAR. Speaking of which, we're hoping you'll bring Sam along to our meeting next week and give us a demonstration. I've seen you two working a trail and we could seriously use you on search and rescue missions." Reaching down to pat his German Shepard, he said, "I'm hoping Gretal here will have what it takes, but we have to make it through obedience first."

"She's doing very well for her age."

"We're a bit behind in our training, what with all the fire outbreaks. Hey, thanks for scheduling this make-up session."

"Happy to help. And I'll try to make that next SAR meeting."

Maggie hummed happily as she finished her chores with Phil Olsen's help and brought the last boarder in from the exercise yard. She was still smiling when Zak rushed up.

"Problem in front," he said tersely.

Maggie thrust the leashes into Phil's hands and hurried to the customer lounge where Nicholas, Howard, and Sylvia had gathered with the rest of the class. Maggie smelled the smoke even before she pushed through the tangle of dogs and owners and saw the remains of an armchair, its cushion smoldering on the floor. Ben Springer, Gretal alert at his side, held one of the fire extinguishers Maggie had placed in the building.

"How did this happen?" Maggie demanded.

"Cigarette," Ben reported. "I'd guess English Ovals." He picked up the cigarette butt. "One of yours, Zak?"

"My brand, but that's not mine."

"Who was smoking in here?"

Silence.

"I swear to you, I wasn't in here," Zak said firmly. "We were outside."

"That's right," another agreed. "Zak was with us."

Maggie swept the room with a glare. "If this is someone's idea of a stupid joke, it's sick," she said bluntly. "Fortunately, the damage is minimal. Next time, we might not be so lucky. If I catch *anyone* smoking anywhere except the designated area outside, you'll be banned from Waterside. Permanently."

Conversation was muted as the group moved toward the training arena. Zak hung back, his expression grim. Claire hovered behind him, her anxious gaze darting between the two adults. Zak reached out to stop Maggie when she would have walked past him. "We need to talk."

She took a deep breath, tried to steady herself, and kept her mouth shut. Her head actually hurt from the effort to remain silent. She grabbed the cushion and dragged it outside onto the gravel, then used a hose to thoroughly soak the fabric. Zak and Claire followed her.

"Okay, you're upset. So am I." Zak stepped close, his voice low as he met her gaze. "Somebody wants to make me look guilty. When you think this through you'll realize that."

"I can't think about this right now," she said, struggling to keep her voice steady. "I have to clean up this mess, and then I have a training class to run."

"I was the one who said to consider everyone guilty until proven innocent, didn't I?" Zak asked ruefully.

"I better go."

"When you're ready to talk, you know where to find me. Let's go, Claire."

"But I wanna play with Sweet Pea!"

"Not tonight, honey."

Maggie watched them leave through a blur of tears.

Howard appeared at her side. "You should know—"

"I've got my hands full here. Can't this wait?"

"It's about Doreen—" he stopped abruptly as Nicholas leaned against the open door.

"Everything all right out here?"

"Perfect. Just perfect," she muttered.

For the next hour, Maggie blocked out everything except the obedience drills and the animals. She moved mechanically from group to group, correcting, praising, applauding in all the right places, but her heart wasn't in it. Even the sight of Delilah looking interested or Sylvia working so earnestly with Charlie failed to dispel Maggie's lethargy. It was a relief when the time was up.

When the session ended, most of the class stored their equipment with a minimum of fuss and departed. As she straightened up the training arena, she heard voices, one sharp with anger, the other a low, insistent murmur. She recognized Howard's strident tone, and she thought she heard Nicholas. That seemed odd; she couldn't recall the two men ever exchanging more than a few words.

What could they possibly be arguing about? She couldn't summon the energy to care. She just wanted everyone to leave. But even as the thought crossed her mind, she heard Sylvia's anguished cry. Maggie threw down the leashes she held and sprinted across the arena, along the hall, and into the lounge.

The last stragglers from class stood in a tight group, staring at Howard, unconscious on the floor. Sylvia knelt beside him as Ben Springer felt for a pulse. "Call 911," he ordered. "Now!"

Maggie complied with shaking fingers. "What happened?"

"Heart attack, or maybe a seizure," Phil Olsen said. "He was arguing with this guy here"—he nodded toward Nicholas—"and all of a sudden he fell over."

"It was hardly an argument," Nicholas snapped, but Maggie could see he was worried. "Merely a disagreement between old friends." He knelt down and touched Sylvia's shoulder. "He'll be all right," he said kindly.

Phil picked up a set of keys from the floor and handed them to Sylvia. "You better hold on to these."

Sylvia stared at the keys listlessly and handed them back. "Those aren't Howard's."

"Anybody here lose your keys?" When nobody answered, Phil shrugged and tossed them onto the counter.

Sylvia insisted on following the ambulance, brushing aside Maggie's offer to go with her. "Take care of Charlie, will you?"

"Of course. Call me as soon as you know anything," Maggie pleaded, hugging Sylvia fiercely.

When the last customer had gone, she refused Garrett's offer to help clean up, needing a physical outlet for the emotional storm within. She straightened the customer lounge, then went outside and heaved the ruined chair cushion into the trash bin. The chair itself went into a storeroom until she could find a replacement cushion. As she worked, she wondered what Nicholas and Howard had been arguing about. Nicholas had brushed aside her questions and left soon after the ambulance set off. She wasn't eager to insert herself into their argument, but the ugly incident in her customer lounge made it her business, whether she liked it or not. She made a mental note to ask Sylvia when things settled down.

She was on her way out when she saw the key chain Phil had found. Strange nobody came back to claim that, she mused.

Maggie was about to put the key chain aside when she saw the purple unicorn and stopped in her tracks. Her hands trembled as she saw the large "W" etched on two of the keys.

She was holding Doreen's missing key chain.

Howard had tried to tell her something about Doreen earlier. Was it about the keys? Why was he carrying them around? Maggie felt dizzy and had to grab the counter to keep from falling down. The scene from Sheriff Malone's office flashed into her head. "She came in as the county's Jane Doe number seven—no purse, no wallet, no driver's license," he'd told her. And no keys, Maggie remembered.

Why did Howard have the dead girl's keys?

Dead girl.

Did Howard Bridger kill Doreen?

ZAK PACED AROUND his living room, worry cramping his stride as much as the small space. He'd been horrified when he heard the ambulance, and only marginally relieved when he raced down the road and saw Maggie in the distance, alive and well, talking to the rescue team. Although he ached to rush over, he turned back to his own house with an effort. She's all right, he told himself. This time, at least. But what about the next time?

That fire was deliberate. He knew it, felt it in his gut, but the motive eluded him. The chair had been discovered before anything else had been damaged. So the intent had been to frighten Maggie. And push her away from him.

The use of English Ovals put a decidedly personal spin on things. Anger roiled inside as he realized, for the first time, he was a target. He'd been in the crosshairs before, but he'd been deployed to a place where being a target came with the territory. He was a world away from that action—or thought he'd been, until tonight. Someone's trying to drive a wedge between him and Maggie, he thought worriedly. Whoever it was, they want her isolated. But why? What could Maggie possibly have that somebody would want so desperately?

Zak was sharply aware of his small daughter's vulnerability. The danger was creeping closer and the violence was increasing. He couldn't live with himself if anything happened to her. Claire may hate him for what he was about to do, but he wasn't taking any chances with the most precious part of his life. He glanced at the clock. It was still early enough that a phone call wouldn't panic his ex-wife.

He debated how much to tell Althea, fearing she'd find the situation too stressful to face. In the end, he compromised, couching his story in half-truths. "I need you to keep Claire for a few days. I have some business and the sitter won't be available. What? No, I'll bring her up myself, save you the trip."

"I'm not sure," Althea said doubtfully. "You know what happened the last time—"

"I talked to Claire about that. She understands you've been under a lot of stress. She loved your present, by the way."

"It might be okay, if you think it will work this time. A day or two, you said?"

"Just a few days," he corrected gently. "I understand this is difficult for you. We all know—Claire knows—you love her."

"Let's do it," she said suddenly, with a firmness in her voice Zak hadn't heard in a long time.

"We'll see you tomorrow."

33

The sky was a sullen gray, the horizon heavy with smoke. The temperature hadn't fallen below eighty-eight degrees overnight. Maggie relieved Garrett shortly after six, unable to sleep. She'd lost track of how much caffeine she'd poured into her system in an effort to get her brain working again. She sat at her desk, sipping coffee and contemplating the key ring she locked in her desk the night before.

Rob arrived at seven, and Garrett took his boat out, intending to join the fire crews working across the lake to contain yet another grass fire. That one had been sparked by lightning—which seemed bitterly ironic to Maggie, given that the same storm clouds hadn't brought any rain.

Bev came in a few minutes later and, after hearing the distressing news of the events the previous night, volunteered to bathe and trim Charlie before attending to her grooming clients. "It's not much, but it might cheer Sylvia up."

Zak had left a terse message on her voice mail, saying he had taken Claire to Springfield to stay with her mother for a few days and could be reached at the co-op in case of emergency. He'd been right to get Claire away from here, she thought. The fire in the customer lounge could have been deadly. If anything happened to that little girl, she knew he'd never forgive her—and she'd never forgive herself.

Sweet Pea sensed her distress and hovered nervously. After Maggie tripped over the small animal for the fourth time, she pushed her outside with her other dogs, saying, "You all need some exercise." Going back into the office, she called the hospital. "Immediate family only in the ICU. No exceptions."

Staring at the key chain, she considered keeping it locked away until she could confront Howard, but the caffeine had cleared away enough cobwebs to make her realize that was a bad idea. The keys had belonged to Doreen, and the sheriff would definitely want them.

She could leave Rob and Bev at the kennel while she delivered the key chain to the sheriff's office and explain where they'd been found. Then she'd go by the hospital and warn Sylvia, give the woman time to prepare herself before the sheriff pressed Howard for details about his involvement with Doreen. As for herself, she wasn't sure she was ready to face the man, not with gruesome suspicions filling her mind.

Decision made, she locked the keys back in her desk and went to help finish the morning chores and then told Bev and Rob her plans. "You can leave a message for me with the sheriff's office or at the hospital if you need to."

"Not gonna happen," Rob said flatly. "My dad will skin my hide if I let you go somewhere alone. Sorry, boss, but where you go, I go."

"I can handle things while you're gone," Bev offered. "I've got plenty to keep me busy here. One of my friends is bringing her Bouvier in this morning to be groomed—in fact, she ought to be here in just a few minutes. Wilma was planning to stay anyway while I groomed Arnold."

"Are you sure the two of you will be okay?"

"Did I mention Wilma teaches self-defense classes?"

"Keep the phone close, just in case."

"I will, I promise. Now go take care of business."

Rob had called ahead; his father was waiting for them at the sub-station outside Eureka Springs. Lucas already knew about

Howard being hospitalized after collapsing—Garrett had called the night before and briefed his father on the suspicious fire and the argument preceding Howard's attack. Now he listened intently as Maggie described finding the keys, and then excused himself to make a phone call, returning with an update on Howard's condition. "Still in ICU, can't be questioned yet."

He offered coffee. Maggie accepted, thinking she'd ingested enough caffeine that morning to keep her awake until Labor Day.

"Ben Springer called this morning, told me he followed the ambulance to the hospital. He talked with one of the nurses, who told him that Howard had a pack of English Ovals and a lighter in his pocket when he was admitted."

"First Zak and now Howard! Are you saying you honestly believe either of them could have set that fire in my customer lounge? I don't believe it!"

"I don't think Zak's involved, no. Look, Maggie, I don't like this any more than you do. But look at the facts. Howard was there when the fire started. He was carrying the same brand of cigarettes found at the scene. That's not his usual brand—he smokes Marlboros. I checked. And now we have the Crowley girl's keys."

He paused to gulp coffee. "Granted, that's circumstantial, and I'm going to need some solid evidence before I arrest his sorry self. Make my job a lot easier if he'd just confess and be done with it. But his doctor's adamant he can't be questioned for at least a day or two, and maybe longer. Once he's stable they're thinking of transferring him to the regional heart center over in Barton County."

"You're sure it's him?" Maggie asked unsteadily.

"We can connect him to the Crowley girl through the key chain. We know he had an affair with her, and we only have Howard's word that it was over. The rest is guesswork. Maybe the girl didn't want the affair to end. Maybe she couldn't handle the rejection and threatened to tell his wife. Maybe he was afraid of what Sylvia would do and he panicked. That's enough motive for me," Lucas said flatly.

"You've been asking a lot of questions," he continued. "Maybe that made him nervous, decide to scare you off. Ruling out the letters, which Bertha Hawkins already admitted to, we can place him at or near the scene of everything that's happened at the kennel. We know he has a boat. And one of my deputies remembered seeing Howard a couple of days ago out by the dam, getting into a black Jeep. Interesting coincidence, if that vehicle belongs to him. You can be sure I'll be asking Howard about that Jeep. If it has a winch on it, I'd lay odds it's the same one Miss Abigail and Bertha Hawkins saw."

He smiled grimly. "Based on what we know right now, I'd say we've got him dead to rights."

34

The following days passed quietly. Angus called, demanding details about the fire and Howard's collapse. After hearing Maggie's abbreviated version and commiserating with her, he added news of his own. "I hear Bertha Hawkins decided to move back to Texarkana," he reported. "You won't have to worry about her anymore."

With Bertha leaving and the sheriff sure of Howard's guilt, Maggie turned her full attention to business. Garrett was still staying at the kennel. Maggie, who'd grown accustomed to having her neighbors' help, was grateful to have somebody sharing the on-site responsibilities.

Zak came by three days later, brushing aside Maggie's stammered apologies. "You had good reason to worry."

"You had some worries of your own. Is Claire okay?"

"She's fine. This visit seems to be going better than the last. When I talked with Claire this morning, she sounded excited about a trip to the zoo later this week."

"I'm glad she wasn't here the night Howard collapsed. She seems very fond of him." Quickly, she brought Zak up to date on what had happened since she last saw him. "I gave the keys to the sheriff. He seems pretty sure he can build a strong case."

"If the sheriff's right, Howard fooled all of us. Have you spoken to Sylvia? This has to be hard on her."

"I've called her a few times. So far, she's standing by her man, in every sense of the word. She won't leave the hospital and insists Howard's being framed. Says she knew about the affair with Doreen, and that Howard knew she knew."

"Wow, that makes my head hurt. But say it's true. That shoots down the sheriff's theory that Howard killed Doreen to keep the affair secret. Unless," he added slowly, "Sylvia's trying to eliminate that as a motive."

"What about Doreen's keys?"

"Did you actually see Howard with those keys?"

"They were on the floor, next to him. And there's more— Howard wanted to talk to me about Doreen that night. Maybe he wanted to give me her keys, I don't know. I was trying to focus on the training session and I put him off until later. Nicholas interrupted us," she recalled. "Those two were arguing after the session and then Howard had that dreadful attack."

"What was the argument about?"

"I don't know. Why? Do you think it's important?"

"They argue, then Howard has a heart attack. Coincidence?"

"I'll ask Sylvia."

"Let me know. I tried calling her but all I get is voice mail. I'd go by the hospital, but I'm due back at the co-op for a double shift. We probably won't be busy but somebody's got to mind the shop. How about you? What's on your schedule?"

"I'm going to visit Sylvia today once Rob finishes the morning run. Tomorrow I have errands and a training session in town, then I'm going to run a demonstration for the Search and Rescue team on the north side of the lake, over by the dam."

"They're still fighting fires up that way. Won't the smoke affect Sam's ability to follow a trail?"

"Depends how heavy the smoke is. The SAR team leader told me we'll be working east of the trouble spots, so I guess it all depends on the winds."

"Well, just be careful out there. I'd come along to watch but I have a follow-up appointment at the VA medical center down in Fayetteville. Nothing major, but I can't reschedule," he added, noting her look of concern. "The drive actually takes longer than the appointments, usually. Hey, how about I use that time calling the Colorado gallery again?"

"I totally forgot about that! This business with Howard has pretty much driven everything else out of my head."

ROB AGREED TO stay at the kennel until Maggie returned from the hospital. "I'd feel better if you were here, to keep an eye on everything," she told him. "That smoke has me a little anxious."

"Yeah, we're getting it from both sides, but we're in good shape here. There's a lot of land and a couple of creeks between us and that Hawk Hollow fire, and we're safe from the one closing in on Eureka Springs. If the wind doesn't shift, the town could be in trouble. Hey, you going to see Mr. Bridger?"

"He can't have visitors except family. I don't want to see him, anyway. I want to see Sylvia and she's spending most of her time at the hospital, so that's where I'm going. No matter what Howard has—or hasn't—done, Sylvia's a good friend, and I need to support her."

"Dad said I was to stick close—"

"It's okay," she assured him. "There's a guard at the hospital and Howard isn't going anywhere. No need to worry now."

IN THE HOSPITAL cafeteria, Maggie guided Sylvia's trembling hands around the tea cup and held on until the woman's grip firmed. "I understand Lucas intends to question Howard as soon as he can speak."

Sylvia shuddered. "He keeps saying the same thing over and over. Asks me to forgive him." Sobs racked her slender frame.

Finally, she quieted. When she spoke again, Maggie had to lean close to hear. "I almost divorced him after that business with your mother. Oh, yes, I knew all about that. We'd just opened the garden center and were in debt up to our eyeballs and he lost the best job he'd ever had, all because he wanted his employer's daughter," she said bitterly. "He told me he and Miles had a fight and that he quit. I never told him I knew different. But I knew, just like I knew about the others he had on the side."

"And you stayed with him anyway."

"When it came right down to it, I decided I'd rather live with Howard, affairs and all, than live without him. I knew he loved me, at least as much as he was able. So I told myself it didn't matter who he slept with, as long as he came home in the end." She wiped her eyes. "All this talk about evidence, and motive, none of that proves anything. Thirty years together, that's my evidence."

Maggie said hesitantly, "I heard Howard arguing with Nicholas just before he collapsed."

"It couldn't have been anything important."

"What was it?"

"Probably my masks. Nicholas wants them for his gallery." She smiled sadly. "Funny how things change. If he'd made that offer twenty years ago, I'd have jumped at it, strings and all."

"What strings?"

"The Crane Gallery offers exclusive contracts provided you agree that Nicholas has the final say in all art decisions. That includes subject matter and style. All or nothing, according to Nicholas. I told him I'd take nothing, thanks very much. He didn't like that."

"I guess he isn't rejected often."

"I suppose that's what makes him successful. When Nicholas wants something, he always finds a way to get it."

35

Nicholas was in his office at the gallery, watching his assistant talking earnestly with a lone customer, but his mind was elsewhere.

He glanced out the windows where the smoke hung heavily over the hills that edged the town. Trucks and vans lined the streets; gallery and shop owners were hurrying to shift as much of their inventory as possible away from the growing fire threat. He was in a better position than most, with one floor of the gallery below ground level and a basement converted years ago into a vault complete with generator and secondary air shafts. He'd already discussed which of the inventory should be moved down, and his assistant would oversee that task.

He had other inventory to shift, things he'd trust to no one else. He'd need his four-wheel-drive for that job. There was always the chance the winds would shift again, he mused, and the fires would bypass the town. But there were also fires to the south. And that could put Eagle Cove in danger. He thought of Waterside, and Maggie.

He called the hospital and learned Howard was now under guard. Nicholas frowned as he thought about the keys they'd found next to Howard's body—proof the man knew more than he'd admitted about that dead girl. If the sheriff could connect Howard to everything that had happened at Waterside, Nicholas would rest easier.

He'd made it his business to keep watch over Eagle Cove in the years since Margaret had left her family. He'd kept his eye on Howard, too. He knew the man was guilty of his share of misdeeds—and Nicholas thought he knew exactly what they were—but murder? Nicholas shook his head. He wasn't sure Howard would have been willing to go that far to keep his secrets safe. Then again, he acknowledged, every man has his breaking point.

Nicholas thought of Maggie. She'd been relentless in her pursuit of the truth. How would she react when she learned the whole story? He glanced at his watch, thinking of everything that still needed to be done, and added a trip to Eagle Cove to his list.

Some things couldn't wait.

36

Claire watched the dark smoke rising above the trees in the distance. The whole sky looked dark and scary and she didn't much like the lightning that flashed now and then but maybe it would rain. Daddy said they needed it bad.

She wiggled her toes and squirmed; they'd left Springfield three hours earlier, and she was tired of being in the Honda. She sat up straight when they turned onto the road going home. She couldn't wait to show Maggie the new Scooby-Doo tee shirt her mom had given her.

"I'm really sorry about cutting our visit short, Claire. I bet you wish you had somebody else for a mother, don't you? I wouldn't blame you if you did!"

Claire reached over and patted her mother's leg. "It's okay. You did real good, better than last time," she said cheerfully. "You're getting pretty good at this mom stuff!"

"Oh, Claire—"

"Don't cry, or Daddy will think something bad happened."

"I don't see his car," Althea said fretfully. "Where is he?"

"He might be at work. But it's okay, we can go to the kennel. There's always somebody there. You'll like Maggie, I know you will. And she'll like you, too," the child said earnestly.

"You really are a sweet child. I think we better save those introductions for another time. If that's okay with you."

"Sure!"

Following Claire's directions, Althea drove carefully down the road leading to the kennel. She'd barely stopped the car when Claire jumped out, grabbing her sneakers and dragging her backpack behind her.

"Bye, Mom," she called.

Althea looked around, frowning worriedly. She heard dogs barking but didn't see anyone. "I thought you said somebody would be here."

Claire shrugged. "They're probably all inside. See, there's Rob's truck, so he must be here," she pointed out. "And there's Sweet Pea! She's always with Maggie. That means Maggie's here, just like I said."

"Well, if you're sure."

"Thanks for bringing me home. I'll tell Daddy how good you did!" She watched her mother drive off before running up to greet the elderly spaniel.

"Let's go find Maggie," she told Sweet Pea. She started toward the kennel, where the dogs were still barking, and then stopped in surprise when Sweet Pea, growling, trotted past her.

"Hey! Wait for me, Sweet Pea! Where are you going?"

The spaniel headed past the house and down the old road toward the lake. Claire followed, noticing a black Jeep parked beside the art studio and the old stone wall. "Is that Maggie down there? Let's go see!" She skipped barefoot toward the studio, laughing as she followed Sweet Pea down the dusty road.

37

After a training session with the Boyden sisters and their Cocker Spaniel Henry, Maggie dropped by the hospital and tried, unsuccessfully, to convince Sylvia to take a break from Howard's bedside. They'd moved him out of Intensive Care but he was still heavily sedated and still under guard. No visitors other than family, she'd been told. Family and hopefully the sheriff, she thought. She was still stunned at the idea that Howard was responsible for Doreen's death, and hoped Lucas Johnson would soon have answers for the many questions she still had.

All things in time, Gran would have said. Maggie pulled out her cell phone and called Zak to give him the latest news. "This not knowing is driving me crazy," she said with a sigh. "It doesn't seem like we're any closer to solving this whole mess."

"Well, I have some good news," Zak offered. "I called the Colorado gallery while I was driving down to the VA. Your mother's agent is back in town. I guess I pestered them enough, because the gallery owner promised me the guy would call me back today."

"Great! Now if he'll just give you a phone number or an address—I swear, right now I'm ready to drive out there and find her myself!"

"I won't take no for an answer," he promised. "I'll call you after I talk with him."

Her good humor restored, she called the kennel. "I'm headed to pick up Sam at the vets, and then we're off to the Search and Rescue team session," she told Rob. "It's over on the north shore of the lake, though, so I won't be back anytime soon. Can you and Bev manage in the meantime?"

"Sure. It's quiet here. Got any other chores you want me to do while you're gone?"

"You can check the supplies we've put on the boat. Take Mr. B along with you, would you? Poor fellow, I haven't given him much attention in the last few days. Sweet Pea can go, too—she loves to play in the water."

She swung around the corner to Angus Sheppard's clinic where she'd dropped Sam off earlier for his annual shots. She paid her bill and thanked the desk staff for keeping him while she visited the hospital. "He's so cool!" said one. "I saw your field demonstration when you had that open house," she told Maggie. "Can you teach my Pomeranian to track like that? She's small, but she's really smart."

"Any breed can compete in tracking. It depends on the dog."

"Hey, she's in the back—want to meet her?"

"I've got another obligation this afternoon, but I'll be happy to schedule an evaluation session for you. Just call the kennel."

"Awesome!"

HOURS LATER, SHE grinned wearily as she heard similar excitement from the county's Search and Rescue team.

"I had my doubts about using a dog in terrain like this," the team leader, Keith Baxter, told Maggie. They had laid a track across bluffs divided by a steep, rocky ravine choked with brambles and deadwood. Scrub pine and juniper clung stubbornly to the limestone bluffs, and deep shadows marked ledges and possible caves. Sam had hesitated at one of those, briefly casting back and forth before moving down the ravine. She'd slipped more than once as the shale underfoot gave way. The leash had snagged repeatedly; Sam, however, seemed to understand the tension on the leash was not a correction and pressed on, intent on the search.

At Maggie's request, the group watching had stayed at the upper edge of the ravine to avoid interfering. She'd encouraged them to talk normally among themselves, explaining that she wanted to simulate an actual search scenario. They broke into applause when Sam finally alerted on the "victim" who was actually a member of the SAR team.

"Ravines and bluffs, that's where we spend most of our time," Keith told her. "Caves, too. Ben Springer said you were good, and boy was he right!"

"Sam deserves all the credit. I'm just on the other end of the leash."

"Modest—that makes a nice change." Keith ignored the jeers and rude comments as his team reacted to that remark.

"We still have to take the AKC tracking test before Sam's certified."

"Who cares about a piece of paper? We need a dog who gets results, and you just proved Sam has what it takes to work these hills."

Maggie turned to the person who'd participated in the search and returned his ball cap, which she'd used to give Sam the scent at the start of the search. "You laid a great track, George; your scent was all over those bluffs. How long have you been out here?"

"Ben said you needed a challenge—"

"Thanks, Ben," Maggie called dryly. Ben waved his cap as he grinned.

"I knew you needed the track to be a couple of hours old, so I came out this morning and played around with my metal detector," George admitted.

"Looking for treasure?"

"Lots of Civil War stuff around here," he said enthusiastically. "I got a solid hit at one spot but I didn't have time to explore the cave."

Maggie nodded. "That explains why Sam seemed to alert there. Your scent stopped at the ledge, so he kept going."

Their conversation was interrupted by a yell from Ben, who'd been listening to a portable radio. As he turned up the volume, cells phones and beepers sounded among the crowd.

"… jumped the firebreak at Hawk Hollow and is now pushing to the northwest. Winds gusting to forty miles an hour have made an already dangerous situation critical. Police are urging residents to evacuate to emergency shelters. Stay tuned for an updated list of road closings."

"That's south of Waterside," Maggie exclaimed. "I have to get home."

Keith hauled out a map. "You'd better take the east route through Hickory Cove and around the lake. Might be some smoke and the road isn't in good shape, but it'll save you having to backtrack all the way around."

Maggie looked at the map. She'd taken that route the day she'd been lured out to the old Corbin place. "I've been that way just once," she admitted, frowning over the map. "There's just that one road, right?"

"That's the only one you'll find on the map, but there are logging roads, too, and lanes leading to houses along the lake. Don't rely on GPS and you'll be okay."

Maggie's cell phone rang as she loaded Sam into the van. She heard Bev's voice, taut with strain. "We've got a problem—"

"I just heard the news report. Tell Rob to call Eric Whitehorse, see if he can still take our boarders. If he can't, you two get everybody ready to move onto the boat. I'm on my way—"

"There's something else."

Maggie had never heard Bev sound so stressed. "Tell me," she demanded.

"I'll save the details for later, but Rob heard a commotion down at your mother's studio. He ran down and saw a black Jeep parked there—"

"That Jeep again! Who was it?"

"Rob got knocked out. He didn't see who did it. When he woke up, the Jeep was gone and Sweet Pea was lying on the floor beside him. He called 911 and then he called me."

"Is Rob all right? And Sweet Pea? Just what the hell is going on? Lucas was sure Howard is responsible for all the trouble we've had, but if he's still in the hospital—"

Bev cut her off. "Wait, there's more. Sweet Pea wasn't alone. I found Claire's backpack—the one you gave her for her birthday, the one with Dalmatians, remember?—on the floor in the studio. The place has been cleaned out, Maggie, and I can't find the girl anywhere."

"Claire! She's supposed to be in Springfield with her mother! Zak told me she's not due back for a couple of days."

"I've called Zak, but the line was busy. I'll keep trying. Listen—maybe Claire came home, saw Sweet Pea and chased after her. Maybe she thought Sweet Pea was just following you like she always does. The child would have gone after her, wouldn't she?" Bev paused, breathing deeply. "We have to consider the possibility that whoever broke into the studio and hurt Sweet Pea and Rob also took Claire."

"Oh my God. If anything happens to that child—" Maggie forced herself to focus. "Keep calling Zak," she ordered. "Then start calling everyone we know who might help. I'm on my way."

38

Zak sighed in relief as he left the VA medical center. The military adage "hurry up and wait" described his day as he'd been directed from one department to the next. He was usually pretty good at waiting, but today he found himself unreasonably irritated by the delays and bureaucratic demands.

"I did all this the last time I was here," he protested.

"Then you shouldn't have any trouble filling out the forms again,' the nurse said tartly.

With the last appointment finally completed, he drove north toward home. Storm clouds were thickening in the west. Zak switched on the radio for a local weather update, but after listening to back-to-back advertising drivel he gave up.

He reached for his cell phone, thinking he'd use the drive time to return a few business calls. And call Colorado, he thought, remembering his promise to Maggie. Twenty minutes later he connected with the agent from the Colorado Springs gallery. His satisfaction didn't last long.

"Sorry, I've never met the woman," Leo Shotweiler said.

"But the gallery owner said you're Margaret Raeburn's agent. You handle all her business."

"Well, yes and no. I am the regional rep, which means I handle the gallery end of things out here. Everything else goes through Ms. Raeburn's national representative."

Zak held his breath, counted to ten, and willed himself to be patient. His phone beeped, signaling an incoming call. He recognized the kennel number but ignored the call. Now that he finally had the agent on the phone, he was determined to learn whatever he could. He'd return Maggie's call when he got the contact information they needed.

Thinking quickly, he decided to try a different approach. "I'm in the art business myself, but I can't say I've run into this kind of setup before. You have to deal with the artist *and* a gallery owner *and* a national rep? Sounds like you have your hands full."

Leo chuckled. "Kinda complicated, I know. What can I say? The woman really likes her privacy, and it's not as if she needs publicity to sell her work, right?"

"Well, even if you've never met her, surely you've spoken on the phone."

"Can't say as I have."

The phone beeped again, and then again. "Seriously? So you don't have a phone number? What about an email? Or a mailing address?"

"I told you, I don't deal with any communications, I'm just involved in the gallery business. Look, why not talk to her national rep? You said you're in the business, you probably already know him anyway—"

"What makes you say that?"

"He's right there in your area. At least, that's the contact information I have for him. Hang on while I flip through the Rolodex."

Zak's phone beeped yet again. He glanced at the screen; it was the kennel number. "Hey, can I call you right back? There's another call I'd better—"

"Found it," Leo said triumphantly. "The guy you want to talk to is Nicholas Crane."

39

The road was worse than she remembered. The sky grew steadily darker, although whether from smoke or storm clouds, Maggie couldn't tell. She had no experience driving the van in bad weather, and the rising wind worried her.

Maggie gripped the wheel tightly and steered cautiously along the rutted surface. In the rear, Sam whined as the van lurched into yet another pothole. "Sorry, boy," she muttered. "I'm doing my best."

After Bev had hung up, Maggie called Keith and, struggling to keep a grip on her emotions, relayed what information she had. "I know the team needs an official request but—"

"I'll call the sheriff right now," he promised. "And I'll get whoever's available—some have gone out on fire calls. We'll be in touch."

Next, she called Rob's cell phone. The ragged tone of his voice told her he was in pain, but he vetoed her suggestion they call an ambulance. "I'm all right," he insisted. "Sweet Pea's hurt more than I am, she has a big lump on her head. I called Dr. Sheppard after I called Dad. They're both on their way."

She forced herself to speak calmly. "Me, too. I'll probably lose the phone signal in a few miles—I'm coming around the east side of the lake—but can you fill me in on what happened?"

"I was looking for Sweet Pea, to exercise her like you said. She wasn't in the office, so I went up to the house but she wasn't there either. Anyway, I was standing on your porch, wondering where she'd got to, when I heard her barking down by the lake. I thought maybe you'd come back early and she was down there with you. Then I heard somebody yelling. I figured you might be in trouble, so I ran down there. That's when I saw the Jeep."

"Did you see anybody?" she asked urgently.

"I saw somebody, but I couldn't see his face. About all I can say for sure is a white guy wearing jeans and a ball cap, like half the population around here."

"Then what happened?"

"I heard Sweet Pea yelp, and then … then I heard somebody scream." He paused, and when he continued his voice sounded more ragged than ever. "I think it was Zak's little girl I heard."

"Oh my God, Rob—"

"I didn't think, I just ran in there—"

"And got hit over the head for your trouble."

"Dad's gonna be furious," he said miserably. "I should have called for help instead of rushing in on my own. By the time I woke up, the Jeep was gone and it was just Sweet Pea and me."

The phone beeped. "Hold on," she told Rob, "there's another call." When she checked, however, she was dismayed to see the "low battery" warning on the screen. She reconnected with Rob. "I don't understand it—I charged this phone last night."

"Not many cell towers where you are. You can run down your power quick if your phone keeps trying to search for a better connection."

"I'm going to hang up now, save my battery." Even as she spoke, the signal faded. With a muttered curse, Maggie tossed the phone on the seat beside her.

She couldn't stop thinking about Claire. Was it possible the little girl had returned earlier than expected? What kind of mother just dropped off a child that age and drove off without making sure she was safe?

Stop right there, she told herself. She didn't know what happened or why. Speculating without the facts was a waste of time and didn't get her any closer to figuring out what happened.

There were some things she could speculate about, though. For instance, how likely was it that Claire would have followed Sweet Pea down to the studio? Very likely, she decided. The little girl adored Sweet Pea. And if she thought the spaniel would lead her to Maggie, then it was highly probable Claire had gone willingly to the studio. And walked right in on—who? It must have been someone Claire knew, or why would they take the child? Why not leave her there with Rob and Sweet Pea?

When Maggie got back to the kennel, she'd see if Sam could pick up the girl's scent. It was a long shot, she acknowledged. It was far more likely that whoever was in the Jeep most likely had taken Claire.

The van hit another pothole and shuddered to a halt. Maggie shifted frantically into reverse and then forward again but couldn't gain traction. She was stuck. Clambering out, she discovered the front passenger tire flat and wedged into a deep hole. There was no way she could shift it by herself, she realized in dismay.

She checked her phone; no service. She hauled out her map and compass, unloaded Sam and filled his portable water bowl from the can stored in the back. While the dog lapped eagerly, she stuck a hastily scribbled note on the windshield, hoping someone would come along and catch up to her.

She tucked her compass in the front pocket of her vest and checked that she had ID, cell phone, and a protein bar along with the items she typically carried in the vest. She dropped three water bottles in the side loops. Setting her cap firmly on her head, she snapped Sam's long tracking leash onto his collar.

"Keith said there were houses along the lake," she told him. "Let's hope we find somebody home—somebody with a land line. And if we're really lucky, somebody with a vehicle. Find 'em, Sam!"

The smoke continued to drift across the way, making breathing difficult for both of them. Maggie was content to let Sam set the pace, mindful of the heat and knowing he had to be tired after that lengthy demonstration. They walked uphill and down for two hours, pausing frequently for water breaks and short rests. Near the top of one steep hill she called a halt and checked her phone again. Still no signal. Please let there be a house soon, she prayed.

She had two water bottles remaining. Pulling out one, she poured water into the palm of her hand for Sam before quenching her own thirst. She was sliding the bottle back into its loop when Sam stiffened and then pulled forward. Trusting his instincts, she increased her pace. "What is it, boy?"

A quarter mile ahead through a break in the trees she saw a clearing along the shore of Beaver Lake. A cabin, a barn, and several smaller buildings stood in the clearing, close to the water. A sleek boat banged against the tires edging a dock; the wind had risen sharply, turning the normally placid lake surly. Someone was moving about the boat, but the swirling smoke made it difficult to see clearly.

"Hello!" she called, raising her voice to be heard against the wind. When the figure in the boat swung around to stare at her, she waved and started in that direction with Sam pulling strongly at the leash. The person she'd hailed jumped onto the dock and hurried toward her.

As he approached, Maggie was shocked to realize the man was Nicholas Crane. She'd never seen him dressed so roughly. Instead of his typical suit, he wore tattered jeans, heavy boots, and a ball cap pulled low across his brow.

"I didn't know you lived out this way!"

"My own little retreat. What are you doing here?"

"My van broke down a long way back, and Sam led me here. Can I beg a ride to the kennel? And borrow your phone? Mine's just about gone—" She broke off as Sam barked and strained forward. "Steady, boy," she ordered.

A dog inside a nearby building barked excitedly in response. "Quiet!" Nicholas shouted. The noise continued unabated. "That's Delilah," he said sourly. "Beautiful, stupid, untrainable Delilah. More trouble than she's worth."

She'd never heard Nicholas talk that way. Maggie felt a spurt of concern for the animal and promised herself she'd follow up later, once the crisis was behind them. Until then, she couldn't let herself be distracted. "I'm sorry to impose on you, but it really is an emergency. There's been another break-in—"

"And a little girl is missing. Yes, I know."

40

Bev's phone call and the news about his daughter had Zak pushing his car to the absolute limit, slowing only for the worst of the curves and cursing when he came up behind another vehicle, blasting his horn relentlessly until he could roar past. His initial panic had settled into an adrenalin burn as his military training kicked in and his mind focused on a single mission: bring his daughter home.

But when Bev told him about finding Claire's backpack in the studio, he'd thought his heart would stop. He'd packed it himself with her Scooby Doo pajamas, Treasure of the Ozarks tee-shirt, her favorite night-light, coloring book, crayons ...

He tried, unsuccessfully, to reach Althea. After the fifth attempt he considered, then rejected, the idea of leaving a voice mail. Anything he said might set her off again, and he had enough to deal with without worrying about her, too. What the hell had she been thinking, just leaving Claire and taking off like that? Did she even think to check that an adult was there?

And what had *he* been thinking? He had to admit there was plenty of blame to go around. Althea had agreed to have Claire join her only because he hadn't given his ex-wife any choice. He'd been so worried about the escalating trouble at the kennel that he'd all but forced Althea to agree to the visit. And look where it got them, he thought now in disgust.

Focus, he ordered himself. Focus on the mission and get it done, one step at a time. Okay, he thought, first step: call up reinforcements.

He took out his phone, hit the speed-dial button for his VA counselor, Mike Jameson. In short, terse sentences he outlined the situation. "I'm heading into the hills, not sure how much longer I'll have a phone signal," he told him. "The community's already stretched thin because of the fires. Barton County, and maybe yours, can send some people, but there's a lot of territory to cover. And no telling how long it's going to take," he admitted. "Sheriff Johnson is going to need more help."

"He'll have it," Mike assured him. "I'm pulling the call roster now, and I'll get the other counselors on it. Hell, I can probably find a couple dozen guys just hanging around here."

"Mike—" Zak had to stop, fight for control.

"We've got your six, man. Give me another call when you get up there and get briefed. Hey, are the feds working this?"

"Nobody's mentioned that and I'm not waiting around to find out. This is our firefight—they'll have to catch up."

HE HIT A roadblock south of Hawk Hollow. "Sorry, pal— fire's jumped the road up ahead," the deputy at the roadblock told him. "Need to get to the lake? Cut back over to Highway 127, then go up by Round Creek."

He slammed the car into reverse and hit the speed-dial button for the kennel as he turned south again. When Bev answered he updated his location. "ETA's about an hour, maybe more if I hit another detour. Let me talk to Maggie."

"She's not here," Bev said shakily. "She was somewhere on the eastern shoreline when we lost contact. She should have been back by now."

"Tell the sheriff he needs to be looking for two people."

"He already knows. He's set up a command post here at the kennel. Keith Baxter called, too—he's the head of the county

Search and Rescue team. He says he showed Maggie the route but he's worried she might have gotten disoriented in the smoke or had vehicle trouble."

Zak was all but snarling, his knuckles white against the steering wheel. "Tell the damn SAR team to get out there and find her! Find both of them!"

41

Maggie was stunned. The man standing before her bore little resemblance to the sophisticated man she knew. "You know what happened to Claire?"

"My dear girl, do you really think a child might go missing without the population of five counties knowing about it?"

"Oh, of course. I told Bev to call everybody she could."

As she spoke, Nicholas closed the distance between them. He reached out toward her, then jerked back with a frown when Sam growled. "Put that animal in the barn with Delilah while I finish loading these supplies, would you? I'd just as soon not be a target for those teeth."

"I can't imagine what's got him so worked up," she apologized. "I guess the heat and smoke has rattled both of us. Or maybe it's the wind. For just a minute there, I thought ... well, never mind," she said, feeling unaccountably flustered.

"It appears to have been a difficult day all round. Never mind, I'll take care of you. Go put him in the barn," he repeated. "He'll be quite comfortable until we leave, I assure you. And then go help yourself to a cool drink while I get organized."

Reluctantly, Maggie led Sam into the barn. She didn't know what to think; Sam had behaved as if Nicholas had been an intruder instead of a family friend. Had the dog picked up on something she missed? She wanted to keep the Sam close at her side, but she didn't want to risk offending Nicholas in his current mood. "I don't like this either," she whispered to the dog. "But we need him to get home. So play nice with Delilah until I can get us out of here, okay?"

Moving toward the cabin, she stuffed Sam's leash in a back pocket of her vest and turned on her cell phone. Please let there be a signal, she prayed—and let the battery hold out long enough for her to place a call. She wondered how far she was from home. If the silence around her was anything to go by, she was a long way from any populated area. She could see only a narrow strip of water; this must be one of the larger creeks that fed into Beaver Lake. An odd place for a man like Nicholas, she mused. Although he'd mentioned being a landowner, she'd somehow assumed he was referring to his gallery or a house in town, and not a cabin on an isolated stretch of land.

The cabin interior, though, didn't look like anything she might have expected to see in the woods. The place was a stylish retreat furnished with fine leather furniture and crystal lamps. Bookcases lined one wall and art work was carefully positioned throughout the room. More GQ than American Rustic—and definitely more like the Nicholas she'd come to know.

Feeling more at ease, Maggie wandered about. Drapes on the windows blocked the sun. Finding a wall switch, she turned on the track lighting suspended beneath the ceiling beams, which highlighted sculptures on pedestals and a collection of paintings along the walls.

One piece above the desk caught her eye. The painting was small, exquisitely rendered, the colors rich and vibrant. A small child knelt among garden greenery, her face turned toward the elderly woman in the background who was carrying a shallow basket filled with herbs. The artist had captured the tranquility of the garden and the obvious bond between woman and child in strong, self-assured strokes.

"Your mother called it The Herb Garden," Nicholas said from the doorway, watching her closely.

Just then, her phone beeped, indicating a signal. "At last!" she exclaimed. "Excuse me a moment, would you? I've been trying to get a signal for hours. I want to let folks know I'm on my way home. They're probably getting worried about me."

Only two bars showed, but it might be enough. As she pressed the speed-dial button for the kennel line, she nodded toward the painting. "The Herb Garden? I thought I saw that name on the studio inventory. That can't be right, though, if you'd already bought it."

"I didn't." Gently, Nicholas took the phone out of her hands and snapped it shut.

42

The parking lot in front of the kennel was crowded. Judging from the tags, law enforcement officials and SAR volunteers from two counties had answered the call. Trucks and off-road vehicles parked facing the road for a speedy exit. Speedboats, jet skis, and a couple of pontoon boats were moored at the dock or secured along the shoreline.

Zak recognized Donnie Ray Bowles and Ben Springer in the crowd milling about the parking lot watching the clouds dropping lower over the rough water. As he passed, he could hear them taking bets on the weather, arguing over the odds of rain. Others he didn't know were helping Rob check water lines and distribute shovels and rakes. The air was oppressively hot despite the rising wind.

Zak paused to grip Rob's hand. Bev had told him he'd been injured trying to help Claire. "How's the head?"

"I've had worse hits in football," Rob said, then added in a burst, "I should have stopped him, I should have done *something*. I just let him take her."

"Hey, none of that. Thanks to you we have a description—"

"Not much of one. White guy, black Jeep," Rob muttered. "What good is that?"

"It's a start. We'll find him, and we'll find Claire. We'll get her back."

Ben Springer stepped forward, gripped Rob's shoulder. "Damn straight, we'll find her," he agreed. "Zak, the sheriff's inside, he'll give you an update."

The sheriff's department had taken over the kennel office, dumping everything except the coffee pot off the counters and table tops to make way for area maps and miscellaneous electronic equipment. Lucas was on the phone, issuing commands. The county SAR team had set up operations in the customer lounge; a small group was there now, checking gear and listening to updates from their team leader. Some were armed.

"Barton County is sending over their mobile command center," Keith Baxter was saying. "We'll use that as our base of operations if the fire pushes us out. Keep your radio on, follow standard protocol. And for God's sake watch what you say. We don't need another PR fiasco."

Zak glanced at Ben. "What's he talking about?"

"A few months back a kid got lost, fell in a cave. Team did their best, but he didn't make it. There was a rookie with us—his first rescue—and he freaked. Got on the radio and, well, half the county heard before we could notify next of kin."

The image of Claire, alone and afraid, somewhere in the dark made him sick. Zak was positive he could feel the blood leaving his head. Heads turned toward him as he swayed slightly. He was having trouble feeling his feet.

Ben stepped closer and gripped Zak's elbow, holding him steady. "I know it's your little girl out there. That sucks," he said bluntly. "I figure you want in on this action, and I hear you were damned good at recon. We need you, man, so get your head together before the sheriff sees you."

"Damn straight I want in." Once he was sure he had his breathing—and his feet—under control again, he nodded to Ben and, emotions locked down, went in search of information. "What can you tell me, Sheriff?" he asked. He kept his tone formal, a holdover from his military days. "Do you have any word on my daughter? And where's Maggie?"

"We're doing everything we can to find both of them," the sheriff said. Taking Zak aside, he quickly filled in the details. "First, your daughter. There was no sign of a struggle, nothing to indicate she'd been hurt in any way. It's possible she interrupted a burglary in progress, and the thieves panicked and took her with them. Right now we're assuming a stranger abduction. Believe me, we're not taking any chances. We've broadcast information about the vehicle and a description of your daughter, and we've got roadblocks up. So do the fire crews."

"Yeah, I ran into one down by Hawk Hollow, had to detour over to Round Creek. Listen, I've got buddies on the way to help. I know you're short on manpower, so tell me what you need done." When Lucas frowned, Zak gave him a level stare. "We both know civilians can be a pain in the ass. And family members are prime suspects. Well, Uncle Sam's my alibi on this one—check with the VA center, verify my movements. Then cross me off your list. And these volunteers aren't amateurs. We all have sand in our boots and we know how to follow orders. So tell me what needs doing, and let's get to it."

Lucas hesitated only briefly before he picked up Claire's small backpack and handed it over. "Right now, I need you to give us as much information as you can. Bev tells me your daughter was supposed to be with her mother. Your ex-wife, right? We've tried the number you passed along. No answer. I called Springfield, asked them to send a unit out."

"I've been calling. All I get is her damned voice mail."

"I have to ask. Any chance she might be involved here?"

"None. Look, she's had some problems, but—"

"What kind of problems?"

"She had a breakdown last year," Zak admitted reluctantly. "But she's been working with a therapist. She's better. And she wouldn't do anything to hurt Claire."

"All right, we'll track her down, get some answers. I'll call Springfield, see if they have a female officer available. And we'll need the name of that therapist, and a phone number."

"It's in the cottage."

"Okay. Meanwhile, do me a favor. Go through this backpack, see if you can figure out what she might be wearing. Any detail at all might help."

It was becoming crowded inside the kennel office. When the door swung open yet again, Zak watched Sylvia Bridger and Angus Sheppard push their way inside. They conferred briefly with Bev before Angus hurried off to treat Sweet Pea. Sylvia headed straight to Lucas.

"Angus was with me when we heard about Claire, and now Bev says Maggie is missing, too. Don't you even try to blame this on Howard. He might have done some stupid things in his life but he would never hurt that poor child, or Maggie either. You just cross him off your list of suspects right now—unless you think he managed to sneak out of the hospital without Deputy Do-Right noticing," she said sarcastically.

"Settle down, Sylvia. And no, I don't think Howard's involved." He turned again to Zak. "Okay, back to what I was saying, it's possible the thieves—"

Sylvia interrupted him. "What thieves?"

"The ones who cleared out the studio," Lucas answered tersely. "Refresh my memory—who knew the paintings were there?"

Zak didn't give a damn about the paintings but he thought he could see where the sheriff was going. "Find the paintings, we find the bastard who took Claire?" he asked, and saw the sheriff nod. He forced himself to concentrate. "Who knew? Maggie. Her parents. Me, everybody who works here. Jake Turner. Her insurance agent ... um ..."

"Frank Taylor," Sylvia supplied the name. "We knew, of course—Howard and me. Angus, too. So did Nicholas. Pretty much anybody who knew the family knows about the studio. It's been here for years."

Abruptly, Zak remembered the phone conversation he'd had before the news about Claire made him forget everything.

"The studio—we keep coming back to that. It's important, I'm sure of it, but damned if I can see how. Maggie's been saying all along that her mother had come back here. She's worried her mother wants to take Waterside away from her. Maybe it's not Waterside she's interested in, but something from the studio."

"If Margaret wanted something, she'd just waltz in here and take it," Sylvia told them. "But she's not the violent type, and I refuse to believe she would hurt a child."

"Maggie's been trying to locate her mother. Dead ends, every time. I've used the contacts I have out west but can't find anyone who's seen or talked to her in years, until today. I finally got a hold of her agent. He's never met her in person, either—"

"This isn't helping," Lucas growled.

"Just wait. The guy told me all communication goes through the Crane Gallery. He said he works with Nicholas Crane exclusively, that Nicholas is Margaret Raeburn's national rep."

"No way," Sylvia said flatly. "Everybody knows Nicholas *wanted* to handle Margaret's work, but she turned him down a long time ago."

"Maybe she changed her mind. All I'm saying is that if she is involved in something around here, Nicholas Crane will know it. And whatever it is he knows, it might help us find Claire."

"There might be a connection." Lucas grabbed his notebook. "I think I told you the feds are talking to Jake Turner about the old Spanish silver he was peddling on the black market. Latest update: he's claiming he works for Nicholas Crane. Hold on, I've got my notes somewhere ..."

Zak felt his control slip. "So they dig for treasure—who gives a damn?"

"The feds do," the sheriff said dryly. He found the page he was looking for. "Okay, here we go. Jake Turner says he's been on Crane's payroll for years, and not just digging up the countryside. Claims he helped Crane move stuff in and out of the studio over the years, even after Maggie fired him. Crane helped himself to whatever he wanted, according to Jake."

Zak slapped his fist on the counter. "The studio inventory that wasn't right." Thinking furiously, he replayed the scene in his head. "There was something on the inventory about the paintings from Margaret Raeburn's show, but we couldn't find them. When Maggie called Nicholas, he said he didn't know anything about them. What if he's been stealing paintings all this time? What if he came back today to finish the job? And Claire interrupted him."

Lucas frowned. "Why didn't he clear out when Maggie re-opened Waterside? Why wait until now?"

"Maybe these fires forced his hand. Or maybe he wasn't worried about Maggie finding out. If you're right, Jake Turner probably told Nicholas about Maggie's every move. Jake knew Maggie hadn't bothered with the studio. She only opened the place after Frank Taylor insisted on an inventory."

"His building burned down right after that," Sylvia remembered. "Coincidence?"

"Maybe not," Lucas acknowledged, writing rapidly. "Let's go back through the time-line. Leaving out Bertha's letters and phone calls, what happened first?"

"Doreen Crowley drowned," Zak said.

Sylvia gasped. "And when Maggie identified the body—"

"She discovered Doreen had Margaret Raeburn's locket," Zak finished. "It all comes back to Maggie's mother. But why?"

"Time we found out," Lucas said.

43

Maggie stared at the painting. She was sure she'd seen that name—The Herb Garden—in her grandmother's notebook. She was equally certain the painting had not been in the studio when she and Zak checked the inventory. She looked at Nicholas, leaning against the door, blocking her exit.

"Gran must have listed that by mistake." She managed to keep her voice steady. "I'd like my phone back, please."

Nicholas shook his head. "So your friends can interrupt us? I don't think so, my dear."

"Stop calling me that," she snapped. She took a deep breath and struggled to control her fear. Stay calm, she warned herself. Don't jump to conclusions. There could be a legitimate reason he had that painting here. Maybe there was more to their relationship than he'd previously admitted. "Did my mother give you that painting?" she asked suspiciously, and was taken aback as his sardonic laughter filled the room.

"Your mother wouldn't have given me so much as a scribble from her sketch book," he said bitterly.

"You didn't buy it. She didn't give it to you," she said carefully. "Why do you have my mother's painting?"

"Not just one," he corrected. "If you don't count the ones already sold, I have acquired all of Margaret's work—including everything from the studio at Waterside."

"*You* broke in—"

"Actually, I have a key."

"Where's Claire, you bastard? If you've hurt her, I swear—"

"Shut up," he said mildly. "The child is fine. I would have left her there along with the idiot boy but she wouldn't stop screaming." He nodded toward the door at the far end of the room. "I gave her a whiff of something to keep her quiet. She's asleep. She's fine," he repeated. "If you want her to stay that way, you'll do exactly as I say."

Maggie dashed into the adjoining room and choked back a sob when she saw Claire, asleep on the bed. She ran her hands gently over the small body. The girl was barefoot and wore shorts and a tee shirt. Maggie pushed her hands carefully through the tangled hair and was relieved not to find any lumps.

"I told you, she's fine."

Maggie spun around, furious to find Nicholas standing right behind her. "She's been kidnapped and drugged and God knows what else you've done to her. You think that's fine?"

Nicholas glared at her. "I did not assault the child, if that's what you're implying. How dare you suggest such a thing? And don't speak to me that way again."

"I'll speak to you any way I like, you son of a—"

"No, you won't." He slapped a cloth against her face.

Maggie smelled something sickly sweet. She struggled but he was stronger and held her easily. She heard him chuckle, and then the world faded to gray.

THE BOAT BACKED away from the dock and moved slowly through the turbulent water of the lake. Forced into a prone position on the deck, Maggie could see only the boat and the sky above. The sun was obscured by heavy clouds, thickened with smoke and ash. A jagged burst of lightning hurt her eyes. Her head ached and she felt groggy from whatever it was he'd given her.

She had a vague recollection of stumbling along the dock with her hands tied behind her. Nicholas had tossed a still-drowsy Claire over his shoulder. Now, feeling small hands pressing against her cheeks, she shook her head to clear it and opened her eyes.

Claire was whispering her name and patting her face. The child's eyes were huge and slightly glassy, her skin clammy despite the heat. Maggie recognized the signs of shock and longed to wrap her arms around the girl, but her hands were still firmly bound behind her back. She twisted her head slightly and saw Nicholas at the wheel. Hate boiled up at the sight of him, and Maggie mentally consigned the man to Hell for all eternity.

As if reading her mind, Nicholas looked down. "Hot, isn't it? Not many boats out here today," he said conversationally. "It's the smoke, I suppose. We should have a quiet ride."

Her throat felt like the bottom of a dry creek bed. Her voice wasn't much more than a croak, but she was damned if she'd let him see her fear. "Oh, so we're just out having a fun day on the lake," she said sarcastically.

"In the unlikely event that anyone does come close, you'll stay quiet and out of sight."

"If I don't?"

"Oh, I think you will." His gaze moved from her to Claire, huddled beside her. "It's a long way to shore."

"You filthy—"

"Now, now, my dear, watch your language."

Claire buried her head against Maggie, her tiny hands stroking and patting wherever she could reach. "I'm scared," she whimpered. "I wish my daddy was here."

"Me, too," Maggie answered. She checked that Nicholas was busy with the boat, then leaned closer. "I don't know where he's taking us. But listen. When we get to shore I need you to be ready to run if you get the chance. Run and hide, okay?"

Claire moaned, tears streaming down her face. "No no no! I wanna stay with you!"

"What's she carrying on about?" Nicholas asked sharply.

"She's scared," Maggie shot back. "She's just a little girl. Untie me so I can comfort her," she pleaded.

"Shut her up or I will. It would be a real shame if she fell overboard, wouldn't it? She can't swim, can she?" He paused before adding, "Neither could Doreen."

"You're despicable," Maggie hissed.

Nicholas shrugged. "Accidents happen all the time."

The boat slowed, and then stopped. Looking up through the haze, Maggie realized she was staring at a steep, rocky bluff covered in juniper, pine, and scrub brush.

Nicholas dropped anchor close to the shore and slung a backpack over one shoulder. "Let's go, ladies."

Claire wrapped her arms around Maggie's leg. She was trembling hard, exhausted, her breath coming in ragged gasps. "Where are we going *now*?"

Maggie leaned against her, wishing she could gather Claire close. She tried to sound calm. "I think we have to climb up."

"Up," Nicholas agreed. "And then we go *in*."

44

Climbing the limestone bluff required every bit of dexterity Maggie could summon. She doubted she could have managed it at all if her hands had still been tied. In fact, she hadn't; she'd lost her balance on her first attempt and slid backward, landing with a bone-jarring thud and banging her head against the rocks at the water's edge.

Cursing, Nicholas dragged her to her feet and jerked the knots loose. "Do exactly what I say, or I'll leave the girl behind."

Unbound, she found she could climb after all. It wasn't the sheer vertical cliff she'd first thought. The steep slope was pockmarked with outcroppings, scrub brush, and small trees rooted in the rock face. She dug her boots in for traction, clinging tightly when the wind tugged and the shale shifted beneath her. Despite the protection her jeans and vest offered, she was bruised and bleeding from a half dozen scrapes before she'd managed twenty feet. All the better for leaving a trail, she thought with grim satisfaction.

Following the man's terse directions, she moved up and to the right, eyes darting left and right as she climbed, searching for familiar landmarks or someone, anyone, out on the lake who might see them on the bluff. Through the haze she thought she could make out a large structure some distance away. Was it the dam? She searched her memory for details of the landscape.

There was a road that ran across the top of the dam; she'd driven it a couple of times when she'd first explored the area. There were scenic overlooks near the dam, she remembered. If anyone was there now, could they see the bluff through the smoke?

She had to get Nicholas away from Claire. But how? She knew the bluffs along this part of the lake were at least a hundred feet high. There was no way they could manage such a distance. She tried to look backward as she climbed, trying to keep an eye on Claire. She was desperately afraid for the child, who was clearly in shock and probably still feeling the effects of whatever that bastard had used on her.

Maggie measured the distance between them, weighed the odds, considered her options. She was strong, she reminded herself. She could kick, knock him off balance, push him backwards, down into the rocks. If she could knock him out, they could get back to the boat, get away, get help.

Pulling herself onto a narrow ledge, her anger burned as Nicholas shoved Claire upward. The child slipped repeatedly, scraping knees and elbows and bare feet. At one point her foot was caught, causing her to cry out. Nicholas, panting heavily, yanked her foot free and dragged her the last few yards up to the ledge.

Maggie grabbed the girl, hugging her fiercely. She ran anxious hands over the small body and was relieved that the cut on her foot seemed the worst of her injuries. The tissues she'd had in her pocket would be a sodden mess after she'd fallen into the water, so she used a corner of her shirt to tend the cut. "Unless you want to leave bloody footprints all over the place, you better let me clean this up." And let him not notice the trail she'd made as she'd climbed, she thought.

"Where we're going it won't matter." Still, he swept his foot across the dusty ledge, eradicating the bloody footprints before once again knotting the rope tightly around Maggie's wrists. He gestured toward the shadows.

Maggie moved forward warily. At the back of the ledge she saw a narrow passage. Beyond the boulders lay complete darkness. She froze. "Where are you taking us?"

"Shut up and get moving. We wasted too much time already."

She looked again at the dark hole, shuddered as he pushed her roughly forward. Another shove and she was past the boulders. The light from the ledge faltered a few feet beyond the entrance; she could barely make out a narrow passage. He shoved her again and she stumbled, falling to her knees against the remains of a crude wooden gate propped against the limestone.

This was worse than any nightmare she'd ever had. "I can't see anything," she said desperately. Her throat tightened. Her heart hammered. She couldn't breathe. If she had to take one more step into that black space she'd start screaming and never stop. She felt small hands clutch her vest and realized Claire had fallen against her and was again sobbing frantically. Hysteria seemed imminent—for both of them, Maggie admitted. "Hold on to me, sweetie," she murmured. Give me strength, she prayed.

The Lord helps those who help themselves, Gran used to say. Maggie dredged up the remnants of her wits. If she could convince Nicholas he'd profit by keeping them safe, there was a slim chance they might survive this ordeal. To do that, she had to let him think he was winning. But how?

Let him think he's winning, she repeated to herself.

"You want us to go in there, fine," she said, matching her tone to his. "But we're not taking one more step without a light. This little kidnap scheme of yours won't get you a dime if anything happens to either one of us. I know you want money—I've seen your fancy suits, the Mercedes, the paintings, the sculptures. Takes a lot to support a lifestyle like that, doesn't it?"

"I have no money worries, my dear." He jerked Claire upright and handed her a flashlight. "She goes first," he told Maggie. "And as much as I hate to disappoint you, I don't plan to stay here waiting for a ransom. I already have one fortune in the bank, and another waiting right here in this cave. Now stop stalling and move."

AT LEAST HE'D left them a lantern in the small cavern before disappearing down a passage. Claire shivered in the chill air and clung to Maggie. "Tuck your hands under my vest," she told the little girl.

"I'm cold," Claire wailed. "I wanna go home."

Maggie's clothes were still wet and she shivered in the damp of the cave. At least Claire was mostly dry; Nicholas had hauled her to the shore. "Me too, sweetie, me too." Maggie was afraid she would start sobbing herself if she said anything more.

She made herself breathe deeply and put all the confidence she could muster into her voice. "Sheriff Johnson, your daddy, and probably everybody we know is out there, right now, looking for us. I need you to be brave a little longer, all right? As soon as we can, we'll make a run for it. Meanwhile," she said cheerfully, "I'm thirsty. I bet you are, too. If you can reach my water bottle we can have a drink."

The distraction worked. Claire tugged one of the water bottles free and drank her fill before holding the bottle up carefully to Maggie's lips. She gulped the cool liquid, thankful she'd been wearing her vest and carrying water with her that day.

She thought of Sam, left behind in the barn, and prayed he'd be found soon. She'd filled a big bucket for each dog, but that wouldn't last long in this heat. And if the fire got close, there'd be no escape. No, she refused to even think about that.

"Curl up here beside me, sweetheart," she invited. "We'll keep each other warm." As the little girl huddled closer, Maggie kept up a soft murmur of words. Within moments the child fell into an exhausted slumber.

A wavering light appeared. Turning her head, Maggie realized the cave must go deeper than she'd thought. Moments later, Nicholas entered, carrying a small crate and a flashlight.

"I apologize for the drab quarters, ladies. But under the circumstances, I had no choice."

"Sorry to have inconvenienced you."

"Sarcasm doesn't suit you, my dear."

"I told you not to call me that. And keep your voice down, unless you want a hysterical child on your hands. She's had about all she can take today, thanks to you," she said bitterly.

He didn't acknowledge her barbed comment, but when he spoke next he was quieter. Setting down the crate, he pried open the lid and extracted a small, rectangular-shaped object. He began polishing, rubbing until it gleamed in the light of the lantern. "Beautiful, isn't it?" he asked dreamily.

"What is it?"

"Silver, of course." He seemed surprised by the question. "Spanish. And very, very old."

"That can't be ... I don't believe you! Those are just stories!"

"Pretense doesn't suit you, *my dear*. Your mother knew all about it, she knew when she gave you that map—the map that should have been mine," he added bitterly. "I've been searching for years with nothing to show for it but a couple of Yokum dollars and a small cache of Confederate coins—and those turned out to be counterfeit. I needed that map to find the real treasure."

Maggie's head was spinning. The day had taken on a surreal quality. Like Alice down the rabbit hole, she thought. "I told you before, it's not real. My mother made that map," Maggie objected, careful to keep her voice low. "It was part of a silly Halloween costume."

"No, it's not. She used to buy old pictures and boxes of junk all the time. She found a letter describing the location of the treasure taped inside one of the framed pictures. She was so excited," he recalled. "She showed it to me, just once, and laughed about making a map. I searched everywhere but couldn't find it. And to think you had it all along."

"Nicholas—"

"That's why you came back to Eagle Cove, isn't it? You wanted to cheat me, just like your mother did!"

They were at the mercy of a lunatic. "I have no idea what you're talking about." She spoke quietly, mindful of the child sleeping deeply beside her. "I give you my word, Nicholas. I am *not* trying to cheat you."

"That's almost exactly what your mother said when she told me she was leaving. Told me she was only taking what was hers. Bad enough that moron Bridger wanted to run off with her, take her away. But for me to lose those paintings, that was the last straw. After I'd given her everything. Everything!"

"So you decided to take the paintings for yourself, after she'd gone? Weren't you worried she'd find out?"

"That wasn't going to happen."

"Why not?"

"Because she's dead."

45

At the kennel, Lucas Johnson organized the law enforcement efforts while keeping an eye on those coordinating volunteer activities. His senior deputy, Jonathan Hoffsteder, had taken over the office computer and was tracking the reports coming in from the patrols Lucas had dispatched. A laptop showed a live feed from the emergency management office, providing real-time data on the wildfires, road closings, and detours. Another supplied the latest information from other regional and national law enforcement agencies.

Hoffsteder typed a short message. Seeing the sheriff's questioning glance, he pitched his voice low. "Somebody flagged our Amber Alert, wondered it was a custodial issue."

The Amber Alert system was intended to mobilize a community to search for a child abducted by a stranger. By Department of Justice standards, abductions by non-custodial family members generally didn't trigger an Amber Alert unless there was a risk of the serious injury or death. Lucas had seen the statistics himself; as much as ninety percent of all reports were false alarms that nonetheless required law enforcement action. He glanced at Zak, hoping he hadn't overheard the conversation.

ZAK HAD TAKEN possession of the counter next to Hoffsteder's equipment. He'd locked himself into a zone, handling every task the sheriff handed him with the same fierce concentration and effort that had helped him survive three combat tours. At the moment he was scrawling notes while listening to one of the military community volunteers who'd responded to his call for help.

He finished the call, tore the sheet from the pad, and handed it to Deputy Hoffsteder. "Latest update from War Eagle Mill; no suspicious activity." He was holding his fear at bay by sheer willpower, knowing if he lost control he'd be ejected from the action. He couldn't let that happen, had to stay involved.

He felt a slight weight press against his leg, and looked down in surprise to see Mr. B nudge him. Zak crouched beside the dog and gently stroked his head. He must miss Maggie and his buddies, Zak thought. "We'll find them, boy," he whispered.

THE SHERIFF'S CELL phone rang. He turned his back on the room, flipped it open. "Sheriff Johnson."

"Gabe Cooley here. I'm out here on Little Jack Creek, about a quarter-mile in from the lake."

"What have you got, Deputy?" Lucas asked. He was careful to keep his voice neutral, conscious of the crowd in the room, and very aware of Zak rising to his feet close by him. If the news was bad, he didn't want the man to hear it this way. Telling a parent his child was dead was the absolute worst part of his job, Lucas thought. He prayed this one would be found unharmed, but as the hours dragged by the odds slid the other way.

"Cabin with a barn, couple of sheds," the deputy reported. "There's a dock, too. No boats. No houses close by. Doesn't look like anybody's here. Knocked on the door, tried to look in the windows, you know, that sort of thing."

"Your point?"

"Yes sir. Like I said, I took a look around. Found a vehicle behind the cabin. It's a black Jeep."

Lucas spun around, grabbed a pen and note pad. Around him, the room fell silent. "Give me the tag number, and the VIN."

The deputy rattled off the information. Lucas scribbled furiously and shoved the pad toward Hoffsteder.

On the phone, Cooley was still talking. "No sign of the little girl, but there's a bunch of pictures—paintings, I mean—in the rear compartment. Could be the vehicle your boy saw, Sheriff."

"Give me your exact location," Lucas ordered. "I'm sending a patrol boat your way right now. Stay with your vehicle and keep your radio on. Do not, I repeat, do not approach the cabin until back up arrives."

Hoffsteder looked up. "Records check shows that the vehicle owner is a Nicholas Crane. Eureka Springs address. Cross-checking now to see if he has other vehicles or property."

"Sheriff," Cooley said, "there's more. I found a couple of dogs in the barn. One of 'em is that big Lab of Maggie Porter's. You know, Sam."

"You're sure it's him?"

"There's a tag on the harness, says Waterside Kennels. But I'd know Sam anywhere. Met him when we took that Dalmatian pup out to Maggie's. Don't know the other dog."

"What about the van?"

"No sign of it."

"Okay, when back up arrives, sweep every building. I'm on my way." He snapped the phone shut. His eyes met Zak's. "We found the Jeep, with the paintings still inside."

"Claire?"

"No word yet. But there's a chance that, wherever she is, Maggie is with her. My deputy found her dog at the property." He didn't voice his fear that Maggie could have walked into a dangerous situation and been forced to drive off, leaving the dog behind.

"I'm coming with you," Zak said flatly. He headed for the door with the Beagle still close by his side.

"I'm coming, too," Angus announced. When Lucas started to object, he added, "I can patch up people in a pinch, if you run short of medics."

"Right." Addressing the others now clustered around him, Lucas said, "I'm switching to Mobile 1. Hoffsteder, you're in charge here until I get back. SAR, be ready to move. Rob and Bev, you handle the kennel. If that fire gets close, follow Maggie's plan to get the animals out of here. Right?"

They nodded.

"Everybody stay in radio contact. We've probably got a long night ahead of us, but we're not giving up. They're out there somewhere, and we're going to bring them home."

46

For years Maggie had believed her mother abandoned her, walked away from everything, everyone she'd known. She'd grown up believing her mother hadn't wanted her, had rejected her in favor of a free and unfettered life. But dead? She'd never, not once, imagined that might be so.

Her mother was never coming home. Never.

Maggie wanted to scream at Nicholas, to charge the space between them and knock him flat. If her hands were free she'd have flung rocks and anything else she could find, hurl them until she wiped that superior, condescending smirk from his face. She wanted to rip out his dirty, thieving, murderous heart.

She glanced down and gave a silent prayer of thanks that Claire was still asleep. Whatever she did, Maggie told herself, she must do it quietly, without inflicting further trauma on the little girl. There would be time to scream and cry and grieve later—if they made it out of here alive. She didn't really think that would happen, not anymore, but even if the odds of escaping were a million to one she was going to cling to that chance.

Keep him talking, Maggie told herself. The longer he talked, the longer they'd live. And maybe, just maybe she'd find a way out. She flexed her hands, concentrating on the rope that bound her wrists behind her. Was it her imagination or did the rope seem a fraction looser? She forced herself to keep her body as still as possible, praying that the dim light would conceal her efforts to break free.

Desperate to keep him talking, Maggie said the first thing that popped in her head. "I don't believe you," she said flatly. "You're just trying to frighten me."

He shrugged. "I might as well tell you. I wanted her to reconsider the contract I offered. I found Margaret packing up her studio. I tried to reason with her, but she wouldn't listen, told me I couldn't have her paintings. Said she was going to offer them to another gallery. I had to shut her up, had to make her stop saying those things. I put my hands around her throat."

He stared at Maggie. "I thought she'd been alone, but then I saw you on the road, staring right at me. I put her body in my car and went after you."

Maggie squeezed her eyes shut as her recurring nightmare flooded back. She saw herself running to the house, down the hallway to the kitchen, tumbling down the basement stairs, trying to hide from the monster.

The monster was here, now, and still talking, words flowing faster and faster as if he couldn't wait to tell his story. "I didn't know how much you'd seen, and I couldn't take the chance you'd talk. So I decided to help Margaret 'walk away' from her life here. I helped myself to her clothes, her suitcases. It was ridiculously easy.

"Of course, I couldn't risk anyone blundering through the woods and coming across her. So I decided a more creative solution was called for."

Bile rose, hot and fast, at the thought of her mother in an unmarked grave in the woods. "Someone will find her eventually," she said hoarsely.

"Oh, she's already been found," he said carelessly. "I made certain of that. Just as I made certain they'd never know her identity. I kept her purse, her jewelry. No one will ever connect that pile of bones to your mother. As far as the world knows, Margaret Raeburn is alive and well in Colorado."

"Bones—"

"Rather famous, in their own way. Your friend the sheriff has seen to that, talking to the press, and that television show. Appealing to the public for help. Touching, in a pathetic sort of way." He sighed. "He might actually succeed, sooner or later, in identifying Jane Doe number one and two. He's persistent, I'll give him that. But you and I are the only ones who will ever know the true identity of Jane Doe number three, won't we?"

Maggie's thoughts stuttered, stopped. Her vision darkened, her chest hurt. Her stomach heaved. "My mother is ... my mother is ..."

"Jane Doe number three, of course. Or perhaps you would prefer to think of her as Bone Woman."

47

It was probably only moments, but Maggie felt as though endless time had slipped by after Nicholas' cruel revelation. The tightness in her chest became actual pain and she realized she'd been holding her breath. She took in huge gulps of air, shuddering as his words struck deep. She lurched sideways as if to avoid the emotional blow. At her side, Claire whimpered.

Maggie froze; she didn't want the little girl to hear any of this; she'd already experienced enough terror to fuel a lifetime of nightmares. If she even had a lifetime ahead of her, Maggie acknowledged grimly.

She bitterly resented not being able to put her arms around the child and hug her close. The most she could do was lean toward her to murmur soothing words and hope the child would fall back to sleep.

It worked. Within moments, Claire's eyes fluttered closed and her body, pressed tightly against Maggie, went limp. When she was certain the girl was asleep, Maggie slowly raised her head and glared at Nicholas, who was once again polishing the small bar of silver.

Rage, burning as intense as any wildfire, shot through her. She knew now that he had no intention of letting them go, guessed he'd led them there so he could retrieve his damned treasure and dump them at the same time. She heard, again, Gran's voice telling her the Lord helps those who help themselves.

Her mind raced, thinking of options. The bluff looked like hundreds of others that dotted the region, but she'd seen the dam, she was sure. If they could find their way out they could make their way up to the road, head for the dam. Somebody would be there.

And if they didn't get out? Would anybody even think to look for a cave? She knew there were probably dozens of places like this surrounding the lake; she'd heard stories about many of them. She seriously doubted Nicholas had trusted anyone with the location of his treasure, and the cave entrance wasn't easily visible from the lake.

The lake.

Nicholas had left his boat at the base of the bluffs. The police would be looking for them. Search and rescue, Zak, friends, volunteers. How long would it take for someone to spot that boat and investigate? Once they found the boat, they'd find the trail she left, realize it stopped at that ledge. They'd look, she told herself, and they'd find the entrance.

There was always a chance, though, that even if somebody spotted the boat they might miss the trail, or go past the ledge and miss the entrance entirely.

She had to believe somebody would find them. They needed time, that's all. If she could keep Nicholas talking, she could buy some time.

She wasn't giving up.

48

Zak stared at the map spread out on the patrol boat's console in front of him. It had been hours since he and Lucas had picked up Sam. It felt like years. He'd kept himself busy, handling radio traffic for the sheriff and checking in with Mike Jameson, who'd driven up from Fayetteville and was now at the kennel, serving as a switchboard of sorts for the veterans who'd turned out to help one of their own. Several had brought their boats and despite the looming threat of a storm were out on the lake right now, methodically checking the dozens of secluded coves where a boat might be hidden.

Even though all reports had so far been negative, Zak envied them. They were on the move, working as a team, while he baby-sat a radio and listened to the weather reports, he thought in disgust. He didn't have much experience in waiting for the fight to come to him; he'd rather be on the offensive.

The sheriff had deployed teams at strategic points around the lake, taking a calculated risk he'd covered the most likely zones. All they needed now was a credible sighting. So far, they'd followed up on three reports and two possible sightings with nothing to show for it. He looked at the unlit cigarette in his hand, and threw it overboard in disgust. "Close to five hundred miles of shoreline across three counties and God knows how many boat ramps and docks. He could be anywhere."

As if sensing his frustration, Mr. B whined and nudged his hand. Zak stroked the dog's head. "You miss it, too, don't you boy?" He looked up at Lucas. "Maybe he's remembering his glory days. He wants in on the action."

"I'll take whatever we can get." They were docked at Indian Creek, following up on another report. This one seemed slightly more promising than the others. Two campers swore they'd seen a man hauling a crying child off a boat. "Looked downright furtive, he did," one of them declared when they were questioned. "What with everybody talking about that poor little girl being kidnapped and all, we figured we'd better call it in."

His wife chimed in. "They headed for the Sugar Mountain trail. My Clive wanted to follow 'em but he's got a bad heart."

"We appreciate the help," Lucas told them. "Now if you folks would give your statement to that deputy over there, I'd be grateful."

THE DESCRIPTIONS GIVEN by the couple at Indian Creek didn't match that of either Crane or the Henderson girl, but Lucas was willing to follow any leads at this point. Hopeful that other tips would come in, the sheriff had asked Baxter to send out a small team to follow up this lead, augmented by the tracking dog sent over from Barton County.

Deputy Hoffsteder was coordinating activity from the kennel and passed along news as he heard it. The fire was still some distance away, but volunteers were patrolling the area just in case. Washington County was sending up two dogs and their handlers. They were en route to the north shore, where they could deploy by road, boat, or on foot as needed.

With little to do, Lucas felt his frustration rising to match Zak's. Every minute the girl was missing was like one more grain of sand sliding out of his grasp.

He hoped the girl's mother, Zak's ex-wife, would provide something that would help. So far, that hadn't happened. When the Springfield police had tried to question her she collapsed and had to be sedated.

The search of the cabin had been a bust, too. They retrieved Sam from the barn and checked the Jeep behind the cabin; Lucas was confident it was the same vehicle Rob had described. There was nothing to indicate Claire had been there, although the vehicle suggested otherwise.

There'd been no sign of recent digging around the cabin, for which Lucas breathed a silent prayer of gratitude. He refused to dwell on the chance Crane might have dumped the girl somewhere between Waterside and the cabin. If he'd buried her somewhere along the way they might never find her.

There was another possibility. A records check revealed one of the vehicles registered to Crane was a new Sea Ray twenty-foot speedboat. Lucas couldn't shake the feeling that Crane was out there on the lake somewhere, and the only logical reason he could think of at the moment was to dispose of his captives. That was not an opinion he'd share with anyone else, but he suspected others had similar misgivings.

He'd sent deputies and reserve officers out checking docks and marinas, and was grateful for the scores of veterans and civilian volunteers who'd turned out to help. He'd warned all of them to pull back and report if they saw any craft resembling Crane's boat. The search wouldn't be easy; the sheer size of the lake and connected waterways meant a long, arduous search. High winds were adding another layer of risk as smaller craft struggled to make headway in the choppy waters.

If there was another reason for Crane to have taken the boat, Lucas couldn't see it. Whatever he was doing, though, the probability was high he'd return to the cabin at some point. He couldn't see the man stealing all those paintings just to abandon them—not to mention all the artwork they'd found inside the cabin. He'd left two deputies there. "Search every last inch of the place again," he'd ordered. "You find anything unusual—anything at all—you let me know."

The radio squawked to life. Zak responded, then tossed the microphone to Lucas.

It was Hoffsteder reporting. "FBI's on their way, boss."

"About damn time," Lucas growled.

"Somebody got their wires crossed, thought this was about some black market silver deal, tried to blow me off. Don't worry, I set 'em straight. They should be here by dark. And, uh ... they said once they're on scene, you can stand down."

"I'll stand down when this operation is over, and not one blessed second sooner," Lucas snarled. "If they're half as smart as they think they are, they'll use the resources we're offering."

"You want I should tell them that?"

"Hell, no. You just keep things together there. And have somebody call the radio and television stations again, ask them to keep broadcasting the descriptions I gave you."

Tossing the radio aside, Lucas glanced around the boat. Zak had picked up a signal and was once again on his phone, this time talking to colleagues from the co-op who'd organized a search through the neighborhoods surrounding the downtown area. From his expression, Lucas guessed they'd found nothing to report.

Where the hell was that boat?

Lucas glanced at the dogs, envying their patience. The Beagle hadn't seemed to move, nor had the big retriever. Since they'd collected him, Sam had stayed near the prow, his attention straight ahead. Angus sat beside him, binoculars in motion, scanning the bluffs that edged the lake. Following their gaze, Lucas could see the SAR team spread out along the bluff, poking the underbrush with long poles and following the Barton County search dog. Watching their slow progress, Lucas picked up his radio. "SAR One, this is Command. Anything?"

"Nothing, Command. We'll keep you posted. Out."

49

Nicholas appeared to be in no hurry. He talked on, pausing now and then to pick up another silver bar to polish. Maggie surreptitiously worked to loosen the rope around her wrists while Nicholas boasted of his elaborate scheme to convince people Margaret Raeburn was alive and well.

Portraying himself as her national representative, he'd hired Leo Shotweiler, purchased a house, furnished it, and stowed Margaret's belongings in the closets. He even set up bank accounts in Margaret's name so payments from the gallery could be electronically deposited. He sold several the first year. "Once I got the press interested, I gave them just enough to establish her reputation as an eccentric recluse. After that, all I had to do was sit back and sell one, sometimes two paintings a year, raising the price all along. Even in this down market, her signature brings in thousands."

"And nobody thinks it's strange they're buying paintings all done twenty years ago?"

"She always put the date on the back of the canvas. A little Gesso, a few strokes, and nobody knew the difference. After all, it's the signature that matters, and I never touched that.

"After the first few paintings with altered dates were well received, I realized I had a talent that deserved to be nurtured. With Margaret's help, of course." He smiled wickedly.

"And you accused us of cheating you!" Maggie sneered.

"She owed me," he shot back. "I saw her potential long before anyone else. Certainly your father never did. He was too busy with his own career to even notice what his wife was doing. No, I was the one who saw what she could become. I helped her develop her talent, damn it. I nurtured her, encouraged her, even bankrolled her first big show. I offered your mother the world when nobody else would take a chance on a backwoods hillbilly. We would have both been famous, and she took that away from me. So I took it all back, on my own terms."

He described how he put his own padlock on the studio door. He'd slipped some cash to Jake Turner to look the other way while he came and went as he wanted. It had been a highly profitable venture, until Maggie inherited the property and re-opened Waterside Kennels.

"At first, I thought it wouldn't matter. You didn't talk about your mother, and you never went into the studio."

"What makes you so sure?"

He smirked. "I had other inside information."

"Doreen," Maggie breathed.

"It was ridiculously easy. All I had to do was give her a few trinkets, make a few promises. After I bought Delilah for her, she couldn't wait to tell me every intimate detail of your life."

"The dog in Miss Abigail's garden—that was Delilah?"

"I told you that animal was untrainable. After that, the stupid girl had to find another place to live. I set her up in a little house I own at Piney Point. I disliked that drive, though, so I brought her to my cabin. I let her keep some things there, closet space, a drawer, a box for her silly trinkets. I gave her a few more little things and she told me whatever I wanted to know."

"She thought she'd found her Mr. Right," Maggie guessed. "But something went wrong, didn't it?"

"She noticed too many details for her own good. She came in one day when I was working on a painting—one of Margaret's paintings," he added pointedly. "I laughed it off, distracted her with another gift. The twenty-four karat kind. I thought that worked, until I discovered she'd gone through my most private possessions. I'd warned her never to touch my things."

"More fool you, to trust someone like that. You bribed her to spy on me, and then were surprised when she snooped through your things? So what did she find that got you so upset?"

"She found Margaret's locket. She thought it was yours, of course, and was going to have it out with you, as she so inelegantly stated. I knew you'd recognize the locket right away. You could have ruined everything. I couldn't let that happen.

"It cost me the better part of a bottle of Chardonnay but in the end she came willingly enough. Or she did, once I showed her a ring and let her think she'd be wearing it soon. Stupid little bitch," he said casually. "As it turned out, she wasn't wearing the locket." He frowned, remembering. "She wouldn't tell me where she'd hidden it, even after I offered to pull her back in the boat. All she had to do was tell me."

Maggie was horrified. "You *knew* she couldn't swim and you just let her drown?"

"It took longer than I expected. She should have gone down right away, but she was tougher than I thought."

"Smarter, too," Maggie couldn't resist adding. "Must have been quite a shock when I told you that I knew Doreen had my mother's locket."

"I was certain she'd hidden it out of spite. I thought it must be at the house in Piney Point—I insisted she leave most of her things there. Then it occurred to me she might have left it in the kennel. What a good thing I kept her keys."

"*You* had her keys all along? But Howard—"

"That was rather clever of me, wasn't it? As it turns out, I didn't need her keys—you'd changed the kennel locks and Doreen never had any to your house. But it worked out in the end, when I decided to make it look like Bridger had them all along. He's gotten in my way rather too often, you see. Setting him up for a murder he didn't commit was poetic justice."

"And did Doreen deserve what happened to her?"

"She sealed her fate when she found the locket." He shook his head. "Of all the people who might have identified her, you were the only one who could have recognized the locket. The police didn't care. They were satisfied it was an accident but you wouldn't let it go. I had to do something. I tried to scare you off, but that didn't work. And when you decided to inventory the studio, I knew I had to move fast. But now other circumstances have arisen making immediate relocation prudent."

"What do you mean?"

"Art is only one of my businesses. I told you I'd been searching for treasure ever since your mother showed me that map. I've hired a few people to dig for me over the years. I couldn't risk damaging my hands, of course. I promised them a share of the treasure and, like the gullible fools there were, they believed me. Jake Turner was better than I expected, and got more results than Howard Bridger—"

"Howard!"

"Useless, in the end. Turner did find a few nice things now and again. One of those finds was a Union soldier's haversack with two very nice silver bars. He found it wedged behind the boulders on that ledge you were on earlier, as improbable as that seems. There was just a corner visible when he came across it. He said he was taking shelter in a storm, but I rather suspect he'd been looking for a quiet place to enjoy his whiskey. But he started bragging about our acquisitions and drew the attention of a group I'd rather not do business with."

"The government's after you," Maggie said flatly. "So you're leaving. Why didn't you just go? Why did you have to do this?" She indicated Claire.

"I couldn't leave without my paintings! As it was, I'd almost finished when the child came in and started screaming."

"And Sweet Pea?"

"That stupid animal bit me." Nicholas rose. "Now, as much as I've enjoyed this little tête-à-tête, I have business to see to.

The paintings from the studio are in my Jeep and there are some things in the cabin I wouldn't want to lose. Then I've got to move the silver. A few more loads, and your map will once again be nothing more than a silly child's legend."

He picked up the lantern and studied them in its light, then knelt and pushed Claire away from Maggie. The little girl came awake with a scream and cowered away from him.

"Leave her alone!"

Nicholas ignored her. He ran his hands briskly over Claire, poking fingers into the pockets of the girl's tiny shorts. Turning to Maggie, he repeated the process with her vest, then her jeans. "Relax, I'm just checking for flashlights. I wouldn't want you getting any ideas and wandering off while I'm gone," he explained.

He found her key chain and pulled it out. "Not much you can do with these, eh?" Next he found Sam's tracking leash. "I don't suppose you'll be needing this, but I'll let you keep it a little longer. A little souvenir of your own," he suggested as he replaced the leash in her vest pocket.

He patted her on the head. "By the way, you can't get those knots loose, but you keep right on trying. It will give you something to do until I come back."

"Damn you!"

He laughed. "I might just keep you around long enough to help me move the last of my treasure. Oh, and don't worry about any smoke that gets in here. I promise you'll be gone long before the fire gets to you. Just like your mother."

50

Without the lantern's dim glow, the cavern was completely black. Maggie couldn't even see Claire beside her; only the child's tight grip on her vest told her she was there.

"Is the bad man gone?" Fear, exhaustion, hunger, and cold shook Claire's voice.

"For now, but he's coming back so we have to work fast," Maggie said, thinking furiously. "I need to you to get something out of my vest for me." Her efforts to shift to a better position prompted frantic shrieks and sobs.

"Where are you going? I can't see you!"

"I'm right here. Remember the flashlight your dad gave me for my birthday? It's in my vest, in that inside pocket. Move your hand up a little more … that's it. Good girl!"

"It doesn't work!"

"You have to press the little button, remember? Just feel around the edge and push hard with your thumb."

"I did it!"

"You sure did! Okay. You hold the light steady while I work on getting my hands free." She'd felt the rope give, just a little, and now she set to work with a vengeance. As she struggled, she realized that he'd most likely moved the boat, which seriously reduced the odds someone would see the trail she'd left. Nothing short of divine intervention was going to save them once Nicholas returned, and Maggie thought she'd used up her share of miracles when Donnie Ray Bowles rescued her from that ravine. If they were going to get out of there alive, it was up to her.

She twisted and bucked until she was flat on her back. By cocking an elbow and straining on the ropes, she was able to painfully work first one hip, then the other, then one leg at a time between her arms, ending with her arms in front of her. The relief was instantaneous, and she lay there for a moment, panting heavily.

"Hand me the light, sweetie, and let's see if there's anything in my pockets to cut these ropes with," Maggie urged.

"There's this funny thing," Claire said doubtfully, holding up the military surplus can opener Maggie carried on her key chain.

"We can try it." After several minutes, she gave up. The P38 hadn't been designed to saw through nylon rope. She resolved to add a knife to her gear, if she lived to do it. "Never mind. Here, hold the light again and stay close. I want to check out that crate, see if there's anything in there we can use."

Inside was more silver; Maggie saw rectangular bars and smaller, odd-shaped pieces. She picked one up, surprised at the unexpected weight. She balanced it awkwardly between her bound hands and dropped it in the large front pocket of her vest. "We need to get out of here." Looking around, Maggie saw there were two passages side by side, and cursed herself for not paying closer attention to Nicholas' departure. "Hold on to me. And keep pressing that button, okay?"

Choosing the passage on the left, Maggie rolled a handful of pebbles in front of her as they inched forward down a steep slope. They'd managed a few yards before a hole loomed in their path and the pebbles dropped out of sight. They backed out and turned toward the other passage, then stopped when they heard the unmistakable sounds of footsteps. Someone was coming.

Maggie looked frantically for another way out. There was no place to run. "Hold the light for me!" Groaning with the effort, Maggie dragged the crate inside the passage. When she felt the crate rock slightly, she backed away.

"Give me the light and get behind that rock!" she whispered, pointing to a large boulder beside the left passage. "I'm going to have to turn the light off, so close your eyes and don't move."

Maggie slumped into a sitting position in front of the rock where Claire was hiding. She heard Claire whimpering behind her. "Hush!"

She dropped the Flashcard between her legs and pulled her knees up in front of her, hoping against hope he couldn't see her hands were now tied in front of her. She tugged the heavy piece of silver from her vest pocket and waited.

As the lantern's glow preceded Nicholas into the cavern, she forced herself to breathe deeply, calmly. She had one chance to make this work.

51

Nicholas was in a murderous rage. "There are police all over. It's your fault, damn you," he shouted. "If you and that sniveling girl hadn't slowed me down I would have been gone by now." He held the lantern high and looked around. "Where is she? And what have you done with my treasure?"

"Don't try to pretend you care about one little girl. It's your precious silver you want, isn't it? Well, I hid it where you'll never find it!" She looked toward the second passage, then looked quickly away.

He followed her gaze, just as she'd hoped, and saw the crate. "Really, my dear, I'm disappointed. I expected something more creative from you." He turned his back on her and holding the lantern strode toward the crate.

As he bent over in the passage, Maggie struggled to her feet and hurled the silver straight at his back. Her aim was off; she landed only a glancing blow to his shoulder. He staggered and, bent over as he was, couldn't regain his footing. He fell heavily against the crate, pushing it over the edge. Too late, he saw what was happening. With a scream of pure rage, he tried to brace himself and seize the crate but couldn't overcome the combined disaster of his own forward momentum and the crate's downward slide.

Nicholas, crate, and lantern plunged downward, the light bouncing wildly as it fell. Maggie heard the impact of body against stone. She forced herself to crawl forward and look down, and choked back a scream when she caught sight of him, lantern still clutched in his hand, lying crumpled on a ledge no more than twenty feet below. He wasn't moving. There was no sign of the silver.

She backed out of the tunnel, crawled toward the rock where Claire was, and groped for the Flashcard she'd left there. She breathed a sigh of thanks when her fingers closed over the plastic cover. Pressing the button, she switched on the light. "It's okay to come out now, sweetheart."

With a cry, Claire rushed toward her. "Is the bad man dead?" Claire's voice was muffled, her face pressed against Maggie.

"I don't know, but he can't hurt us anymore. Now, you hold the light and let's get out of here!"

The passage was narrow, forcing them to walk in single file. Claire led the way, walking slowly and holding the light out in front of her. The passage twisted and turned before climbing upward. Just when Maggie thought she couldn't climb anymore, they reached a level place and saw the passage forked.

The light went out, then flashed on again. "Sorry," Claire said in a small voice. "My finger slipped." She held the light up against the wall, illuminating arrows chalked in both directions. "Which way?"

"I don't remember," Maggie admitted. She looked at the exhaustion stamped across the little girl's face. "I'll bet your fingers are getting sore, aren't they? Why don't we switch off the light and rest a minute?"

"But it'll be dark!"

"We'll hold hands." Maggie forced a cheerful note into her voice. "We'll close our eyes and pretend the light's still on."

"Promise you won't let go?"

"Promise." The small hands quivered with fear as Maggie held them firmly. They sat quietly for several minutes. She was about to suggest she take a turn with the flashlight when she felt the cool touch of air on the right side of her face. Startled, she opened her eyes and looked right. Unless she was hallucinating, there was a faint brush of air coming from that direction. It had to be a way out.

There was a genuine smile in her voice now. "Let's go this way, sweetie."

Minutes later, they reached the entrance, only to find Nicholas had set the wooden gate against the boulders, effectively closing them in. After struggling to shift the heavy barrier Maggie nearly conceded defeat. "If my hands were free, I could move it, but I can't do it like this," she said in frustration.

She forced herself to breathe slowly and evenly. "Maybe there's a way around it. Climb up on my shoulders and see if you can squeeze through that hole." Faint light came in through a gap in the rocks above the barrier. Kneeling, she waited until Claire had climbed on her shoulders, then she slowly straightened. "Hold on to the wall for support," Maggie directed. "Can you reach it?"

"It's too small," Claire wailed. "We're never gonna get out!"

"Steady, sweetie." Moving carefully, Maggie reversed her actions and the little girl clambered down. Slipping her wrists over Claire's head she pulled her into a tight embrace. "We're not giving up. What we need is a plan. What did you see when you looked through the hole?"

"Rocks and trees. And water. And lights. Like Christmas."

"Christmas lights and water." Maggie was puzzled, then she had it. "You must have seen boats out on the lake! If you could see them, they might be able to see us!" Excitedly, she rummaged through the pockets she could reach. "Check my back pockets. We need to get their attention," she explained. "See if there's anything in there we can use."

Claire pulled out Sam's tracking leash. "How about this?"

"Good! And here's the orange flag I used in the search demonstration." That was just today, she thought in amazement.

"Okay, I'm going to tie this around the end of the leash. Then I want you to climb back up on my shoulders and push it out the hole. We don't want it to fall all the way out, though. Can you loop it around that piece of wood up there?"

Claire agreed eagerly. The orange flag disappeared through the opening. "It's getting dark. Can anybody see it?"

"It's a long shot, unless we can get their attention." Maggie studied the opening above their heads. "If I hold your ankles tight, do you think you can stand on my shoulders and blink the light, like this?" She flashed the light in three short bursts of light, then three longer bursts. "It's important to do the same thing, over and over, so anybody watching will realize it's a signal and come investigate."

"And we'll get out!" Claire said excitedly.

"That's the plan, sweetie. Now, up you go!"

52

There were only eight passengers waiting for the last tour of the *Ozark Queen*. If this keeps up, Adam Mackenzie thought sourly, I'll be back bagging groceries at the Sak-n-Sav, and the bank can add another boat to its auction list.

But until that happened, he was determined to give his customers their money's worth. He'd decorated the boat with colorful lights and streamers, offered sodas and snacks, and kept plenty of seat cushions on hand.

He knew some of the other charter operators hated giving the same spiel over and over, but Mac honestly enjoyed it. He pointed out the wildlife refuge on Deer Island, where bucks had been known to swim to on the first day of hunting season, and entertained his customers with stories of catfish "as big as a man" hiding far beneath the surface.

As he approached the dam the turbulence increased, causing several passengers to clutch the rail for support. He nodded to his partner, who had the awnings ready to roll out in case those clouds delivered. God knows they needed the rain, he thought, but he doubted his passengers would appreciate being caught out in a storm. The water could be unforgiving in rough weather, and the wreckage of many a boat littered the lake bottom. He didn't want the *Queen* joining them, so he changed up his route a bit, brought them closer to shore, just in case. Even though the drought had dropped the water levels lower than he'd ever seen, there was still places along the bluff with deep pools and room to navigate safely.

Cruising along the bluffs, he noticed a fancy boat tied close in and a peculiar light blinking about halfway up the bluffs. Must be a ledge there; damned odd place to camp, he thought. Dangerous, too; there were warning signs posted all over those bluffs. Kids, he supposed, looking to make some mischief. He smiled, thinking of his own teen-age years. Some things never change.

SPARKEY'S MARINA WAS crowded that evening. There were still a few tourists hanging around, ignoring the evacuation orders, but it was mostly locals coming in for gas and beer and news. Tonight was no different, and Beau Bronson relaxed in his rocker by the window, one ear tuned to his customers and the other listening to the scanner his nephew Paul had brought in. Paul, at the register, was talking to Adam Mackenzie. Beau caught the end of their conversation.

"Mind you, I climbed those bluffs myself, back in my wild days," Mac was saying. "We had to hike in, though. Never had a fancy boat like that one I saw."

"Do you suppose they're camping up there?"

"Don't know. But that light was strange. Never seen anything like it, blinking off and on like that. Real steady, like." Mac paid for his purchases and headed for home.

The scanner had picked up plenty of chatter about that little girl missing from Eagle Cove. And there'd been something about a boat, too, he thought. Beau looked at the wall where photographs of his own children and grandchildren were proudly displayed. What if one of his babies was out there?

He reached for the phone.

53

Maggie heard the sound of powerful boats coming closer. "Somebody's coming! Keep flashing the light until we're sure they see us!"

Claire bounced on Maggie's shoulders, shrieking with joy. Her sudden movement caught Maggie off-balance, and she stumbled, bracing her bound wrists against the wooden barrier in an effort to keep her footing. "Don't—"

Claire reached out to steady herself against the wall but misjudged the distance, cracking her elbow against a rock and dropping the Flashcard. Blackness descended. Shrieking, the girl grabbed fistfuls of Maggie's hair and pulled hard.

Moving slowly, terrified Claire might tumble off her shoulders and be seriously hurt, Maggie sank to her knees. "Climb down, honey. Put your hand on my shoulder. That's it."

Finally Claire slid down, breathing heavily. "I want you to take slow, deep breaths," Maggie directed. "Stand right where you are while I find the light."

Groping blindly, she finally felt a corner of the plastic casing, but couldn't pry it loose from the crevice where it had fallen. "I can't get it out."

"They're never gonna find us. We're gonna die and it's all my fault," Claire sobbed.

"They'll find us," Maggie said firmly. Her mind raced furiously as she considered their options. She fumbled through her pockets, hoping against hope she'd find another light, a match, anything. Nothing.

Claire was still crying. As Maggie thrust her hands inside the lower pockets of her vest, her fingers closed around a familiar object. Her field whistle!

"They can't leave, they can't!"

Maggie smiled as she dropped the braided cord around Claire's neck and pressed the whistle into her hand. "They won't," she promised. "Keep the same rhythm going as the light. Three short, three long. We'll take turns."

Claire puffed on the whistle, heard a faint sound. She tried again. This time, a definite whistling sound, although it was probably still too faint to be heard from a distance.

"Once more, and then I'll try. Now take a deep breath and blow really hard!"

54

The man at Indian Creek turned out to be a young father carrying an overtired toddler. Lucas was backing away from the dock when the call from Sparkey's Marina came in. He ordered all teams to converge on the dam area and was relieved to hear Keith Baxter and the primary SAR team were en route.

Dispatch reported the Washington County team was already in the vicinity, as was a state police unit. "Send 'em over to Miz Sternes' place. That's the closest access point. And call Miz Sternes, tell her they're on the way," he added, belatedly remembering the woman's attitude about trespassers. "We're about twenty minutes behind them."

Zak relayed the information to Mike Jameson as the boat plowed through the rough water. Thunder prowled around them and lightning flashed through the columns of smoke rising across the hills as they raced toward the north shore. Light rain began falling as they neared the bluffs and saw Baxter's team pull up next to a boat anchored close to the shore. One of the deputies riding with the SAR team keyed the radio and relayed the vessel registration number.

"Dispatch, check that against DMV records," Lucas ordered.

Silence, and then the dispatcher's voice came through loud and clear. "That's a match with our suspect, Sheriff."

Lucas and Zak moved at the same time, leaving Angus to manage the radio as they dropped over the side and followed the SAR team to shore. There was no path along the water's edge; the only way to go was up. The rain was falling faster.

Behind them, Zak saw more boats converge on their location. "Reinforcements are here," he told Lucas, who waved his thanks when the new arrivals aimed powerful search lights on the bluff.

"We got a trail here. Fresh tracks," one of the SAR members called out. "Ya'll watch your step—this shale gets slicker than owl shit when it rains."

Following his lead, the team climbed, moving carefully, testing each hand hold before shifting their weight. Zak made the mistake, once, of looking down to the jagged rocks at the base of the bluff. There's no way Claire could have managed this on her own, he thought bleakly. He prayed Lucas was right and that Maggie was with his daughter. She'd be all right with Maggie, he told himself. He wouldn't let himself think otherwise.

From the top of the bluff came the sound of voices. "More reinforcements," Lucas said with satisfaction. "They'll rappel down, search the whole cliff."

From the boat, Mr. B barked sharply. And barked again. And again. Then Sam joined in.

Seconds later, they all heard what the dogs' keen ears had already picked up: the shrill notes of a whistle.

And then, a shout: "We found them!"

55

In the days following, Maggie repeated her story until she was heartily sick of it all, and wanted nothing more than to erase the horrible experience from her memory. She couldn't ever forget, though, the wonderful people who'd done so much to find them and bring them home.

The wooden barrier Nicholas had wedged between the boulders at the entrance of the cave proved no match for the determination of the rescue team, and she and Claire were freed just moments after the first SAR member reached them. People crowded onto the ledge and into the tunnel, all talking at the same time. And then Zak was there, sweeping his daughter into a tight embrace before reaching out to drag Maggie into the shelter of his arms. The rope on her wrists was cut away and somebody—she thought it might have been Ben Springer, but rain and tears blurred her vision—checked her over quickly.

"Take care of Claire," she insisted. 'I'm okay. I just want to go home."

Going home, however, turned out to be a lengthy process. While the SAR team worked on a plan to get her and Claire off the bluff, she gave the sheriff an abbreviated version of events. Chatter has risen around them, but the word 'treasure' got everyone's attention.

"We'll get the details later," Lucas assured her. "And we'll take care of Crane. Right now, let's get you out of here."

The SAR members at the top of the bluff rappelled down with Stokes baskets and conferred with Keith Baxter, who was directing the rescue. Claire appeared to be on the verge of complete exhaustion; she clung to her father and refused to let go. After a hurried consultation they sent Zak up with her in the first basket. Maggie followed in the second and found EMS vehicles at the top of the bluff.

At the hospital, Dr. Coventry was waiting. "We have to stop meeting this way," the doctor said with a gentle smile. "Now, let's see what the damage is this time, shall we?"

Maggie couldn't tell them what substance Nicholas had used to render them unconscious, so they'd drawn blood and run tests before settling them in a room upstairs. Two headaches, one case of shock, a concussion, a few sprains, and "a bucketful of cuts and bruises," according to the nurse who'd rolled a cot for Zak into the room Claire and Maggie were sharing. "I hope you're planning to take a few days off."

Remembering the last concussion she had, Maggie shook her head carefully. "I have a kennel to run."

"That's covered," Zak told her. "I called while you were in with the doctor. Bev and Garrett have worked out a schedule, plus a few of my buddies are camping out there."

"But the storm—"

"A little rain won't bother them. They're Army."

"Nobody's sleeping outside when I have a big house right there. Garrett has the keys. Tell everyone to make themselves at home."

"Okay. Now get some sleep."

"I need to tell you—"

"Claire's safe. You're safe. That's all that matters. Everything else can wait."

THE STORY WAS front page news locally. When the tale of Margaret Raeburn's murder hit the wire services, the national press descended on Eagle Cove en masse. And when rumors about treasure leaked out, bedlam ensued. The phone rang endlessly as the concerned, the curious, and the just plain nosy clamored for details. A deputy was sent out to control traffic on the roads leading to Waterside, turning back the media while waving residents and customers past the roadblock.

Even the rain, still falling steadily, couldn't deter the prying eyes. Television camera crews were everywhere, interviewing anybody who would give them the time of day. The *Ozark Queen* did a booming business giving tours of the bluffs. Business at the local marina was brisk as enterprising reporters and photographers rented boats and trolled along the shore, shooting footage of the kennel and the studio. Trespassers, however, were few, thanks to the roving patrols organized by Garrett and Zak.

"Vultures," Maggie said when she heard about the media's activities. She'd retreated to the house and taken refuge in the kitchen after a hectic morning in the kennel. The steady stream of genuine well-wishers had both humbled and exhausted her. She'd lasted two hours before Bev gently booted her out and sent her back to the house.

Claire was asleep again, curled up on the hearth cushions. Sam and Mr. B were there, too, close to the basket where Sweet Pea dozed. Zak was finishing a call when Maggie walked in.

"I asked my counselor for a referral," he told Maggie. "The VA center here doesn't have any pediatric specialists, but he gave me the name of someone in Rogers. She's going to see Claire tomorrow, but she said it's common for kids to sleep so much after an ordeal."

The doctor at the hospital had examined Claire the morning after the rescue. There'd been no evidence of sexual assault but the emotional trauma had taken a heavy toll on the child. The doctor encouraged him to seek professional support, and Zak had immediately agreed.

At the moment, he and his daughter were staying with Maggie. Looking around the kitchen, he told Maggie it felt like coming home. "Claire seems to think so, too."

"She's amazing, you know. I'm her number one fan."

"You and the entire SAR team, and all my buddies. They've named her group mascot and are demanding visitation rights."

That comment sent Maggie's thoughts straight to Althea. She'd had more than a few sleepless hours thinking about his ex-wife and the blame she'd heaped on the woman's shoulders. Gran would have told her it's not her place to judge. She had to believe the woman loved her daughter. Whatever happened, trust Zak to handle it, she thought.

He'd spoken briefly with his ex-wife on the phone a couple of times in the past few days. After calling to report their daughter was safe, he'd been reluctant to call again. He probably wouldn't have if his counselor hadn't intervened.

Maggie had overheard the counselor's words. "She's been through a different kind of hell," Mike Jameson had told Zak the night before. "We can talk about it when you want, but right now how about you take the first step and reach out to her? You said it yourself: she'd never intentionally hurt your daughter."

Now, as they sat in the kitchen watching Claire sleep, Zak said, "She talked to her mother this morning." He shrugged. 'We'll take it a day at a time."

They both started when Mr. B jumped to his feet. "I've never seen him like this," Maggie said.

'I told you, he's ready for a new career." Zak snapped his fingers. "Okay, boy, let's go check it out."

From the front porch they saw the sheriff's four-wheel-drive making its way to the house, followed by the veterinarian's truck. She was pleased to see Sylvia with them.

"We've come bearing gifts," Angus called cheerfully. 'Well, we did anyway. No telling what Lucas is up to."

Laughing, Maggie held the door wide and invited everyone back to the kitchen. She inspected the box Sylvia handed her.

"Krispy Kreme doughnuts! I had no idea they were sold around here."

"They're not," Angus informed her. "I drove over to Rogers, stocked up. Got a few dozen out in the truck. Had more, but I dropped some off at the hospital. Picked Sylvia up there, talked her into coming out with me."

"Angus, I think I love you," Maggie said sincerely.

The vet grinned happily and reached for a doughnut. "I brought gossip, too. Now that the story about the treasure is all over town—"

"All over the country, more like," Lucas said sourly.

"You're probably right," Angus admitted. "Have you heard the latest? Some are saying the silver wasn't old treasure at all but probably loot stolen from a government transport—you know, something the Yankees brought through here during the war."

"Stolen and stashed it in a cave. And I suppose the thieves just forgot to go back for it?" Sylvia asked skeptically.

"Who knows? Maybe they died, or if they were soldiers they just moved on. Even if they came back after the war, things probably looked different. Maybe they couldn't locate the cave again."

"Well, I for one don't care where it came from," Maggie declared. "I never want to see it again."

Angus looked at the sheriff. "Have they found anything yet?"

"Not so I've heard," Lucas answered. "I've had an earful, though, from Miz Sternes, who's insisting that anything in there belongs to her, says her property goes clear down to the lake. The Corps of Engineers disagrees, of course. They're making some noise about the Government Property Line—the boundary markers for which," he added dryly, "have mysteriously disappeared."

Lucas glanced toward Claire and lowered his voice. "I do have some other news, though. I just came from the hospital myself. Crane is busted up pretty bad, but he'll live to stand trial. The prosecutor's talking about two counts of murder, attempted murder, abduction, and theft, for starters."

"Does this mean Howard's been cleared?" Sylvia demanded.

"Yup. Crane wanted a fall guy, and your husband was the perfect choice. From what we've learned, the only thing Howard's guilty of is adultery, and that's between the two of you."

He paused. "I talked to your family's dentist this morning, Maggie. He's sending us your mother's dental records, so we can make a positive ID of the Jane Doe remains. With Crane's confession to you and the evidence we found in his cabin, I'd say we already know."

They'd found a box while searching the cabin. Inside was a wallet with Margaret Raeburn's driver's license and credit cards. There was also a wedding band; Maggie had confirmed the date inscribed was her parent's wedding date.

The search had also turned up another box, this one filled with cheap trinkets and other items. "Doreen's souvenirs," Maggie suggested when she'd been asked about them.

The sheriff's office announced they'd made an arrest in the death of Doreen Crowley but declined to release details, calling it an ongoing investigation. Now, looking at her friends, Maggie said quietly, "The press doesn't seem to care at all about Doreen, but I do. If she hadn't come to work here, she might never have recognized that locket. She might still be alive. She must have been terrified, out there in the water alone, knowing she was going to die at the hands of the man she thought she loved."

Maggie took a deep breath to steady herself. "Taking my mother's locket meant Doreen's death. But her actions started a chain of events that brought a killer to justice. And for that, I'm thankful. Wherever her spirit may be, I hope she knows that."

"Amen," Lucas said quietly.

After the others had departed, Zak looked at Maggie. "What are you thinking?"

"I've spent most of my life believing my mother didn't love me, that she'd willingly ignored me all my life. And now that I know the truth, I should feel different. I should feel something besides anger. But I don't. All I feel is ..." She groped for the right word. "Empty," she said finally.

"Give it time," Zak advised.

Epilogue

Raindrops clung to the grass in the Eagle Cove cemetery where Margaret Raeburn was laid to rest beside her parents. The same minister from Gran's funeral was again present, his voice gentle as he began the service.

Tears misted Maggie's eyes as she glanced across the grave at her father. Charles had arrived last night and would be leaving that afternoon; that he'd come at all gave Maggie hope for their future. They'd spoken briefly, awkwardly, by phone several times in the last few weeks.

There had been a public memorial service, organized by Sylvia and a cluster of older women from Eureka Springs who'd turned up "to do what needs doing," as Miss Abigail had told her. The event had again drawn the national media's attention, and Maggie was grateful to the community that had closed ranks around her, protecting her.

Hundreds had turned out for that event, but today's service was private, known only to those closest to Maggie who had been her staunch supporters since she first reopened Waterside Kennels. Zak stood close by her side. Sylvia and Howard were there, and Angus, and Lucas with his sons Garret and Rob. Bev was there too. Her parents were minding the kennel so the whole group could be together.

As the service concluded, Maggie closed her eyes in a brief prayer of farewell and breathed in the heady scent of fresh-cut flowers. Her mother had often painted the wildflowers of the region, and Maggie had ordered a spray to be placed on top of the casket. A formal wreath from Charles lay beside them.

Maggie slipped her hand from Zak's comforting clasp to collect the cards from the floral arrangements that surrounded the grave. One card was unsigned, but Maggie knew it had been Lucas who'd left the single white lily that accompanied the card. She didn't have to glance down to remember what it said.

Rest in peace, Bone Woman
Never forgotten — finally home.

ABOUT THE AUTHOR

SUSAN HOLMES IS a writer, editor, and college professor whose work has appeared in academic journals, military publications, and other media. She makes her home in Arkansas, where she is currently working on the next book in the Waterside Kennels Mystery Series. Her novels are available in print and e-book editions.

TO LEARN MORE about the mystery series, the world of dogs, and life in the Ozarks—including a look at the places used in this series —visit Susan's website at dogmysteries.com.

Made in the USA
Lexington, KY
14 June 2014